KINGS OF COUNTRY
JACE

SASHA SUMMERS

sourcebooks
casablanca

Dedicated to those who face their fears and seek justice.
Your voices heal our wounds.
Your strength gives us hope.
You are not a victim. You are a survivor.

Published by Sourcebooks Casablanca, an imprint of Sourcebooks
P.O. Box 4410, Naperville, Illinois 60567-4410
(630) 961-3900
sourcebooks.com

Printed and bound in the United States of America.

OPM 10 9 8 7 6 5 4 3 2 1

Chapter 1

"ARE YOU KIDDING ME?" THEY COULD NOT BE SERIOUS. Krystal glared at her daddy, country music legend Hank King, in pure disbelief. "Why would this be *great* news? For me, anyway." Blood roared in her ears and a throb took up residence at the base of her neck. She slipped the leather strap of her favorite Taylor spruce acoustic guitar from around her neck and placed the instrument tenderly on its stand. "It's great news for what's his name—"

"Jace Black," her manager, Steve Zamora, said.

"Whatever," she snapped, shooting a lethal gaze at the balding little man. "I'm sure he's ecstatic. He gets to sing my song, my *best* song. With the one and only Emmy Lou King." She downed a water bottle, parched from singing for almost two hours straight.

"Come on now, Krystal. They're singing one of *your* songs," her father soothed. But she wasn't ready to forgive him. Or see any good in this. And when he added "You know Emmy will do it up right. She always does," it stung.

Unlike me. Her spine stiffened and her fists tightened. She and her twin, Emmy, were different as night and day. A point her momma was all too happy to point out at every opportunity.

"Don't get your feathers ruffled, now. You know I

didn't mean anything by that." Her daddy tipped his favorite tan cowboy hat back on his forehead, crossed his arms over his chest, and frowned.

Poor Daddy. He said the women in his life were the reason he was getting so grey. It wasn't intentional. She didn't like disappointing him—he was her hero. But, dammit, he couldn't pull the rug out from under her and expect her to smile and thank him. She wasn't a saint. She wasn't Emmy.

Steve tried again. "This is a win all around, Krystal."

"No, it's not. Not for me," she argued. Blowing up wasn't going to change their minds, but maybe reminding her daddy how special this song was. "Daddy, you know this song means something to me, that it's…important. I'm connected to it, deep down in my bones. I can sing it and do it justice." She hated that her voice wavered, that sentiment seeped in. This was business. And while the business loved raw emotion and drama in its music and lyrics, they weren't fans of it from their performers.

"Now, darlin', you know how it works. It's all about timing." Steve used his soft voice, the please-don't-let-her-start-screaming-and-throwing-things voice. Like lemon juice in a paper cut.

"Timing?" she asked. The only thing Steve Zamora cared about was kissing her legendary father's ass and managing Emmy Lou's career. "It's been my sister's time for ten years now."

Not that she begrudged her sister an iota of her fame. It wasn't Emmy Lou's fault that she was the favorite.

She had that *thing*, a megastar quality—that universally appealing sweetness that the world adored. Krystal had a real hard time with sweetness.

Why the media, fans, even the record company labeled Krystal the rebel, a black sheep, the wild child of the King family was a mystery. Marketing, maybe? The good twin, bad twin thing? Whatever. She had her days. And her very public breakup with Mickey Graham hadn't helped. To hear him tell it, she was a selfish prima donna who'd broken his heart. It'd hurt like hell that everyone was so willing to believe the worst of her. But her pride had stopped her from telling the truth— the real truth, not Mickey's version of it. His tall tales cemented her bad-girl image, so she'd embraced some of the freedom it gave her.

"I get you're disappointed, Krystal, but there will be other songs." Daddy's hand cupped her cheek, his smile genuine and sympathetic.

He did not just say that. His easy dismissal cut deep. Yes, there would be other songs, but this one *mattered*. People might chalk it up to her breakup with Mickey. She knew better. The song had come from a wound that wouldn't heal. A wound that haunted her dreams and reminded her to guard her heart, to never let anyone in. Every scribbled note, tweaked word, chord change, or key finagle had led her to both love and hate the finished product. But it made her proud.

Her daddy had said he was proud, too. Just not enough. While she'd never asked her father to plead her case at their label, Wheelhouse Records, she realized, deep down, she'd hoped he would—for this song—without her having to ask. But if he had championed her, she'd be cutting the single, not Emmy and some new music reality TV star.

"You good?" her father asked.

No. She glared.

He sighed. "Breathe, baby girl. Don't want you spitting fire at folk for the rest of the night."

She didn't need to be reminded of the Three Kings fans lined up outside. This had been her life for the past ten years. It was more than singing side by side with her twin sister and older brother, playing her guitar until her fingertips hurt, or waking up humming a new melody, new lyrics already taking shape. It was making people *feel*. The only thing that mattered was the fans. Was she upset? Yes. Hurt? Most definitely. But when she left her dressing room, a dazzling smile would be on her face—for them. After the meet and greet would be another story.

Her father let out a long, pained sigh. "Might as well go ahead and send him in."

Send who in? Her dressing room was entirely too crowded already. Not that protesting would make a bit of difference. She flopped into the chair before her illuminated makeup mirror, all but choking on frustration, and rubbed lotion into her fingers and hands. Hands that were shaking.

Steve leaned out her dressing room door, calling, "Come on in, Jace. She's looking forward to meeting you."

Jace. She froze. As in Jace-the-song-stealer Black? She was *not* looking forward to meeting him. Some wannabe singer from a no-count TV talent show. *American Voice*? Or *Next Top Musician*? Or something else gimmicky and stupid?

In the mirror, she shot daggers her father's way. He was pushing it—pushing her. She applied a stroke of bloodred color to her mouth, jammed the lipstick lid back on, and pressed her hands against her thighs before risking a glance in the mirror at the man who'd stolen her dreams.

He was big. *Big* big. He had to stoop to get through the door of her dressing room.

"Mr. King, sir." Jace's voice was deep and smooth and impossible to ignore. But that didn't mean he could sing. "It's a real honor." He extended a hand to her father. Polite. That was something.

"Good to meet you, son," her father answered, shaking his hand and clapping Jace on the shoulder.

Tall *and* broad-shouldered. A weathered black leather jacket hugged the breadth of his shoulders and upper arms. As he pivoted on the heel of his boot, her gaze wandered south, revealing a perfect ass gloved in faded denim. She blew out a long, slow breath. Very nice packaging. *But* a great body didn't mean diddly when you were performing live, in front of an audience of thousands.

He glanced her way then. It was a glance, nothing really, but it was enough.

Oh hell.

Of course he was drop-dead gorgeous. Thick black hair, strong jaw, and a wicked, tempting grin on very nice lips. *Dammit.* He shook hands with her weasel manager, Steve, before giving her his full attention. A jolt of pure appreciation raced down her spine to the tips of her crystal-encrusted boots. *It's not fair. None of this is fair.* She fiddled with her heavy silver Tiffany charm bracelet and tucked a strand of hair behind her ear, too agitated to sit still.

Talented or not, it wouldn't matter. Not when he looked like that. Which was exactly why he was here. That face. That body. Jace Black and Emmy Lou King? His dark, dangerous good looks and her sister's golden sweetness? They'd make quite a pair onstage, singing her song…

Her song.

Her temper flared, quick and hot. She didn't give a damn what he looked like. Or if he had manners. He hadn't earned the right to her words, not by a long shot. And since he was a big boy, she'd take it upon herself to show him how tough this industry could be. Starting right here, right now.

His gaze locked with her reflection. "I can't tell you how…amazing it is to meet you, Miss King." That velvet voice was far too yummy. "I know every word to every song you've written." He needed to stop looking at her so she could stay pissed off and feisty.

But he didn't. And the longer he looked, the harder it was to overlook the way he was looking at her. Admiring her as a singer and songwriter was one thing. But right now, something told her he was appreciating more than her music.

Too bad she couldn't like him. At all.

She ignored her daddy's warning look and stood, turning to face Jace. Her momma raised her daughters with a deep understanding of female charm and the power it could wield. With a dazzling smile, she shook the hand he offered, fully intending to use her powers for evil. But the brush of his calloused fingers against her palm threw off her concentration. It had been a long time since she'd been even slightly attracted to a man. But this time, there was nothing slight about what she was feeling. *No, no, no. Stay mad.* "Oh, I doubt that, *Chase.*"

"Jace," he said, grinning.

Oh hell, this is bad. That smile. She knew his name, but still… "Right." She bit into her lower lip, drawing his attention to her mouth.

His nostrils flared just enough to make her insides soften. Not the reaction she was hoping for. He cleared his throat and tore his eyes away, that square jaw of his clenched. Tight. That was a weakness of hers—a man's jaw muscle. Only two things made a man's jaw tick like that: anger or desire. And, right now, she was pretty sure Jace Black didn't have a thing in the world to be angry about. But she did. Big-time. The slow, liquid burn taking up residence deep in her stomach was beyond inconvenient.

Steve said something original like, "What did you think of the show?"

"Incredible. Y'all are even better live, I think, if that's possible," Jace said. "I'm a little starstruck—guess you can tell."

Was he? She couldn't tell—his hotness was getting in the way. No way she was going to let a pretty face and tingles lead her astray, not this time. "That's always nice to hear." If it was true.

"I want to thank you," Jace said to her father—of course. Only someone like Hank King could get a nobody reality star this sort of break. "I know how lucky I am to get this opportunity." He had *no* idea. His luck was her loss. Not that he could know or understand how much his words stung. His gaze returned to her when he said, "Your music has always meant a lot to me—a lot of folk, I'm sure. But your new song—"

"*My* song?" She couldn't take it anymore. His reminder lodged a sharp spike in her throat. "From what I hear, it's yours now." She ignored her daddy's disapproving frown and the panic on Steve's face. Like her temper was totally unexpected? They should have thought about that before bringing *him* in here seconds after crushing her hopes and dreams. The sting of tears infuriated her further. None of them would ever see her cry, dammit. Ever.

"It's a good song." From Jace's expression, he knew something wasn't right. But he kept right on talking. "It's one of the best things you've written. When I read it—" He broke off, shaking his head. "I'm still in shock I get to sing it."

"That makes two of us," she whispered. But at least he got it, about the song, anyway.

He hesitated, then stepped closer. If she'd had room, she'd have stepped back. Because Jace Black up close was even better—worse—than Jace Black at a distance. Good skin. Even, white teeth. And a holy-hell amazing scent that had her toes curling in her blinged-out ostrich-skin boots.

"I'm guessing I wasn't your first pick?" His gaze never left her face, waiting for an explanation.

She shrugged, wondering why she'd suddenly lost her ability to fire off something quick and biting.

"And you're not happy about it." He swallowed, the muscles in his throat working.

She heard him—she did. But the air between them was crackling something fierce and it was taking total concentration not to get lost in those light brown eyes. After spending the last two years avoiding men, she wasn't sure what, exactly, was happening. Only that she needed to keep her guard up and as much space as possible between them. Pretty words and even prettier packaging might have made it easier for him to worm his way in with other people, but it wouldn't work on her.

What did he want? Beyond singing her song, of course. She studied him openly, exploring his face and searching his gaze for some nervous flutter or guilty flush. Mickey's eyes tightened when he was hiding something. Just a little, mind you, but when she saw it now, she knew it was a red flag. And Uncle Tig... *No.* She swept thoughts of him aside.

But Jace?

The flash of pure, unfiltered male appreciation in

those incredible eyes had her insides fluid and hot. If only they'd met under other circumstances...then it would be okay to get tangled up in bed somewhere—and have one hell of a time wearing each other out.

She swallowed, the images all too tempting. Too bad she had to hate him. "Don't you worry over me, *Jason*. I'm tough."

She wasn't feeling very tough at the moment. The sooner today was over, the sooner she was done with Jace Black. Which was better for his career, anyway. Even though she was pissed he'd taken her song, it wasn't in her to intentionally sink his career just to spite him. No, that was more her momma's MO—and she was nothing, *nothing*, like her momma.

Enough. She was tired and irritable and on the verge of coming undone. Her fans were waiting and they deserved the best her she could muster. She turned, glancing at her reflection and smoothing a wayward strand of long blond hair into place. Crystal chandelier earrings and a beyond-blinding crystal necklace—Momma was all about the bling—accented the plunging neckline of the concert's final costume change. The ultrafine black suede fringed dress felt like silk and was cut to perfection, clinging in all the right places.

From the tightness of Jace Black's jaw, he noticed.

Maybe she could muster up the energy to mess with him a little, for the hell of it. "Time to go meet the fans." A dazzling smile just for him. Yep, that floored him. "You are planning on tagging along, aren't you?"

His gaze narrowed—confused. Maybe even a little nervous.

"We weren't staying—" a man in the corner said.

"Well, that doesn't make any sense." She hooked her arm through Jace's. A warm, very thickly muscled arm. Not that muscles mattered. "And who are you, anyway?"

"My manager. Luke Samuels," Jace said.

A weasel—like Steve. He had hair and was dressed better, but there was no denying the similarities: too eager to please and dewy with anxious sweat. "Miss King, it's an honor, a real honor—"

"Sure. But since you're here and all, might as well come meet some fans. Since our fans will be your fans soon enough." She beamed up at Jace again, but this time around, he looked downright suspicious. So he was smart, too?

"If you want—" Luke began.

"I do," she said, tugging Jace along. "Besides, you should meet Emmy, maybe get a few pics of the two of you." She didn't know why she was torturing herself. Seeing her sister and Jace together, paired up to sing her creation, wasn't going to improve her mood. But there was no going back now.

Smile in place, she walked into the hall to the sound of those fans that paid extra money for the backstage passes and meet and greet. "You know how to work the crowd, *Jake*?" she asked, emphasizing the name. His delicious grin told her he hadn't missed it. "Now's a good time to get some practice."

Now that she'd led him into the lion's den, he could fend for himself. With a wink, she let him go—but he followed closely—his scent still teasing her nostrils. Best to ignore him and focus on doing her job.

She enjoyed this part of it. This was what it was about—these people loved their music, loved them. Their enthusiasm was contagious and reassuring. As much as she'd like to deny it, she wanted to be liked, maybe even a little bit adored, the way her sister and brother were.

And Jace Black? Apparently, people knew who he was and, from the way they screamed his name, liked him.

If he wasn't stealing her song, she'd have considered being a fan, too. But he was, so she wasn't. Still, from that wicked grin to those beautiful eyes, there was a whole lot about Jace Black to like.

———————

Don't screw this up. Jace tore his gaze from Krystal King.

If he was smart, he'd hang back and watch the Kings work the room. He could only hope to handle a crowd like this with half their composure. When someone recognized him from *Next Top American Voice*, he got red-faced and tongue-tied. He wasn't sure why he'd gone along with Krystal—he just had. And now? He sure as hell hadn't expected to be recognized. Women were screaming his name, waving their cameras at him—some of them were *crying*. Crying?

It made him uncomfortable as hell. Here he was, blushing and stumbling over what to say, and these people knew his name, thought he was talented, wanted to touch him and get his autograph.

"Smile and wave," his little sister, Heather, had told him. "Pretend like you're having fun. Like you're going fishing." He wished she were here, poking fun at him, keeping him grounded. Since she wasn't, he'd follow her advice. He leaned into the crowd and smiled at the dozens of phones snapping pictures.

He didn't know if he'd ever get used to this. To him, it was overwhelming. Crazy. And *part of the job*—the Wheelhouse Records PR department had assured him.

Krystal's husky laughter set the hair on the back of his neck upright. Out of the corner of his eye, he saw her hugging a fan. The tenderness on her face was unexpected— and oh so real. He'd been warned about Krystal King. She was guarded. Check. Had a bit of a temper. Check. The spark in her green eyes confirmed that, too. No one had to tell him she was sexy as hell—he'd always known that. But nothing, *nothing*, had prepared him for how fiercely he'd respond to her.

To say he was attracted to the rebel King was an understatement.

But there was more to Krystal King than what the media, Wheelhouse Records, and his manager had to say. Anyone who could write the lyrics she did or create music that made him ache was more than cold and angry. Her music was her voice—weighted with real passion.

The sort of emotion that had him wearing out Three Kings CDs in his old truck and singing along whenever one of their songs was on the radio. His favorite songs? The ones she wrote. Not only did he admire her music, but he admired how she handled the bad-girl persona and public character-bashing she was regularly subjected to. He never believed the tabloid headlines or talk show gossip, but if she was angry and guarded, she had plenty of reasons.

Was he one of them now?

The way she'd looked at him...he hadn't been prepared for that. He couldn't tell if she was all angry fire or sizzling from of a different kind of flame. Wishful thinking. There was no way someone like Krystal King was interested in him. All he knew was looking at her too long had him burning in a way that set warning flares off in his brain. Watching her now, blond hair hanging down her back and the fringes of her black minidress swinging around a pair of long, toned golden legs, had him wishing. Hard.

Bad idea. Don't screw this up.

"Jace." A woman grabbed his hand. "I love you. Your voice is perfect." Her cheeks were flushed. "You're perfect. I voted for you every night."

"I appreciate that. But I'm not perfect," he said, smiling. "I can promise you that."

"You are. You are. And I love you," the woman insisted, her grip tightening.

"And he loves you, too. You have to share him with

the rest of us," Travis King, the only male member of the Three Kings, gently pried the woman's hand loose. "But he's real glad you came out to meet him. Got something for him to sign?"

The woman nodded and offered him a poster of the Three Kings. He glanced at Travis and signed the corner, feeling like a fraud. He handed it back, smiled, and moved on. "Thanks," he murmured to Travis.

"Clingers are hard," Travis said, signing and talking and not missing a step. "One woman jumped over the tape and into my arms. She was no lightweight, either. Pulled a muscle in my back and had to get one of them to help her back onto the other side of the tape."

Jace looked in the direction of Travis's nod. Three men and one woman wearing "King's Guard" shirts. *Clever.* "Security?" he asked, smiling in spite of himself.

"Always," he said. "I hear my sister roped you into sticking around?"

"Not sure how it happened," Jace confessed.

"Krystal has a way of getting what she wants." Travis laughed. "Come on, take a break in the greenroom. Then it's time for group pics and hanging with the money." He led Jace down the hall, all the while smiling and waving.

Krystal joined them, no sign of her earlier tension present. She sort of…glowed, happy and excited. "You two stand together too long and we might have a riot on our hands."

Was that a compliment? It sure as hell sounded like one.

"Just own it, man. Own it and enjoy every minute."
Travis grinned. "You'll never have to sleep alone again."

"Travis, there are times I'm ashamed to call you my
brother." Clearly, she didn't appreciate her brother's attitude. By the time they entered what resembled a small
conference room, Krystal was back to being tense and
quiet.

One wall was lined with mirrors and floor-to-ceiling
folding screens. Jace was blindsided by the photographs
hanging on the wall just inside. He wandered, reading
autographs and shaking his head at the impressive display of talent that had visited the Chesapeake Energy
Arena before him. Willie Nelson. John Connelly. Loretta
Lynn. And a smiling, younger Hank King. Here he was,
a west Texas roughneck, surrounded by reminders of
everything he wasn't. Sooner or later, the rest of the
world would snap out of it and he'd be back on the grass-
hoppers, drilling for oil from dawn till dusk.

Might as well enjoy it.

On the opposite wall, a long table was covered with
trays of pastries, fruit, and cheese. He almost took pictures for Heather—almost. She'd love to see this—the
fancy sparkling water bottles in large glass bowls full of
ice. Above that, three large televisions played, muted.
The room and its occupants seemed to be on fast-
forward, while he was stuck in slow motion.

He shook his hands out and did his best not to stand
out.

His manager, Luke, was waiting with Mr. Zamora,

looking almost as nervous as he felt. Jace had taken a gamble hiring him, but Luke had grown up in the business and knew all the right people. Like CiCi King. He had no idea Luke's mother and Hank King's wife played bunco together, but he suspected that was how he'd ended up here. His voice was only part of it—having the right connections sealed the deal. Still, standing against the wall as the room filled with the chart-breaking, award-winning King family and the entourage that cared for them had his insecurities kicking in. Sure he sang some, for himself—or at the bar in town. But he had nothing, *nothing*, like the talent in this room.

Sure, they talked and laughed just like normal folk—but there was nothing normal about these people. He didn't belong here. This was not his life. This wasn't real; it couldn't be.

It didn't help that Krystal kept glancing his way. Even standing there, talking to her brother, she radiated a sort of defiance that was hard to ignore. Hell, if he was honest with himself, he didn't want to ignore her. He'd prop himself up right here, against the wall, and look his fill if he could. No woman should look this beautiful in real life. But she was.

Her eyes narrowed, the slight tilt of her chin baiting him. Damn it all, he couldn't help it—he winked at her. And saw vibrant color bloom in her cheeks.

"Jace?" Luke waved him over.

Probably a better idea than staring at Krystal. With a sigh, he joined Luke. "What happens now?" His ears were buzzing from the noise of the crowd and the concert earlier.

"Hydrate, snack, relax until the Kings say it's go time," Steve Zamora said, tossing him a water bottle. "Through those doors, the big spenders are waiting. The kids mingle, rub elbows with the power-players or their die-hard fans, take pictures, then make their getaway. Thirty minutes, more if you're having a good time. Just waiting on Emmy."

"As always," Travis sounded off.

"I'm here, Travis, be nice." Emmy Lou King made her entrance. There was no other word for it. She sort of glided into the room, drawing every eye her way.

"You shake everyone's hand, Sis?" Travis asked, making a show of checking his nonexistent watch.

"Course you did, darlin'." Hank King draped an arm around his daughter's shoulders and steered her his way. "Emmy, this is Jace. Jace, Emmy. He'll be singing a duet on the next album."

Just when he thought he was getting a handle on things, he was knocked for another loop. First, he was standing in the room with a man he'd grown up idolizing—he'd stomped around in his daddy's boots and hat singing Hank King songs until his parents had hollered for him to stop. Now he was shaking hands with the man. Meeting Krystal. Then Travis. And now the enormity of what was happening hit him. He was singing a duet with Emmy Lou King.

Hell no, this wasn't his life.

"He's new, so try not to dazzle him too much," Travis said.

Jace chuckled. "Good to meet you, Miss King. Tonight has been…unreal." He broke off, shaking his head. They'd grown up in the public eye, so they had no idea how surreal this all was.

"Daddy has that effect on people." Emmy Lou did have an incredible smile.

Hank King looked at his daughter with true adoration. "I'm pretty sure he was talking about you three."

"Or maybe he's still thinking about the women crying over him. Oh, and the one holding on to him with a death grip. That gets to a man," Travis said, biting into an apple.

He might be a little overwhelmed by all the introductions, but the thing that "got to him" the most tonight had nothing to do with his career and everything to do with a woman. Since he'd walked into Krystal's dressing room and they'd locked eyes, he'd been trying to recover. That wasn't what tonight should have been about. But, damn it all, he had no idea how to make it stop.

"We need to get you some security." Luke frowned. "I'll get on that now." He was already typing something into his phone.

"The first time someone grabbed hold of me, I panicked," Emmy said.

"You were sixteen. Being grabbed by a stranger at sixteen is panic worthy," Krystal said. "Don't let it get to you, Jace. Keep on smiling and, if it gets too intense, flag your guy over."

His name had never sounded husky and sexy as hell until she'd said it. And she'd said it right this time. *Jace.* He cleared his throat and took a swig from his water bottle.

"Looks like you've already got your own fan base." Hank scratched his temple. "I don't know much about the show you won, but people seem to already know and love you. That's a good thing."

"Your sales are only as strong as your fan base," Emmy Lou said. "They won't buy you if they don't love you."

"Guess you all don't have much to worry about," he said. Three Kings were a fixture on the charts. And Emmy Lou King? She had an army of fans dedicated to her.

Emmy Lou shook her head. "I always worry. People are watching everything I do or say—it's a lot of responsibility. I don't want to mess that up."

"That's why people adore her." Krystal's gaze flicked his way. "She's just as loyal to them as they are to her."

Seeing the sisters side by side was a surprise. The sisters were identical twins, but he had no problem telling them apart. Krystal was in her signature black, tight and seductive. Emmy was in pale pink and white, lacy and flowing. But the attire wasn't what did it. Maybe it was their mannerisms or their voices or the fact that one sister grabbed, and held, his interest.

Travis tossed his apple core into the trash. "And why she doesn't have much of a social life."

"*Social life?*" Krystal's smile hardened. "Like you? I'm

pretty sure taking groupies back to your place doesn't count. Besides, they might not be a fan when the *party* is over."

Jace did his best not to laugh, but damn, she was good. Even her father was laughing.

"Beware." Travis leaned closer and pretended to whisper to him. "My sister has a razor-sharp tongue. Don't get on her bad side."

Jace had a sinking feeling he was already on her bad side—for reasons unknown.

"We really appreciate the time you've given us tonight, but we'll be heading out." Luke was shaking Steve Zamora's hand. "We'll wait for your call on the scheduling."

"Monday morning, our Austin studio, nine a.m. Right, Hank?" Steve asked. "Let's get this project in the works."

Krystal missed a step, teetering enough so that she braced one hand on the wall. It wasn't much—but it was enough for Jace. She didn't want him singing her song. The look on her face only confirmed it. She *really* didn't want him singing it. He had one choice: prove he'd do it right.

"Already set up," Hank replied, nodding his goodbye and disappearing through the door.

"Jace?" Luke asked.

Jace nodded. "I'll be there."

Steve nodded and followed Emmy Lou through the door.

Krystal finished off her water bottle and turned to

face him. Those eyes of hers were blazing. If he'd had time, he'd have tried to talk to her, to calm her fears. It was one of those songs—important, special. He'd damn well make sure anyone listening to it knew it, too.

The first time he'd read the lyrics, he'd been drawn in. After the soul-crushing loss he'd suffered three years ago, "Ashes of My Heart" said all the things he'd never been able to. While he thought Krystal's soulful rasp was a better fit for the song than Emmy Lou, it wasn't his call. Something told him Krystal wouldn't care about his opinion of the lyrics or her voice. She'd think he was sucking up.

Still he couldn't help himself. "Meeting you…well, tonight's been my lucky night. I hope I'll see you again." And he meant it.

She shook her head. "Do you? Guess we'll see, *Jack*." Without another word, she followed her family into the next room.

Chapter 2

"Aw shit." Krystal heard Travis about the same time she slammed into his back.

"Travis?" she asked, pushing against her brother's back. "What's wrong?"

He turned to face her, his hands on her shoulders. "I need you to keep it together. There are witnesses." He shook his head. "Are you listening to me?"

"Not that you're making a lick of sense." She brushed his hands off her shoulders and walked around him, into the room of waiting VIPs. Now she needed to get her mind off Jace, his light brown eyes, and all the witty comebacks she should have tossed his way before leaving him tonight. Chances were she'd never see him again. She chewed on her lower lip, unexpectedly disappointed. No, it was good. Jace Black was bad news, period. She had no use for him.

Unless it was in the bedroom. She'd give him whatever he wanted there... Her body ached to do just that. Contrary to what the media said, she wasn't the sort of girl to have a fling. Still—she blew out a slow breath—that man had kicked her long-dormant libido into overdrive. Every time his heavy-lidded gaze drifted her way, the temperature seemed a good ten degrees hotter, and it had nothing to do with the anger she'd hoped to hold on to.

Someone bumped into her, their murmured apology a reality check. Here she was, in the middle of a room full of people, imagining Jace Black in her bed? Talk about bad timing. As Emmy pointed out, these were the folks who shelled out a minimum of twenty-five hundred dollars for tickets and deserved their attention. For that low, low price, they got floor seats, *free* drinks and food, an autographed picture, a picture with the band, and a guaranteed thirty minutes of cocktails and socializing. Some were true fans, others were big-spending friends of their family or the record label.

Unfortunately, her mother was also there. Because her momma *never* missed an opportunity to collect information that might benefit her later. Krystal had no illusions when it came to her mother: CiCi King was not a nice person. The only thing her mother cared about was keeping Three Kings on the charts and the front page. If there was a way to get Three Kings more press, she was all for it. Her big eyes, bright smile, and charming laugh might have the rest of the world fooled—Krystal's daddy included—but she knew the truth about the woman who'd birthed her.

That was one of the reasons she and her momma had a...*strained* relationship.

Travis hovered beside her. "You look way too calm. It's freaking me out."

What was wrong with him? Had her mother done something she didn't know about yet? Worse than handing off her song, that is? Somehow, deep down, she knew her mother had had a hand in that.

If she were the one singing the song with Jace, she wouldn't be upset. She paused then. Of course she'd be upset. Jace's talent was unknown. What if he couldn't sing? What if he butchered her song? No one knew what the song meant to her—but she did. Soulful eyes, glorious black hair, and a killer grin could only do so much on the charts.

"You sure you're okay?"

"I'm fine, Travis. Give me some room." But then she saw exactly why Travis was freaking out.

Mickey Graham.

The son of a bitch was here. Laughing with her mother and her friends. Drinking beer and rubbing elbows with *her* VIPs.

"What the hell? Why is he here?" she hissed, grabbing onto her brother's arm.

"There we go." He covered her hand with his. "I don't know why. But he is. And people are watching." He patted her hand.

Krystal stared down at the concrete floor, fighting for composure. Nausea and fury clamped down on her lungs and heart and stomach until it was hard to breathe at all. The last time she'd seen him in person had been at the Awards for Country Music. He'd had the nerve to try to get a picture together. That hadn't ended well—for her. Apparently stomping your heel so hard it punctured his boot and sent him to the ER for a few stitches in his foot was press-worthy.

Of course there was not a single picture of his hand

on her ass. Or a sound bite of what he'd said about how
he considered her voice her second-best asset and what,
exactly, he wanted to do to what he considered her best
asset. Not one. Instead, every radio show and entertainment magazine and TV show said Krystal King was out of
control with bitterness over their breakup. And she was,
but not the way they thought. He'd used her, publicly,
mercilessly, and managed to turn her into the bad guy.

But it was her fault. She'd let him in. Believed him.
Trusted him. Let her hunger for acceptance, for love, blind
her. If she'd kept her guard up, he'd never have been in a
position to launch the campaign that made him and almost
destroyed her. She knew better. She'd been a fool. Again.

Now he was here, invading her world again. And it
made her blood boil. Travis was right to warn her. An
audience might just prevent her from totally losing it. But
it didn't change the fact that he had no right to be here.
How had he even gotten in without an invitation?

An invitation.

She knew. Damn it all, she knew. And the veins in her
head began to throb so that she pressed her fingers to her
temples. "Momma?" she asked, her throat so tight it hurt
to say the word.

"She wouldn't, Krystal." But there was doubt in her
brother's voice. "No...she wouldn't. Would she?" He
glanced at her.

"She would. And you know it." Krystal cleared her
throat. "And we're all going to find out why soon enough."
Because her momma knew doing things in public, with

an audience of highly connected people, was much harder to undo.

"What are you two talking about?" Her daddy hugged her into his side. "Should I be worried?"

"I would, if I were you," Travis said, nodding at their mother, her friends, and Mickey Graham.

"What the hell is that rat bastard doing here?" Her father's whisper was lined with outrage.

That's right. Her daddy loved her. He'd get offended on his little girl's behalf. But what would he do if he found out his wife was the one who'd invited the rat bastard?

"Keep your distance, Krystal," her daddy warned. "If you can't hear him, he can't say anything to set you off. And we both know the man lives to set you off."

"Fine by me," she replied.

And that's when their mother spotted them. For a split second, her mother looked at her. In that blip of time, there was no doubting her mother's excitement. Or her smug little smile of victory. Whatever CiCi King was up to, Krystal was at the center of it. And since Mickey Graham was smiling her way too, she was pretty sure she wasn't going to like it. Not one teeny tiny bit.

"Hank." Her mother held out one perfectly manicured hand, diamonds sparkling. "You look good, honey." She tipped her face so Daddy could give her the obligatory kiss on the cheek.

He did. "CiCi, ladies." He was all smiles for the women circled around his wife. But he turned his back to Mickey.

And Krystal loved him for it. So, so much.

"Wanna drink?" Travis asked, steering her away from her parents and Mickey.

"No," she said, arm tightening. "And don't you dare leave me."

He sighed. "Can we at least walk to the bar then, maybe talk to some people?"

"Sure." She followed his lead and gave it her all. If Mickey knew she was ready to pounce, he'd love it. And she didn't want to give him any more power over her. She was done with that. With him. At least, she thought she was. Until Momma dragged him back into the mix.

Forget about Mickey. She smiled and turned all her attention to the fans and their questions. No, she'd never been to Alaska, but she was sure it was mighty cold in the winter. Yes, she had seen the new Tom Cruise movie but thought it was overrated. She did still have her three-legged Chinese crested dog, Clementine—an Instagram star with a huge following. And she was excited about the tour and how well tickets were selling.

At the moment, she wished she were back home in the rolling Texas hill Country. She could use a little peace and quiet, a long ride on her blue mare, Maizy, and lots and lots of wide-open space.

"Bad news about Josephine and Frankie." His name badge said John. "Did you see it?"

Krystal had no idea what he was talking about. "Did I see what?"

"The arrest?" name badge Irma added. "Backstage, right before you went on."

She blinked. Arrest? Josephine and Frankie? They were the opening act, a sweet couple who played a unique blend of bluegrass, folk, and classic country. They were low drama, something that was a rarity in the music world. "No…no, I didn't see a thing."

"It was all over the news, livestreaming," John said, launching into the drugs found on their tour bus. Lots of drugs apparently.

"Who will be opening for you now?" Irma asked.

"No idea," she said, but as soon as the words were out, she knew. *No. No. No.* Her momma wouldn't do that to her. Mickey? She couldn't. She was her mother, for crying out loud. The blood drained from her cheeks. Daddy wouldn't let it happen. Surely. Her gaze flew across the room, searching for him.

Mickey Graham winked at her. He winked. And he smiled that lopsided smile that used to turn her insides to goo. Now it made her want to throw up. Preferably on his favorite pair of calf-skin boots. He loved those damn boots.

"Pictures," Emmy said, leading her to the step and repeat wall. A drape of royal blue fabric, their logo—a cowboy hat with a hatband covered in crowns—and "The Three Kings" repeating every few feet. She, Emmy Lou, and Travis took at least a dozen pics before she noticed her father. He was angry in his own way. He didn't scowl and yell. No, his cheeks turned red, his blue eyes narrowed to slits, and the muscle in his jaw locked tight. Like now.

When the cameras stopped and people started saying their goodbyes, she made her way to her daddy's side. "You okay?" she asked, smiling up at him.

"Krystal," Mickey Graham said, sneaking up from behind. Like the snake he was.

Her daddy squeezed her hand in warning.

She nodded, then sucked in a sharp breath. "Mickey," she said, refusing to look at him.

But her mother pulled him around, into her line of sight. "Oh, sugar, isn't it nice that Mickey stopped by to see the show?" her mother asked, watching her closely.

Krystal didn't say a word.

"I've always been a fan, you all know that." Mickey's aw-shucks twang was too much. How had she ever dated him? *Thought* she cared about him?

"Of course you have." Her mother was still smiling, still watching. "It's been quite a night. First the whole drug bust, then Jace Black, and now, you."

Why was one of her mother's friends taking pictures? Holding up her cell phone. Was she recording this? Whatever. If she ever fully understood the way her mother's mind worked, then she'd have reason to worry.

"You know, that Jace Black is all over the place right now. Have you heard him sing?" her mother asked.

Mickey stiffened at the mention of Jace's name. Maybe she'd find a way to like Jace after all. He was sure as hell easy on the eyes. And, when he'd looked at her, there'd been nothing but warmth in his light brown gaze. Nothing like the way Mickey was looking at her now.

"Never heard of this Jace Black till tonight," Mickey said to her mother, his posture defensive. "My manager didn't mention anything about him when he said you'd called."

"Me call?" Her mother rested her hand on her surgically enhanced chest. "Sugar, I never make phone calls. I have people for that."

"Well, someone called," Mickey said, glancing her way. "I thought it was too good to be true—me opening for you all. Especially after what happened between us, Krystal." He stepped closer, his hand reaching for hers. "But at least I can say what I've wanted to say for a while now."

Krystal stared at her hand, caught in his clammy hold, and fought for control. Mickey couldn't be their opening act. And her mother—what was she thinking? The urge to scream at them, to yank her hands away, almost choked her. But she wouldn't cause a scene—no matter how perfectly her mother had laid her trap. Instead, she bit into her lip so hard she tasted blood.

Everyone was staring at her, waiting. Even Emmy Lou looked nervous. So she managed to say, "There's nothing to be said."

"Maybe not for you, Krystal, but I have a lot to say." His gaze bounced between her, her mother, and the camera.

She had to leave. Now. She gently but firmly withdrew her hand from his. "You'll have to find someone who wants to hear it." And she left the room as quickly and calmly as possible.

"Whoa," Luke said for the fiftieth time. "I just keep saying it, man."

Jace nodded. They'd left the VIP room, walked out of the stadium, and stopped in the parking lot, talking strategy and schedules. He couldn't help but worry that, once he got into his truck and drove away, this would all disappear. He'd wake up tomorrow morning at five, head to the factory, punch his time card, and singing would only be his hobby again.

"It doesn't feel real," he confessed. Tonight had been weird...and a whole hell of a lot of awesome. He couldn't wait to tell his sister all about it. Heather would want details, too—down to what they were wearing, who was there, and any gossip.

"It's real, all right. We're just getting started," Luke said, glancing at his ever-present cell phone. "I'll pick you up around seven thirty? We can get coffee on the way."

The side door to the stadium opened, slamming loudly into the side of the building, and Krystal pushed out, her leather fringed skirt swaying. Seconds later, a man followed her. Even from this distance, he could tell Krystal was upset. Her hands clenched, arm held out, keeping distance between them. What was going on and who was giving Krystal trouble? When the two of them paused under one of the massive parking lot lights, he knew.

Mickey Graham?

Where was Krystal's bodyguard?

From all the tabloids, headlines, and talk show interviews Heather kept up with, he knew their relationship hadn't ended well. Krystal King, country royalty, fell for an up-and-comer on the circuit. Once they'd broken up, Mickey spilled his guts to the world. Krystal had ended it, cheated on him. And she was mean to Emmy Lou and Travis, fought with her mother and father, and was spoiled rotten.

Krystal had never said a word about any of it—not Mickey's accusations, their relationship, or their breakup.

Jace had never believed it. Ever. Her music told him all he needed to know. She'd been hurt, deserted, and betrayed.

Still, Mickey's song "Lie to Me" had released not too long after their split and shot to the top of the charts. He said it was about losing Krystal. But Jace couldn't shake the feeling that Mickey was milking his short-lived romance for all it was worth—and it had been worth a lot. The single had gone gold regardless of the fact that Mickey Graham had no real musical talent. He ran around in sleeveless shirts and spray-painted-on jeans, his voice was nasally, and he had no range—he was all flash and no substance.

None of that mattered right now. Not when Mickey was up in Krystal's personal space—so much so that Krystal was backing away.

When he'd started heading her way, he didn't know. But she was upset and on her own and he wasn't going to stand by and do nothing. He wasn't wired that way.

"This could get ugly," Luke said, following.

"Why won't you go away and stay away?" Krystal's voice rose. "I don't want to see you. Get it through your thick head—I don't like you."

"You used to," Mickey replied.

"I was an idiot." She shook her head. "Why are you really here? Why?" The pain in her voice had Jace moving faster.

"You think I'd pass up an opportunity to open for the Three Kings? Hell no." Mickey sighed, shaking his head. "Then your dad goes and screws it up. What the hell is he thinking? Bringing in that wannabe?"

"Talk to him about it," she snapped. "Go on." She pointed behind him. "Now."

He chuckled. "You can't tell me we wouldn't have fun on the road together. You know we would."

"Are you serious?" Her voice shook. "Why did you follow me, Mickey? Is there a camera out here somewhere? Looking for more PR at my expense? I'm tired of getting you more headlines."

What was Mickey talking about? The Three Kings had one hell of an opening act. And why had her mother called him? From the way Krystal was staring at Mickey, she was just as surprised as he was.

"I'm not about to apologize for doing what it takes to get a platinum record. You've always known my career came first." He shook his head. "Hell, it wasn't all bad. Being in your bed. Mm-m. You remember, too. Don't you? Miss me? I know you do."

He and Luke were so close—but not close enough. Krystal's hand shot out, the slap echoing in the still parking lot.

"You really are a bitch, you know that?" But Mickey was laughing.

The son of a bitch deserved more than a slap; Mickey Graham deserved getting his ass handed to him. Jace would be more than happy to teach him a lesson in manners. If the bastard didn't step away from Krystal, class was about to be in session. Still, Krystal was upset—for good reason. Instead of busting heads, he'd get her out of here. He reined in his temper, ignored Mickey Graham, and stepped between them, facing her.

"Krystal?"

She was shaking, staring blindly at his chest.

"Krystal?" he asked again, his voice low. "Hey, it's Jace."

"You're Jace?" Mickey asked, still behind him. If the son of a bitch was smart, he'd stay there.

Krystal finally looked up at him, dazed. He searched her pale face. "You okay?" She didn't look okay. She looked terrified. Frozen in place and shivering.

Her eyes widened, truly seeing him for the first time. "Jace?"

"Yeah. Hi. Need a ride somewhere?" He grinned.

She blinked rapidly, running a hand over her hair. Her hand trembled like a leaf.

Damn, her fear had his stomach in knots. And his hands fisting. "Or a human barrier between you and the asshole behind me?" He tried, he did, but there was no denying the edge to his words.

She smiled, surprised. "Yeah," she breathed. "I do… Thank you."

"Taking her back to her hotel won't get you any-where," Mickey snorted.

Jace spun on his heel, fists clenched, jaw tight. Being tall had advantages—like towering over assholes with big mouths. "You want to get punched? You keep talking, you will."

Mickey's mouth hung open in shock, but he didn't say another word.

Jace turned back to find Krystal's eyes closed, her face crinkled up tight, and her hands fisted at her side. He could only imagine all the things she wanted to say and do right now. Her restraint was admirable. His, on the other hand, was fading. It was time to go.

"Mr. Graham, isn't it?" Jace heard Luke say. "I'm a fan, a big fan. Are you in the market for a new manager? If you are, maybe we could go get a beer?"

Jace didn't wait to hear Mickey's response. He glanced back at Luke, nodded, and led Krystal away. He hadn't felt the need to fight in years, but right now, the urge to punch Mickey Graham was all-encompassing. Hard enough to wipe that smug grin off his face and land him on his ass. Though Krystal had landed one hell of a slap. "Let's start walking. I'm parked out in the south forty."

It was a smaller smile this time, but a smile nonethe-less. "Lead the way, Jake."

He laughed. "Now, you're working at it. You know my name."

She glanced up at him, peering up at him through her thick lashes. "Do I?"

Damn she was pretty. And feisty. And talented. "My name is Jace Michael Black. But most people just call me Jace."

"Michael's a good name. Why didn't you go with that?"

He chuckled. "Jace is a bad name?"

She shrugged. "I'm not sure yet."

"You let me know when you figure it out." Once they reached the jacked-up rental truck Luke had saddled him with, he opened the passenger door for her. The truck had a hydraulic lift, making that first step a doozy—especially for someone wearing a short, skin-tight miniskirt.

"A gentleman?" she said, taking his hand to step up into the large four-wheel drive.

"Yes, ma'am. Thanks to my grandmother."

Try as she might, there was no way she was going to get into the truck cab without showing a lot of skin. Considering his grandmother wouldn't take kindly to how much he was already appreciating the view of her long legs as she attempted to climb into his truck, he did what any gentleman would do.

He'd intended to lift her up and into the truck. That was the plan. But her scent slammed into him with dizzying impact. And once his hands settled on her waist, his brain short-circuited. Her fringed costume hid the fact that her midriff was exposed. Now, her skin, smooth as silk, electrified the tips of his fingers and had him seriously rethinking the gentleman thing.

She stared up at him, all emerald fire and pure temptation. A temptation he'd do well to resist. Getting caught up in Krystal King would be the stupidest thing he could do. He wasn't stupid. With a heavy sigh, he lifted her, set her on the truck seat, and released her before he did something he'd regret. Regret washed over him the minute he let her go.

"You *are* a gentleman. I'll have to thank your grandmother," she said, smiling. "The gentleman is a dying breed."

"I'm sure she hears you." He winked, pushed the passenger door shut, and made his way around the front of his rental truck.

"I'm sorry," Krystal said when he climbed into the driver's seat.

"Don't be. It was a long time ago. Good to talk about her, keeps the memories alive." He started the truck, his gaze sweeping the parking lot. No sign of Mickey Graham or Luke.

"They're gone?" she asked, her voice rough.

"Looks like it." He glanced at her. "You okay?"

"Fine. I'm tough, don't you know?" She looked at him, an edge to her voice. "Hard and cold and…unfaithful and irrational. I'm sure, somehow, tonight is—will be—all my fault." She crossed her arms over her chest and stared out the window.

"I was there." He assured her. "His fault."

She didn't respond, but he thought he saw a glimpse of a smile on her face reflected in the truck side-view mirror. She had every right to be upset; he was fired up and it wasn't even his problem. But if he could distract her, he would. "How'd the VIP thing go?" he asked. "Anything exciting?"

"That was it." She shuddered. "He was there, hanging on Momma's arm, smiling that sleazy smile."

There was so much wrong with that statement he didn't know where to start. No matter how hard she denied it, she was hurting. So changing the subject might be the best option. "You always play acoustic guitar?"

She looked his way then. "Yes."

"You use it when you're composing?"

"It's what I learned to play on." She nodded. "One of Daddy's old ones, all scratched up and faded teal. But when he gave it to me, it was the prettiest thing I'd ever seen. And it's still the best present I ever got."

He respected Hank King. Anyone who knew country music knew about the man's humble roots, his determination to succeed, and his independence. His marriage to oil-princess CiCi Beaumont didn't slow his drive or sway his ambition—he'd turned his career into a family affair. And, clearly, it had worked well for the family. "He knew what you had inside."

"What do I have inside?" The tone of her voice changed, softening.

"Music." He glanced at her then. "Your sister and brother can sing, but you...channel it, you create it. It lives inside of you. And when you sing, people feel it. Anyone who watches you would say the same thing."

She stared at him, her gaze sweeping over his face before locking onto his mouth. The longer she stared, the harder it was to concentrate on his driving. When she bit the red fullness of her lower lip, he was damn near breathless.

He cleared his throat. "What?"

"I'm trying to decide what you want?" The question was soft and thin.

He frowned, unsure how to proceed. Right now, with her looking at him, he wanted something. Her. Not as Krystal King from the music videos, TV interviews, or songs that filled his truck to and from work. But this Krystal King, sitting here in the dark with him, staring at his mouth, wanting him. Like he wanted her. Badly. "Right now? Directions to where I'm going."

There was that smile and her husky laugh. When she looked at him again, he pretended not to notice. "My bus." She shook her head. "Back the other way. Through the security gate."

He turned around and followed her directions to one of the large black buses waiting.

"King's Coach?" he asked, put the truck in park, and opened his door. He jumped down and came around to get her.

She slid out of the truck cab and into his arms. "Yeah, we get a lot of mileage out of the whole King thing. Never gets old." She smiled up at him, her hands resting on his chest.

Every breath she took pressed her curves more tightly against him, kicking his pulse into overdrive. The slow smile on her lips was all it took to make him rock hard and aching. Did she know how bad he wanted her? Having her in his arms was a sweet sort of hell.

Her eyes narrowed, just a bit, setting off warning bells. Was this some sort of test? For all he knew she was toying with him—and loving every minute of it. Either way, this had to stop. Now.

It took effort to ease his hold, to lift his hands from the warmth of her bare flesh. But he did it. *Damn it all.* "Night," he whispered, stepping back and giving her space.

With a nod of her head, she walked the short distance to her bus—fringes swinging in time to the sway of her hips. He bit off a groan, leaned against the truck hood, and shoved his hands into his jeans pockets.

But when she reached the bus, she paused and looked back, studying him. "I guess this is goodbye, Jace Michael Black. Thanks for the ride." She wavered, as if she had more to say, then thought better of it. With a flounce of fringe and sparkling boots, she disappeared inside her bus, the thud of the doors closing echoing in the parking lot.

"Well, hell," he ground out, resting his head on the hood of the truck until he could think straight again.

Chapter 3

THE BLACK WINDOWS OF THEIR SUV WERE HEAVILY tinted, but the bright Texas sun filtered through—not helping the pounding in Krystal's head. She'd already asked their driver to slow down a little, the world flying by making her stress-headache nausea that much worse. She didn't need to be here. Nope, she *needed* to be barricaded in her nice dark bedroom between crisp, clean sheets with her dog, Clementine, at her side, pretending that the best thing she'd ever written wasn't being recorded without her. But Daddy put his foot down, insisting she come along as "creative consultant." Maybe he thought keeping her involved in the creative process would make this hurt less.

He was wrong. She'd had two days to accept she wasn't singing her song, but making her watch Emmy Lou and Jace do it was mean.

It didn't help that her nightmares had been worse since her run-in with Mickey. Not that Mickey had ever hurt her, but still. Being alone with him. Having him invade her space. He dragged her back to a time and place she didn't want to go to—trapped, in the dark, knowing there was no one to hear her. Or stop what was happening. She'd pushed and fought only to jerk awake, crying and drenched in sweat.

Jace's timing had been perfect. Jace—who her sister had been chattering about since they left the ranch and made the drive into town.

"He is gorgeous," Emmy Lou said. "Don't tell me you didn't notice."

Krystal sipped her skinny vanilla latte. She'd noticed, all right. Since meeting him, Jace Black had starred in far too many daydreams. But it was purely physical— because he was hot. So hot she wished he'd followed her onto her bus. She'd waited inside, hoping against hope, holding her breath until the lights of his truck and the roar of his engine told her he'd driven off. He was, apparently, a real gentleman. It was surprising in a good way. And disappointing. Sleeping with him would have been a colossal mistake. But she was pretty sure it would have been worth it.

"I thought we were off men together?" she asked, leaning against her sister. Even though it had been years since Emmy's breakup with football player Brock Watson, her sister hadn't moved on. Emmy rarely mentioned her ex. Partly because it still hurt to talk about him and partly because talking about him brought out Krystal's super-protective side.

Brock had been the one. Well, everyone had thought he was, anyway—especially Emmy Lou. He was a too-cute, all-American, Mom-and-Dad-approved, apple-pie-loving, high school sweetheart and soon-to-be professional football star. Emmy had given one hundred percent of her heart to him, and he'd shredded it into a million tiny pieces before chasing after his dream—a dream Emmy Lou had always supported.

Things went from bad to worse when her sister had learned about his engagement and subsequent over-the-top wedding to a lingerie model. Emmy had cried and cried and Krystal had vowed never to let anyone hurt her sister like that ever again.

"Not all men are like…Brock." Emmy drew in a deep breath. "Anyway, Jace seems nice." Emmy glanced at her sister. "What did you think?"

So far, yes. He *seemed* nice. But she wasn't ready to buy the whole gentlemanly, nice hot-guy thing. He seemed a little too good to be true. "My head hurts. It's seven thirty and I'm having my first cup of coffee, Emmy." She dodged. "I'm not thinking about anything. Except my coffee." Which was a lie. Thanks to her sister, she was definitely thinking about Jace. His smile. His laugh. The crinkles at the corner of his eyes. That smooth-as-velvet voice. The touch of his fingers against the skin on her back. And the way his faded jeans hugged an ass worthy of notice. She'd definitely noticed him.

Emmy laughed. "Well, he seemed to like you."

Krystal almost choked on her coffee. If he'd really been interested, she wouldn't have slept alone. "You have an overactive imagination, Emmy. He was in shock, like a deer in headlights."

To be fair, he'd handled himself pretty well, all things considered. No matter what he was feeling on the inside, he stayed cool and collected, barely tripping over his words when he talked to her father. And after, with Mickey. If he hadn't shown up, what would have happened? She owed him a thank-you. She could think of a dozen or so ways she could repay him. One or two of them might be clothing optional. She smiled as she sipped her coffee. "But he's nice. Maybe."

He was still an ass for stealing her song.

"I'm sorry your head hurts." Emmy looked pointedly at her choice of attire. Her sister looked perfect, as always. She didn't leave the house unless she was ready for a photo shoot. Hair, makeup, actual pants versus yoga pants or leggings, and some cute, ruffled blouse.

"Don't get all judgy on me." Krystal stared down at her cheetah print leggings, black Converse, and oversized black T-shirt. She adjusted her black cap and pushed her sunglasses up her nose. "It does hurt. I'm upright, wearing clean underwear and a bra. I'm not trying to impress anyone. Besides, I'm only here as a technical adviser." Something she'd tried to get out of. The song was done. Since she wasn't singing it, they could do what they damn well wanted with it. A point that had already been made perfectly clear to her since she wasn't singing it.

"What do you mean?" Emmy turned to look at her.

Krystal peered over the edge of her sunglasses. "Um, you and Jace."

"Me and Jace what?" Emmy Lou froze. "You mean… Wait. But I thought you were singing—"

"You thought wrong." A sharp spike formed in her throat, so she sipped her latte.

"But this is your song." She shook her head.

Krystal didn't say a thing. It *was* her song.

Emmy chattered away. "Momma said it was the best thing you'd ever written it. She was so excited about it."

"Momma says a lot of things. What she means is something different," she interrupted. Her dear, precious mother. The incident with Mickey had only reinforced how much she *disliked* the woman who'd birthed her. It was wrong, she knew it, but CiCi King brought it on herself. What sort of person tormented her child for profit or attention? How would that help the band? She would do anything, *anything*, to keep the Three Kings front and center. Like bring the man that forever tarnished her reputation to a VIP mixer hoping to stir things up. And suggesting he replace their opening act. She wouldn't put it past her momma to have planted the drugs in Josephine and Frankie's bus. But that seemed far-fetched, even by CiCi King standards.

Then again, it wasn't completely implausible.

This was the same woman who'd dismissed her accusations against Tiger Whitman all those years ago. Krystal, according to her mother, was "looking for attention" and lying to get it. Her mother was furious—with her—for making up such vile, dirty stories about a dear family friend. Tiger, Uncle Tig to those who knew him, was a fine, upstanding pillar of the country music business. He'd helped so many careers along the way, including her daddy's. The man was practically family. He'd never ever hurt her—Momma refused to believe otherwise.

But Krystal knew the truth. She lived with it every day.

Panic gripped her, pulling her muscles tight and pressing the air from her lungs. And she hated it. Hated the slimy bastard. Hated the weakness. Hated being locked in her head—in fear—when she was safe and sound sitting by her sister.

"Oh, Krystal." Emmy took her hand. "I can't do it," she whispered. "How could she?"

Because it's what Momma does. Stir things up. Keep drama front and center. As long as she was in charge, she was happy. Somehow, she knew her mother had pitched it to the Wheelhouse Records VP, a man she had firmly in her pocket, as a vehicle for Emmy Lou. She wanted to believe her father hadn't played a part in that. Her daddy was a businessman, but he loved his children and that always came first.

How Jace Black wound up part of the deal, she didn't know.

The car came to a stop and they made their way inside the studio her family owned. Between her father and the Three Kings, it had made more sense to build one than rent one every time they needed one, which was often. Of course, her daddy had a pretty open-door policy, when he or the Three Kings weren't working on something.

She nodded at the sound manager and sipped her latte, wishing the caffeine would take the edge off. But there wasn't enough coffee in the world for that. Mickey, her mother, her song—the song she'd written hoping to put some of her demons to rest…

"Are we late?" Emmy whispered, nodding toward the recording booth.

Jace Black was already waiting. *Still way too hot.* She pretended to take a long, slow sip of coffee to give him a thorough once-over.

His faded jeans did only good things to his perfectly sculpted ass. And the worn John Deere tractor shirt hugged his upper arms just right, hinting at his impressive muscles. The throb in her head was challenged by the throb of want flooding her veins. It'd help if he wasn't smiling at her. Or he wasn't so tall. Or so bone-meltingly gorgeous. The things she was imagining right now, with painstaking attention to detail and in slow motion, took more of the bite out of her headache.

"Morning," he said, all dimples and white teeth.

She grunted.

"Jace," Emmy Lou whispered. "Nice to see you."

"You too," he said.

"Krystal, rough morning?" her daddy asked. "Headache?"

She nodded, sipping her coffee.

"Before we get started, there are a few things we need to work through. You've all heard about Josephine and Frankie. We had a few guests step in the last two concerts since their arrest, but we need a solid opener." Her daddy sat on a stool. "Jace, with the duet and all, Luke thought you might be interested."

Krystal choked on her coffee. There was a vague recollection of him being mentioned that night, with

Mickey, but she'd been too distracted and upset for it to register. Until now. Jace. On the road. Being nice and funny. Too hot for his own good. Driving her out of her mind—wanting him. In close quarters.

But her mother's alternative—Mickey Graham— would make her life a living hell.

"Are you serious?" Jace asked, stumbling back a step to sink onto a stool.

Her father nodded.

Krystal was struck by Jace's reaction. The man was truly shocked that her father would suggest such a thing. And, for some reason, it touched her. She had yet to discover if Jace was talented, but her father saw something in him. That spoke volumes.

Jace stared around the room, glancing at Emmy Lou, then her father, before his grey eyes locked with hers— and held. His gaze fell away, and he rubbed his hands on his thighs. He stood, eagerly shaking her father's hand. "Thank you."

Why had he looked at her like that? Was he going to say no if she objected? She should. Really. Nice or not, he made her nervous. Not about him, but about the way she reacted to him. "If he said no, we'd be stuck with Mickey?" she asked. Surely there were other options— less complicated options.

"Of course not." Emmy Lou cleared her throat. "Daddy would never do that to you. To us."

She smiled a hard smile at her sister. "*Daddy* might not."

"But you *are* interested?" her daddy asked Jace again.

"Yes, sir. Without a doubt."

"We're good." Her daddy stood. "Luke said you have enough songs to start putting together a few singles? Let Krystal take a look at them, tweak things up." He glanced at her. "Okay?"

She nodded. Sure, why not? What she really needed was more time with Jace. That way they could really torment each other. She sighed. Maybe Jace was working with her mother. His job was to drive her to distraction. Because if he was their opening act, she'd get to see him all the time and want to stay with the Three Kings versus exploring a solo career. Not CiCi's best plan—but not her worst.

"Daddy." Emmy Lou spoke up, making a big production out of coughing. "My throat is hurting something fierce."

Hank King frowned. "Need to rest your voice then. Krystal, you up to running through the song with him a few times? Let him get the feel for it?"

Her headache melted away. She pulled off her sunglasses and shot her sister a heartfelt thank-you smile. "I'm up for it." There was nothing wrong with Emmy Lou, and they both knew it. Her sister was giving her the chance no one else would.

"Then you two start warming up," her daddy said, disappearing into the sound booth, Emmy Lou following, sending her a good-luck wink.

"You ready?" Krystal asked, climbing onto the stool.

Five seconds ago, she had wanted to lock herself in the bathroom and cry. Now, she was here, about to sing her song—with Jace. And she'd know if he could sing.

He nodded, clearing his throat. "Nervous as hell."

"Just pretend you're singing in the shower," she said, the imagery immediately amping up the aching throb deep in her belly.

"Pretend I'm in the shower? With you?" His cheeks turned dark red.

"You're blushing, Jace Michael Black." Her smile grew. "What in the world are you thinking? And here I thought you were a gentleman." She'd be okay with him being a little less of a gentleman.

His gaze swept over her face. "I'm a gentleman. But I'm a still a man."

She knew that all too well. Her daydreams had carried out what would have happened if he'd followed her into her bus. It—they—would be incredible. All she had to do was look at him to remember—and ache.

His dimple was just too much. "You started it."

"No one ever said I was a good girl," she managed. What would being a bad girl with Jace Black be like?

They sat there, staring at each other, the air growing charged. If she could go back, she'd drag him into her bus and get him out of her system. Maybe that's all they needed. She was fairly certain that's what she needed. She wasn't going to kid herself. His fascination with her would wear off as soon as they hit the road. A man was hard pressed to stay faithful when there were willing women every time he got off the bus. Travis would be more than happy to tell him all about that.

Jace Black was no different than any other man.

She might take a man to her bed, on her terms, but she'd never ever let one near her heart again.

She frowned, turning her attention to the sheets of music before her. Her lyrics. Her music. Her pain and humiliation. This was going to be harder than she'd thought. Baring her soul didn't come easily. But, for this song, she'd let go and sing. From that place inside.

Jace stared at the words on the page. He'd read it a hundred times, knew it by heart, and now it was showtime. It was bad enough that Hank King was in the sound box, bad enough he'd have to sing with Emmy Lou. But now it was Krystal—and that changed everything. She'd written this. The look in her eyes when they'd met, the anger and resentment, was for this song. She wanted to protect what it was, what it meant to her. It meant a *hell* of a lot.

He couldn't screw this up.

"Stop it." Krystal's voice threw him.

He looked at her. "Stop what?"

"You're getting in your head." Her brows rose. "Am I right?"

He shrugged. "There's a little pressure here." This was nothing big for her; her family owned the recording studio he was sitting in for crying out loud. But for him, this was huge.

She laughed. "Why? Because you're hoping to prove that you're worthy of being on a record with my sister?"

This recording contract was important, but the Three Kings had never been part of the original deal. Singing with Emmy Lou guaranteed him instant fame—but he'd rather sing with Krystal. Not that he'd say so. Hell, he was just happy to be here. But there was so much riding on this. A future for Heather, for one. Financial security. And, if he was lucky, a career that wouldn't age him before his time. "It's more than that."

She put her headset on the music stand and sat back. "What then? You need to have a clear head so you can focus on the music."

"And them?" he asked, pointing at the sound booth. To her, they were family. To him, they were country music stars. Chart-toppers with the kind of power and connections he couldn't begin to imagine.

"They'll wait." She crossed her arms over her chest. "Talk."

She was sexy as hell when she was bossy. Sexier. Was it possible for her to be sexier? He laughed. Right or wrong, he'd spent far too much time wishing he'd knocked on her bus door. "I'm supposed to make Hank King wait on me?"

"Yep." She nodded. "Tell me what you'd be doing now. If you weren't here."

He sucked in a deep breath, imagining his daily

routine. "Six months ago, I was working in the oil fields of Odessa, Texas. Money's good—or it's not. Leave there, bone-tired, and head to Bail Bonds. Late nights, lots of drunks and stupid people wanting a 'get out of jail free' card. And, occasionally, I'd sing at the local honky-tonk."

"How'd you get here?" she asked, a smile on her face.

"My sister. She entered me in that reality show and everything changed." He shook his head. "All this"— he pointed around the studio—"is still a shock to my system. Your dad in there. Your sister. Being opposite you. Singing with you?" His voice deepened. "I *am* in my head a little."

Her expression shifted, from curious to...concerned. "I'm guessing there's a reason you're working so hard?" She cleared her throat. "Wife? Kids?"

"No." *Not anymore.* Thinking about what he'd lost still tore him up inside. Talking about it here, now? No way. "Little sister. A lot of medical bills to pay off." He didn't elaborate. "She's a freshman in college now." He ran his fingers through his hair. "She's a kid. A good kid. Deserves having her chance."

"What about you?" she asked. "Ever stop to think this is *your* chance?"

This was definitely his chance. But he'd been putting Heather first for so long, putting her first now just made sense. "A chance I can't afford to screw up," he replied.

She grinned. "Jace Michael Black. My daddy thinks you can sing. And if my daddy thinks you can sing, you can't be all that bad."

He laughed. Was it wrong that hearing her say his name felt good? And her grin. Damn but she was a pretty thing. Even without all the makeup and fancy clothes she'd been wearing the other night. If anything, he preferred her like this—young, natural, casual. And then he realized, she was relaxed, all the defensive tension and anger gone. She loved this, loved music. They had that in common.

"What's your sister's name?"

"Heather," he said.

"She's named Heather and you get stuck with Jace?" She shook her head.

"Still not over the name yet?" he asked, his gaze falling to her long neck.

"Told you, I'm not sure what I think yet," she said.

"I'm fine. I mean, I'm ready now." He rolled his head. He could do this.

"You sure?" she asked, picking up her headphones. "We could go once, no music. If you want?"

He shook his head and put on his headphones.

Krystal gave the sound booth the thumbs-up and a slight hum flooded his ears. The yearning strains of the guitar flipped a switch inside. The melody was sweeter than he'd expected. And when the lead-in notes rolled over him, he closed his eyes and sang, "I remember you, standing in the sun, smiling at me, and suddenly the world caught fire. Blinding, beautiful fire."

The music kept going, but Krystal was silent.

He opened his eyes to find her staring at him, her lips parted and her eyes wide. He'd screwed up? His gaze bounced from the pages to Krystal. She just kept right on staring. Shit. What had he done? He glanced at her, skimmed the lyrics, then turned to the sound booth. "Aw, was my timing off?" As far as he could tell, he'd been spot on.

Hank King chuckled. "No. You were great. You just blew her socks off, son." He was still chuckling. "How about we start again? Will that work for you, Krystal?"

Jace looked at Krystal then, really looked at her. There weren't many musicians he admired like Krystal. She was the real deal, what singers and songwriters should strive to be. And he'd impressed her. *He'd* impressed *her*? "Did I?" he asked, disbelieving. "Knock your socks off?"

She shook her head but didn't say a word.

"I did." He sat a little straighter, more than a little pleased.

"Don't let it go to your head," Krystal teased. "Besides, I'm not wearing socks." She smiled at him. "You keep singing like that and you're going to do just fine." She blew out her breath. "Okay. Let's do this."

One minute, he was feeling pretty damn proud of himself. The next, he was drowning in the heat of those green, green eyes.

"Let's go," Hank said.

He slid his earphones back on, the swell of the music flooding his ears. She liked what she heard. And this time, he didn't close his eyes. He watched her. "I remember you, standing in the sun, smiling at me, and suddenly my world caught fire. Blinding, beautiful fire."

She blinked, green eyes flashing before she closed her eyes to sing, "I remember you, taking my hand, holding me close, and suddenly my world caught fire. Blinding, beautiful fire." Her voice—damn, her voice. It reached inside and grabbed hold of him.

"You were everything. My breath, my home, my night, my day. Didn't care what people said. Didn't need a thing but you," he paused a beat. "Till the flames inside burned too hot, and you tried to run from the heat."

"You were everything. My hope, my fear, my night, my day. Didn't know my heart was gone. Didn't know you took it all." The words gutted him. "And your words, your lies, your promises were the sweetest pain of all."

The chorus was together. Her gaze met his then, locked together as the words hung in the air between them.

"Love isn't love when the flames burn it down. There's no hiding or forgiveness from the damage that it's done. When the smoke clears away, you'll still find me searching here. Searching for the ashes of my heart."

He was lost in her green-eyed gaze by the time they'd finished the second verse. And the chorus, together... Singing with her was more than he could ever have anticipated.

Her lyrics were powerful and real. He knew what it was to love someone and suffer betrayal. The anger and pain took some of the joy out of life. If he thought about Nikki and Ben too long, the pain made it hard to breathe. How many times had he replayed that night, over and over, wishing he could go back and change it? Not that he could bring back his wife or baby boy. They were gone and it was his fault.

The crackle in his headphones brought him back to the here and now. Now, opposite Krystal, studying him closely. There was a new respect on her face. An appreciation for him. Not him, his voice. But it was a start.

"That was incredible," Emmy Lou said from the booth, and sniffled.

"Are you crying?" Krystal asked, all smiles.

"She is," Hank King answered. "A lot."

Emmy Lou sniffed. "You two were—"

"Perfect," her daddy said. "Damn it all. You two are gonna make things hard." He sighed. "We're gonna make a copy of it and send it to Wheelhouse. Baby girl, this is your song. The two of you, together, were meant to sing this song. Any fool listening would recognize that."

Jace watched Krystal's expression as her father was talking. She lit up from the inside, so damn happy he couldn't help but smile, too. A few things were certain. Krystal loved and respected her father. She was damn talented and damn gorgeous. And Jace was going to have to be real careful about keeping his feelings in check. If Krystal King knew what he thought about her, she'd either slap his face or, worse, invite him to bed.

Chapter 4

"You're good." Krystal hugged her sister close. "So good I almost believed the whole sore throat thing."

Emmy Lou hugged her back, hard. "I don't know what you're talking about."

"Uh-huh. Sister-girl, you still can't lie to save your life." She pressed a kiss against her cheek. "And I love you for it." She stared into emerald eyes that matched her own. "Thank you." Her voice wobbled just enough to tell her twin all the things she'd never be able to put into words. She prided herself on powerful lyrics, but speaking from the heart—one-on-one emoting—was way outside her comfort zone. Even with her twin.

"It's your song." Emmy's long, perfectly curled locks bounced with the slight shake of her head. "No one could do it justice." Her gaze darted to Jace. "But he sure came close. Guess Daddy knew what he was doing when he picked him, huh?"

Krystal nodded, doing her best not to ogle the impressive specimen of a man with the voice of an angel. If an angel was big and ripped and sexy as hell. The thick tattoos covering the inside of his left arm and snaking up under his sleeve only added to the bad-boy thing. "He usually does." Which was one of the reasons he was who he was. Between his talent, never-fail instincts, and business savvy, her daddy knew a good thing when he saw one.

The only exception to that? Her momma. If her daddy had one weakness, it was his unfailing loyalty. In most people, that would be considered a good thing. But she knew better. Her daddy stayed married because he took every vow and promise he made as gospel. Her daddy always said a man was only as good as his word. He lived by that—whether it made sense or not.

"No point," her daddy was saying now. "It's something CiCi and I started when the kids were young and I was on the road. If we're under the same roof, we sit down for a meal. A home-cooked meal at that. We always have more than we need."

Her daddy also believed in having an open door—meaning he'd just invited Jace back to their place for dinner.

"Momma's got her charity planning luncheon," Emmy Lou added. "So Krystal and I are in charge. Travis said he'd help but—"

"That boy isn't allowed in the kitchen," their father cut her off. "Took months to get the smoke smell out of the house."

Her brother was a genius. He'd been volunteered to make dinner once—once—and he'd burned the lasagna to a crisp. The smoke had rolled out so thick and black, neighbors had called the fire department. Of course her mother had turned it into a photo shoot. Nothing like a little kitchen fire to get some press-worthy pictures of her daughters serving the cute firemen slices of Krystal's special lime sour cream cake. Two things had come out of that day: Travis's permanent ban from cooking and a potential cookbook deal for a Fit for a King Cookbook—a project her momma had shelved, much to Krystal's disappointment, because she felt it didn't fit their brand.

"If I'd known all it took was a little smoke to get me booted out of the kitchen, I'd have put tinfoil in the microwave years ago," she teased.

Jace laughed. Damn it all. If only he'd snorted. Or had a horselaugh. Or did something to make him less…less.

"Don't let her fool you." Her father had his hands on his hips, giving her his long-suffering-daddy look. "That girl knows her way around a kitchen. Spends more time cooking than anyone else in the house—and we have a cook. I'd be round as a hay bale if we didn't spend so much time on the road."

Cooking cleared her mind. When she was elbows deep in bread dough, some of her best songs took shape. The smell of cinnamon and nutmeg had helped her write a couple of the Three Kings original Christmas carols. Not that anyone knew that. The last thing she wanted was someone tampering with her creative process.

"That's right, Daddy." She hooked arms with him, teasing. "And someday I'll make some big, strong man a good little wife. Imagine it. Me, barefoot and pregnant, tending an organic vegetable garden and making all our food from scratch. While I sing happy songs and have help from my talking animal friends."

Her father chuckled. "Whoever marries you better have a hell of a thick skin. Or your razor-sharp tongue will end him in no time."

Krystal nodded. "If he really loves me, he'll love all of me." Because her razor-sharp tongue was the only way she could cut through the crap. She had yet to meet a man who wanted *her*. No, they all wanted what she came with: travel, fame, and money. "Besides, you know how jealous Clementine can get."

Clementine had been an impulse adoption at a pet rescue event. The near-starved, furless Chinese crested puppy had been pulled from an overcrowded puppy mill. The runt of the litter, she'd been tiny and pathetic and recovering from her leg amputation. One look in her big chocolate brown eyes had Krystal snatching her up and taking her home. She'd never regretted it. Not only did her baby make her laugh out loud but Clem loved her unconditionally. And the pup was a pretty good judge of character. The one time she'd run into Mickey with Clem, the dog had peed all over his feet.

The memory always made her smile. Something about Mickey's red face and stunned horror as his boots were soaked.

"I'll bring Jace along in a bit. I figure I'll hear a few of his songs, since we're here." Her father looked Jace's way. "If that works for you?"

The look of pure surprise and, likely, nerves on Jace's face would have been near impossible to fabricate. Maybe he wasn't faking. Maybe he really was a good ol' boy who'd won his big break. Maybe he was starstruck by everything. Or maybe his good looks and her body's well-hello-there response were clouding her judgment.

"Yes, sir," Jace mumbled, cleared his throat, and tried again. "Yes, sir, that works for me."

"Go easy on him, Daddy." Emmy Lou pressed a kiss on their father's cheek.

"Nah," Krystal argued. "Put him through the wringer. Make him work for his dinner."

Jace stared at her, laughing again.

"Be nice, Krystal." Her father sighed. "He's gonna be singing with you a bit now. Might want to try to play nice."

"Now, Daddy, you know better than that." She rolled her eyes. "I wouldn't know how to play nice if I tried. Why start now?" She was teasing, sort of. But it was easier this way. If she acted tough, acted like none of this mattered, it was easier to bury the eventual disappointment deep, deep down. "Besides, just because you're sold on the two of us doing the song doesn't mean the label will be."

"Your daddy's got some pull, baby girl." He patted her cheek. "I'm gonna use it."

He meant it. She could tell. And it filled her heart to the brim. *Don't cry. Don't cry.* Damn but her eyes were burning. Easier to look away—at Jace—than face the well of untapped emotion she struggled daily to avoid.

He was watching her, his beautiful eyes searching hers. Searing and invasive. Not with hunger, what she'd expected. It was deeper than that. If she didn't know better, she'd think Jace Black saw the pain and anger and shame eating away at her insides. And if he did, then what? She barely knew this guy. So far, he seemed okay. But things were rarely, if ever, as they seemed. Hot or not, decent or not, Jace Black was just another singer looking for a way to launch himself into stardom. He didn't give a shit about her or her personal demons. And she'd be wise to remember that—not so easy to accomplish when one lingering look had her breathing hard with want.

"We'll see you at home." Emmy Lou took her hand and tugged her to and out the recording room door. "You keep that up and Daddy might rethink this whole duet thing, Krystal."

There was no point pretending she didn't understand what her twin was saying. Still, it wasn't in her nature to roll over. "I didn't do anything."

"Not yet." She shot her sister a look. "But you were thinking about it. That much was clear."

A handful of snappy retorts rose up, but she swallowed them down. "Whatever. It's not a big deal. He is… good-looking."

Emmy smiled then. "Yes. I noticed."

How could she not notice? His wow-factor was undoubtedly one of the reasons he'd won his reality show. And his voice. Because, holy crap, his voice had totally blown her away. Hearing her words through him… She hadn't been prepared for how incredible he… it…the song really was. But it was. As long as the record label cooperated, she might have her first single outside of Three Kings.

Once inside the car, Krystal dozed off to the sound of Emmy Lou playing some candy game on her phone. When she woke, the faintest whispers of a new song were hovering on the edges of her mind. They parked and Krystal all but jumped out, pushing through the oversized wooden doors and into the showplace foyer with the mile-high ceiling and art deco light fixture her momma had pushed for. When it was on, the whole floor sparkled—courtesy of the mica chips and crystal veins in the marble flooring. It was over-the-top, just the way her momma liked it.

But the click of nails against the tile had her smiling and she dropped to her knees as Clementine came sliding around the corner, hobbling on three legs, rear end wagging and in full happy mode. "Did you miss your mommy?" Krystal asked, scooping up her dog. "I missed you, too. You would have been proud of me, Clem. Mommy sang her heart out."

"And got all goo-goo eyed over a guy," Emmy joined in. "If your mommy had a tail, he'd have her wagging it."

Krystal laughed so hard she almost dropped Clementine. "You are hilarious, Emmy Lou."

"Deny it?" her sister asked, hands on hips, waiting. But Krystal was still laughing too hard to answer. Emmy nodded. "I didn't think so."

Krystal stood, holding Clem. "Don't you listen to her. We're going to make something yummy." She carried her dog into the kitchen, still smiling.

"Clementine is not going to help you cook," Emmy Lou argued. "You're going to put her down. *And* wash your hands."

"See how grumpy Auntie Emmy is, Clem?" She giggled as Clementine gave her chin several wet doggy kisses. "I think you'd be a good little sous chef."

Clem grunted and wiggled.

"After you have a potty break. Maybe? We'll convince Auntie Emmy, don't worry." Krystal carried Clementine to one of the large french doors leading out into the rose garden. A faint melody was taking shape, hints of a connection forming. A solid tempo. Yearning fiddle. She stood in the door, pondering, the heat from the Texas sun and the whir of the cicadas so deafening she lost her train of thought. "Nothing like a Texas summer to remind a gal how blessed she is to have things like air conditioning," she said over her shoulder.

"If Gramma were here, she'd tell you to stop letting all the bought air out," Emmy answered.

Which was true. Gramma had been a child of the Depression. Waste not, want not. And letting ice-cold "bought" air drift outside was a pet peeve of hers. "Hurry up, Clem, before Gramma comes back to haunt us." Krystal laughed as Clem came barreling back across the lawn and inside, heading straight to her water bowl. "I know, it's hot out there, isn't it?"

Clementine sat, staring up at her with adoring eyes.

"I know, Clem. I love you too, baby." She blew the dog kisses, mentally flipping through some of her favorite recipes. "I'm thinking buttermilk biscuits and apple pie?" They were two of her specialties—not that she was out to impress anyone. No way. No one to impress. Not at all. If she were, she'd make her lime sour cream cake. Or her turtle chocolate truffle cake. But she wasn't. So extra-flaky, extra-sweet, and extra-gooey apple pie would have to do.

"Good." Emmy opened the fridge. "Roast chicken? Baked potatoes? Salad?"

"Perfect." Krystal began pulling ingredients: flour, baking soda, buttermilk, eggs. Her favorite ceramic mixing bowl. The melody picked up.

A few words popped up. A male voice was singing. That stopped her. She frowned into the bowl of sifted flour, one cracked egg in her hand. She didn't write songs for men. Sometimes Travis got a line here or there—part of the chorus—but never a full-out song. And yet the words were definitely masculine. A ballad. Heartfelt and raw.

She's dancing in his arms now...

She hummed a few notes to get the feel of it.

Just friends. Easy to say. But I miss you. Every damn day...

"New song?" Emmy asked, sounding far away.

She nodded, using two forks to cut the shortening into the flour. No matter how many fancy gadgets her daddy bought her, she insisted on cooking the way her gramma taught her. A dash of this, a pinch of that, and a whole lot of butter. It calmed her, helped her focus.

Tonight's about them. Not about us. Exchanging their vows. And pledging true love.

He kisses his bride. They both cut the cake. They smile and they laugh, but my damn heart aches.

And seeing her now, on the dance floor, smiling that smile, makes me want more. And all I can say is how I feel.

She dumped the ball of dough onto the marble countertop and rolled it out, sprinkling a bit of flour on top, before smoothing it out with the roller again and pressing the dough into the pie plate.

"It's got a good melody." Emmy Lou handed her a large bag of green apples. "I like it."

"You do?" She smiled at her sister, prepping the apples and swiping the peels and cores into the bag to take to the stables later.

Emmy nodded. "Sad, though."

Krystal laughed. Most of her songs were sad. It's not like she set out to write heavy, emotional things—they just sort of fell out of her head and onto sheet music. "You know me."

Emmy nudged her. "I do." Emmy wore her heart on her sleeve—and her face. Every single one of her thoughts and emotions were on display for her fans, friends, or family members to see, manipulate, or dissect as they saw fit. That was one of the reasons the world loved her— Emmy's sweetness and lack of guile was irresistible.

All reasons why Krystal was so protective of her.

Apparently, she wasn't alone when it came to worrying about her sibling. Emmy Lou was wearing her "concerned" face, her blue-green eyes studying her a little too closely—a mix of sympathy and anxiety.

"Don't give me that look," Krystal sighed. "I'm fine."

"I'm not giving you any look." Emmy Lou's brow wrinkled. "Fine isn't good. I want you to be good. I worry—"

"Well, stop it," she interrupted. "I don't want you to worry. Least of all over me." She grinned. "Besides, it'll give you wrinkles. Momma would have a fit if you gave yourself wrinkles over me." And she'd likely blame her, too.

Emmy Lou shook her head, but she was smiling.

They worked alongside each other, the large state-of-the-art kitchen warming from the dual stoves working overtime. While Krystal knocked out another verse for her new song, Emmy Lou continued to hum the new melody. By the time dinner was done and the smell of cinnamon and apples flooded the house, Krystal was ready to pluck out the song on her favorite guitar, play around with chords, and find just the right words.

"Add another place," Emmy said, carrying another plate and silverware into the dining room.

"Who's coming?" she asked. With Daddy, there was always one more.

"Momma's meeting wrapped up." Emmy glanced her way. "She'll be home in time for dinner."

Now she was doubly glad she hadn't made one of her signature desserts. If she had, she'd be putting a target square on Jace's back. Her momma was all charm and grace when it came to *useful* people. Considering he'd unintentionally blocked her attempt to get Mickey on the road as their opening act, Jace Black had a strike against him. Another strike for singing the duet with her—not Emmy. One more strike, and Jace Black would officially be on CiCi King's blacklist. And that was one thing she wouldn't wish on her worst enemy.

"You can't be nice to him," Emmy Lou said.

She nodded. If she liked him, her mother would eat him alive.

"You can't be mean to him, either," Emmy Lou added.

Because if she didn't like him, her mother would become Jace's biggest fan.

"What am I supposed to do?" she asked, frowning as Clementine circled her. "Ignore him? Fake a headache?" Maybe that was the best option.

But the front door opened, followed by the sound of boots on marble. And the clickety-click of her momma's designer heels.

By now, Jace should be used to feeling out of place. Almost like he'd snuck into a party and now he had no choice but to pretend he'd been invited or he'd get his ass kicked to the curb. He was standing in Hank King's house, talking about Hank's favorite Texas football team and their chances at the playoffs in what could only be described as a man cave.

Out of place? More like on another planet.

Framed concert posters. A few encased guitars signed by some of country music's greatest talents. As if that wasn't enough, Hank's impressive display of platinum, gold, and silver albums covered an entire wall of the room.

They sat on overstuffed leather couches, a massive television screen opposite them—on but muted. In the far corner was a wet bar. Travis was there, pulling longnecks from the refrigerator.

"Their preseason stats are looking pretty good," Hank said. "We got so damn close last year."

"Momma was sure you were going to have a heart attack," Travis laughed, handing them each a beer.

Jace took the beer and grinned. When you lived in Texas, football was part of your DNA. And the Houston Roughnecks were the favored team. Last year, he'd screamed and cussed through most of the Championship Bowl, too. "Terrible ref. Bad call."

Hank nodded, slapping his thigh. "Damn right."

"Don't get him started." Travis chuckled. "How'd it go? Singing with my sister?"

Hank shook his head. "I'd seen some of the clips from your show, so I knew you could sing, and today you didn't disappoint."

Just when he thought things couldn't get more awkward, Hank King goes and gives him a compliment. What the hell should he say? Thank you? Nothing? Aw, golly, gee shucks? Considering they were both staring at him, he had to say something. "I can't quite wrap my head around this. All of this," he managed.

Hank smiled. "Stay humble, son. That's probably the best advice I can give you. You remember where you come from and you'll never stop appreciating where you are or what you have."

"Dinner's ready." Emmy Lou poked her head in. "What are you watching?"

"You just missed him," Travis said. "Played good, but they pulled him early."

Jace glanced at Travis, then Emmy. The girl was red cheeked. "I wasn't asking about Brock." She sighed.

Travis cut his eyes her way. "Okay, sure."

"Travis." Hank shook his head.

"I asked what you were watching." Emmy's smile wavered.

The three of them turned toward the television. A woman in a wedding dress was sobbing in the middle of a fancy shop, a group of people on the couch looking disappointed, while some guy in glasses was trying to put a veil on the crying woman.

"Guess the game's over?" Jace had been too caught up in the conversation, the room, everything—to notice.

"I have no idea," her father said. "Why is she crying?"

"Do women cry like that when they go wedding dress shopping?" Travis asked. "Why? It's a dress."

"What did that say? Fifty-five hundred dollars?" Hank asked, pointing at the television.

"For a dress?" Travis asked.

Jace was laughing now; he couldn't help it. He knew exactly what the show was; his sister, Heather, loved it.

"My first car cost less than that," Hank went on.

"Oh, for crying out loud." Emmy Lou sighed, taking the remote from her father. The television went black. "Food's getting cold." She shook her head, one eyebrow cocked. "Momma will have a field day if she hears you were watching wedding shows."

Hank slid an arm around his daughter. "Maybe I was just getting ideas for you or your sister's big day. You think you'll want a fifty-five-hundred-dollar wedding dress?"

Jace followed, half listening as they wandered through the massive home. Through open doors, he spied an office, a music room with a baby grand piano, back through the showplace foyer, down the hall to the dining room.

CiCi King was there. Smiling. She had a…predatory smile. One that made him nervous. "You sit by me, Jace." She sat, patting the chair next to her.

He swallowed, doing his best not to frown. Or run. Instead, he nodded, hoping like hell he wasn't sweating half as much as it felt like he was. "Yes, ma'am."

With her platinum hair, perfectly enhanced body, and Southern charm, she was something to look at. But she had a shiny, brittle quality that put him instantly on edge. Her blue-green eyes were hard, no matter how big her red-painted smile was. "I want to hear all about your recording session. What do you think of Hank's li'l ol' studio?"

Travis snorted.

A swift kick to the shin had him darting a look across

the table at Krystal. She didn't make eye contact, but she wrinkled her nose and her brows rose high. What the hell was that about? If she was trying to tell him something, it wasn't working.

"I don't have a lot of experience, Mrs. King, but today has been beyond incredible." Which was a little too aw-shucks-golly but true.

"You call me CiCi now, you hear?" She patted his hand. "Sounds like we'll be seeing a lot of you. No point in keeping things formal." She stared down the table at her husband, her smile softening. "You get things squared away?"

Hank nodded. "We wrapped up the paperwork at the studio. Jace will be with Three Kings for the next ten shows." He cut into the chicken, put a serving on one plate, and passed it along. "We only got through three of his songs before we ran out of time, but I can't wait to hear the rest."

By the time everyone had their plates and serving dishes were traveling, Jace risked another look Krystal's way. She, however, was staring pointedly at her plate, stabbing her potato with the tips of her fork.

"I must say, I cannot wait to hear you two together," CiCi gushed before staring into the basket. "You make these biscuits, Krissy?"

Krystal nodded.

"They look a little dry," CiCi went on, passing the basket on to him, her fingers brushing along the back of his hands.

He wasn't sure what bothered him more: her maybe-accidental-maybe-not touch or how easily the woman belittled her daughter.

Jace nodded, grabbed two biscuits, and passed along the basket. "We sound good, if I do say so myself." Hank had played back some of their recording and it had set the hairs on the back of his neck straight up.

"You should." Hank nodded. "Good to recognize talent when you hear it. You two were meant to sing that song together. Sent a cut to Wheelhouse already. Ethan heard it, loved it, can't wait to get it out."

Krystal looked up then, the sweetest smile on her face.

"See, Krissy?" CiCi nodded, cutting her chicken into tiny pieces. "I know you were upset over the way things worked out, but if Ethan loved it, then it's a surefire hit. I may never have been on that stage, but I do know this business. Wouldn't hurt you to listen to me every once in a while."

Krystal's smile faded. Her gaze bounced his way before returning to her father.

"I made a call, CiCi." Hank's voice dipped, drawing all eyes his way. "Krystal is singing with Jace. It was the right call. They sound…well, it was radio gold. And Ethan was smiling like the cat that ate the canary."

CiCi carefully laid her silverware on her plate, her gaze locked with her husband. "I'm so glad everything went so smoothly. I'd hate for Jace or his agent to be upset, since we agreed he'd sing with Emmy Lou."

Jace opened his mouth, but Krystal landed another

solid kick to the shins under the table. A warning. That much he got. Clearly, there was some tension between the mother and daughter. Or maybe CiCi was used to getting her way. But the idea of letting CiCi King chip away at Krystal's high—his high—was just plain wrong. "I guarantee you Luke will be happy. If I'm happy, he's happy." He sliced the biscuit open and spread on the butter, ignoring the narrow-eyed look the older woman shot his way.

"You should have heard them, Momma." Emmy Lou smiled. "They had me in tears."

CiCi shoved her plate away. "I hope our fans aren't too disappointed. Hard to sing along to a song if you're crying. And you know how our fans love to sing along." Her smile was strained.

Jace considered himself a pretty easygoing guy. He wasn't quick to make assumptions or judgments because it bothered the shit out of him when people did it to him. But sitting here, watching CiCi King at work, was a challenge. He didn't know what to make of her. This woman was Krystal's mother, wasn't she? She should be proud of her daughter— both her daughters—and support them. He didn't know what the hell she was doing, but he didn't like it.

"I'm a fan," Jace said, smiling. "I have every CD. Listened to them all so many times I've got them all memorized." He shrugged. "As a fan, I'll say this song? The one I—and I can't believe I'm saying this—I got to sing with Krystal King? The fans will love it." He kept staring at Krystal, willing her to look at him. She didn't.

"Damn right." Travis held up his green-cut glass. "Cheers to Krystal and Jace and their new song."

CiCi was the last to toast, but she did it—reluctant or not. Once that was done, conversation turned back to neutral topics like football, the latest top-ten chart, and the possibility of bringing on a new costume designer. Jace did his best to engage, but he couldn't shake off the bitter taste in his mouth. His mother had been gone so long she was more a faded angel than anything else. But he treasured what he remembered: her soft voice and gentle smile. To have her slight Heather like that was beyond imagining.

He was offended on Krystal's behalf—so much so that he ended up eating five of her biscuits. They weren't the least bit dry. They were delicious. If there'd been any more in the basket, he'd have probably eaten those, too.

"What time is our flight in the morning?" Krystal asked, standing to clear dishes.

"Travis, get up and help." Hank pointed at his son. "You better not start breaking dishes to get out of it, either."

Travis shrugged and started to stand, but Jace cut in. "Let me. It's the least I can do after your hospitality."

"He's right." Travis smiled and leaned back in his chair.

"Everyone want pie?" Krystal asked.

"You made pie, too?" Her father patted his stomach. "You know I do."

"A small piece for him," CiCi said. "None for me."

Because you're hard-hearted.

Jace kept his smile in place, balancing plates and his temper all the way to the kitchen. But once the door swung shut behind them, all bets were off. Still, this was her family and, after that, the last thing he wanted to do was upset her. "It's been a while since I've done the whole family-dinner thing, but I don't remember it being so…"

Krystal put her plates on the counter and faced him, brows high and arms crossed. "Warm? Supportive? Full of love and laughter? Welcome to my world."

He wasn't sure what to say, but after that, he had a whole new respect for her.

A ball of wispy white hair hobble-ran through the dog door, emitting a few yipping barks and whines, weaving between Krystal's legs until she crouched to give the animal her full attention. "Hey, baby. I'm sorry I have to keep you locked up in here." She knelt, cradling the dog's head in her hands. "Don't want you upsetting Gramma CiCi any more than usual."

The dog looked at Krystal with pure adoration.

"This must be Clementine." He smiled. He'd seen dozens of photos of Clementine on Instagram. One of the ugliest damn animals he'd ever seen. So ugly, she was cute. Mostly furless, she had a pom-pom on the top of her head and the tip of her tail, giving her an eighties-rock-star vibe. With her unsteady walk, she was an eighties rock star recovering from an all-nighter. Heather was a big fan of the three-legged Chinese crested. And Krystal.

Krystal looked up at him. "The one and only." She

stood. "Clem, this is Jace. Let me know what you think of him."

Clementine sat, looking back and forth between the two of them. She seemed undecided so Jace squatted, holding out his hand toward the little dog. Clementine continued to sit, staring at his outstretched hand without interest.

"Come on, Clementine," he coaxed. "Don't leave me hanging here. You're making me look bad."

Krystal made an odd choking sound.

"Come on," he tried again.

Clementine yawned, stood, and trotted his way. Her dainty nose sniffed up and down each finger and all along his hand and forearm before she whimpered and lay on her back, exposing her tummy.

"You hussy." Krystal was outraged. "I can't believe you."

Jace chuckled, obliging the dog with a thorough tummy rub. "Heather is going to be jealous. She's one of your biggest fans."

"She is?" Krystal asked.

He nodded, standing.

"Here." Krystal scooped up Clementine, thrust the dog into his arms, and pulled out her phone. "Hold her up and give me a smolder. Chicks dig that, big-time. Hot guy with cute dog? Oh yeah." She held her phone up. "Come on, Clementine. Smile for Mommy."

The baby voice she used on her dog had him grinning, too. Of course, the hot guy reference helped.

"Nice. Good one." She held the phone out for his inspection. "I'll post it."

He shook his head; things like Internet fame and social media were things he was hoping to avoid. Krystal was the pro here. If she wanted to do it, he wasn't going to stop her. "Whatever."

"Uh-huh." She typed away on her phone, then shoved it back in her pocket.

"You have a right to be happy. About today." He cleared his throat, her green eyes meeting his. "I don't know about the rest of it, it's none of my business. But I do know that much."

She stared up at him, arms crossed over her chest, blond hair over one shoulder, green eyes blazing.

What was she thinking? Did he want to know?

"You should leave the stubble." Her voice was husky, her gaze traveling along his jaw to his mouth. It was pretty damn easy to figure out what she was thinking then. Her lips parted just enough to make him start thinking about all the things he shouldn't be thinking when it came to her.

Dammit.

"Where's the pie?" Hank King's voice carried, only slightly muffled by the swinging kitchen door. Clementine barked in answer, planting two serious doggy kisses on Jace's chin.

"Coming, Daddy," Krystal called back. "He has a weakness for pie. Especially my pie." She shook her head, nodding at Clementine. "She likes you." She spun on her heel to pull a stack of small plates from a cabinet.

He rubbed Clementine's head, doing his best to rein in the still-rapid beat of his heart. "She strikes me as a pretty friendly dog."

The sugar-crusted flaky crust she placed on the counter made him wish he'd stopped at three biscuits instead of five. When she slid the piece from pie dish to plate, the apple cinnamon sweetness temptation was undeniable. "You made that?" he asked, stepping closer to inhale deeply. He groaned. "I'm beginning to see why your dad might be partial to your pie."

She pointed at his mouth. "There might be a little drool, right there."

"Very funny." This close, it was a toss-up between what was sweeter: the pie or Krystal.

She moved to the other side of the island. "Clementine is a good dog, for the most part. But she'd let you know if she didn't like you." She plated another piece of pie and glanced his way, smiling. "She peed on Mickey. All over his jeans and boots."

Jace rubbed Clementine's head and ears. "You and I are going to get along just fine, Clementine."

Chapter 5

"THAT TAG WAS A BAD IDEA," KRYSTAL WHISPERED TO Clementine.

With every step, her little dog's metal tag bounced off the clasp of her collar, the merry jinglejangle echoing in the quiet, sleeping house.

Clementine smiled up at her, tongue lolling, knowing full well she'd get a treat once they arrived at their location. When Krystal had the odd night home during a tour, the two of them had turned midnight snacking into part of their routine.

Tonight, she wanted pie. Warmed up, with ice cream. Without the heaping side order of guilt and disappointment her mother was always so eager to serve up.

She pushed through the kitchen door, flipped on the light over the stove, and opened the refrigerator. Can of whipped cream. Gallon of milk. Pie. She turned, depositing her load on the massive marble-topped island in the middle of the kitchen.

"You beat us." Travis stood there, hair mussed and smiling.

"Shit," she hissed, her heart slamming into her chest. "I didn't hear you."

"Us" meant Travis. And Jace. Because her daddy had insisted he sleep over since their flight was at four a.m.

and it made more sense for him to stay here than waste time driving back and forth. Which did make sense. Until she was face-to-face with him, his black hair falling onto his forehead and his heavy-lidded eyes weighted with sleep. Jace, yawning? Adorable.

Really, Krystal? Get a grip. He's yawning. She placed the cake server on the marble top with a little more force than necessary, causing both Jace and Travis to startle.

"I thought we were being quiet?" Travis yawned.

She was being quiet. It was his fault. And Jace's. Jace with his sleepy grin. And his...his presence. Who slept in a skin-tight white undershirt anyway? His tattoos all look-at-my-big-manly-arms. And pajama pants resting low on lean hips... At least they were an improvement over his jeans. He didn't seem to own any that didn't showcase his ass. And thighs. And ass. *Way to get it together.*

"You snuck up on me," she whispered—more a hiss than anything. He was right. The kitchen was crowded enough. Still, he was her brother—she couldn't let him have the last word. "It's a dick move."

"Language." Travis tsk-tsked. "And why would you hear me? I mastered the art of stealthy sneak-outs in high school." He reached for the pie.

"Nope." She snatched it away. "Mine."

"Sharing is caring," Travis replied, coming around the island.

"Stop." She cradled the pie close, her whisper as force-ful as she could make it. "I mean it. I didn't get any—"

"Your fault, not mine." Travis reached around her, grabbing for the pie.

"I will stab you with a fork." She snapped, glaring up at him. "Since you're invading, why don't you make yourself useful and get the ice cream? Then, maybe, I'll give you some pie."

"Fine." Travis held his hands up in mock defeat. "Fine."

"And be quiet," she added, glancing at the door.

Travis made a show of pretending to lock his lips.

"What are you? Five?" But she was laughing.

Jace was watching her. And dammit all, she was staring right back, cradling a sticky apple pie against her chest like a moron.

"Your dog wants something." Travis nudged her, pressing the gallon of ice cream against her arm.

"Travis," she jumped, the shock of the cold sending her a good two feet in the air.

"You're jumpy." He laughed.

"You're an ass." She put the pie on the counter, smacked his arm, and turned away, cooing down to Clementine. "What is it, baby? I didn't forget you. You want a treat too?"

Clementine did a little dance, her back end and tufted tail wagging with excitement.

"I can get it," Jace volunteered. "If you're worried he'll steal the pie."

She spun to find Travis about to do just that. "Dammit, Travis."

He laughed.

"Thanks, Jace. You'll get an extra big slice." She glared at her brother. "The treats are in the pantry."

"On it."

From the corner of her eye, she saw him walk across the kitchen floor. Bare feet. And pajama pants sliding even lower on his hips. Low enough to make her hold her breath as he bent to get Clem's treat jar.

Really? Was she really that hard up? Had it been so long that one look at a well-muscled back and sculpted ass turned her into a pile of quivering goo? Apparently.

She sliced into the pie, cutting two large pieces and placing them on plates. The last piece was small. Like sliver small. She held the plate out for her brother.

"Krystal," he moaned. "Come on, now."

"Why are you here?" she asked.

"He wanted pie." Travis pointed at Jace. "Hospitality and all that."

Her gaze bounced to Mr. Temptation, looking even more damn adorable crouching down to give Clementine her treat. Clearly, she wasn't the only one suffering from this bizarre Jace Black fascination. Clem seemed downright smitten. "And?" There was more to it; she knew her brother too well to believe this was purely about pie.

"Emmy Lou said something about you humming?" Travis said, serving himself a bigger slice and putting the plate in the microwave.

She and Emmy might be twins, but the three of them rarely kept things from each other. Growing up on the road and in the spotlight had strengthened their connection, siblings and best friends. But there were times, like now, when that was inconvenient. "I do that. Hum, I mean."

"When you've got a new song rolling around up there." He poked her head, pulling his plate from the microwave. A scoop of ice cream and mound of whipped cream was added to the pie. "Here." He held it out for Jace. "And you were baking. Baking? Humming? New song."

Jace stood, listening with interest. "Thanks." He took the plate and sat on a nearby stool.

"Look at you, using your manners," Krystal teased.

"Look at you, dodging the question," Travis said, putting another plate in the microwave. "Since you're not talking, it must be something good."

"Maybe she's not ready to talk about it?" Jace eyed his pie, fork hovering. "Sometimes, things need to…roll around a bit? Before they come together."

Exactly. Wait. "You write songs?" This was news to her.

He winced, then shrugged. "Hard to say I write anything when I'm sitting here with you. But I try." He took a massive bite, moaning with appreciation. "This is the best pie I've ever had. Ever. My grandma's probably rolling over in her grave to hear me say it, but it's true."

"I told you it was even better the second time around," Travis said around a mouthful.

She was still mulling over the latest pro on the Jace Black pros and cons list. It was getting to be a little too pro-heavy for her. That in itself triggered warning bells.

Life had shown her time and again that, when it came to people, the only thing to count on was disappointment. Anytime now, Jace Black was going to let his true colors come shining through. And when that happened, she'd be ready. "Will you be singing your songs when you open for us?"

He nodded, swallowing. "A couple. The record label has set me up with a few, too." He shrugged. "That takes some getting used to—singing what you're told to sing versus what you want to sing."

Travis paused. "Hell, I'm always singing what I'm told to sing. Singing what I want to sing? What's that?" He winked at her.

She stuck her tongue out before turning back to Jace. "I get the impression Wheelhouse is willing to invest a lot of time and money into your career. Meaning they're going to give you songs that will put you on the charts." With her fork, she speared some cinnamon-covered apple. "Once you get on the charts a few times, you'll have more say-so in your song choices."

He stood, carrying his plate around the island and rinsing it in the sink. "People keep talking about careers and charts and tours. I'm still waking up at four for work. In the oilfields." He put his plate in the dishwasher and leaned back against the counter, his tight shirt and bed-head hair on display.

"You miss it?" Travis asked, shoveling in a last, massive bite.

Jace chuckled, running a hand along the back of his

neck. He grinned, almost embarrassed as their eyes met. "Miss it? Hell no. But knowing I could go from this back to that—"

"That's not going to happen." She hadn't meant to say it out loud. For one thing, she didn't want Jace to know how talented she thought he was. She didn't want him to know she thought about him at all. For another, she didn't want her brother to get all wide-eyed and suspicious—like he was now. "Between Wheelhouse and my daddy, you've got everything you need to make it in this industry."

"And you," he added, his voice thick. He cleared his throat, his gaze falling from hers. "Your song, I mean. I'm not sure what I did to wind up here, but I'm grateful."

Either he meant it, or he was really good at lying. After Mickey, she wasn't sure she was the most reliable judge of character. He did *look* like he meant it, that he was thankful and aware of how damn lucky he was. The thing was, she was thankful, too. And when he'd sung her words, they'd come to life. A person couldn't fake that, could they? The look in his eyes. The yearning in his voice. It had been real. And whatever he'd suffered transformed her melody into something beautiful and haunting.

"Which reminds me," Travis said, pointing at her with his fork. "Your song. The new one you were humming in here?"

She sighed, scooping up Clementine and pressing a kiss on the tip of her downy soft head.

"We know the drill, Krystal. You bake, we get new songs." Travis served himself another slice.

"You do realize you're a pain in the ass?"

"And you love me." He tugged her into a hug. "Don't try to deny it."

"I won't." She sighed, smiling up at her brother.

"The more you avoid talking about it, the more likely it is I'll make your life hell until I get answers." He smiled. "And when I say hell, I mean tickling you."

She tried to pull away, but he was too strong and she didn't want to jostle Clementine.

"Come on, now." Travis used a baby voice. "Emmy Lou already hummed some of it."

She groaned as her brother started humming her song. Emmy hadn't held anything back because he hummed through most of what she'd worked out.

"Nice." Jace nodded. "A lot of soul."

"Krystal can't write any other way." Travis released her. "She might have a bad attitude most of the time, and a short temper, and no patience, and a hell of a lot of opinions—"

"Really?" She elbowed him.

"But deep, deep, *deep* down inside, she's a world-weary, fragile, and emotional soul." Travis winked.

"Did you just quote our review from *Entertainment Monthly*?" She was laughing.

"Did you just admit that you read the review in *Entertainment Monthly*?" Her brother shook his head.

"Wait a sec." Jace was frowning. "*Entertainment*

Monthly said all that? What the hell sort of review is that?"

"They just said the deeply fragile and emotional soul part. Went on about how Krystal was underrated and truly gifted as a songwriter. Blah blah blah." Travis grinned. "The bad attitude stuff is all me."

"The song you're working on." Jace's fingers were tapping a beat on the marble island. "It's got a little bit of your dad's song 'Bring Her Home.'"

She shook her head. "Not really. Beat's close but I'm thinking slower." She closed her eyes and hummed it through, pausing now and then to adjust the pitch.

"Damn." Travis was shaking his head when she was done. "Nice."

"You had doubts?" She teased, setting Clementine on the floor and refilling the dog's water bowl. "You hear that, baby? First, they want to hear what I'm working on, then seem surprised it's any good."

"Lyrics?" Travis asked.

She glared up at her brother. "Don't push it."

"Fine. I'll get it out of you before long." He yawned. "We're heading to the airport in, what, four hours?"

"Yup." She glanced at Jace. "You ready for tomorrow?"

Jace shook his head. "You mean flying to Charleston to sing, onstage, with Krystal King?" He kept shaking his head.

Travis laughed. "Enjoy the ride. And the perks." He chuckled. "There are so many perks."

"And by perks, he means groupies." She tried to keep

the edge from her voice. Tried. And failed. "Whatever. Go ahead and catch an STD. Catch two. Collect a whole bunch even. You'll need your rest then, so you boys go off to bed and I'll clean up here." The sooner they were gone, the sooner she could stop thinking about Jace, in his tight white shirt, enjoying the *perks* of the road. It shouldn't bother her. It shouldn't. But it did.

She covered the pie with foil and tucked it into the refrigerator, dodging Clementine to reach back for the ice cream and milk. When the food was packed away, she turned to load the dishwasher. It wasn't the way the muscles of his back worked that got to her. Or the way he'd simply stepped up to help clean without being asked. No, it was the sound of his deep velvet voice humming the tune of her newest song as he worked that left her hands unsteady.

Jace sat in the last row of the chartered airplane, his lucky baseball cap pulled down low and his leather jacket folded up behind his head for a makeshift pillow. He was worn out. Being in the King house surrounded by all the things he never knew a person needed made him uneasy.

The shower operated with a remote. A remote control. He'd taken a picture and sent it to Heather—who'd instantly sent him a string of rapid-fire texts demanding pictures of everything.

He'd texted: **Why are you awake? It's almost one in the morning.**

College student. Cramming. Send pics. I'm freaking out here, she'd fired back.

He'd smiled, yawned, and texted, **Pics tomorrow. Get some sleep. Love you.**

You better. Break a leg tomorrow night, big brother. Wish I was there to cheer you on. I love you. Her text had ended with a string of kiss and kissy-face emojis. Heather was an emoji fan.

The remote hadn't just turned on and off the shower. Hell no. That would have been too easy. It turned on the in-floor heating, a variety of nature sounds, mood lighting, and a whole slew of different water pulses. He'd given up, stood on hot tiles, the sound of whales echoing off the walls, under alternating pink-and-purple lights, with water shooting him straight in the chest. Damn hard, too. Why the hell would anyone want that sort of water pressure? Eyes pressed shut, he rubbed his chest, wondering if he was bruised.

"Jace?" Krystal stage-whispered.

He opened one eye to find her standing in the aisle next to his seat. Her heavy-lidded eyes, too-big T-shirt, zebra-striped leggings, and worn-out John Deere tractor cap might be his favorite look yet. "Krystal."

"You look like you pulled an all-nighter."

"Didn't sleep." He opened both eyes, looking at the enlarged picture on her shirt. "Is that Clementine?"

She stared down at the image and smiled. "Yeah. A fan made it for me. Isn't she the cutest?"

Clementine was on her back, her tongue lolling out

the side of her mouth, in a blinged-out sweater that said "Mommy's Little Angel." "She's something, all right." He stifled a yawn. "She coming on the road with you?"

"Of course. She's asleep in her kennel up front." She cocked her head to one side, her green gaze sweeping over his face. "Why didn't you sleep? Eat too much pie?"

He liked her like this best. Teasing. Smiling. No tension. "Is that a thing? I'm pretty sure it's not."

She laughed. "Well, I hate to do this but…you're in my seat."

He tipped his cap back. "We have seats?"

"Not officially." She shrugged. "But I always sit back here. It's quiet. You go up there and you'll be forced to listen to Travis. He snores like a freight train. I pity his wife—if he ever stops screwing around and finds someone willing to take him on."

"Great." He yawned, shrugging. "Guess it's a good thing I can sleep through practically anything."

"Or you could just ask," she said.

"Ask?" he repeated, gathering his jacket and well-worn duffel bag.

"You're going to have to learn to stop being so agreeable, Jace. You're going to get eaten alive." With a sigh, she flopped into the seat beside him. "Fine."

"What?" He was confused.

"You can stay." She yawned. "You go up there, you won't get a lick of sleep. And I don't want you falling over when we sing tonight."

He wasn't about to argue.

"It's not just Travis. Emmy will be on Instagram or Snapchat or doing something super-productive so you'll feel guilty for not being productive." She yawned again, her eyelids drooping as she curled up in the oversized seat. "Even though it's human to need sleep. Emmy's devotion to her fans is ridiculous. But maybe that's why she's the popular one, I'm the screwup, and Travis is the playboy."

"You're not a screwup." Guarded, definitely—even a little detached. Considering the press she'd received in the last eighteen months alone, both made sense. Survival skills were required in a hypercompetitive industry. And, apparently, in the King household. He hadn't spent much time with CiCi King, but in that time, he'd learned quite a bit. And gained a whole new level of empathy and respect for the King children. Especially Krystal.

Still, Krystal shifted in her seat to study him. "Thanks, random reality TV winner guy who's known me for like five minutes."

"You're welcome." He chuckled.

She rolled her eyes. "Sarcasm. Something else you'll need to acquaint yourself with."

"Lucky to have your help on that." He rolled his jacket back up and closed his eyes as he rested his head.

"We have pillows."

"I'm good." He yawned, vaguely aware that the plane was taxiing down the runway. "So you know, I'm a good judge of character."

The dismissive snort-laugh she made had him

opening both eyes. "I'm not so sure about that. Don't you read the newspaper? Or watch the news or listen to the radio? If you did, you'd know all the mean and selfish and horrible things I've done." She was studying him again. "I am a bad person. You've been warned."

What was she looking for?

He waited, searching for the right words. Because, right now, he needed to be damn careful. "You know that game? Where you go around the circle, whispering the secret to the person next to you, and they whisper to the person next to them, and on around until the last person says the secret out loud?"

She nodded. "Telephone?"

"Yeah, that's it. Telephone. Every person hears some of it and fills in the rest? By the time it comes out, some words have changed. Some so much that it doesn't resemble what it started out as—hell, it might be unrecognizable. Definitely misunderstood. Or out of context. I think it's more like that. Might be simplifying it a bit, but you get what I mean." He held his breath, watching her.

"I get what you mean." Her grin was full of mischief. "But I did stomp on Mickey's foot. Hard. Made him bleed and ruined his boots." And she didn't feel an ounce of remorse over it, he could tell.

"I'm betting he deserved it." He shrugged. "And that he loved the attention he got out of it."

"And he got *plenty* of press." She lowered her voice, almost mumbling. Her gaze slipped from his. "Did anyone see him stick his hand under my skirt? No. Did anyone hear what he said to me?" Red seeped into her cheeks. "Of course not."

Anger clocked him right in the throat, squeezing tight enough to make breathing a chore. "What?" He'd had the chance to punch the son of a bitch square in the jaw, to lay him out cold in the damn parking lot that night. He should have. Hell, he wasn't opposed to doing just that next time he came face-to-face with the bastard. "Why not tell someone?"

Her jaw ticked, her smile going hard. "No one listens, Jace. Especially when it's something they don't want to hear." She closed her eyes and slumped back against the seat.

Try as he might, he couldn't relax. And, from her white-knuckled clenched fists, she wasn't asleep either.

Who the hell wouldn't listen to that? To her? It's not like she wasn't surrounded by people almost every second of every day. Surely, one of them would believe her? Everyone needed someone—a person they could rely on. He had Heather. Heather had him. He'd be damned if he ever turned his back on her, no matter what. "Krystal—"

"Don't." Her green eyes popped open, cutting him off. "Don't you dare start feeling sorry for me." She shot him a look.

He held his hands up in mock surrender. What he was feeling at the moment had nothing to do with pity. Pissed off? No doubt. Frustrated, too. And fiercely…protective? Of Krystal? Well, hell, she wouldn't thank him for that. Not one little bit.

With a nod, she relaxed—a bit. "Where does Heather go to school?"

"Oklahoma." He paused. "She works hard—on the dean's list. I'm damn proud of her." He smiled. "But I haven't seen her in a bit."

"Miss her?" She nodded. "Sounds like she got all the brains and you got all the looks?" she said, teasing, turning so she was curled up and facing him.

"Oh, no, Heather's gorgeous." He grinned. "Too."

She laughed that time. "And, out of the two of you, she definitely has the better name."

"We're still on that?" he sighed. "Jace isn't a bad name."

"But is it a *good* name?" She smothered a yawn. "Now shush so I can sleep, since I didn't get much earlier, either."

"Have problems with your shower too?" he asked.

"What? My shower?" Confusion clouded her altogether too pretty face.

And damn, she was pretty. "Forget it." Thinking about her in the shower was a bad idea. He pulled off his cap and ran his fingers through his hair. "Something keeping you up?"

She nodded, looked like she was going to say something more, then thought better of it.

"Music help?" he asked. "I do that. Work through it. Over and over?"

She pressed her eyes shut.

He started humming her song and was instantly rewarded with a smile. She kept her eyes closed, but she was definitely smiling.

"No," she interrupted. "Like this." She took it down a note, softened the tempo a beat, leaning closer to him. "Don't you think?"

"Yeah." He stared into those green, green eyes. "Better."

Her gaze fell to his lips. "You think you're charming, humming my song, being polite, and looking...like you do." Her brow rose high, and she stared at him for a long time before adding, "But you're up to something."

She thought he was charming? And what the hell did that mean: *Looking like you do?* Was that a good thing? It didn't sound like it, even though he was pretty sure it could be a very good thing. If she trusted him. Why would she? She was wary of people, men—especially those looking to use her as their ticket to fame—most of all. Maybe, when they'd known each other for more than a week, she'd start to believe that, with him, what you saw was what you got. That didn't mean he wasn't curious to know what sort of diabolical plans she thought he had. "Like what?"

"I'm still working that part out." She yawned, her eyes drifting shut. "Just know I'm watching you."

He smiled, watching her features soften in sleep. Try as he might, sleep eluded him. With his legs stretched out in front of him and his head propped on his jacket, he was comfortable enough. His brain wasn't cooperating.

Might be because tonight's concert was important. It was the first time Krystal's new song was being performed. Also, they'd be singing it together.

In one week, he'd be the Three Kings opening act. His own show. His own band. His own music. *Shit*. Was he ready for this?

He blew a slow breath out, staring out the small window at the lightening sky. The black was giving way to a deep blue, shot through with deep purples and the hint of pink. A new day. A new world. All good. It was up to him now. And he wouldn't let Heather or Luke or Krystal or Hank or Emmy Lou or any of the people counting on him down.

Chapter 6

"YOU WERE BASICALLY SLEEPING IN HIS LAP." TRAVIS scratched the back of his head. "Cuddled close and all."

She scowled at him. Had she fallen asleep on Jace? Yes. Had she woken up with her head on his chest? Again, yes. How he'd gotten his arm around her was a mystery... But she had not, *absolutely* not, been all over him. Had that stopped Travis from teasing her the entire time they'd been rehearsing for tonight's show? Not in the slightest.

"All over him." Travis clucked, shaking his head.

Unintentional or not, she *had* sort of been all over him. Legs in his lap. Head buried against his chest. Arms around his waist. And he'd been holding on, keeping her wrapped up tight in his big, strong, tattooed arms. He'd smelled like heaven and felt twice as good. It had been a hell of a way to wake up.

But it would have been better without an audience.

"Uh-huh." Travis picked up his guitar.

Don't ask. Don't acknowledge. Don't even respond. But the look on his face had her asking, "Uh-huh, what?"

He plucked a few notes. "Nothing." But his grin said otherwise.

"Travis." Emmy Lou was doing her best to keep them both on task. Poor thing. Didn't she know that was impossible? By now, she should trust that, solid rehearsal or not, they'd manage to put on a great show. Once the lights were on and people were screaming their names, they all understood the responsibility they had to their fans. "We were all tired. They fell asleep. That's all. Leave it alone." The look she shot him was intended to be firm—maybe even intimidating.

"Sure. Sure." He winked at Emmy. Still, his tone said something entirely different.

That *was* all. Neither one of them had made the conscious decision to become a sleeping pretzel. She had *tried* to extricate herself from their tangle of limbs without waking him. And failed. One second, he'd been all dead weight and deep sleep. The next, he'd pulled her close, smiling at her with his bedroom eyes.

"I'm just making an observation. Krystal might not hate him after all." He chuckled. "And he didn't seem too put out to wake up with her all up in his personal space."

No, he hadn't. He'd *seemed* happy to see her. Until the sleep had cleared from his eyes and he'd sat bolt upright, knocking their heads together and drawing every eye on the plane their way—those that weren't already staring at them, that is—before mumbling an apology and disappearing into the bathroom.

Emmy Lou looked back and forth between them. "I'm not sure what you're hoping to accomplish, Trav. I think it's best if we all get along—since we're going to finish out the rest of the tour together."

"Right, exactly. Get along." Travis was all smiles. "And

you two seem to be. You're crushing on him. I even have a picture here of you two, *getting along*." He held up his phone.

"You do not." Krystal sighed. At least, he better not.

Her brother lived to get a rise out of her. This was what he did. After hours of traveling and rehearsing, Travis got restless. Why he thought picking on her about *Jace* was a good way to pass the time, she didn't know. Teasing, as a whole, was his preshow process.

"Something tells me I'll have a whole album full of you and Jace getting along." He shrugged, staring at his phone. "Might even post it online. Can't hurt launching this song."

She shot him a look. Whether he meant to or not, he'd struck a nerve. The last thing she'd ever do was exploit her personal life for work. "Not funny."

"I wasn't exactly joking." His eyebrows rose.

"Are you kidding me?" After everything she'd been through with Mickey, there was no way she and Jace—if that was even a thing—would become part of their marketing plan. People ended up getting hurt. Meaning she'd wind up getting hurt. Again.

"Hold on a minute." Travis shifted the guitar strap on his neck. "You want this solo thing, I know you do. Use what you've got, Krystal. A good song. An interested guy fans approve of. And obvious attraction." He shrugged. "Before you go there, you have to know Jace is nothing like Mickey. Jace is a seriously nice guy."

All she could do was stare at her brother.

"The song is enough." Emmy Lou spoke up. "More than enough."

"Thank you." Krystal hugged her sister.

"It is." He nodded. "*We* know that. Sometimes record labels and charts and sales need a little push, though. I'm not saying it's a good idea one way or the other, I'm just saying."

"You're starting to sound a little too much like Momma for my liking, Trav."

"I'm not the one who posted a picture of him holding Clementine, now am I?" he asked. "You didn't think that'd cause a reaction? Because it did. Might as well use it."

She frowned. "That was for Heather. His sister."

"And a few million of your closest Instagram and Twitter followers," he murmured.

Even Emmy nodded at that. "The post got serious attention and reposts and all sorts of fan love. Not just for Clementine, either."

She wasn't the social media guru her sister was. When Krystal posted, she tended to throw whatever caught her fancy out there. Like Jace. And Clementine. Together. Adorable. For the whole world to see and jump to conclusions.

"You three ready for makeup?" Misumi, her and Emmy's assistant, asked. "The label wanted to do a few shots of you three and Jace when they announce Jace is joining the tour."

Krystal didn't miss the look her brother sent her. All smug.

Curling irons, hairspray, and false eyelashes were her immediate future. Travis teasingly called their makeup regime "battle gear." The last few years, her look had gone darker—smoky eyes and bold lips—while Emmy Lou stayed pink and soft and innocent. As if anyone could confuse the two of them?

Her colors were dark—black, navy, the occasional splash of red. From fringed suede, her favorite, to sparkle-heavy sequin-covered dresses, her costumes fit like a glove but allowed her to move. When someone came to a Three Kings concert, they were blown away by the energy and production values of their show.

Last, but definitely not least, came the jewelry. Bling was important to her image. Crystal chandelier earrings, a crystal collar necklace, and crystal-covered bangles on both wrists. Not to mention her boots—even the boots sparkled. After she was deemed photo ready, she attempted damage control by shoving Clementine into the arms of everyone on her crew. The pics were posted instantly, witty comments and obnoxious photo stickers, too. Maybe now her post with Jace wouldn't matter so much?

With Clem in the arms of Misumi, she endured a final makeup touch-up and followed her siblings into a staged room for the photo shoot. Bright lights beat down on the pristine white backdrop, their electric hum audible over the handful of conversations taking place as props were brought in, removed, rearranged.

Jace was there, doing his best to make her trip all over herself by standing there looking good enough to eat. That's all he was doing, standing there, but it was enough. She smoothed her hands over one of her favorite curve-hugging, black suede dresses, the jangle of nerves in the pit of her belly unfamiliar.

If he thought she was going to let him get to her, he was wrong. She knew better. *Dammit.* She did.

"Channeling your inner Johnny Cash?" Travis asked, giving Jace a head-to-toe sweep.

"Black." He shrugged. "Jace Black."

Black was his color. Black Stetson. Black boots. Skintight black T-shirt to match the tattoos, and faded black jeans that should be downright illegal for the things they were doing to the man's ass... She swallowed, fiddling with the fringes of her skirt.

"Clever," Travis chuckled, glancing her way. "Now you two match." He was enjoying this way too much.

Dammit. Dammit. Dammit. Don't look at him. Do. Not. Look. At. Him.

She did, of course. How could she not? He had some sort of internal magnetic thing that zapped her into full-on stare mode—whether she liked it or not. And what did he do? Smiled at her. And tipped his hat like a real cowboy gentleman. Before heading her way.

"Think this was planned?" Jace asked, dodging a lighting assistant and stepping that much closer to her in the process.

Not looking at him would help—if she could manage it. But that wouldn't stop her from inhaling his delicious denim-leather-sandalwood-aftershave scent. Especially this close. Her gaze darted to his chest. Right at her eye level. There was no denying there were some heavy-duty muscles underneath that cotton shirt. She didn't need to look to know that since she'd used him as her personal pillow. And enjoyed it.

Dammit.

If her clueless brother had picked up on the combustible pulse between them, others would, too. If they hadn't already. This was bad—for both of them.

Add on the imminent arrival of the surprise she'd arranged for Jace and she knew she'd messed up. Big-time. What had she been thinking? It was too late now. *Damn it all.*

"You know what they say, imitation is the best form of flattery." She injected as much hard-ass venom into her words as possible. With a toss of her perfectly tousled curls, she put as much space between them as possible—without sparing him or his angled, stubbled jaw or perfectly cut bod a single look.

The fan was turned on, the lights were angled, and the posing began.

Performing onstage was one thing. It was in the moment. Constant movement. The crowd and music stirred her in a way that made things natural. Posing for pictures? Turning her chin another eighth of an inch to the right and down. Not smiling, smiling more, smiling but no teeth. Tossing her hair. A fake laugh. The fake laugh thing was the worst… Definitely outside her comfort zone.

Still, she did her best. At least she had Emmy and Travis to interact with. He was great at cracking them up and Emmy always seemed to know when she needed an encouraging smile or nudge. All the while, the photographer offered up suggestions, the camera shutter clicking away.

"Watch the shine on Emmy's nose," the photographer called, waiting until Emmy's nose had been dusted before he took a few more shots. "Jace. Come on up."

That's when she risked a quick look. And regretted it. Poor Jace. He looked downright nervous.

"Let's have Jace, Emmy, Travis, and Krystal." The photographer nodded. "Squeeze in. Smiles." A few dozen clicks. "Good. Now Jace and Krystal."

Whatever sympathy she'd been feeling for Jace evaporated at the sound of her brother's laugh. It wasn't completely unexpected. They were singing a song together. A duet. These pictures were marketing for the song. Her *song*. Nothing else.

"Face each other," the photographer said.

She blinked, the weight of the photographer's stare growing. *Really? Fine. Dammit.* She spun on her booted heel, took a deep breath, and glared up at Jace.

Jace burst out laughing. Full-bodied, dimple-inducing, from-the-toes laughter. Adorable and real and impossible to resist.

It had been a long time since she'd laughed like that. For a split second, she could forget the lights and cameras and people milling about. A second. And then Jace

Black did something he shouldn't have. Still smiling and breathless, he reached up and smoothed a curl from her forehead.

"Good," the photographer said. "Let's get the guitar in the shot."

Just like that, the lights and cameras and people were there again. No doubt watching and analyzing every reaction or expression.

It had been an accident. One of those unexplained impulses. Nothing calculated. Or planned. Jace wasn't the sort to do something like that. Was he?

"Here." Jace handed her the guitar. "You okay?" It was a whisper.

No. Hell no. Nothing like getting blindsided by dimples and a nice ass to shake your confidence all over again. If she didn't keep it together, she'd be swallowed up by a panic attack. Right now, that would only add to this mess. She strummed the strings, wincing at the sound the instrument made.

He chuckled. "Needs a little tuning."

She nodded, staring at the guitar. Keeping her emotions in check and her face blank wasn't going to be easy, but it was necessary. Jace might not understand the sort of fallout a simple look could trigger, but she did. Since she'd already unintentionally opened the door to speculation about their relationship…well, chances were he was about to find out how one picture, one look, could change everything.

"Hold on," the photographer said, stepping back to review the proofs on screen.

"Are you breathing?" Jace whispered.

She glanced at him, searching his brown eyes for any telltale cause for alarm. The problem was, everything about Jace Black was alarming. Her reaction to him was visceral. One look from him had her insides melting. Like now. Right here, with cameras at the ready.

There was also that misguided little voice in her head wanting her to give him the benefit of the doubt. She didn't know much about Jace Black, that was true. But what she did know was he was nothing like Mickey Graham; Travis got that part right.

It was important he stay that way.

Having their personal lives linked might be a good thing for her but not for him. For her, he'd be damage control. For him, she'd be the powder keg that invariably blew his career to shreds. Didn't he get that? Didn't he know that she was the wrong King sister to get involved with?

The longer she stared at him, the more his smile faded.

"You two want to come look at these?" her father called out. "I'd say we're good, but I'd rather get your approval before we send any of these out with the press release."

"Sure." She tore her gaze from his, shoved the prop guitar into his hands, and hurried to her father's side.

"Gonna be a hell of a challenge to pick the right one." Her father crossed his arms over his chest, his gaze fixed on the monitor.

"Right?" the photographer nodded. "Solid gold, if I do say so myself. Every shot."

She wasn't sure what she'd expected, but not this.

Oh no. No. No. No.

The photographer had picked up on everything. Every tiny, infinitesimal detail. How she looked downright tiny next to him. His jeans—those jeans and that ass. Jace was…well, it was understandable that he already had fans. Now that she'd heard him sing, she knew it wasn't just because of his smile. Or his laugh. Or those dimples. Or his incredible, work-hardened body. Hell, the overall gorgeousness of everything about him.

That part was good—for Jace.

But the rest was not.

That thing, that chemical reaction between them, was there. Recorded forever. For all the world to see.

The look on his face when he touched her. Her heart felt heavy, compressed inside her chest.

The look on her face when their eyes met. Her smile. *No.* Her lungs emptied and the anxiety she'd been grappling with came crashing in. *No.*

"These won't work," she whispered, the words getting stuck in her throat. Not that anyone was listening to her. Even if they had, they wouldn't have taken her seriously. No, every one else seemed thrilled by the shoot.

"This one." Her father tapped on the monitor, enlarging one shot of the four of them. They were all smiling and excited. "And this one." Another click, this one of her and Jace. They were smiling, caught up in one another, leaning close, one of Jace's heavily muscled tattoo-covered upper arms extended forward as his fingers brushed her temple.

It was too intimate.

"Maybe this one too?" her father asked, looking her way.

Jace didn't know much about photo shoots, but he was pretty sure it had gone well. At least, everyone in the room seemed happy. Everyone except Krystal. He wasn't sure what he'd done, but he'd sure as hell done something.

"Jace." Hank waved him over. "I can't guarantee your opinion will influence the outcome here, but I'd like to hear it all the same." He chuckled.

Jace handed off the guitar to the prop master and stood beside Emmy Lou. Emmy Lou, who was shifting from foot to foot, shooting worried looks at her twin. So he wasn't the only one to notice Krystal's agitation.

The pictures were awesome. Every single one of them. He looked like a starstruck idiot, but that's because he was. The pictures were honest—too honest. He was beyond starstruck. If there'd been any doubts about his interest in Krystal King, they were gone now.

"You look good." Travis clapped him on the shoulder. "No one would know this was your first rodeo."

"People are going to freak out." Luke was smiling from ear to ear, like a kid in a candy shop. "Freak."

He shook his head, doing his best not to stare at the picture Hank King wanted to use of him and Krystal. But, damn, she looked beautiful. And, together, they made one hell of a team.

"Daddy." Emmy Lou tugged his arm. "Are you sure about this?" She lowered her voice. "It's a great shot, but—"

"It's a picture." Travis shook his head. "And they look—well, look at them. It's a damn good picture. And they are singing a ballad. It's good marketing."

"You don't think it implies…something else?" Emmy asked.

It was there, staring them all in the face. Jace saw it—felt it. The live-wire spark between them.

"A platinum single?" Luke was teasing, his enthusiasm unaffected by Emmy Lou's concern.

Hank shot him a look, one brow arched. "Jace?" Arms crossed, eyes narrowed, Hank King was sizing up Jace, waiting for his reaction.

"I'm with Emmy on this one." He shook his head. "The song will stand on its own."

Travis moaned, running a hand over his face. "Are you looking at the same picture I am?"

Luke jumped in. "Jace, Hank knows what he's doing—"

"I know." Jace cut him off. "You asked. Use a different picture. There's plenty to choose from."

Hank shook his head. "I respect your opinion, son. And that you speak your mind. But I've been doing this a hell of a long time. See this?" Hank asked, tapping on the picture. "That's something you can't stage. The song is good and I believe in it. But you have to use every angle to set it apart." He glanced at Krystal. "Okay?"

Krystal was motionless, the color drained from her face and her hands pressed flat against her upper thighs.

"I'll take that as a yes." Hank grinned, then looked his way.

Luke nodded. "This will get people talking—and buying the single."

Jace was pretty sure it wasn't a yes. They might be comfortable moving on without her weighing in, but he wasn't. "Krystal? Are you comfortable with this?"

The room fell quiet and all eyes shifted to Krystal.

She spared him a glance, shrugging. "It's just business. That's all. You want to sell records, don't you?" There was an edge to the question. "That's what this is about."

While Hank picked out a few more pics, Luke was talking his ear off about a late-night show spot he was trying to book and a possible endorsement deal from a boot maker. Jace only half listened. Between the photo shoot and the show tonight, his adrenaline was pumping.

The show. Krystal's song. Their duet. It was a big deal. And she was counting on him not to blow it.

No pressure.

"You look green, man." Travis nudged him. "Nervous?"

He nodded.

"Nerves are good. Keep you on edge. Give you energy." He grinned. "Keep moving, keep singing." He nudged him. "Own your talent, man. You can sing. You wouldn't be up there tonight if my dad didn't think so."

Travis's attempt at a pep talk wasn't doing much to settle Jace's nerves.

"Besides, it's not like you'll be doing this alone." His gaze settled on Krystal. "Follow her lead. She knows what she's doing."

Krystal was still staring at the computer monitor covered in photos from the shoot. "I think you just gave me a compliment."

"Don't let it go to your head." Travis chuckled.

"Wouldn't dream of it." Krystal spun away from the monitor and stared, hard, at him. What she was looking for was the mystery. Was it the song? His performance? Did she still resent him like hell? Did he blame her? Whatever it was, it weighed on her. There was a slight crease between her brows. And a tightening around those full, bright red lips. The only way to know what she was thinking was outright asking her. Right now didn't seem like the right time. For one thing, he wasn't sure he was up for dealing with the fallout from the answers she'd give him. Not and still manage to do what he needed to do tonight.

After the concert, after he'd done her and her song proud, he'd ask her what was on her mind.

After five minutes of staring, Jace's nerves were strung tight. "What?"

She shook her head. "Nothing." Her curls shook, one falling across her temple to rest against her cheek.

Travis snorted but scurried away when she shot him a lethal glare.

"I get that I'm not your first choice." He kept his voice low, aware that there were others in the room. "Hell, I probably wasn't on your top fifty list."

Her chin thrust slightly, defiant, and her brows rose, but she didn't argue with him.

"But I promise you I won't let you down, Krystal." The urge to smooth that curl had his fingers itching. "Old-fashioned or not, I'm a man of my word."

"If anyone else had said that, I'd be laughing." The corner of her mouth curved. "Not that it wasn't all kinds of corny—because it was—but for reasons beyond understanding, I sort of believe you."

"Sort of?" He pushed.

Her brows rose higher, if that was possible.

"How do you sort of believe something?" He couldn't stop looking at that curl. "You either do or you don't." Those red lips, full-on smiling at him now.

"Why does it matter?" Those green eyes traveled over his face, still searching.

That was the question. And there were a whole lot of possible answers. He went with the easy ones. "I admire and respect you and your family, always have. I know you're taking a chance on me—"

"A big chance." She nodded.

He smiled. "Yes, you're taking a big chance on me—"

"Risk. I get the feeling, with you…maybe *risk* is a better word?" Her green eyes locked with his, her smile going hard.

They weren't talking about music anymore. "Krystal…"

She stepped back, blinking, her gaze falling from his. "You might want to go warm up some. The show will be starting soon."

He stood rooted to the spot, while she walked out of the room, her black suede fringes swaying around her thighs with every step.

"Not a good idea," Luke murmured, appearing at his elbow.

"Neither is sneaking up on me." He sighed.

"Whatever." Luke pointed at the monitor. "That makes for record sales. That look." He pointed at the door Krystal had just walked through. "That is biting the hand that feeds you."

Jace stared at his manager.

"The show is over. The Kings are giving you a chance at an actual career." His voice lowered. "We need to stay on CiCi King's good side here, Jace. I don't think it's a good idea for you to be mixing business with pleasure."

"No one is mixing a damn thing." He frowned. "I don't need help managing my life, Luke. Just my career."

Luke smiled—it wasn't a real smile. "Believe me, I don't want to. So don't get them mixed up, okay?"

For the next hour, Jace warmed up with the band Hank and Luke had pulled together. He'd spent time jamming with Travis and Sawyer, but this was different. This was the real thing. Jace had been more than a little awed to have some industry staples backing him. Scotty Reed, his drummer, had covered for Hank and the Three Kings a few times. Rafael Fuentes, guitar and keyboards, and Tommy Glenn, bass guitar, had been touring since Jace was in high school. In a couple of weeks, when he was officially the Three Kings opening act, they'd be his band, and it blew his mind.

So did being led around backstage, to watch the show from the wings.

He'd never seen the Three Kings live. He'd managed to get Heather a ticket once, a couple of years ago, for her sixteenth birthday but he'd had to work. Seeing them up close, hearing them harmonize, the easy rhythm and seamless delivery were awe-inspiring.

He sang along when they sang the crowd-pleasing drinking song "One More Round," tapped his foot to "Cut and Run," and wound up staring when Krystal pulled out all the stops for "I'm Leaving First."

"Ready?" a woman asked. He should know her name but he was drawing a blank. She handed him his guitar. "Jace?" she repeated. "You ready?"

Hell no. He nodded, slipping the strap over his shoulder and running his hands along the familiar, worn leather strap. But this wasn't some honky-tonk truck stop in West Texas. And it wasn't some reality show with folks screaming, hoping to get themselves on television. This was it.

The big league. His big break. The beginning. Or the end.

"We've got a real treat tonight," Travis was talking. "Some of y'all might have heard a rumor about my little sister Krystal teaming up with a certain singer?" He paused, letting the roar of the crowd rise. "Any ideas on who I'm talking about?"

It started out soft but rose. Over and over, a little louder each time. His name.

Jace. Jace. Jace.

"Hear that, Krystal?" Travis asked. "Guess the cat's out of the bag." Travis turned and waved him forward.

The crowd went crazy.

He didn't remember making the conscious decision to walk, but he was moving. Without tripping over the spiderweb of cords and cables that covered the stage. Without being blinded by the white spotlight narrowing the stage to one spot.

Krystal, seated on a stool, and an empty stool beside her. For him.

She patted the stool, smiling at him like this was an everyday sort of occurrence.

He tipped his hat, earning a few screams from the crowd, and sat on the stool beside her. He looked out over the crowd, a mass of dark shapes and a few hundred telltale lights from all the cell phones recording. "Evening," he said into the mic on the stand in front of him.

More screams had him shaking his head.

He strummed his fingers over the strings of his guitar

and turned to Krystal. The stools were close enough to see her, close enough to feel the heat and energy rolling off of her. She was nervous. No, the look on her face said something else. She was...terrified?

This wasn't about him. This was about her. And this song. It mattered to her, maybe more than he could truly understand.

He winked at her, took her hand long enough to offer a reassuring squeeze, and began to play in earnest. He drew a deep breath and sang. "I remember you, standing in the sun, smiling at me, and suddenly my world caught fire. Blinding, beautiful fire."

The audience went crazy.

"I remember you, taking my hand, holding me close, and suddenly my world caught fire. Blinding, beautiful fire." Her gaze stayed on him, the husky notes of her voice wavering and rich and mesmerizing.

A few notes, his fingers moving on their own. "You were everything..." He sang his part then he paused a beat. "...you tried to run from the heat."

Krystal swayed with the music, raw and anguished; she didn't hold back. "...the sweetest pain of all."

All he could do was stare, the words and music tying them together as they sang. "Love isn't love when the flames burn it down. There's no hiding or forgiveness from the damage that it's done. When the smoke clears away, you'll still find me searching here. Searching for the ashes of my heart."

If he woke up tomorrow and this was over, he'd

be satisfied. He was a roughneck. A midnight bail-
bondsman. A blue-collar man with a beat-up truck and
a mobile home with a leaky roof and a groaning air conditioning unit. But tonight, he was singing a damn good
song with Krystal King in front of a few thousand people
screaming his name.

He stood, playing through the extra notes she'd added
for a guitar solo. He'd thought she'd meant to play it.
Instead, she'd told him to. "Girls love guys who play the
guitar," she'd said. He hadn't argued.

From the screams and whistles of the audience, she'd
been right.

But they weren't who he was looking to impress. She
was right here, next to him. He shot her a smile and she
slid off her stool, coming to his side. Her hair was mussed,
her cheeks were red, and her eyes flashed. Whatever jit-
ters she'd been feeling, they were gone. The music carried them both.

He stepped closer, his fingers stilling on the strings of
his guitar.

She smiled up at him, breath a little uneven, the flash
and shimmer of her earrings catching the lights. All of
her sparkled—she was lit up from the inside, proud and
happy and so damn gorgeous he didn't want this moment
to end. The whole coliseum seemed to be holding their
breath, waiting. Krystal pushed a wayward curl from her
shoulder and held her mic with both hands, her eyes
never leaving his face.

He nodded, stepping close enough to share her mic.

"Love isn't love when the flames burn it down. There's no hiding or forgiveness from the damage that it's done. When the smoke clears away, you'll still find me searching here. Searching for the ashes of my heart."

She hummed a note and repeated, softer and husky, "Searching for the ashes of my heart."

It was his turn to hold his breath. Exhilaration mixed with a healthy dose of doubt settled hard and tight in the pit of his stomach. He waited, staring into her green eyes as the lights went dim.

The noise was deafening, rolling out of the dark and slamming into them. The crowd's applause and screams and whistles swept over them like a wave of living, breathing energy. The sense of uncertainty he'd been grappling with for most of the day fell away instantly. This was good. Not just good, awesome. He knew it, felt it, and—according to Travis—needed to own it. When the high he was riding crashed, he'd consider it.

For now, he was sweaty, breathing hard, and, damn it, feeling pretty good. When Krystal threw her arms around his neck, it went from good to great. Right, even. And he held on to her. Tight.

Chapter 7

"YOU DID IT," SHE WHISPERED AGAINST HIS NECK, true happiness welling up inside her.

"We did it." His voice was muffled and gruff. He shifted his guitar behind him, so his arm could hold her against him in the best way possible.

We. The meaning of the word, applied to them, didn't bother her the way it should have. There was no *we* here, not in the long run. This was a duet, a business arrangement—a collaboration. That's all. She understood that. Well, her *brain* understood that.

The rest of her...that was a different story. Dammit, it wasn't like she had a choice. Her reaction to him was instinctual. It wasn't just warm fuzzies he stirred; it was the far more electric and bone-melting impact he had on her that was the problem.

And it was a problem.

Like now.

When she was hugging him in front of a crowd of several thousand fans and she was in no hurry to let go. When his scent made her dizzy and the crush of his chest against hers did nothing to dampen the whole bone-melting problem. If anything, the brush of his breath against her neck and the press of his hand against her back had her aching in a way that would lead to serious consequences. Enjoyable but far too complicated and severe consequences.

So much for her frantic attempt at damage control over her Jace and Clementine Instagram post.

"Y'all were awesome." It was Emmy who hooked arms with her and pulled her, gently, away from his embrace.

Krystal nodded, Jace's dark silhouette moving quickly offstage before the bright white lights kicked on.

"You good?" Emmy's hold tightened. "It was amazing, Krystal."

"I know." She tried to laugh, but she couldn't bring herself to make light of it. Not yet. It had been amazing, special—too special to dismiss. She wasn't one for sentimentality but *this*, she wanted to cherish.

The rest of the concert went like clockwork. They hit their marks, pulled out all the stops, and delivered everything their fans had come to expect from a Three Kings show.

"Where's Jace?" Travis asked. "He should come out for the finale."

Lori, the stage manager, managed to find him and send him out in time to sing their hit "Forever My Home." The audience approved, making Jace blush and shake his head and amp up his appeal to every woman in the room.

Krystal couldn't remember a time when she wasn't onstage. Right or wrong, she'd grown up in the spotlight. Now, it was second nature. Not so for Jace. Still, he rallied when she smiled his way and laughed when Travis whispered something in his ear. And then they were singing and he was fine.

It was odd how easily he fit, riffing off Travis's guitar and playing along on his beaten-up wooden Taylor guitar. He knew the words, of course; he was a fan. And "Forever My Home" was a Three Kings favorite. Upbeat and catchy, Jace had no problem jumping right in. Fans loved it, especially the way he tipped his hat at the crowd when the song ended. Because he was a gentleman.

How long would that last now? She'd like to think Jace wouldn't fall victim to the women, parties, drugs, and alcohol followed by a round of bad choices…but it seemed to be part of the process. How far he'd fall and how well he recovered was up to him.

Not that she needed to worry tonight. Even though her surprise wasn't an intentional groupie-blocking move, there was no denying that was the end result. One more night to hold on to gentleman Jace.

She smiled. *Gentleman Jace.* It was catchy.

His light brown gaze met hers and when he smiled right back, his dimples appeared. The dimples. That skin-tight shirt. The tattoos. The bod… And the voice. Jace Black was pure temptation.

Good thing she was strong.

But, to play it safe, no more staring or smiling or leaning in or spontaneous hugs. She tore her gaze from his and headed offstage, gulping down a bottle of cold water Misumi offered and heading toward the greenroom. "She here?"

Misumi nodded. "She's waiting."

"Did she see the show?" Her excitement didn't make sense. But she was. Excited.

"Got her a shirt, too. Figured that was okay? She's a big fan, you know?" Misumi chuckled. "She even brought Clementine a treat."

Krystal smiled at that. That was why Heather was here. She was a Three Kings fan. This was her brother's first performance with them. Heather should be here to support her big brother and have a little fun in the process. Yes, Jace was missing his little sister and that might have had the slightest impact on her decision to fly Heather in for tonight's show. But, primarily, this was for Heather.

"It's trending," Emmy said, holding up her phone.

"Glad that whole 'no phones' thing is being reinforced," their manager, Steve, snapped.

Krystal rolled her eyes. Steve didn't seem to grasp the significance of their fandom. Without their fans, he'd be out of a job. Leaked videos and pictures normally helped keep them relevant and on the charts.

"It's you and Jace," Emmy added.

Krystal paused then, glancing at the phone. There they were, singing. Leaning in…invested in each other, in the moment and the song. Her chest grew heavy, her lungs light. The hum and buzz they'd ignited onstage instantly sparked to life. It had been an incredible performance. Vulnerable and raw. And, possibly, revealing. Or maybe she was just being paranoid. Hopefully, she was. First the pictures, now this. It was all an illusion. She'd been at this game long enough to know that.

"Views are climbing." Emmy Lou nodded. "Looks like you've got a serious fan base, Jace."

"Bet ninety percent of them are chicks." Travis chuckled. "You've increased your *dating* pool by a few thousand."

"Travis." Emmy Lou's disapproval was adorable—because she was always adorable.

Krystal was not. With her nerves on edge, it wouldn't take much to trigger a full-on vent at her brother. Which he would love. Going off the handle now would only give Travis more leverage in the whole crushing-on-Jace thing.

But the truth was something different. There was no crush. Crushes implied something sweet and innocent. Her response to Jace Black was anything but. She was a woman—he was all man. That was why she couldn't give in to the urges and cravings he caused. Because it would be all too easy to lose herself in Jace.

In the end, this whole good-guy thing wouldn't last. It never did. She was too smart to set herself up for a guaranteed heartache. She would be strong. Resist.

"Good job, man, good job." Jace's agent was all smiles. Unlike Steve, he still had that new agent giddiness. "Killer show. All of you."

Krystal's hand was shaking when she reached for the greenroom door. What if Heather didn't like her? What if this was just a colossal mistake? Travis was going to make this unbearable.

"Krystal?" Travis asked, brushing her hand aside and opening the greenroom door.

"I can't believe this!" It was almost a scream. "Ohmygawdohmygawd...seriously?"

It was the look on Jace's face that set her mind at ease.

He was smiling ear to ear, hurrying into the greenroom. She followed.

Jace was spinning Heather around, still smiling like a fool.

"His sister?" Travis asked, watching.

She nodded.

"You did this?" Emmy Lou's voice wavered. She had enough sentimentality for the three of them. "Krystal." She hugged her sister. "You did a good thing."

She hugged her sister back, watching Jace and Heather's reunion. "He missed her."

"Little sisters." Travis sighed, draping an arm over their shoulders. "You're pests, but you're our pests."

Krystal smiled and swatted his chest. Emmy Lou smiled and rested her head on his shoulder.

"I can't believe I'm here." Heather was beet red and staring. "I can't believe you're here." She clung to Jace's arm. "This whole night."

"Right there with you." Jace nodded. "Pretty unreal."

"You were amazing." Heather smiled up at him. "I was all, that's my brother—who swears he can't sing. Up there. Singing with Krystal King." Her brown eyes met Krystal's. "You're like the single coolest person ever." The way Heather was looking at her, she almost believed the girl.

Travis pushed her forward. "She has her moments."

Krystal smiled. "It's nice to meet you, Heather."

Heather hugged her. "Thank you, so much. I wanted to be here, but there was no way. Thank you."

Krystal hugged her back. "You needed to be here."

"This is amazing. Being here and you guys. Seriously,

thank you." Heather stepped back. "I did that. I just hugged Krystal King. I am so sorry. You're like *you*. I'm seriously sorry."

Krystal laughed.

"It's just...I like, sort of idolize you, you know?" Heather paused. "Is that creepy? That is totally creepy, isn't it?" She glanced back at her brother.

That's when she realized Jace was staring at her. It was a new look. One she wasn't sure what to make of.

"Am I messing things up?" Heather asked, covering her face with her hands.

"No, you're not. He's so happy you're here, he's speechless." Travis stepped forward. "I'm Travis."

"Oh, I know." She was wide-eyed and blushing. "You're way cuter in person—I didn't think that was possible."

"I like her," Travis said to Jace.

"Liking is okay. Anything else is not allowed," Krystal cut in, stepping between Heather and her brother with a narrow-eyed look of warning.

Travis was laughing.

"Heather, I am so glad to meet you." Emmy Lou was all smiling charm and sweetness.

The inevitable glaze of awe descended on Jace's little sister and Krystal risked another glance at Jace.

His light brown eyes met hers. *Thank you,* he mouthed, nodding at his sister. When he looked at Heather, it was with so much love. He seemed...calm. Relieved. Excited. It made sense, needing to have someone he knew by his side. Someone unconditionally on his side he could share this with.

And right then, Krystal knew the truth. None of this was for Heather. She'd done it all for Jace.

"How do you not freak out every single day?" Heather was shifting from foot to foot, barely containing her excitement. "That is Hank King," she whispered. "I mean, Jace. We are talking about *the Hank. King.*"

Jace nodded. "That *is* Hank King. Right there. Believe me, I know. I'm not used to it. I'm not sure I'll ever get used to any of…*this.*"

"How could you? I'd never get anything done. I'd just stare. Like that guy. Who is that guy?"

"His name is Sawyer." He nodded at the man. "He's security. Mostly for Emmy and Krystal."

"Then I guess he's allowed to stare at people and stand in corners like that. Still, sorta freaky, though." Heather let out a little squeal and took his hand in hers. "Emmy Lou is super nice. And oh so pretty. But Krystal…" She sighed, a dreamy sort of sigh he was familiar with. "She is *it*, you know? Just, everything."

"Yeah." He knew, all right.

"She did this. I mean, her assistant, Misumi, called me two days ago and, boom, here I am." She shook her head. "She really likes you. Taking that picture of you and Clementine was just about the biggest stamp of approval she could give you."

Which was news to Jace. Poor Clementine had been

passed around like a hot potato, which led him to doubt his sister's summation of the whole photo op.

But Heather wasn't done. "I mean, you two sounded so, so good. Not good. It was…it was incredible." Her smile grew. "Do you even know how amazing you two sound?"

He shrugged. Maybe. Yes. He wanted to think he did but…nothing about tonight felt real. Beginning with that photo shoot, ending with hearing Heather's profuse thank-yous to Krystal.

"Come on, Jace." She tugged at his hand. "This is your life now. How is this happening?"

"Which means it's your life, too." He squeezed her fingers. "How's school?"

"Nope, nuh-uh, we are *not* talking about school." She squealed again. "Is that…is that CiCi King? I have read a lot about her." His sister's tone was both awed and intimidated.

That was most definitely CiCi King. The change in the air was palpable—from euphoric to braced. It didn't help that she was looking at Jace, and Heather, with a smile that had him checking for exits.

"She's pretty," Heather murmured. "In a mean-girl sort of way. Like, mess-with-me-and-I-will-cut-you thing? Wait, did I say that out loud?"

He laughed. Luckily, the room was noisy and they were far enough away that no one would have heard her. Krystal's comment about Heather getting all the brains played through his head. She might be young, but she was razor-sharp. And perceptive. CiCi King was a mean girl—worse, a mean mother. He might not know the details of what soured her and Krystal's relationship, but there was no denying it was hanging on by a thread. A thread neither of them seemed ready or willing to save.

"What do you do now?" Heather asked. "Something cool?"

He chuckled. "Me? No. I'm pretty tuckered out, Heather. Let me check in with Luke, and if we get the all clear, I could go for some pizza?" He paused. "And a shake?"

"It's like midnight." She made a show of looking at her phone.

"I didn't realize there was a pizza and shake cutoff time." He winked. "You're not hungry?" To him, she seemed skinny. Too skinny. One night of pizza and a few milkshakes wouldn't fix that, but it would have to do. For now.

"I could eat." But she wasn't paying attention. Krystal walked in—with Clementine. He wasn't sure what Heather was more excited about: Krystal or the dog. He had to admit, Clementine was growing on him. He'd come to admire the little dog's fearlessness, even when she was sliding into walls or stumbling in a full run. Must get that from her owner—the woman holding the dog. She was something else. Something soft pretending to be hard. Something vulnerable pretending to be strong.

Her green gaze bounced off his, but she smiled Heather's way. Why did she do that? Did she honestly believe he bought her whole indifferent thing? He didn't.

There was no way she could deny the current between them—it was too big, too live, too damn electric to ignore.

"Krystal King is smiling at me," Heather whispered, her grip painfully tight. "Smiling."

"You did sort of tackle her."

Heather stared up at him in horror. "I did. I really did."

"I was teasing, Heather." He hugged her close. "Give me a sec." It didn't take long for him to hunt down Luke. He was on his phone, as always.

"We're going through Salt Lake tomorrow. From there, we're in California. I've got you on that late late-night show with the guy that does the singing?" He looked up from his phone. "The funny one?"

Jace nodded, not entirely sure who Luke was talking about but assuming it was a good thing. Promo was always a good thing, wasn't it? Especially now that he'd be the Kings' opening act. How hard could it be? Sitting in a chair, talking about how damn lucky it was to be him right now. He was the luckiest bastard alive and he knew it.

"This is good, man, awesome." Luke slapped him on the shoulder.

"Okay for me to take off?" he asked. "Heather's here."

"Check with Hank, will you?" Luke's phone buzzed. "I don't think he has anything else planned, but I don't want to step on anyone's toes. Especially his."

"Agreed." But the sight of Krystal beside Heather, Clementine in his sister's lap, had him heading their way. "Satisfied?"

"Um, no. I'm overwhelmed. Can I just quit school and

be her dog nanny?" Heather was smiling, Clementine bathing her cheek in doggy kisses. "We don't have to rush off, do we?"

"Where are you rushing off to?" Krystal asked, smiling at the ferocity of Clementine's wiggles.

"Someplace where there's good pizza. Maybe a few milkshakes?" He paused. "If you want to join us? After the meet-and-greet thing?"

He wasn't sure who was more surprised. Heather was practically bouncing in place. Krystal was staring at him like he'd grown another head. Or the fact that he'd asked her to come along.

"Did I hear milkshakes?" Travis asked, joining the group. "Sawyer was telling me about this place off the highway. Not sure about the pizza, but the burgers and shakes are good."

"I'm not averse to a good burger." Jace nodded.

"My stalker Sawyer?" Krystal asked.

Travis pointed. "Krys, he's your security guard. He's decent."

Jace took another look at Sawyer. Stalker? He grinned, thinking about Heather's earlier assessment. Weren't security guards supposed to be stony-faced, muscle-bound guys? The "King's Guard" shirt did make it hard to take him too seriously, though.

"Why don't I recognize him? I like Jerome better; he's not intense all the time." Krystal's gaze narrowed. "Besides, isn't he a little young to be a retired Special Ops guy? Dad's a firm believer in hiring veterans."

"Don't know. But he's cool." Travis yawned. "Pretty good on the guitar, too. Food? Yes?"

"Sounds good. Can you watch her until this dog and pony show is over?" Krystal sighed, smoothing the crazy white tuft on top of Clementine's little head.

Heather was speechless, staring between Krystal and Clementine with wide, wide eyes.

"Pretty sure that's a yes," Jace answered for her.

"Y-yes." Heather nodded. "I'll take the best care of her."

"I know it." Krystal gave Clementine a final pat, then followed her family into the room of big spenders and potential sponsors. Jace and Heather encountered a few stray fans on their way out of the stadium. Awkward or not, he signed the shirts and pics and notebooks held his way and posed for a pic or two. Clementine's presence didn't go unnoticed, so he hurried Heather along, thinking the little dog's presence, with him, might be best avoided. They poked around his bus while the Three Kings did their thing. He had time to shower and pull on a favorite T-shirt, worn jeans, and a hometown feed store baseball cap.

"You don't look like Mr. Fancy-Pants Jace Black anymore." Heather sat on the floor, Clementine running back and forth across her legs, chasing her squeaky toy.

Jace looked down at his outfit. "I've worn this a hundred times."

"Right. As Jace, my brother. Working two jobs, sweaty all the time. Leaves his dirty socks by the hamper—not in the hamper." She smiled down at Clementine. "I'm not complaining. I love you either way."

He shook his head. "Good, because I'm the same person. Your brother?"

Heather laughed as Clementine rolled onto her back. "It was weird. You didn't look like you. I mean, you did, sort of, but you didn't."

He sat on the floor beside her. "How do you think I feel looking in the mirror?"

She patted his leg. "But you're happy? Aren't you?" She rubbed Clementine, but her brown eyes were searching his.

He nodded. "Of course I am." For the first time in his life, he had a chance to make life easier for them.

"You sure?" Her voice broke. "I worry about you."

"You don't need to, you hear me?" He caught her hand in his. "It's my job to worry about you, not the other way around."

"I'm pretty sure it doesn't work that way." She squeezed his hand. "After Nikki and Ben...I guess I'm always going to worry about you." Her head rested on his shoulder. "That's not something a sister just forgets, seeing her brother like that."

He'd been a mess after the accident. For weeks, he couldn't let go of what should have happened. He should have remembered the milk and eggs Nikki had asked him to bring home. If he had, Nikki would never have packed Ben into his car seat and headed into town. But he hadn't remembered. He'd been too tired to notice she wasn't steady on her feet or the empty case of beer in the back of the pantry—until after. Her car swerved into oncoming traffic. They'd been hit, head-on, by a semitruck.

Ben had died on impact.

Nikki had hung on for three weeks, a bunch of wires and machines working to keep her alive. He'd never felt that kind of pain—or anger. At Nikki. At himself. When she died, he didn't know what to feel or do or think. Work, and Heather, kept him going. To pay Nikki's hospital bills and keep food on the table, he had to work doubles.

His biggest regret? Shutting out his little sister. He'd lost a wife and son. She'd lost her nephew. Heather had loved that boy with her whole heart. Losing him had gutted her, too.

He pressed a kiss to her temple. "I guess that's what you do when you love someone. You worry."

She nodded. "But if I know you're happy, I won't have to worry so much."

"Then stop worrying, kiddo." He pressed another kiss to her temple. It had been two years. Two years of shutting out the what-ifs and regrets and clinging to things worth protecting. The laughs and hugs and the feel of Ben in his arms... He didn't want to forget any of that.

Days got easier and life kept on going.

Once Heather entered him in that television show, his world was stuck on fast-forward. Everything was different. What that meant, he wasn't exactly sure. Not yet. But he wasn't about to worry his little sister. Was he happy? He didn't know. Was he thankful? Hell yes. That was enough. More than enough.

By the time Emmy Lou, Travis, and Krystal showed up, Jace had been ready to call it a night. He was an early-to-bed, early-to-rise man. It was way past his bedtime.

"You look beat," Travis chuckled, leading them across the well-lit parking lot to the waiting black SUV.

"I am." He didn't argue.

"We can skip it, if you want." Heather all but drooped with disappointment, still holding Clementine.

"Are you kidding?" He wrapped an arm around her. "I didn't get all cleaned up for nothing."

"I'm not sure you could call that cap clean," Krystal replied.

Jace pulled off his cap. "I've had it for ten years. Just about got it broken in."

Krystal laughed, shaking her head. Her face was scrubbed free of makeup, the tight-fitting dress traded in for faded jeans and a blue plaid button-down shirt two sizes too big. Her boots still sparkled something fierce, making him grin. She looked young and carefree with her long hair caught back in a ponytail and a smile on her face.

"What?" Her smile dipped.

Dammit. He'd been staring. And she'd noticed.

"Your boots." He fumbled for an excuse.

"What about them?" She stared down at her boots.

"Right. Boots," Travis said, he and Emmy Lou going to the other side of the vehicle.

"Not exactly ranch gear." He shrugged, then opened the door of the SUV.

"Good thing we're not going to the ranch." Hands on hips, her brows rose. "Besides, I like these boots."

"They're some boots."

"They're custom-made," Heather said, looking back and forth between them. "All the etching and crystals and design work—just for Krystal."

Krystal's smile tightened and she stared down at her boots, a V forming between her brows.

"Ladies first." He gave Heather a hand up into the SUV.

"Thank you." His sister was all breathless excitement again, holding on to Clementine like the dog was a national treasure.

"Always the gentleman." Krystal took the hand he offered, the starch back in her spine. "She's sweet." There was a hint of sadness in her voice. And regret.

He held on to her longer than necessary, wishing like hell she'd let him in and knowing the chances were slim. "Some people would say bringing my baby sister here for me was sweet."

"Maybe." Her gaze fell to their joined hands. "Others might think I did it because I was after something." She slid onto the leather seat and pulled the door shut without another word.

He climbed into the front passenger seat and nodded at Sawyer, their driver, all the while wondering what the hell her comment meant. Was she trying to warn him away again? Or was she hoping to reel him in? Hook, line, and sinker.

Chapter 8

"STRIKE!" KRYSTAL DID A LITTLE DANCE ACROSS THE polished floor of the bowling alley.

"Way to not be competitive." Travis crossed his arms over his chest.

"You know better." She leaned forward, smiling at her brother.

"Glad you're on my team." Jace high-fived her, his dark hair falling onto his forehead. "That puts us in the lead, doesn't it?"

His grin made her forget about her brother and the need to rub his face in the fact that they were kicking his and Sawyer's butts. Just like Jace's laugh made her insides go all soft and warm. And the heat of his hand on her back had her leaning, just a bit, into his touch. Until tonight, she'd thought bowling was boring.

Travis rolled his eyes. "You're both poor sports, then? Awesome. Something else you have in common."

"Maybe we should call it a game?" Emmy Lou sat at a table behind their lane, with Heather and Clementine. "Food is here, anyway."

"Fine." Travis scowled.

"Wait, hold on." Krystal held her hand up. "Are we calling it as in Jace and I win? Or calling it and tomorrow you'll say it didn't count?"

Travis rolled his eyes.

"That's not an answer." She glanced at Jace. "Is that an answer?"

Jace laughed. She was growing far too fond of that laugh.

"My ice cream is melting." Travis pointed at what appeared to be whipped cream piled high on a large ice cream shake.

"Then you'd better answer." She pushed. "We win as is, or we play through?"

"You win," Travis grumbled softly.

"Sorry, man, even I'm going to have to ask you to repeat that." Jace shook his head.

"Really?" Travis sighed. "Fine. You. Win. But we're kicking your ass next time."

Krystal flopped into the chair beside Heather, smiling as Clem jumped into her lap and planted two doggy kisses on her chin. "Are you proud of your mommy, Clem? Putting Uncle Trav in his place like that."

"Give it a rest." Travis shoved a handful of cheesy fries into his mouth. "Mm, good."

Jace sat beside Krystal, reaching over to give Clementine a gentle scratch. "Hey, Clem."

Clem's little tail went fast motion.

"Clementine," she pretend whispered. "A lady should pretend to play hard to get."

Jace shook his head. "I prefer a straightforward woman myself." His gaze met hers. "No games."

"Chocolate shake. Your fave." Heather slid the

milkshake toward her brother and yawned. "Do you guys do this sort of thing often?"

Emmy Lou glanced at the clock on the back wall. "Is it really three?"

"I don't think we've ever bowled at three in the morning." Krystal took a fry from the plate Jace offered. "Thank you."

"Guess we're getting special treatment, Heather." Jace winked at his sister and took a sip of his shake. "Damn, that is good." He ran his tongue along his lower lip and took another sip. "Want some?" He held the cup out, the straw sliding around, tip toward Krystal.

The idea of putting her lips on the very place his had just been kick-started a pulse in the base of her belly. She shook her head.

"You're missing out."

She reconsidered the whole climbing into his lap thing but got ahold of herself before she did something she'd seriously regret.

Jace offered the tall glass to his sister. "Heather?"

They passed the mountain of food around, sharing bites and relaxing. Krystal ate one piece of cheese pizza, a handful of cheesy fries, and the better part of her vanilla milkshake before exhaustion hit her. While Travis had launched into one of his never-ending monologues on the importance of a four-by-four off-roading package for any self-respecting truck owner, she was sliding down in her chair.

She didn't know when Jace had moved closer. Or

when he'd slid his arm around her so she could rest against his shoulder. If Travis hadn't yelled, "Rematch?" and jolted her awake, she probably would have stayed blissfully asleep. Against Jace. Again.

But this time she only had her arm draped across his waist. She sat up quickly, her head smacking into Jace's chin with an audible clack.

"Ow," she hissed, rubbing her head.

"Yeah." Jace was rubbing his jaw.

"Hard headed. I told you." Travis laughed.

"Sorry," she murmured, still rubbing her head.

Jace wiggled his jaw back and forth. "You okay?" His fingers slid through her hair to feel for a knot.

She shivered. He was warm, his touch, his gaze—all of him. She wanted his warmth. Badly. If there hadn't been an audience, she would have crawled into his lap right then and there. Between the heavy stubble on his jaw, his heavy-lidded gaze, and his scent still clinging to her hair and cheek, she was ready to throw in the towel and surrender to this wildfire hold he had on her.

But they did have an audience. Her siblings. And his little sister. Heather was watching with wide eyes.

She leaned away from him. "I'm fine. Thanks."

"Travis." Emmy shook her head, but she was smiling. "That was mean."

"It's a brother's prerogative." Travis was staring at Krystal, looking like the cat that ate the canary. "More pics to add to my ever-growing collection."

"Who's playing?" Emmy asked.

"Go ahead." Krystal waved her away.

"This is sort of like a dream." Heather continued to stroke a softly snoring Clementine. "I mean, no one would believe this. This sort of thing doesn't happen to normal people." Her brown eyes widened. "Not that you're not normal. You are way...better than normal. What am I doing? I so need to stop talking... Sorry."

Krystal smiled, stirring the remains of her perfect vanilla shake with a long red-striped straw. "Don't be. I get it." She shrugged. "Honestly? I'd be okay living a normal life."

Heather frowned. "Why? I mean...why? When you have this?" She pointed at Travis, Jace, and Emmy, staring at the illuminated scoreboard over their lane of the deserted bowling alley. "You guys rented out a bowling alley. After hours. And the kitchen opened." She nodded at the table, covered in pizza crust, cheesy fries, empty burger wrappers, and a variety of soda and ice cream shake cups.

Krystal felt bad about this. The bowling alley had been closing up when they got there, but Travis had knocked on the door, and, suddenly, the whole place was at their beck and call. Money was a powerful incentive. And the bragging rights. They had taken a handful of pics with the owners—a small thank-you for the immense accommodation considering the late hours and cleanup the owners would be facing after they left. "Travis tends to get his way when he turns on the charm."

"I don't think they mind." Heather smiled at the older couple watching them, smiling, from the counter that ran the length of the bowling alley.

Krystal was too busy watching Jace bend forward to pick up his ball to answer. No doubt about it, tonight had turned her into a bowling fan.

Jace turned, winked at Heather, and smiled at Krystal.

"My brother likes you." For the first time all night, Heather's smile wobbled.

Krystal wasn't sure what was more worrisome: Heather's observation or her vanishing smile. What was she supposed to say? What was there to say?

"It's just that, after everything he's been through, I'm a little overprotective of him." Heather shrugged. "The television show sort of dragged it all up again. They thought his story made for good drama." She shook her head. "Like it was a story? And just when he was starting to get over it. Well, maybe not over it—I don't think he'll ever be over it." She blew out a long breath, her brown eyes locking on her brother's back. "But, you know, it was everywhere."

Krystal had no idea what she was talking about. Maybe if she'd watched the tapes her father had sent her, she'd know what the show had brought up and what Jace was starting to get over. "You lost me."

Heather frowned, studying her long and hard before her expression cleared. "You have no idea my brother was married?"

"No." It made sense. Jace was a good guy; she was beginning to believe that. "What happened?" If the rest of the world knew, it didn't seem like too invasive a question. Besides, what sort of woman would let Jace Black go?

"They died." Heather's voice dropped, wavering.

The air in her lungs grew thick and heavy, and heat crawled up the sides of her neck and into her face. White-hot. All the ice cream and pizza and french fries were a bad idea. She didn't want to know. She didn't. "They?" It was a whisper.

"My nephew." Heather sniffed. "Ben. He was almost two."

Krystal stood up. She didn't know where she was going or why, but she had to move. That wasn't the answer she'd expected. His wife and her boyfriend maybe? That would have been good drama. His wife and son? That wasn't a story. That was a tragedy. A night-mare. One there was no waking up from. "I'm so sorry, Heather." Jace had lost a wife and son. Heather had lost a sister-in-law and nephew. "I had no idea."

Heather nodded, watching her. "I guess I thought the whole world knew by now."

She shook her head, trying, and failing, not to look Jace's way. "I feel… I've been so hard on him. Teasing him." Relentlessly. If she wasn't glaring or throwing verbal grenades his way, there was the other thing—the visceral, near-electric arc connecting the two of them and threatening nuclear meltdown.

"Maybe that's why he likes you so much. You treat him normally."

He must have known she was staring at him because he turned to look their way. A quick double take between her and Heather almost had him heading over, but Travis stopped him, pointing at the scoreboard and pulling him back into the game.

"I know you like him too. And I'm glad. I mean, hello, he might be my brother, but I know he's one of the good guys and he deserves like a really, *really* good woman. Who will love him more than anyone or anything else, you know?" Heather cleared her throat. "If that's you, and I think it might be, just know that about him. That he's been through a lot. Like a lot, a lot. And it wouldn't be fair for him to go through something like that again. Right?"

Krystal nodded. Heather was a sweet kid but she couldn't be more wrong. *It's not me.* The heat in her face was drying her throat until the urge to cough was overwhelming. She picked up her shake and finished it off, closing her eyes against the telltale sting.

"Come on, Heather," Emmy Lou called out. "Girls against the boys."

Heather sat Clementine on the cushion at her side, watching as the dog yawned, stretched, and curled into a ball before dropping back into a deep sleep. She cast a nervous glance at Krystal. "Should I have told you? He really likes you, is all. I mean, really. But, I mean, you're Krystal King. Famous and beautiful, and well, he's just my brother. A normal guy who's had his heart broken." She paused. "Jace always said your songs said the things he couldn't, that your words made him hurt a little less. Like, maybe you could understand what he's been through?"

Krystal couldn't answer. Not yet. Jace had lost his wife and son. She'd only lost…herself.

"Writing a song about something doesn't make you an expert on it." Her father had said it time and again. "Living life—that's the best way to make your music real." That was why she didn't write happy love songs. She didn't know what that meant, and contrary to what her mother said, lying didn't come easily to her. All she knew about love was pain and hurt and betrayal and loss.

Jace Black deserved a better song, and a better love, than that.

Heather's gaze fell from hers. "I definitely should have stopped talking like fifteen minutes ago."

Anxiety laced the girl's words, so somehow, Krystal was saying, "I'm glad you told me." She was. Sort of. Now she needed time to process it. Alone, preferably. "You go play…er, bowl. I'll be back." She did her best to smile as she hurried to the restroom.

Washing her hands in ice-cold water helped. But coming eye to eye with her reflection had her gripping the sink.

"It's not always about you." It was something her momma had said over and over. *"Other people have feelings, too. You need to think about what you say and do, about how your words and actions will affect everyone involved— not just you."*

"You're right, Momma," Krystal whispered.

Whatever this was between her and Jace didn't matter.

It wouldn't last, so why waste time starting something that would wind up causing them both pain? This was about him, about the break he deserved and the life he could have. She wasn't going to get in his way. The best way to do that was to stay out of his way—better yet, stay away. She and Jace had to spend time together onstage but, from now on, that was the only time they'd spend together.

"Try this one." Calvin Laramie had a close-trimmed beard, a brightly colored plaid button-up shirt, and spray-painted-on jeans with shredding on one thigh— something the man hadn't earned from a day's hard labor. His jeans were tucked into ostrich boots that cost as much as Jace had spent on his last truck. This was the stylist CiCi King had hired to "give Jace a look that would set him apart." Luke had about fallen over when he'd heard the news. CiCi, Luke said, was a genius when it came to this industry. She knew the right people and stayed ahead of the trends—hell, she'd started a few. If she thought Calvin was the man to help Jace make his mark, Luke was on board.

But even Luke was eyeing the jacket with suspicion.

Jace stared at the metal-studded black leather jacket the man held out for him to try on. In what world would he wear that? "Pass."

"I do know what I'm doing." Calvin shook the jacket. "It's my business to create a star."

Jace didn't answer. He wasn't one to complain, but the afternoon was wearing on his patience. Leather pants? Damn no. Boots with a silver-tapped four-inch heel? What the hell was that? Jeans with fancy designs and shiny crap? Was CiCi King out to make a fool out of him? Or did she honestly believe this was what was needed to "take him to the next level."

He was pretty sure spending ten hours a day with his band was the best way to take him to the next level, but he wasn't going to argue with the woman. The sooner this ordeal was over, the better. He'd probably change back into his own clothes, anyway.

"This?" With a sigh, Calvin pulled a black snap-front button-up from the rack.

It was a traditional black cowboy-cut shirt with pearl snaps. No embroidery. No leather. No shiny beads to make his eyes cross. Still, the glossy sheen on the pearl snaps were not his style.

"Come on, Jace," Luke encouraged. Poor guy was stuck between a rock and a hard place. He wanted to take care of Jace, but he also wanted to stay in CiCi King's good graces. Jace was pretty sure a choice was going to have to be made and, possibly, Jace would wind up looking for a new agent.

"Fine." He tugged his worn grey T-shirt over his head and tossed it onto the dressing room table.

A quick knock and the dressing room door opened.

"Travis?" Krystal leaned in.

His eyes met hers in the mirror and the air arced electric, giving his heart a jolt.

In the four days since Heather's visit, Krystal had all but run at the very sight of him. Onstage, she sang her heart out. The connection she was fighting was there, stronger than ever, binding them together, and driving him crazy because he knew she felt it too. He saw it every time she stared into his eyes and leaned in close to share the microphone. And every time, he wished the song was a little longer. Once the lights dimmed, she was gone. He'd reached for her, called her name, even followed her from the stage, but she'd managed to elude him. It wasn't like he could stand onstage and demand answers in the middle of a concert. Hell, he had no right to demand a damn thing from her anyway.

It didn't stop him from wondering what had happened to turn something that felt like the start of something good into the end of something that never was.

Not that he was ready to give up. That wasn't who he was. He was stubborn.

Emmy Lou waved. "Hey, Calvin. Getting Jace ready for tonight?"

There might be a conversation going on around him, but all Jace saw was Krystal. Standing, staring, on the verge of flight.

"Trying." Calvin didn't even try to mask his irritation. "He's not nearly as easy to work with as you two."

"Well, you've still got…two hours?" Emmy smiled. "Though less is more with Jace, Calvin. He's more like my daddy when it comes to fashion. Don't you think?" She turned to Krystal.

"I guess." Krystal blinked, her gaze darting around the room as she murmured, "Oh…looking for Trav…" Her gaze bounced to his chest. "Sorry." She grabbed Emmy's arm and pulled.

"What? Are we leaving?" Emmy asked.

Krystal slammed the door shut and whatever was said next was muffled by the cinder block walls of the stadium.

"Shirt." Calvin held out the shirt. "I would definitely say this is less than everything else I've suggested."

Jace grabbed the shirt. "Dammit." He pulled open the door and ran out.

Krystal was a few feet away, leaning against the wall, eyes pressed shut and hands fisted at her sides.

"You need to talk to him," Emmy was saying.

If the "him" was him, Jace totally agreed. If she didn't want to talk, maybe she'd listen. He had a lot to say. But the sound of his boots on the concrete hall had her eyes fly open and her feet moving—away from him.

"Wait," he called out. "Please."

Emmy Lou smiled. "Hey, Jace."

Krystal hesitated, then spun on her heel, the tilt of her chin giving him all the warning he needed. "What?" Her gaze slid over his bare chest. Was she blushing? Krystal King? He rattled her and he liked it. He more than liked it. "We're busy."

"Krystal." Emmy Lou sounded more like a disapproving mother than a twin sister.

He couldn't help but grin. "I know it."

Krystal shifted from foot to foot, drawing attention to her pink zebra-striped tennis shoes. "Jace—"

"I could use a little coaching." He paused, including Emmy in the conversation. "Tonight, I'll be up there alone, and I'll admit, it's got my guts all twisted up. It's one thing singing with someone." He shrugged. "But solo?" It wasn't a lie. Eight to ten songs, time depending. Forty minutes of just him. Forty never-ending minutes of him singing on a stage—with no Krystal or the Kings there to make it effortless. He could make a damn fool of himself. "And there's this." He held out the shirt, pearl snaps and all.

Krystal looked at the shirt as if seeing it for the first time. "That's not right—that's not your…style. Your brand."

He nodded.

"What was wrong with what you wore to the photo shoot?" Emmy asked, taking the shirt and giving it a once-over. "I mean, this isn't bad but… Try it on."

"It's not good, either," Krystal finished. "Do what you want. Wear what you want. Make sure it's something you like because that's what people will expect to see you in from now on."

He nodded, shrugging into the shirt and snapping it up.

"Actually." Emmy's brows rose. "It looks good on."

But he was watching Krystal, waiting for her response.

Her lips pressed tightly closed and her eyes narrowed. "Yeah. But…" She glanced at his face before she stepped forward and began rolling up the sleeves of his shirt. "You want to show these off." She nodded at his tattoos. "Your fans will want to see them."

He stared down at her, the top of her golden head bent as she tugged his sleeves and made them even. His throat clogged with all the words he wanted to say. Words. And a melody. Soft and slow and sweet, playing through his head.

She looked up at him, eyes wide and breath unsteady.

"Good?" He could reach out and touch her. He sure as hell wanted to.

She nodded.

"It works." Emmy agreed.

"No more pearl snaps." Krystal tapped the pearl in the middle of his chest, her hand remaining. "All black."

He nodded, resisting the urge to take her hand. He was vaguely aware of Emmy, practically sprinting to his dressing room with a "I'll go tell Calvin" called back over her shoulder.

His dressing room door slammed shut and they were alone.

Her hand fell from his chest.

"You've been hiding from me." It wasn't a question. Or an accusation. Just a fact.

She swallowed but didn't say a word.

"Why?" He pushed, needing to know.

She stared at the top pearl snap on his shirt. "I never pegged you as someone with such a high opinion of himself, Mr. Black. Why on earth would *I* be hiding from *you*?" But her bite was halfhearted and she couldn't meet his gaze.

He tipped her chin back, waiting for her to look at him. "That's what I'm asking."

But staring into her green eyes made things go hazy around the edges. She did that to him, put the rest of the world on mute so she was all that registered. The heat in her gaze was countered with something wary—something fragile. Unless she talked to him, he'd never know what she was struggling with.

"It doesn't matter, Jace." She cleared her throat. "Don't let the song we're singing confuse you. This is business. Work. I'm the first duet you've had. I have no doubt, *no* doubt, there will be plenty of others."

He knew good and well they weren't talking about their song. Did she really have such a low opinion of him?

"It's music. When it's good, it should stir things up inside." Her voice faded to a whisper.

"You're telling me what I'm feeling isn't real?" He knew better than that.

She blinked, her mouth opening. "Feeling?"

He nodded once, his heart damn near beating out of his chest. *Yes, dammit, feeling.*

"No." She shook her head, stepping away from him.

She was scared. Of this? Of him? Of the feelings she was hell-bent on denying?

She tried again, her voice thick. "It's not." She kept shaking her head, determined to shut him down. "It's a good song."

The panic on her face was unexpected.

"I need to go. I was looking for my father." She tore her gaze from his and made a show of staring down the hall in both directions.

"I thought it was Travis?"

She glared back up at him. "Travis, too. They're together." Her gaze fell from his.

She was a terrible liar. "I'll tell them if I see them." He ran his hands over his shirt front. "No pearls snaps? They're growing on me."

A ghost of a smile crossed her face. "If it makes you feel better, you can pull it off."

"As long as the ink shows?" he clarified.

She stared long and hard at the black that covered most of the inside of his forearms. The cross covered up the skin graft he'd had from a pipe explosion on a rig. He'd been lucky. Two others had ended up with permanent disabilities and another dead. His other arm was covered with the day his son was born and the day he died, in roman numerals. A reminder, always, of how precious time was and to make the most of every second. Like now. This moment.

"Yup. Play up your strengths. You are hot." She shrugged, that hard coldness seeping in, stiffening her posture and turning her voice brittle. "Follow my brother's lead and you'll learn how to make the most of it. Like he said, you'll never have to sleep alone."

He stepped closer, closing the distance between them. "Don't get me wrong, I like your brother but that's not who I am, Krystal. If you'd stand still long enough to listen to me, to give me a chance, you'd know that."

Emerald green eyes sparkled up at him. "A chance at what? Making a mistake? One I promise you'll regret?"

His chest pressed in, squeezing the air from his lungs. "Krystal—"

She covered his mouth, her gaze falling to her hand. "Leave it, Jace. You've got a show to worry about. Fans to dazzle. A career to build. That's what you should be thinking about right now. That's what matters. A lot of people are counting on you. Heather. My dad. Don't screw this up." She stepped around him and walked quickly away.

Fine. She was right—a lot of people were counting on him. He'd put on one hell of a show. But he wasn't letting this go. He stared after her, waiting for her to disappear at the end of the hall before heading back to his dressing room.

"I like it." Calvin nodded. "The sleeves. The tats. Good call." He paused. "We need a hat."

He had a hat. He didn't need a new one.

Luke glanced up from his phone long enough to nod.

"Where's Krystal?" Emmy looked around him.

He shrugged, shaking his head. "Looking for your dad or Travis or the nearest exit."

"Can I be honest with you?" Emmy Lou studied him. He nodded.

"I think you scare her."

"Me?" He frowned. "But—"

"It's nothing you've done. Being alone is...safer. She's

waiting for you to prove her right—that it's better to be alone than risk getting hurt."

Which sort of made sense. He knew she'd been hurt, knew she'd been used. It made sense she'd keep the rest of the world at arm's length. And if he wasn't falling for her, he'd walk away. It would be easier, that's for sure. But... "I guess I'll have to prove her wrong."

Chapter 9

KRYSTAL WOKE TO A LOUD THUMP AGAINST THE WALL. She rolled over, pushing pillows out of the way, to peer at the green LED clock. Three forty-five in the morning.

A man laughing. Another thump and a door slamming into the wall. Not next door but close.

She rolled over, pulling a pillow over her face. "Are you frigging kidding me?"

Her head had started throbbing about midway through the last set. She was seeing stars and feeling nauseous by the meet and greet but managed to keep it together. When Travis wrangled Emmy Lou and Jace into going to an after-party, she waved them off and headed to her hotel room. A long soak in a hot tub. Turning down the temperature to subarctic. Sticking her feet in ice. Then, when all else failed, the eventual migraine prescription. Normally it knocked her out for a good six hours.

Normally there wasn't some asshole falling into the wall of her hotel room.

Another round of laughter and a crash had her sitting up and kicking back the blankets.

"Oh, baby, don't leave me," a high-pitched, definitely drunk voice rang out in the hallway.

"Seriously?" She was up, unlatching the door and pulling it wide. She winced from the overhead fluorescent lights, the throb behind her eyes spreading around her head and down her neck. Whoever woke her had no idea the sort of shit storm she was about to unleash on them.

Jace.

Coldness leached into the soles of her feet and crept up, numbing everything—except her heart. Jace? She blinked, rubbing her eyes with the back of her hand before risking another look.

It was Jace. In his undershirt. He held his button-down shirt in one hand and propped himself on the hotel doorframe with the other. "I gotta go to bed. I'm exhausted."

A pillow came sailing, hitting Jace in the face before falling to the floor.

Jace laughed, stooping—and wobbling—to pick up the pillow and tossing it back inside. "Night." He pulled the door shut. With a groan, he leaned forward, resting his head against the door. "Damn. It."

If she was smart, she'd move before he saw her but she couldn't move. She couldn't. She couldn't believe it. Didn't want to.

Why was she surprised?

He was a guy. A single guy. One who didn't matter. At all. This didn't matter. It didn't.

She was a terrible liar—even when she was lying to herself.

Jace pushed off the door and turned, his surprise at finding her there almost comical. If he hadn't been leaving the hotel room of the woman he'd just slept with. But he had. He'd just left her—right there, across the hall.

"Hey, Krystal." His smile was off-center and his eyelids drooped.

"*Hey?*" It erupted from her like a cannon shot, echoing down the hall and leaving a resounding ringing in the ear. What was wrong with her?

He winced and braced himself against the wall. "Isn't it late?" he asked. "How's your head?"

"Are you kidding me?" She was shaking. And yelling. At three forty-five in the morning. In the hallway of her hotel. Because he'd slept with someone. Jace. *Jace*... He'd gotten drunk and partied and... He'd walked his one-night stand back to her hotel room because he was a gentleman.

"Oh shit," she hissed, pressing her hand to her head. This hurt. To breathe. To think. Why did it have to hurt? Nothing had happened between them. Nothing. She couldn't care about him. She didn't. Dammit. Her eyes were burning and her nose began to run.

"You okay?" The fact that he looked concerned for her made it ten times worse.

She pressed her lips together, but a high-pitched sound forced its way out, like a teapot screaming when the water was boiling. She was boiling, all right. It didn't make sense and she had no right, but that didn't seem to matter. *I believed you. I did.*

Her gaze fell to his shirt, wadded up in his hand. "You could have gotten dressed." Images of Jace rolling around in bed with some faceless, nameless person sleeping right across the hall from her took over. Bile burned her throat.

He and his warm brown eyes and worried—gorgeous—expression managed to make it to her door. "Krystal. What's wrong?"

"Nothing." She sucked in a deep breath. "Why would anything be wrong?" She sniffed. *I am not going to cry.* She pointed at the room he'd just left. "I'm glad you enjoyed yourself tonight. Now go away—sleep it off. Take a shower." At least she wasn't yelling anymore.

He was close enough she could see the utter confusion on his face. "What?"

Her heart twisted. No, her heart wasn't allowed to react to Jace Black. Her heart was off-limits to him—to any man.

"You lost me." He pressed a hand to his head.

No, you lost me. Her voice broke. "For your sake—and her sake—I hope you wore a condom." That last part definitely climbed back into the yelling category. She slammed the door, a solid thud echoed.

"Ow, shit," he groaned.

He'd been standing so close, she'd probably hit him in the face. Instead of making her feel better, she was close to tears. If she cried—which she didn't. Besides, she had no reason to cry. It was her head that hurt, not her heart.

"Krystal, let me in." He knocked.

"Go away." Her words were too garbled to understand.

"Let me in. You don't understand—"

"I do, believe me, I do." She couldn't even be mad at him. This was what she wanted, wasn't it? It wasn't as if she'd given him any reason to wait for her. If anything, she'd gone out of her way to make sure he understood they would never ever happen.

He'd found someone to spend the night with. So what?

Her head was pounding again, nausea strong enough that she ran for a glass of water.

"Krystal." He pounded on the door now. "Are you okay? Please let me in."

She didn't bother answering. There wasn't anything to say at this point. Her head was hurting, and she needed quiet and the dark and a hot bath to calm her nerves.

A bath helped. She stayed mostly submerged in near-scalding water for an hour, refilling the tub to keep it hot. Not that lying in the dark, in hot water, could erase the mental image of Jace doing all the things she'd imagined him doing to her—to someone else. Every time she started crying, she'd submerge herself in water and come up coughing.

At five, she slipped from her hotel room and made her way to the buses. She ignored the questions on Sawyer's face, left a note for Misumi to get her things from the hotel before they left, and barricaded herself in her sleeping compartment with her guitar and a bucket of Red Vines. Clementine roused herself long enough from her velvet doggy bed to climb up by her side before curling into a ball of white fluff that snored.

The knocking began around nine.

"Krystal, breakfast." Emmy Lou was first.

"Headache," she called back.

"Still?" Emmy Lou paused, whispering to someone. "Daddy wants to talk to all of us. You get some sleep and we'll all have lunch together. Okay?"

"Fine," she mumbled. With any luck, "all of us" wouldn't include Jace.

"Mommy can't face him, Clem." She picked up her beloved pooch and held her nose to nose. "I did a very bad thing." But she couldn't say the rest of it out loud. Admitting she had feelings for Jace to anyone, even Clementine, wouldn't change a thing. Better not to say the words out loud.

At eleven, the bus came to a stop.

"Baby girl." Her father knocked on the door. "You take your medicine?"

"Yeah," she answered.

"You okay?"

Maybe it was because she hesitated. Maybe it was because her daddy always seemed to know when she was upset. Or maybe it was because she hadn't locked the door—but her father opened the door and peered inside before she could come up with a reason to keep him out.

He stood there, hands on hips, looking at her. "What's going on, Krystal?"

She shook her head.

"Now I don't believe that for one second." He sighed, crossing the room to sit on her bunk. He offered Clementine a quick scratch behind the ear. "Had to pry Travis out of his bed this morning, nursing a powerful hangover. Found Jace asleep outside your hotel room door, but he's a little hazy on the rest. And you're playing hide-and-seek when we have business to discuss."

"I'm not hiding." She knew he was goading her.

"Then what are you doing?" He waited. "And why?"

She shook her head.

"Your head hurting?" He pressed his hand against her cheek.

"Not really." Which wasn't true. She might not have a migraine anymore, but getting zero sleep had left her with a dull ache.

"Think you can manage to sit and discuss the Austin Country Music Festival?" He paused, waiting for her reaction. "They're looking for a host. Or two."

He wanted her to be excited, she could tell. And, since it was her daddy, she did her best to smile and nod. "Oh?" She swallowed, pulling Clem into her arms.

"Come on, now. Emmy's got your vanilla coffee thing out here waiting for you." He stood, holding his hand out to her.

"Is Jace here, Daddy?" She had to know.

He stared down at her, an odd look on his face. "He is. Is there something I need to know?"

"No. Nothing. Nothing at all." She shook her head. "I need a minute."

"You've got five."

Once he left, she splashed cold water on her face, twisted her hair into a sloppy bun, and tugged on a massive black sweatshirt that made her feel invisible. Her eyes were red and bloodshot. In general, she looked like hell.

"Not like there's anyone to impress." She flipped off the light, scooped up Clem, and ventured from the shelter of her dim bedroom into the overcrowded cab of the bus she shared with her sister.

"Here." Emmy pressed the tall paper cup into her hands. "I'm sorry you're feeling bad. It seems to be going around."

Armed with her dog and her coffee, Krystal dug deep for the sass she needed to survive. "Pardon me if I don't shower them with sympathy." She squeezed into a chair with Emmy and did her best not to look at anyone else in the room.

Not Travis or Emmy or Jace. Especially not Jace. Even though she could see him from the corner of her eye, even though he was staring at her.

"What's the plan for ACMF, Daddy?" Emmy was the only one who seemed excited.

He clapped his hands together, smiling broadly. "They want the three of you to host the awards show. And they want Krystal and Jace to sing the new single."

"Dad," Travis moaned.

"I'm with your sister on this one, Son. I don't take kindly to paying for damages to hotel rooms." Her father wasn't happy. "You're a King, boy. I need you to remember that before you pull something else like this, you hear me?"

Krystal glanced at her brother. There was a green cast to his skin, his lips dry and pale. "You look like crap."

"You're not exactly little Miss Sunshine yourself this morning." Travis shot her a look. "What the hell was last night about?"

She sipped her coffee. "Last night I was taking

migraine meds while, apparently, you were trashing a hotel room."

"I broke a table. I—we—fell into one." Travis glanced at Jace. "Sorry, man."

Jace nodded.

Of course Travis would be the one to take Jace out partying. Drinking. Breaking shit. Picking up women. Maybe the whole "Gentleman Jace" moniker wasn't going to stick after all.

"You were the one yelling at Jace in the middle of the night," Travis continued.

Yelled. Slammed the door. Loud enough for everyone to hear. She'd acted like a fool. For what? She looked at Jace then.

His light brown gaze was waiting.

All the hurt and anger and frustration she'd been drowning in since three forty-five this morning threatened to rear its ugly head again. Since she didn't relish the idea of getting upset—worse, crying—she decided retreat was the best option. "I'm not really a hundred percent, so y'all work out the details and let me know, okay?" She stood, pressing a kiss to her father's cheek. "This is super exciting, Daddy. Really. Thank you."

He hugged her close and whispered, "Whatever this is, I need you to work it out. The only way to do that is to talk to each other."

"Talking won't fix this, Daddy. But I'll try. I promise, I'll try to let it go."

———

Jace shook hands with Guy James and sat in the chair opposite the iconic desk for the late-night talk show. He had never felt more out of his element—hopefully it wouldn't be too obvious.

"Good to have you here, Jace." Guy smiled. "Once it was announced that you'd be joining us, we sold out. I'm pretty sure we have an all-female audience tonight."

The screams from the audience made Jace shift uneasily in his chair, but he chuckled anyway.

Guy shielded his eyes. "Wait, there's one man, way up there. Hello, sir."

Jace looked out over the audience. There were plenty of men, but he let it go. Guy James was about the laughs.

"Congratulations on the single," Guy said, glancing at one of the cards before him on his desk. "First song and it's expected to climb the charts when it releases officially."

"Thank you." He nodded at the applause from the audience. "I'm not sure any of this is real. Not a day goes by that I don't wake up expecting to be back in the oilfields."

Guy nodded. "Big change?"

Jace laughed. "Yes, sir. But I'm not complaining."

"No, I imagine not." He paused. "Your duet, with Krystal King. Tell us about that."

Jace took a sip from the coffee mug on the desk. He'd expected questions about her. She was far more interesting than he was. If anything, this was his chance to set the record straight on a few things—like who Krystal King really was.

"You're getting to spend a lot of time with her?" Guy pushed.

He nodded. "I am. I always loved their music—I own every album. Working with her?" He shook his head. "She's a good partner, we sync well, I think. I hope. I'm pretty sure there's not a better songwriter out there. She has a way of layering in the emotion, lyrics and music working together. And her voice, well, you've all heard her. I'm blessed."

"We have a picture." Guy turned, looking at the screen behind them. "You two look like you get along."

Jace studied the picture. The day of the photo shoot. Him smoothing her hair. Her smiling up at him. Seeing it now still made his heart rate pick up. She was beautiful. No doubt about it.

"You want to tell us about this picture?" Guy asked.

Jace grinned. "What's to tell? Damn good picture."

The audience laughed.

"And this one?" Guy pointed at the screen again. A different picture. "That's Clementine, isn't it?"

Jace stared at the Instagram post. "Yes. Krystal took that for my sister, Heather." He waved at the camera. "You better be studying for your finals, Heather." He looked back at Guy. "Krystal found out my sister was a fan and took the picture. She does things like that."

"Interesting." Guy nodded. "What about this one?"

Jace wasn't prepared for the picture that popped up. Krystal was asleep on him in the bowling alley, his arm around her and her head resting on his shoulder. He'd turned a little, his nose resting against her temple. The look on his face. "That's a new one."

The audience reaction was a flutter of squeals, some light applause, and a few gasps.

"I know, right?" Guy asked. "This is some development. You've become *friends*?"

Jace nodded, tearing his gaze from the picture that painted a picture all on its own. "We have. I respect her—and I like her. A lot."

"We can see that. But we had Mickey Graham on the show a few weeks back." Guy leaned back in his chair. "He doesn't seem to share your…generous opinion of Miss King."

"He wouldn't. And I have a few choice words for Mickey Graham." He smiled. "But I'm pretty sure I can't say them on network television."

Guy sat forward. "You don't say? Maybe you could paraphrase?"

Jace shrugged. "No man likes rejection. But twisting the truth to get his songs on the chart and his picture on a magazine cover? To me, that makes the man a real rat bastard."

"Probably best if I stop you there." Guy was smiling. "Let me play devil's advocate here, Jace. Some people might think you're doing the same. Or that this relationship with Krystal King is some sort of damage control for her? Pictures like that circulating—looks awful convenient. People love you. After the show, they feel like they know you and want the best for you. I'm sure I speak for most of the audience when I say I'm sincerely sorry for your loss."

"I appreciate that." He nodded. He hated this part of

it. Hated the constant reminder of that truly awful day. How would people react if they knew how angry he was? Not at the truck driver but at Nikki? She'd been drinking and she'd still gone. She'd taken his son away. Forever. He cleared his throat. "It means a lot."

"People want you to be happy. They see you with Krystal King, and they worry."

Jace nodded. "I am happy. I can't predict what the future holds, but I'm blessed that she and her family are a part of mine. It's important to say that Krystal doesn't need damage control—the real Krystal, that is, not the one the media has created. I'd ask people to listen to her songs, read her lyrics, you'll see what I'm saying. She has a huge heart and a good soul. But if being damage control means I get to spend time with her, sign me up."

"You can't fake that kind of chemistry." Guy pointed at the picture on display. Jace and Krystal, leaning in to sing their song together during a concert.

"No, sir, you can't."

"It was a real pleasure to meet you, Jace. I wish you nothing but success."

He shook Guy's hand. "Thank you."

"I hear you're going to sing something for us?" He stood, leading Jace to a stool on the far side of the studio's stage.

Jace nodded, sat, and picked up the guitar. He'd been working on the song for a while, played it through with his band, but he'd never performed it for an audience. "I'm going to play something new for you. I hope you like it. It's called 'One Boot at a Time.'"

He ran his fingers over the strings, smiled out over the crowd, and began to play.

I put my boots on one foot at a time
Work the daylight hours
And earn every damn dime
Life's not easy, but I figure it's fair
And it's all more than worth it
'Cause now she's waiting there

She sings in our kitchen but can't cook a thing
Builds our kids up and believes in their dreams
She likes tractors and my dog and long starry nights
And coming home to her makes everything right

The guys who I work with don't have a clue
They party and hell-raise
Like I used to do
But life took a turn when I met her
And I can't say I miss what came before
'Cause now she's waiting there

She sings in our kitchen but can't cook a thing
Builds our kids up and believes in our dreams
She likes tractors and my dog and long starry nights
And coming home to her makes everything right

When I'm tired or weary or feeling beat down
It's her laugh that lifts me

And turns me around
I'm one lucky man
One smile from her and I'm home
'Cause now she's waiting there

She sings in the kitchen but can't cook a thing
Builds me up and believes in my dreams
Nothing is better than those long starry nights
And, she swears, being mine makes everything all right

"Jace Black, everyone." Guy James shook his hand again and a woman escorted him offstage.

"That was awesome, man, awesome." Luke was pumped up. "Love the new song. Drinks?"

"I'm beat, Luke." He shook his head. "I'm calling it."

"I'll get you a car." Luke pulled out his ever-handy phone.

In five minutes, Jace was headed for the hotel, dozing against the car door. He couldn't remember the last time he'd been up all night. He was bone-tired and determined to avoid Travis King once he got to the hotel. He didn't have the energy to deal with that sort of trouble. Or the hurt Krystal's accusations had caused him.

He stared out the window at the palm trees, fighting to keep his eyes open. He propped himself in the corner of the elevator up to his room and started kicking off clothes as soon as his hotel room door clicked shut behind him.

A hot shower later and he was on his way to bed.

Until the banging on his door started.

"Hold up." He wrapped the towel around his waist. "Travis, man—"

But it was Krystal, wearing the same gigantic black sweatshirt she'd had on this morning—no makeup and a tangled mess of curls on the top of her head.

"Hi." He stared at her, stunned. "You wanna come in?"

She hesitated. "For a minute." She slipped past him and into his room, rocking from foot to foot, her hands shoved into the pocket of her sweatshirt. "I saw you on Guy James tonight." And she wasn't happy.

He closed the door and stood, barefoot and wet-headed. "Yeah." She had more to say, he could tell. After last night, he braced himself.

"What was that? What was with the knight-in-shining-armor crap?" She wrapped her arms around her waist. "I don't need you being all…noble. You can say, 'Hey, Guy, I'm here to talk about me tonight.' Or just tell him to mind his own business. It's not your job to champion me. And those pictures are just pictures. That's all."

"Hold on." He ran a hand over his face, wishing he had a large cup of coffee. And that he was wearing clothes. "We need to back up a little."

Her brows shot up. "No. We do not."

He held a hand up. "I don't know what you thought was going on last night—"

"I know exactly what was going on last night." She rolled her eyes, refusing to look at him. "You can screw whoever you want. I don't care about that."

It had been a long time since anger damn near choked

him. But her easy dismissal tipped the scale. "I carried your drunk-ass brother to his hotel room last night. Got knocked into a table hard enough to break the damn thing." He pointed at the purple-green ridge down his side. "It gets better. He waits to pass out just long just enough to throw up on my shirt."

Krystal eyed the bruise. "And?"

"That's what I was doing last night. That was his room I was leaving, Krystal. His—Travis's. Travis threw the pillow." He paused, watching her. "I leave him, sore and covered in vomit and whiskey, to see you leaning out of your room. And I'm happy all of a sudden because I get to see you before I go to bed. Make sure you're okay. That your headache was better."

She opened her mouth, then closed it. He didn't miss the slight tremor in her hands or how unsteady her breathing was. But she tilted her head, thrust out her chin, unwilling to bend.

He ran a hand through his wet hair. "And then you jump down my throat for hooking up with someone who doesn't exist. It's easier to believe the worst. Is that it? Hell, I think you *want* to believe I'm that guy. But I'm not. If that's your reason for acting like this thing between us doesn't exist, then you're out of luck. I will *never* be that guy. And now you know."

Chapter 10

SHE COULD BREATHE AGAIN. LAST NIGHT HAD BEEN... devastating. Wrong. Why she'd let him get to her, she didn't know. It was like she wanted to set herself up for disappointment over and over. And now...she was disappointed, all right. In herself.

She'd jumped to all the wrong conclusions—because she needed Jace Black to be an asshole. She needed a reason to keep her distance. He was dangerous.

After his interview, she had no choice. She'd been prepared to tell him off, convinced he'd been all doe-eyed and protective to come off looking good. But, no, he was just being Jace. A gentleman. Noble. Honor bound to come to her defense. *Dammit.* He was too good a guy to go down in flames defending her.

"I'm happy for you. Being virtuous and honorable and all that." She swallowed, using her best bitch voice and eye roll. "Why do I care?" *Don't look at him.*

"You don't?" The question was low, gruff, and hard. "Or you won't admit the truth?"

"The truth?" She shrugged. Fine, she'd tell him the truth. Part of the truth. "I've thought a lot about you. You and me. In bed. Hot and sweaty. It turns me on. How's that for truth? It sounds really good." *Don't look at him.* "But more than that? No thank you."

"Sex?" He sighed.

It was getting harder to breathe. "What else? Come on, Jace. Wake up. You're right, there is an attraction, but it wouldn't take much to get you out of my system." It would take so much more than that. Jace was...more. *He deserves better.* She had to say it—and make him believe it. "Honestly, I sort of hoped you were banging some fangirl. You're getting a little too fixated on me." It was hateful; she was hateful. That's who she was. It was best for everyone that way.

Silence.

"Why are you here?" The words were brittle.

"To make things clear." She stared straight ahead. At his chest. His beautiful, sculpted, tattoo-adorned, all-muscles chest. The thorn-covered vine inked around his upper right arm seemed a safe enough focal point.

More silence.

"Then let's do this."

The tattoo blurred and she was staring up into his face. His beautiful, rigid, angry face. This was not expected. He should be disappointed, a little disgusted even, but keep his cool. That whole gentleman thing he did so well. A gentleman would show her to the door and that would be the end of it.

This Jace looked nothing like a gentleman.

Did she want him? More than anything. Ached for him. So much. "Now?"

He nodded, the muscle in his jaw rolling.

She'd hurt him. Good. He needed to believe her. If he

hated her, she'd done her job. There was only one way to make sure he believed her. "Fine." In the seconds it took to pull her sweatshirt off, she tried to shut off the part of her brain protesting her stupid, stupid plan.

The other part of her brain? Oh so excited. Craving this. Craving him. That was the part of the brain she was going to listen to. She dropped her sweatshirt on the floor and kicked it aside.

His nostrils flared, his gaze going molten as his attention fell to her bright fuchsia bra. Hands fisted at his sides, he seemed to be fighting her. Why? This was his idea—an idea she was going to enjoy to the fullest.

Was he waiting for her to chicken out?

No going back. She didn't want to. Tomorrow she might regret this, but she'd worry about that then. Tonight, he was all hers. She was going to make every second count.

Impatience kicked in as she toed off her shoes and shimmied out of her leggings. His knuckles whitened at the sight of her tiny black thong, but the rest of him remained frozen. Her heart was tripping over itself, but he couldn't know that. When she closed the distance between them, she ran her hands up his arms…slowly. She took a deep breath and met his gaze.

He was breathing hard, his nostrils flared, muscles strung tight. The blazing hunger in his eyes burned through any hesitation. She pressed herself against him, wrapped her arms around his neck, and brushed her lips to his.

The contact, skin on skin and mouth to mouth, flipped a switch.

She threaded her hands through his still-wet hair, pulling him closer and tracing the seam of his lips with her tongue. His arms were around her, all muscles and warmth, wrapping her up in Jace. Spicy soap and minty shampoo. The coarse stubble on his jaw. His calloused fingers trailed along her spine. The brush of his lips against the corner of her mouth, teasing. When his lips covered hers again, she was lost, arching into him, her curves crushed against the wall of his chest.

His broken groan shook them both. Lips parted, his tongue slid deep, his hand bracing her head so his kiss could go on and on. She was sucking his lower lip, nipping the soft skin, gripping his shoulders to stay on her feet. Breath and tongues, teeth and lips, they came together with unexpected ferocity.

Years of playing guitar and hard work had left his hands strong and his fingertips calloused. And every rough caress was more potent than the last. His touch slid between her shoulders and down her back, coming to rest on the curve of her hip. She pressed tightly against him, wanting more—needing more. She was so close, but not close enough. Not yet. She reached behind her, frantic to unhook her bra but his hands were already there.

The hook popped free and he slid the lacy straps aside. Seeing the muscles of his jaw working, the flare of his nostrils, had her shaking with anticipation. Yes, he wanted her—like she wanted him. Once would never be enough.

The brush of his thumb on her nipple stole her breath. And his gaze blazed into hers. Over and over, he stroked and teased, his lips pressed to hers and his tongue sliding deep. She was holding on, barely breathing, and frantic for more.

The plane of his stomach was rock hard. Her fingers dipped lower, closing on the towel at his waist and tugging. In seconds, her panties were on the floor and he was on his knees in front of her. The heat of his breath on her skin was too much for her.

"Jace." She gripped his shoulders, pulling him up. "I want you. Now."

In a matter of seconds, she was on the bed, staring up at him—throbbing for him. He stood on the side of the bed, staring down at her with a hunger so raw she felt it.

He watched as his fingers trailed down her breasts, across her stomach, around the curve of her hip, and toward her knee. And then his magical fingers reversed direction, teasing the sensitive skin behind her knee, featherlight up the inside of her thigh, to hover between her legs. The ache was near painful when he touched her. But it was worth the wait. The things he did with his fingers, his hand. She reached up, holding on to the headboard and turning her face into the pillow.

The pillow disappeared.

"If I'm doing something right, I want to know." His voice was low and gruff and delicious against her ear.

"You are." She gasped. "Soon, everyone on this floor will know."

He was smiling one of those smiles that melted her from the inside. Once was definitely not going to be enough. "Let 'em," he said against her lips. His mouth closed on hers, his tongue stealing her breath, and his fingers, those magical fingers, sent her free-falling into pure bliss. He muffled most of her cries with his kiss but he was still smiling like a fool when she opened her eyes.

Something about Jace over her, his hair falling onto his forehead and his eyes still on fire—for her—caught her by surprise. It was a different kind of longing. Better to focus on the here and now than long for the impossible.

She was panting from her release.

It was his turn. She sat up and grabbed him, pushing him back on the bed before he knew what was happening. The surprise on his face was priceless. But nothing was more gratifying than the groan she pulled deep from his chest when her lips found his very impressive, very hard proof of arousal.

His body was incredible. While her mouth was occupied, she let her hands explore. But it was too much for him. "Krystal. Come here." He was breathing hard, his hands fisted in the comforter and the cords in his neck rigid.

She smiled at him, crawling slowly up to straddle him. "Condom?"

He blew out a long, unsteady breath and pointed at the bedside dresser. In the top drawer was a huge box of condoms, a bottle of pain reliever, some Band-Aids, and antacid tablets.

"Looks like you're covered." She held up the mega-pack of condoms. "Maybe." She pulled one out, tore the corner of the package, and placed it gently on the tip of what guaranteed a pleasure-filled evening.

Jace was having a hell of a time breathing. He watched her—straddling his thighs—roll on the condom. With her hair wild and crazy and her lips swollen from his kisses, she was the hottest damn thing he'd ever seen in his life. Her body was beyond imagining: curves, strength, and pure femininity. Touching her. Tasting her. Seeing and hearing her climax for him—he was rock hard and hurting too much to draw this out. Next time, they'd go slow. Next time, he'd drive her out of her mind until she was loud enough to wake the whole damn hotel.

But not now... His hands settled at her hips, lifting her up, telling her what he needed.

Her green eyes blazed as she braced her hands on his chest and eased onto him. His fingers convulsed against her flesh. She was tight. Hot. Incredible. Being buried deep inside her was heaven. She was breathing hard above him, her hair falling forward around them. He reached up, smoothing her hair away and twisting it around his hand to bring her close enough to kiss.

Then she began to move and he damn near lost his

mind. "Dammit," he hissed. The force of her thrusts, the slide of her body gloving him again and again, was already too much for him.

One look at her face steadied him.

As much as he wanted his climax, he wanted hers more. And she was working her way there. With every thrust, every moan and grind, she was closer. One hand in her hair, the other gripping her hip, he met her thrust for thrust. Powering into her. Hearing her growing cries. Feeling her body quiver. Driven. Wild. Finally, the clench and pulse of her muscles constricted around him, signaling her release. She was beautiful. Her face. Her cries. Her body.

She held on as he rolled them over, moaning softly when he slid deep. The mix of hunger and bliss in her green eyes shook the very core of him. This was where she belonged. With him, like this. Whatever it took, he'd prove that to her. They were good together, in and out of bed. Not that he was in a hurry to finish this. He wrapped her legs around his waist, cradled her face in his hands, and kissed her. He moved slowly, sliding in and pulling out, until they were both frantic. And still, he kissed her. He stared into her eyes, so she'd know he was making her feel this way. This was what they, together, could be. He was loving her like this. And she'd miss him, miss this. He didn't want to believe tonight was all he had with her. But if it was, he'd make damn sure she didn't forget.

Her legs tightened around his hips, holding on as she

climaxed again. "Jace. Yes, oh, Jace." It was broken and raw and all he needed to let go.

He moved, hard and fast, until his release slammed into him. He called out, broken words he didn't hear or understand. It was too sharp, too big, the force of this—of her. It went on, rolling over him, draining him, until he was propped on trembling arms, grasping for breath.

She was just as stunned as he was, eyes blinking, cheeks red, her mind working through what had just happened. Which was good. It would have been damn awkward if he was the only one shell-shocked by how good they were together. Not that it would change her mind. She was too stubborn for that. When he rolled to his side, he fully prepared for her to bolt from his bed and his room.

Instead she turned to face him.

He slid his fingers through her long hair, smoothing it away from her face, but didn't say a thing. Words, right now, were a tricky thing. If something was going to be said, he'd let her take the lead. For him, for now, this was enough.

She was studying him, assessing things. Did she have any idea how expressive she was? From uncertainty to fear to excitement, her features shifted until they settled into the beginnings of a smile. "I'm hungry. Are you hungry?"

Which was pretty much the last thing he expected her to say.

"Room service?" she asked. "Then you can tell me about the song you're working on."

Another surprise. Not that he was complaining. If they were talking music, she wasn't going anywhere. "Which one?" There were a few knocking around inside his head.

"Exactly." She was smiling now.

"Hold up." He loved the curve of her smile. "You first. The one from the plane? Finished it?"

Her eyes narrowed and she went back to studying him. "Maybe." And then she was sliding to the side of the bed. "Where is your room service menu?"

Menu? What menu? She was searching his room, naked, and he was appreciating the view. He didn't give a crap about the menu. Or eating. Or getting out of this bed anytime soon.

"Jace?" she asked, peering back at him.

"Yeah?" He propped himself up on the pillows.

Hands on hips, she faced him, all sass. She was sexy as hell. "Menu?" But there was laughter in her voice.

"I'm thinking. Give me a minute." He didn't bother pretending he wasn't giving her a thorough once-over. He was—and enjoying every minute of it.

She laughed. "Food."

"I'm not that hungry…for food." He paused. "Seems I have one hell of an appetite for you." She had a powerful effect on him, one he had no interest in denying. His body was definitely rising to the challenge.

And she noticed. "Really?" It was breathless.

"If you're too worn out…" He shrugged.

"You think that's going to work?" She shook her head,

but she was heading back to his side of the bed, standing beside him—close enough to reach. The look on her face? She wanted him to touch her. He could do that.

"What?" he asked, his hand stroking up the inside of her thigh.

It was a sigh. "This." She leaned into him.

"No." He ran his fingers between her legs and groaned. She was warm. So damn soft. "Maybe."

She didn't waste any time. Once a new condom was in place, she was straddling him, her breath powering out of her as she slid down his rigid length. Her hands gripped the headboard, his steadied her hips. It was hard, fast, and face-to-face. She didn't shy away from him but held his gaze. Thrust for thrust, he soaked up every hitch and moan, the hot slide of her body and the sway of her breasts.

"Jace." She was close. He caught her face, swallowing her near-screamed release with a kiss and powering into her until his followed.

She slumped forward, gasping for breath, her cheek against his shoulder. He wrapped his arms around her, stroking the length of her back. This was right. He couldn't imagine anything better than this. Holding her close and breathing her in.

"You feel good." It was true.

She didn't respond.

"Hungry?" Another stroke, another shudder.

She nodded but didn't move.

He leaned back against the headboard, content to stay

wrapped up in her for as long as she wanted. For the first time in a long time, there was no push to hurry through or get something done.

Even in his dreams, she was there. Her silky arms around him. Scent flooding his nostrils. Her hair spread across his chest. He slept hard and woke up refreshed. So waking up to an empty bed, no sign of Krystal anywhere, was a kick to the gut.

It's not like he'd hoped to find her smiling up at him in his bed... No, hell, that's exactly what he'd hoped. Why wouldn't he? Last night had been all good. She'd felt it, too. Maybe that's why she'd cut and run? The only way Krystal seemed able to process feelings was through song—either writing them or singing them.

Which gave him an idea.

He downed a pot of coffee and stood under scorching hot water to ease the crick in his neck, but he was dragging when he climbed into the elevator.

A text alert pinged his phone.

Heather. She sent a selfie. She was holding up a magazine. The Kings were on the front but a small headshot of him was in the corner.

Proud of you, big brother.

He smiled. **Miss you.**

How's it going? She in love with you yet?

He stared at the picture. Krystal's smile was all attitude. Damn, but he'd hoped it was an act. Part of him—the stupid part of him—still hoped it was. **Think I'm out of luck on that one, kiddo.**

There was a long break, followed by another picture. This was the pic from the bowling alley. Krystal asleep, draped across him. Him holding on to her like...like he had every right to hold on to her. It wasn't the same pic they'd showed on Guy's show; this was from a different angle. It was closer. And what he saw made him ache.

Falling for Krystal King would be the stupidest damn thing he could possibly do. Not that there was any choosing involved in matters of the heart. Anyone who said there was had never been in love, not really. He wouldn't have chosen Nikki. She was happiest in a group, hanging out, having fun. Responsibilities? The mundane day-in, day-out stuff? She couldn't be bothered. Maybe that was why her drinking got out of hand. Her frequent disappearing acts become more frequent as well as her defensiveness. She knew what she was doing wrong, especially after Ben was born, but she never tried to stop. His grandmother always said she'd lead him to heartbreak. But no one could have guessed just how cataclysmic that heartbreak would be.

Read this. It was a link. Ten ways to win a woman's heart. He clicked on it. The first suggestion? Send her flowers and her favorite candy. Really? He didn't think that would work with Krystal. He shook his head and closed the article.

Hell, did he want to win her heart? He might want

to answer that question first—and seriously consider the consequences of his answer.

He shook his head, walking out of the elevators. Thanks. I'll read it on the road.

He stared at the picture of Krystal. He didn't believe last night was all there was between them. Maybe he was kidding himself but…he'd seen the look on her face, the spark in her green eyes. It wasn't just sex. It wasn't.

"Damn stubborn," he ground out, heading to the front doors.

"Jace?" It was Emmy, right beside him. "Talking to Heather?"

He nodded. "Sorry." He hadn't even noticed her.

"No problem." She smiled. "Tell her I said hi."

He nodded, typing in the message and hitting send.

"How'd it go?" Emmy asked, wrinkling her nose. "Krystal stormed out of the hotel room last night, so I'm guessing she wasn't very nice to you? I thought you were sweet. She just sort of blew her top."

He wasn't sure what to say. "I survived."

She nodded. "Glad to hear it—we've got a sold-out show tonight."

They were driving to San Francisco. After tonight's show, they'd drive up the coast to Oregon. "Looking forward to it." He nodded. "Can I ask you a question?"

She nodded. "Sure."

"Krystal." He cleared his throat. "She have a favorite flower? Candy?"

"Red Vines and daisies." She patted his arm. "I'm

rooting for you. I've told her you're a good guy, but you can't really blame her for being suspicious. Krystal... well..." Her expression closed. "If you hurt her, you'll have to answer to me. And Trav. And my daddy, too."

It wasn't the first time he suspected there was more going on than he knew about. "I don't suppose you want to enlighten me on anything?"

Emmy Lou looked at him long and hard, then shook her head. "Krystal doesn't share secrets with anyone. Not even me."

"I respect that." And he did. "And if she had, I wouldn't expect you to tell me. A word loses its power when it's broken."

"That, right there. You don't know how many times it's been broken for her. In big, nasty ways. The kind a person, sometimes, can't heal from." Emmy shook her head. "That sounds like one of her songs, doesn't it? She writes a lot, uses her songs to get stuff out."

He did the same.

"Be good to her, please. She needs someone like you to... to make it better." There was such sadness in Emmy's voice.

"She's not exactly making this easy."

"And she never will." Emmy shrugged. "You should know that from the get-go."

"Message received." He smiled.

"Morning." Travis was walking toward them with a box of pastries in hand, a half-eaten donut sticking out of his mouth. "You two look like you're up to something." He trotted the rest of the way. "What's happening?"

"Swallow." Emmy Lou made a face. "You were raised with manners. I know, because I was there."

He opened his mouth, chewed up donut and all. "Talking about me?"

"And my ribs." Jace nodded.

"Bad?" Travis tugged up Jace's faded grey shirt. "Shit. That looks bad."

"Feels pretty damn bad, too."

"Y'all get a move on." Hank King waved them on. "We've got six hours and not a lot of leeway. I've got some news about ACMF we need to talk about. And a tour extension."

"Does that mean we get to ride on the fancy bus?" Travis asked, following his father. Travis's bus was low-frills and he made sure his father knew how much it irritated him every chance he got. "With its custom leather, high-tech audio-video security system, big-screen televisions, damn near gourmet kitchen—"

"Just get on." Hank rolled his eyes and pointed at the girls' bus—the "fancy bus," as Travis called it. "You too, Jace. Got a song I want to play for you."

"I got a quick phone call," Jace said. "I'll be right there." He dialed quickly. "Luke. I need you to do something for me. I need daisies and the biggest box of Red Vines you can find delivered to the San Francisco venue tonight." He paused. "Krystal's dressing room." He talked over Luke's protests. "Can you do it, yes or no?"

"I can do it." Luke sighed. "But you're playing with fire."

"Yeah. I know."

Chapter 11

"Looks like ACMF isn't going to work out." Her father leaned against the bus wall, slowly spinning his hat in his hands.

"What happened?" Travis stopped mid-chew, midway through the box of donuts he'd brought with him. "I thought we were emceeing? Now we're not even going?"

"Nothing happened." He shook his head. "We got an invite to Australia. Figured you might want to go?"

Something had happened. ACMF was one of her father's favorite events—he credited the festival with him getting his start. To miss it? He was keeping something from them. "And?" Krystal pulled the box away from Travis. "Some of us haven't had one."

"Some of you might want to rethink having one." Travis stared at her rear.

"Rude." She pinched him, hard. "Daddy?"

Hank smacked his hat against his thigh, shooting a glance at Jace.

She was doing her best not to look at Jace. Not to say she wasn't aware of his every move. She was. Or the fact that his faded grey T-shirt hugged the incredibly sculpted chest that she'd enjoyed a little too much the night before.

But her Daddy's expression set her nerves on edge and flooded her stomach with ice. Whatever Daddy wasn't saying, he wasn't sure he wanted to share it in front of Jace.

"Spill." Travis pushed. "I'm not buying it."

"Tig Whitman is getting an industry award." His blue-green gaze met hers. "Doesn't sit well with me."

She handed the box back to Travis. Her daddy was doing this for her.

"Australia, here we come." Emmy Lou was all smiles. "I've always wanted to go."

"Okay." Travis stared into the pastry box, frowning.

She had no idea what her siblings knew. She'd been packed off to the Wellness Ranch for six weeks on intense therapy and counseling—to break her "destructive habit of lying" and "learn why she needed extra attention" and why she "wanted to hurt her parents." In time, she realized she was there to learn to lie better. Uncle Tig had never touched her, never hurt her. No, she'd said those things because she was overshadowed by her sister's success. At least, that's what she picked up as her expected response—and no one thought to question her.

Once she'd returned from her Wellness Ranch visit, no one mentioned Uncle Tig, what he did or did not do to her, or the sudden severing of his and her father's relationship. Something had happened: Uncle Tig was a regular in the King household; then he wasn't.

Travis had brought Tig up once, unleashing sobs and a full-blown panic attack. After that, neither of her siblings brought him up again.

But this was one of those things they couldn't pass up.

Them. Not her. "I can skip it," she offered, sitting cross-legged on the kitchenette bench and pulling Clementine into her lap. "It's not a big deal."

Her father shook his head. "That's not how family works."

"This is business." She smiled at him. "It would be a mistake, Daddy. Y'all have to go to ACMF."

"People will talk." Travis's jaw was locked. "You can't just not show up. We are the Three Kings. You know?"

"Travis." Her father's voice was gruff. "I need everyone to be on board with this. Hell, to feel good about it. And I'll be turning on the damn security system, too. Every time, something goes missing. Not this year."

Krystal smiled. "If that will make you feel better, Daddy."

He nodded. "But you don't have to go, Krystal."

"Make something up." Emmy Lou shrugged. "Laryngitis? That'd keep her from performing. And talking."

"How about we work out the details later." She looked at Jace—and regretted it. "You have a song for Jace, Daddy?" Her gaze fell to Clem.

Her father nodded. "I do."

Clementine's tail wagged and her little tongue brushed the underside of Krystal's chin. "Thank you, baby."

"Here." Travis put the box on the table and slid into the seat opposite her. "Going to Australia wouldn't be the worst thing in the world."

She smiled at him. "Australian women superhot?"

He grinned. "I'm game to find out."

"The new album comes out next month," she pointed out. "This is where we need to be. You know Daddy. He'll get the Australian dates pushed back."

Travis was staring at her, posture going stiff, his green eyes troubled. He had questions. One day, he'd want answers.

"Working on that new song." She cut him off. "Wanna hear?"

He nodded, his posture easing.

She gave him Clementine.

"She doesn't have to be held twenty-four hours a day," Travis grumbled, rubbing the white poof of hair on the dog's head. "You are one spoiled dog, you know that?"

Clementine was all wiggles.

"Just ignore him, Clem," Emmy said, sitting on the seat by her brother. "He only wishes he'd get half the attention you do."

"Poor Travis," Krystal cooed, mussing her brother's hair before she headed for her guitar.

Her daddy caught her hand as she walked past to her room. She paused long enough to kiss him on the temple.

"You know I mean it." He squeezed her hand.

She nodded and did her best to smile. Her daddy loved her—even after all that had happened. She squeezed his hand, hating how her smile wobbled. Better to roll her eyes, pretend it wasn't a big deal. She tried, then hurried to the storage compartments at the back of the bus. It was quieter there and she needed space to clear her mind. She opened the cabinet and pulled out her guitar, her heart hammering against her chest. *Damn Tig Whitman.* Two deep breaths. Resting her forehead against the cool wood compartment. Thinking of her happy place—her grandfather's kitchen, elbow deep in biscuit dough with her grandmother singing to whatever song was blaring from her radio.

It helped. But *he* was still there. Tig Whitman. Her personal boogeyman, waiting to pop out and scare the shit out of her when she thought he was gone for good.

It wasn't as though she were a fragile sixteen-year-old anymore. She had a firm grip on reality. Life wasn't a love song. Being a hero meant doing the right thing, and they were a rare breed. Tears were a waste of time and energy. The people who loved you could hurt you worst of all. Uncle Tig. Her mother. Her father—though he'd done his best to make up for that. And, finally, some wounds would never fully heal. The Wellness Ranch taught her that—the place had taught her a lot, actually. Mostly, how to survive. And lying to hide the nasty truth was the only way everything would be okay. Not for her—but for the rest of the world.

The only time she'd slipped? Years ago. Why her mother thought a "Welcome home from Wellness Ranch" party was appropriate, she still didn't know. Uncle Tig showed up. He'd forgiven her for the horrible things she'd said about him, he said. He'd make sure she knew she was his special girl, he said. But his hug, his hands on her, pressing her close, had been too much. She'd thrown up all over his fancy custom suit and run for her bedroom, refusing to open the door to anyone. Her daddy had to take the door off the hinges to get inside. He'd taken one look at her, hiding in the back of her closet, and told her mother Tig was no longer welcome in their home. Not his name nor his presence. It was the one time her father had laid down the law with her mother.

Her mother had never forgiven her for it. And Krystal could never forgive her mother for deserting her when she'd needed her most. A daughter should be able to rely on her mother, shouldn't she? She tried to be strong, she did. But sometimes, she ached to have someone to turn to.

Her daddy was already too tormented by the past.

Her sister? Or brother? She wasn't about to dump her garbage on them. Assumptions had been made, sure, but nothing had been confirmed. Emmy Lou would be devastated. Travis? He'd want to go for the jugular. She wouldn't drag her siblings into this or tear her entire family apart instead of just her relationship with her mother.

"Krystal?" Jace. Of course. He cleared his throat. "I need to get something."

"Go ahead," she murmured, setting her guitar case on the floor at her feet and closing the compartment. The latch on the door wouldn't stick. She tried again. No luck. And again. "Shit."

"Need help?" he asked.

"No." She shoved harder, slamming with more force than necessary.

He squeezed behind her, warm and solid. "Excuse me."

She stepped back, against the wall of compartments, frazzled by his nearness. By him, reaching for the overhead compartment and how his shirt lifted just enough to reveal a sampling of his seriously ripped abs. *Forget the damn latch.*

How she wished their night together had cooled her interest in him. If anything, it had the opposite effect. The two or three times she'd dared to look his way, she'd been back in his bed, his hands on her skin, buried deep inside her. Now was no exception. She'd give just about anything to rewind and replay their night together.

His light brown eyes met hers, his jaw muscles working—clenching—tight. "You okay?"

She nodded. She'd be better if he was touching her. Kissing her. "Did you need something?"

"Your dad was looking for his harmonica. Said it might be here?" He paused, those light brown eyes fixed on her. "Any idea where it might be?"

She nodded, bending to open the drawer that stored her father's excessive harmonica collection. "Which one?"

He was closer behind her. "Not sure."

She pulled out his favorite, a silver Hohner Super Chromonica, from its velvet-lined box, pushed the drawer shut, and stood, facing the cabinets—not Jace. It was safer that way, wasn't it? Not getting lost in his eyes or the curve of his mouth. Much safer. Or not. Her ass was pressed tight against what felt like the beginnings of just the sort of thing she'd been thinking about—dreaming about—since she'd left his hotel room.

"Here." He reached around her, the back of his hand brushing a far too aroused nipple, and closed the compartment she'd been fighting with, pushing until the latch caught. His hand stayed there, open and flat against the wood, his arm braced taut, against her side, close to holding her. But not.

She was breathing heavily, willing him to touch her, aching for it.

"Krystal." The roughness in his voice sent a shudder down her spine.

No, no. If he started talking, she'd listen. And he was too good at saying all the right—wrong—things. She spun to face him, injecting as much irritation into her "Here" as possible while holding out the harmonica.

His gaze narrowed, falling from her face to the harmonica—to her impossible-to-miss nipples straining against her shirt. He closed his eyes, blew out a long, slow breath, and took the harmonica. She waited, not sure what to hope for but hoping all the same. Finally, his eyes opened, blazing. Beautiful. Hungry. For her.

And he walked away.

She almost slid down the wall to the floor, almost called him back, but knew that was a bad idea. It, they, couldn't happen again. Being alone with him was way too tempting. He'd know what she wanted now, but being the gentleman he was, he'd never act on it without her permission.

She splashed some cold water on her face in the restroom before carrying her guitar back to the eat-in booth built into the bus. Travis and Emmy Lou were reading over her notes, instantly engrossed by her new song. But Jace was singing and his voice did things to her. She set her guitar aside and gave up pretending she wasn't listening. Her daddy joined in, harmonizing. Travis picked up her guitar and joined in, the three of them turning one song into another—until a full-on jam session was underway.

This was how music should be—full of joy and laughter. So much so that parking at the Civic Center was almost a letdown. Not because they had a show, but because the rest of the world existed again. And in that world, she had to keep her distance from Jace Black. No matter how hard that was going to be.

———————

Jace heard the roar of the crowd and smiled. He was a long way from comfortable with his new gig as the Three Kings opening act but this, his duet with Krystal, he looked forward to. When the lights went dim, he made his way carefully to his waiting stool. Now, it wasn't just the song or getting to sing with her. This was the only time he had with her. Since that day on the bus, she'd gone out of her way to avoid him. Hell, she'd barely even look at him. Except onstage.

Onstage, she looked at him like he was someone special to her. Sang her heart out for him.

He sat, his fingers plucking out the first lines of their song. The audience went crazy.

When the lights went up, she was sitting beside him—a microphone in her hands.

"I remember you, standing in the sun, smiling at me, and suddenly the world caught fire. Blinding, beautiful fire," he sang.

Her eyes met his and he was lost. Her voice poured out over the audience and wrapped around his heart. She'd given his flowers to a fan and distributed the giant box of Red Vines among the band and crew, never once acknowledging they were from him. He'd handed her the music to the song he'd been working on and been met with a blank expression and a curt "I'll take a look at it."

But he didn't let it get to him. If anything, it was starting to make sense.

Being alone with him was too risky. She wanted him and, damn, he wanted her. With no one else around, she was worried about what would happen. But in front of people, a few thousand of them preferably, she had no problem letting it all out.

He took her hand in his, the chorus rising up from the audience as they slipped from their stools and stood, face-to-face, to share her mic. He didn't bother pretending he wasn't staring. He was. And he loved what he saw. Her skin dewy with sweat. Eyes huge. Excited smile. Red lips—she was chewing her lower lip now. And the hitch in her breath, the tightening of her hand in his.

He leaned forward, so close their foreheads touched.

"Love isn't love when the flames burn it down. There's no hiding or forgiveness from the damage that it's done.

When the smoke clears away, you'll still find me searching here. Searching for the ashes of my heart."

The crowd was deafening when the lights went dim.

Not that he noticed.

She was kissing him. Arms around his neck, fingers
tangled in his hair. Desperate. He couldn't think, he was
grabbing on, kissing her back—pressing her tight against
him.

Just as quickly, she was pushing him away and running from the stage, almost falling. He stood there, like
an idiot, wondering what the hell to do now. Go after
her? Make her talk to him?

Now was not the time.

The lights were about to come up and he couldn't be
standing there, so he did what he always did at this point
of the show—went and watched from the wings of the
stage. Only this time, he was getting looks. There was just
enough light for anyone watching the stage to see what
had happened. Most of the crew had a job to do, too busy
to notice. But the crew weren't the only people onstage.

"Please tell me I didn't see what I just saw." A vein in
Luke's forehead was bulging.

"You might need to get that looked at." He pointed at
his manager's forehead. "That can't be normal."

"You're hilarious." Luke wasn't smiling. "We've been
over this before—"

"We have." Jace nodded, crossing his arms over his
chest. "I'll refresh your memory this time. You handle
my career. Period." For a minute, he worried Luke would

lose his cool. He liked the guy enough, respected his dedication to the job…but his personal life was his business. Even when a celebrity was kissing him on a concert stage in front of a live audience.

Luke snorted. "This isn't going away."

Jace didn't say a thing.

"Someone probably got a picture." Luke sighed. "Or video."

Which was probably true. The lights came up and the Three Kings were onstage. He'd seen the show a dozen times already but it never got old. The three of them were master performers. And Krystal? Hell, he could watch her sing all day.

"You like her that much?" Luke asked.

"Are you going to lose it if I say yes?" He faced his manager.

And realized Hank King was standing not two feet away, listening to the entire conversation. "Don't mind me. I figured I'd wait around to hear your answer, too."

Jace felt like a son of a bitch then. He'd earned his contract through *Next Top American Voice*, sure, but Hank King had given him this—all of this. Hank might respect his talent, but did he respect him as a man? A man for his daughter? "Yes, sir." He cleared his throat, knowing there was only one answer. The truth. "Very much."

Hank smiled, nodded, and clapped Luke on the shoulder. "Well, there you go."

Luke's attempt at a smile was more than pathetic.

"Don't you worry, son," Hank assured him. "It'll all come out right in the wash."

Confusion descended on Luke's face, but he still nodded, as if he understood exactly what Hank was talking about.

"City folk," Hank said, shaking his head before he walked around a drop-down wall and out of sight.

"What the hell did that mean?" Luke asked.

"It'll all work itself out." Jace laughed.

"Why didn't he just say that?"

"Probably to see the look on your face." He pointed. "That look."

Luke scowled. "Whatever. In the morning, we need to talk strategy. We should be looking at lining up some projects for just you on the way back to Austin. Once you get there, you'll be in the studio getting the album done."

Just when he thought he was getting a feel for things, Luke had found some new opportunity to shake things up. Better to remember the album was the original deal. Wheelhouse Records had signed him for one year and one contract. Everything else? That was up to him—and Luke.

"Oh shit, I forgot." Luke smiled. "You wear cologne?"

Jace frowned. "Not normally."

Luke's smile grew. "You might be. We'll talk."

Two hours later, Jace was in his dressing room downing a bottle of water when his phone started vibrating.

Heather. Not a text like normal.

"What's wrong?" Jace asked.

"Nothing. Why does something have to be wrong?" She paused. "Breathe, Jace."

"I'm breathing. You're calling, so something has to be up."

"Well, it's just…don't get mad, okay?"

He sat on the small sofa in his dressing room. "Okay?"

"These reporters showed up today." She sighed. "I didn't talk to them, much. But my roommate, the one I thought was my friend, she might have talked to them."

He sat back, pressing the cold water bottle to his head. "What might she have said?"

"Probably a whole bunch of stuff that I said—when I thought she was, you know, actually my friend." Her voice broke. "Jace, I'm sorry. I am such an idiot. I don't even belong here—"

"Hold on now." He sat forward, resting his elbows on his knees. "You know I can't handle it when you cry, Heather. Especially when you're this far away."

She took several long, shuddering breaths.

He stood and paced the dressing room. "Talk to me."

"I don't know. I'm used to having you to talk to. I thought Brenna was someone I could talk to. And it was more stuff that I hoped would happen, you know? You and Krystal and how I wanted you two to get together. I told her that. I'm so stupid. Trusting people."

"Trusting people isn't stupid." He sighed. "It's knowing who you can and can't trust."

"I guess." She sniffed. "I went to see about getting a new roommate and Brenna started crying because she was sorry—"

"Heather, if she's sorry, maybe you can work this thing out?" He turned to see Krystal in his dressing room, leaning against the door, an odd look on her face.

"Why would I want to?" Heather sniffed again. "How would I ever learn to trust her again?"

"Trust takes time." He tore his gaze from Krystal. "People mess up, you know that. If you don't think there's a way to work this out, then I'll see about getting you moved to another room. If you do, you should give it a try."

She sighed.

"You remember what Gramma said?" He was smiling. "Nothing worth a thing will come—"

"Easy." She sighed again. "I know. And she is acting sorry. Like crying a lot."

"Talk to her, then call me back. Okay?"

"Okay. I love you, Jace."

"I love you, too."

"Call you later. Probably tomorrow?" she added.

"Sounds good. Bye." He hung up.

"Nothing worth a thing will come what?" Krystal asked, rearranging the various brushes and sprays and powders the makeup team used on him before the show. The damn counter was covered in things he'd never known existed before.

"Easy." He set his phone down. "Nothing worth a thing will come easy."

"Heather?" Her gaze met his, then fell back to the counter. "She okay?"

"She will be." He did his best not to stare, but it was damn near impossible.

She was wearing the last costume of the evening. Black denim dress, little cutouts of stars around the bottom of the short skirt and the top. It was sleeveless, so her shoulders and an eye-catching display of the top of her breasts had him holding his breath every single time she bounced or leaned forward during a song. Her eye makeup was dark, smudged from the last three hours of exertion, bright red lips, and long curls falling down her back. She was, as always, beautiful.

She'd kissed him. He'd kissed her back, then told his manager and her father he cared about her. Which was probably why she was here. But she'd kissed him, she'd ignited *this* all over again. And now, what? Her ramrod posture. Avoiding his gaze. None of it meant anything good.

She drew in a deep breath and looked at him.

Damn it all, but she was gorgeous. Her breath unsteady, breasts shaking, eyes blazing—demanding his attention. He couldn't look at her without wanting her.

One minute she was across the room, the next, she was pulling him toward her.

He should stop her, say something, anything. Instead, he backed her up against the door. His kiss wasn't gentle—he hurt too much. His tongue invaded the warmth of her mouth and she moaned, her nails biting into the back of his head. She matched him, kiss for kiss, on and on, until he was breathless and hungry for more.

Her hands yanked his pearl-snapped shirt wide.

He tugged the top of her dress down.

The crush of skin on skin knocked the air from his lungs, his lips latching on to her neck, making her gasp.

Her fingers fell to the waist of his jeans, unbuttoning. Unzipping and reaching inside. Her fingers closed around him, stroking. He arched into her hand, pressing an open-mouthed kiss—and a damn near growl— against her neck. The salt of her sweat lingered on his lips and tongue.

He tried to pull up her tight skirt while his mouth sucked the tip of one breast, his tongue and teeth working her into a frenzy before he did the same to the other.

She was moaning, wriggling, releasing him, and pressing her hands over her head, against the dressing room door.

With a less-than-gentle tug and the faint sound of fabric splitting, her skirt was up and around her waist, and her panties were gone. He grabbed her hips and lifted her, her thighs silk around his waist.

Reason found him before they made a mistake they'd regret. "I don't have a condom."

"I'm clean," she said. "I get shots. Birth control." Her ankles pressed against his hips, the only encouragement he needed, but her whispered "Please, Jace" made him frantic.

One thrust. "Dammit," he ground out, pressing her against the door, squeezing her hips.

She was holding on to him, her green eyes fluttering open.

He thrust again, savoring her heat, tight around him. Then he was moving, powering into her, harder and faster.

Her lips parted, panting and gasping and clinging to him. Her eyes closing.

"Look at me," he ground out.

She did, her body instantly shuddering, clamping down on him from the inside. He caught her cries with his kiss, his mouth sealed to hers until she was panting. But her legs tightened around his waist and she latched on to his neck, licking and kissing, making sure every nerve ending was strung tight and pulsing. He came, groaning loud and long, burying his face against her neck and thrusting deep. He held on to her until the world started to take shape again.

He waited until she was steady on her feet before stepping away.

She had her dress into place before he was done buttoning up his shirt. "Did you mean what you said?" she asked.

He smiled. "About? I've said a lot of things."

"Nothing. It doesn't matter." She shook her head, her hand on the doorknob.

"Wait." His hand covered hers.

"Jace." She sighed. "It's nothing. It is what it is."

"What the hell is that supposed to mean?"

Her gaze fell to his chest, his pants—open at the waist—and shuddered.

Instantly, he understood. "You mean me and you?" He paused but she didn't look at him or respond. "This is it? This is what you want? You want me when you want me, but only then?"

She glared at him, her red lips opening. But she stopped, her gaze falling from his. "I guess that won't work for you?"

He put a hand on either side of the door. If this was the only way to spend time with her, to get close to her, it was a start. Not like he minded making love to her, not one little bit. "What about me?"

She looked at him, a little surprised, a little uncertain. "Maybe this is a bad idea."

"Probably," he agreed. "But we both know it's going to happen again."

She stiffened, that defiant tilt of her head making him smile.

His lips brushed the side of her neck, taking his time, nipping and licking and making her quiver. More kisses, up the curve of her neck, then sucking her earlobe into his mouth. She softened, her hands resting on his chest, then grabbing the front of his shirt. "It's going to happen again," he said against her lips.

"Fine," she whispered.

"Fine?" he repeated. Maybe this would be easier than he thought.

She nodded. "If you…are…want…how will I know?"

He smiled, stepping back. "Believe me, you'll know."

She shook her head and turned the doorknob.

"You've got a rip." He pointed at the seam along her hip. "Might want to get that taken care of."

Her brows rose high. "You should be more careful."

"Next time?" He grinned. "Pretty sure you wouldn't like that near as much." His phone started vibrating.

"You might want to answer that. It could be Heather." Her hand slipped off the doorknob.

He headed for his phone. "It's Luke." He silenced his phone and stuffed it into his pocket.

Her phone started ringing. She pulled it out of her boot. "Emmy." She answered. "What's up?"

Luke texted.

> Video of you and Krystal kissing. TNM is on it.
>> Someone close or onstage. No doubt who it
>> was.

"Thanks for the heads-up," Krystal said. "Daddy? Fine. Thanks." She hung up.

"What's *TNM*?" he asked.

"That sleazy entertainment news show, *Tabloid News Media*. Luke?" She nodded at her phone. "I'm guessing he called for the same reason Emmy did."

"Video?" he asked. "Luke says…" He read the text out loud.

"I guess I owe you an apology." She shook her head, her long curls swaying. "Wheelhouse Records has already called Steve. Steve's already freaking out to my father."

"This going to require damage control?" he asked.

"More for you than anyone else, I'm sure." Her eyes

widened and she crossed the room, picking up the pair of panties he'd kicked aside not ten minutes ago. "Guess I should take these with me."

His phone started vibrating again. "Luke."

"You should talk to him." She headed for the door. "I guess I'm giving you your first scandal. Who knows? Maybe you'll wind up with a platinum album, too."

"You know that's not what I'm after here, with you. A hit record." He needed her to believe that.

"I know. That's what scares me." She yanked the dressing room door open. "Emmy Lou said we'll have breakfast in the morning, get on the same page, go from there."

He was staring after her, shocked by her honesty. His phone kept on vibrating. "Yeah?" He answered the phone, frustrated and tired and exhilarated, all at once.

"We're meeting in the morning." Luke sighed. "I know you don't get how serious this is, but Wheelhouse is worried. They want you to have a certain image and they're worried that will change if this thing with Krystal progresses."

"Certain image?" he asked, chuckling. "I'm supposed to be, what, a monk?"

"It would be different if this were Emmy we were talking about." He cleared his throat. "There are a lot of rumors about Krystal. Some true, some not. Look, Jace, this is a big deal. She cost the label some serious money about ten years ago. I don't know all the details, it's all some big secret, but it was touch-and-go as to whether Wheelhouse would keep Three Kings. Bottom line, they see you as a moneymaker and they don't want that to change."

How the hell had she cost them money? Ten years ago, the Three Kings were still teen stars, rosy-cheeked and on the rise. He hadn't kept up with them—but Heather had. Maybe she'd have some idea why Wheelhouse was losing their shit over this. Krystal was part of one of the most consistently chart-topping bands in years. "Guess we'll sort it out in the morning."

"Jace, I'm asking you to be open-minded here. We both want the same thing—a career for you. You need to think about what that means. What sort of compromises and sacrifices you might have to make in order for that to happen. I know you like her. I do. But is she worth you losing a contract renewal? You're only signed for a year, Jace. I know you and Heather don't want to go back to the way it was before you won the show."

Jace couldn't argue that. The winnings had paid off Nikki's hospital bills and a good portion of Heather's tuition, but not all of it. Going back to days on the oilfields and nights at the local Bail Bonds wouldn't be the end of the world, for him. But it would impact Heather's future. He'd made peace with the life they'd lived, but he sure as hell wanted better for her.

"Think about it. Really think about it. I'll see you in the morning." Luke hung up.

Jace stared at his phone.

She'd kissed him and he wasn't about to regret it. Well, they'd done a hell of a lot more than that, but no one knew that part of it. How could kissing her cause so much trouble? What the hell had happened to make everyone so skittish about Krystal? And vice versa. He knew the Kings had secrets—that had been obvious from day one—all families did. But most family secrets didn't involve or impact a high-stakes, multimillion-dollar company, in a billion-dollar industry. He wasn't one to go digging into a person's private affairs, but this time, he might have to make an exception.

Chapter 12

"THIS IS BIGGER THAN YOU." HER MOTHER WAS ALL fired up. "And don't feed me some line about caring for him, either. If you cared about Jace Black, you'd stay away from him."

Krystal couldn't argue with her—not on this. She'd tried to stay away from him. Sort of. But she couldn't. And now, this. What the hell had she been thinking? She hadn't been thinking. She'd been feeling. She'd missed him. It was that simple. Missed his touch and his kiss. Jace the Gentleman withdrawal.

"What about his sister? And all his dead wife's medical bills?" Her mother waited. "You realize he worked two, sometimes three jobs and was still facing bankruptcy when that show came along? He finally has a chance to better himself—and his sister. Why would you take that from him?"

Bankruptcy? Medical bills? Was she telling the truth? Or manipulating things to make her feel worse?

"Mom, chill." Travis ran a hand through his blond hair. "I don't see why this is such a big deal. It was a frigging kiss. Period. No one saw much of anything. Besides, Mickey survived just fine. Why is this different?"

"It *is* completely different. How do you think people will react to Krystal breaking Jace's heart? Or Three

Kings? He's…wholesome. A widower. The man lost his baby boy, Travis. Pretty much the entire country feels protective of him—a good portion of that wants to go to bed with him."

Krystal took a sip of coffee. When her mother was irrational, it was easy to brush her off. But right now, her mother sounded all too rational.

"Your daddy was working on a new album. Did you know that?" She was pacing. "It's been three years since his last one. You think having our name trashed all over the place, again, won't impact how the label supports him? It will. Guess it was too much to hope that we'd steer clear of more troubles with the record label. Last time about ended the Kings' music legacy." She waited just long enough for Krystal's stomach to twist, hard. "Now this nonsense about not going to ACMF?"

"Momma," Emmy Lou jumped in. "We're going."

"Yes, I know. And Krystal will get some mysterious illness and bow out?" Her mother shook her head. "I know all about your little plan and I'm disappointed. Beyond disappointed. We don't hide from our fears; we face them. You're never going to let this go until you talk to—"

"Momma." Krystal glared up at her, stunned that her mother was prepared to go there. "We should wait until Daddy gets here."

"He'll see it my way, Krystal. I don't know why you're always so determined to think otherwise." She sighed, frowning at her. "He respects my industry savvy and the powerful friends I have. Friends who have stuck with us through the good times and the not so good times."

"Fine." Krystal drew her legs up, cradling Clementine against her chest. "He'll side with you. And what did the two of you decide?"

She smiled. "Well, what if he'd been kissing Emmy Lou?"

"Emmy vaulted across the stage, in the dark, to tackle-kiss him right after he sang with Krystal?" Travis was smiling. "That makes perfect sense."

Krystal stared down at Clementine, trying not to smile.

"Travis, I don't need your smart mouth this morning." CiCi sighed. "It wouldn't take much to make it look like Emmy's been singing with him the whole time, not Krystal. Some sort of fun and games, switching? The twin thing? It wouldn't be the first time you two had done that. Steve is all over it. I'm sure we can put a believable spin on it, especially since Krystal has never done a duet or single before." It would be a double win for her mother, pretending Krystal had never had her minute in the spotlight and giving Emmy Lou her song.

"That was one concert when we were, what, twelve?" Travis asked.

Emmy Lou frowned. "Besides, I'm not sure Jace will be okay with that, Momma. He's not the smoke and mirrors type."

He was all about being up-front and honest—Krystal had firsthand experience with that.

"Which is why the two of you make sense." There was nothing but disdain on her face when she looked at Krystal. "And you two do not."

"Kinda like a debutante and a ranch hand who'd sing in pool halls on the weekend?" Krystal pushed back. Her mother did not come from humble beginnings. Their father had.

"That was different." Her mother paused, eyes hard and focused. "Now, wait a minute. Hold everything. Are you saying you're in love with Jace Black?"

There was no right answer. If she loved him, which she didn't, her mother would have a heart attack. If she didn't love him, her mother would continue to push this whole Emmy Lou/Krystal switcheroo thing.

"Come on, Momma. Lay off," Travis said. "Why would Emmy Lou pretend to be Krystal? Why would Krystal be okay with that? It won't work."

The sound of the bus doors opening silenced them all. Seconds later, her father, Steve Zamora, Luke, and Jace joined them.

"CiCi." Daddy wasn't pleased. "What is going on?"

Her mother smiled. "I thought I'd get the ball rollin'."

"Food." Jace held out a large cardboard box of bagels. "And coffee."

"Are you really okay with this whole switching-places thing?" Travis jumped right back in. "What's the point, anyway?"

Her father leveled a hard stare at his wife. "CiCi—"

"If I left everything to you, you'd sugarcoat it.

They need to know," her mother interrupted. "About your new album and your song and Jace's career—*she* needs to know her little stunt has put us all in a serious predicament."

"Mrs. King." Jace stepped forward. "I appreciate your concern, but I feel confident this will all be forgotten in a day or two."

"Jace, *honey*, you haven't been at this all that long." Her mother smiled. "Hank and I have been doing this since before you were born. There's so much more going on here than you realize."

"CiCi." Her father shook his head. "We've got this. Steve is going to take you to the airport. We'll be in Austin in a few days."

"I appreciate that, sugar, but I have a stake in this, too. This is my family. My business." Her mother stood her ground, eyes slightly narrowed—voice tight.

"Fine." Her father shrugged. "We hammered out the details on the way here. All we need is Krystal on board and we're good."

"On board with what?" Travis was slathering cream cheese on a bagel. "An out-of-body experience that made her attack you? She was drunk? Someone slipped something into her water? She fell on you, lips first, and you caught her?"

"We're a couple and we're tired of hiding it." Jace was looking at her. "Out front, in public. It can't hurt when the single drops. And, when we decide, we'll break it off."

"He'll dump you," her father said. "So you're the wronged one—but it'll be a mutual thing versus what one of you did to the other."

She looked back and forth between the two of them. "I'm confused. I thought being involved with him was a bad thing."

"It is, if it's presented in the wrong light. But you two, bringing your relationship out in the open, all hearts and doves and love songs?" Luke nodded. "You'll have to really sell this to make it work."

She frowned. "What does that mean?"

"You'll have to smile a little more at me. And scowl a little less." Jace winked, grinning. Because he was enjoying himself. He was getting exactly what he wanted—and loving every minute of it.

It took a lot not to laugh.

"I'm supposed to act like I...I love you?" The words seemed to hang there.

"Shouldn't be too hard." Travis took a bite. "I have a whole bunch of pictures you can use."

"Pictures?" Luke asked.

"Of those two crazy kids." He shot her a look. "Young and in love."

"Are you okay with this?" Krystal ignored her brother, knowing how Jace felt about lying.

"Not ten minutes ago you were telling me he'd have a problem lying." Her mother wasn't happy. "Don't you think this seems a little risky?"

Her father was studying the two of them. "No."

"Wheelhouse is okay with this?" Her mother's eyes narrowed.

He nodded.

"Well, I have a *serious* problem with this." Her mother grabbed her purse. "It's going to backfire. When it does, you remember I told you so. Steve." She didn't stop to give goodbye hugs and kisses as she climbed down the bus steps and out onto the concrete parking lot.

"I'll be back." Steve trailed behind her.

"You're sure about this?" Emmy asked Krystal, beyond concerned. "You've never been the...hearts and doves and love songs type."

As far as Krystal knew, she hadn't agreed to a thing. Yet.

"What's the problem?" Travis asked. "You two get to keep doing what you're doing anyway—only you don't have to hide it anymore."

Which was exactly why Jace looked like the cat that ate the canary.

"Good." Her father glanced at his watch. "The *Good Morning USA* people should be here in about fifteen minutes, so get yourselves pulled together."

"What?" This was all happening a little too fast. "Now?"

"Before this story gets too much of the wrong kind of traction." Luke glanced at his watch. "The sooner the better."

"Come on." Emmy Lou pulled Krystal up. "You need to get dressed."

"Not too much." Her daddy smiled. "This doesn't need to look like a show. This needs to look real."

But she saw the concern on her father's face. "What aren't you telling me?"

"Wheelhouse isn't fine with it." Her father pulled her up from her chair. "No one likes lying, baby girl. You do this, you give it your all. If fans find out, it'd be a bad thing."

"Do you really have a new album in the works?" she asked.

He shrugged. "We'll see how it goes."

Which was the only answer she was going to get.

Fifteen minutes later, she and Jace sat on the stage, facing Molly Harper and her crew from *Good Morning USA*.

The makeup and wardrobe people had done their best to make her appear soft and sweet without making the Emmy Lou resemblance too strong. Black lace sleeveless top, distressed jeans, and her trademark sparkling boots. Her hair was brushed soft and free, glossy lips, not red. She wore crystal-covered hoops, a crystal heart pendant, and a leather and crystal wrist cuff so there was no confusion about who she was. Crystals were her thing.

Jace? He was in black from head to toe and looked good enough to eat. His long legs were encased in painted-on black jeans and his hat sat at just the right angle. She eyed the black snap-front shirt with interest and caught him smiling at her.

"I remembered you like snaps." He leaned her way,

sliding his chair as close to hers as possible and whispering, "Nervous?"

She nodded, taking the hand he offered her. Couples held hands. If her daddy thought this was the way to handle it, she'd do it. They were a couple. And, dammit, holding his hand helped. "You're enjoying this too much."

He grinned, eyebrows raised. "So?"

She rolled her eyes, too tense to come up with a quick retort.

"I've got an idea." His thumb trailed across the back of her hand.

"What?" she whispered back.

His hand was soft against her cheek, almost as soft as the brush of his lips against hers. He lingered, pressing another kiss—and another—until she was leaning into him.

"I hate to interrupt." Molly laughed. "We're on in about thirty seconds."

Jace tucked her arm through his, his fingers threading with hers. She could do this. They could do this. All she had to do was act like she…loved him. Even though she had no idea what being in love was like. She'd written more than a dozen songs about it—might as well tap into them now.

Someone counted down from ten.

"Good morning. Last night a very interesting video was leaked from the Three Kings Concert here in San Francisco." Molly smiled at the camera. "I'm here, live, to set the record straight with country music sensation Krystal King and heartthrob Jace Black."

Krystal was so nervous she almost giggled.

"You two look pretty close," Molly began. "Does that mean the video was, in fact, of you two?"

Jace looked at her.

She was still in danger of dissolving into giggles. What was wrong with her?

"It's true." He nodded. "We've been trying to keep it quiet but, well, you can't fight something like this." His light brown eyes met hers.

Her heart slammed into her chest. "Why would you want to?" she asked softly. It was the question she asked herself every time he looked her way.

He smiled that bone-melting smile. "Exactly."

"I guess, after your recent breakup, there were some concerns?" Molly asked her.

"Yes." Krystal forced herself to look at Molly. "You might have heard that things didn't end well with Mickey." She smiled. "But, honestly, Mickey and I only went on four dates, and I think people wanted us to be a couple, so they took it hard when we weren't a good fit."

"Mickey was one of those people," Jace said.

"You were quick to defend Krystal on Guy James's late-night show." She paused. "Are you saying he's lied about the breakup?"

Jace nodded. "Yes, ma'am."

Krystal squeezed his hand. "I'd rather not talk about Mickey, if that's okay?"

Jace tugged her hand into his lap. "Here's the thing about Krystal. She doesn't talk about people. Good or bad, she's private. It's one of the things I respect about her. So, yeah, I get a little defensive because he's made stuff up, and since she won't lower herself to his level, people assume he's telling the truth."

Molly appeared to be listening sincerely. "Why do you think Mickey Graham has said some of the things he's said? He's painted a pretty unflattering picture of you, Krystal."

Krystal nodded. "I know. I think, sometimes, it's easier to blame someone else when things don't work out. Instead of owning your part in it." Which was true. It was also true that Mickey Graham was just an attention-seeking bastard, but she'd keep that part to herself.

Jace pressed a kiss against the back of her hand. It would be easy to fall in love with Jace Black, if she were the sort of person who could do that.

"Viewers, I wish you could have seen them before the cameras were rolling. These two can hardly keep their hands off each other." Molly shook her head, smiling. "But, you know, a lot of your fans are worried about you, Jace." Krystal knew what was coming. "Most of the country was devastated when they heard your story. Your wife, Nikki, and your son, Ben. It must be hard to move on."

Jace held Krystal's hand in both of his, clearing his throat. "Yes, ma'am."

Her heart ached for him. "He has this way of looking at things. Finding the best. Kind and...supportive. He's a gentleman," Krystal said. "I tease him a little—Gentleman

Jace—because I've never met anyone like him." More truths. Maybe this wouldn't be that hard after all.

"When we met, I felt like I knew her. I could probably recite most of the songs she's written—they helped me get through losing my grandmother. And my wife and son." He shook his head. "Singing with her is special."

"I've heard the two of you." Molly nodded. "Your chemistry comes through. Why do you think you two clicked, Krystal?"

"Well…" She took a deep breath. "He wouldn't give up, for one thing. I was worried, like his fans, about hurting him. I mean, he's him. He has the biggest heart." She looked at their joined hands. "He is the only person who sees me for who I am and believes in me."

"He won you over?" Molly asked.

Krystal nodded, wishing this interview were over. It was a little too honest, felt a little too real. Because everything she was saying and feeling was real.

"Jace, are you excited to be performing at the Austin Country Music Festival? This is a pretty big deal for you."

He nodded.

"Being onstage with some of country music's biggest names. You'll be singing your duet, won't you?"

Which was news to her. She'd been planning on ducking out of the event. An impossibility if they were singing together.

"Yes, ma'am," he answered.

"It has to be overwhelming, coming face-to-face with so many music legends."

"Having coffee and donuts with Hank King?" He shook his head. "Kissing her?" He chuckled. "Not sure I'll ever get used to it."

He was so much better at this than she was. More comfortable.

"There's a lot of buzz about Tiger Whitman's award, a man so instrumental in so many performers' lives." She paused. "What do you think of his new protégé, Becca Sinclair? People are talking about how talented she is, for someone so young. Have you heard her?"

Krystal spent most of the time trying not to think about Tig. And, for a while, he'd laid low. But she'd never thought about this. He was mentoring a new singer? Her blood went cold. For a few seconds, her brain shut down. No hearing or thinking, just a terrible heavy coldness sinking into her bones. She'd let this happen.

"What do you think?" Jace asked, pressing a kiss to her forehead.

She blinked. Jace's kiss helped pull her back to the present.

"We'd love to hear part of the single," Molly said.

"Sure." She forced a smile, doing her best not to panic when Jace let go of her hand. She had to fight against the panic, the crushing weight against her chest, until they weren't in front of the cameras.

Jace was handed his guitar.

He turned his chair to face her. "Good?" He knew something was up.

She nodded.

They sang the first verse through, singing the chorus twice before Molly started clapping.

"I have to say, I wish you both the very best. It's nice to see the two of you so happy." She shook their hands. "I have a feeling you guys have a bona fide hit on your hands."

A few seconds later, the cameras cut, and they stood to have their mics removed.

"Thanks for inviting me," Molly said. "I was sure it was all a stunt until I saw you two together. It's refreshing, honestly. I hope it all works out."

Krystal let Jace do the talking, doing her best to nod or smile or act like she was listening. When her father joined them—after offering Molly tickets to the evening's show and escorting her and her crew from the coliseum—Krystal wanted to go, but her feet were too leaden to move.

"What's up?" Jace smoothed her hair from her shoulders.

She stared up at him.

"What's wrong?" His hands caught hers. "Your hands are like ice, Krystal."

"Nothing." *Everything.* She was pretending to be a normal woman in a normal relationship—neither of which was true. Her personal nightmare had appeared again, but this time, he was targeting someone else. "We did good, right?" she asked, trying to hold it together, but her mind wouldn't stop. Maybe she was wrong. Maybe he'd changed? There was no guarantee he'd try that again. He'd never touched Emmy Lou. It was possible he'd learned his lesson, right?

Jace was rubbing her hands. "You don't need to worry."

"Good." She nodded.

"You ready?" It was her father, his warm arm around her shoulders. "Jace, let's give her a hand."

Something about his touch hit a nerve. Because he knew—she could see it on his face. He was thinking what she was thinking. "Daddy." She stared up at him, nausea and regret choking her.

"I know." His jaw set. "Come on, now. Let's get you some water."

Maybe it was the sympathy on her father's face. Maybe it was Jace's confusion. Maybe it was the self-loathing that she'd never thought about her choices beyond her family. Whatever the cause, a surge of anger had her shaking them off. "I'm fine." She sighed, forcing a smile. "I'm fine." It was a lie; chances were they both knew it. But she didn't care. She had to get to her bus. Somewhere alone, where she could find the strength to do what needed to be done—confront her fears.

Jace sat in the window seat of the bus, the fluorescent streetlights casting flashing patches of light as they passed. Tomorrow, they'd reach Austin and a few days of rest. Heather would be flying in for the weekend; he'd already got a weekend pass to ACMF for her. She was more excited to see the Kings again than the festival—but he figured that would change when she saw the lineup.

She was thrilled about his relationship with Krystal.

Krystal.

Since this morning, he'd been trying to figure out the common denominator between the back-and-forth about ACMF and Krystal's fast escape after the interview. CiCi had never come right out with it, but he'd filled in the blanks. Tig Whitman. Once Travis had crashed in the recliner and Hank had taken one of the bunks in the back of the bus, he'd been scrolling through articles that mentioned Tiger Whitman. Or Uncle Tig, to his friends.

The man was a legend.

He was a big guy. Barrel-chested with a great smile. Balding on top. Fond of cigars and vintage cars. There were plenty of pictures of the man. The pictures of him with celebrities were even more impressive. He seemed to know just about everyone. He had been especially close to the Kings—until ten years ago. He was the one who'd discovered Hank in a little honky-tonk on the Texas/Oklahoma border.

There were pictures of him at concerts. Pictures of him with the King kids. Pictures of him shaking hands with the heads of Wheelhouse Records on the day the King children became the Three Kings. And pictures of him with Hank when he won one of his many awards.

He'd been a fixture in their home—downright chummy with CiCi. And then he wasn't.

The bus slowed and Jace peered out at the brightly illuminated gas station.

"We stopping?" Travis tipped his hat back.

"Looks like it." Jace powered off the tablet and set it aside.

Travis stood and stretched. "Where are we?"

"Middle of nowhere." Jace ran a hand over his face, rubbing his eyes. "Guess we're getting gas."

"I could stretch my legs." Travis rolled his head. "Get some snacks. You in?"

Jace nodded.

The bus parked and he and Travis climbed down. Other than a few big rig trucks and one church youth bus, there were only a handful of cars.

"Guess the girls are sleeping." Travis nodded. Their bus was here, their driver was pumping gas, but no sign of Emmy Lou or Krystal.

Inside, Jace hunted down some Red Vines, sour gummy bears, a box of chocolate-caramel chews, and two cherry colas. And a bag of dog treats. If she was asleep, he'd leave it for her to find in the morning.

The checkout lady gave him his total, then looked back and forth between them. "Ohmygawd. Ohmygawd. You're that guy—the one that won that show. I voted for you every week. You can sing, you deserved to win. And, now, I saw you and Krystal King together. Saw you two this morning, all sweet together. And you're…" She clapped her hands. "You're Travis. Ohmygawd. *The* Travis King."

"That I am," Travis offered. "He's Jace."

"Right, Jace." The woman was all smiles, eyeing the stash Jace had deposited on the checkout counter. "You sure got a sweet tooth."

"It's not all for me." He held up the dog treats.

"Those are for Clementine, aren't they?" The woman nodded. "And everyone knows Krystal's favorite candy are Red Vines." She held up the bag. "Smart fella, to keep his woman happy."

Travis eyed his stash. "Guess you're not riding with me?"

Jace smiled. Hopefully not. But there was no predicting how Krystal would respond to his shameless bribe. He might end up walking the rest of the way to Austin.

The woman grinned. "You be safe on the roads."

Jace paid and nodded his thanks. "Not getting anything?"

"Still looking." Travis shook his head, searching the end rack of artificially sweetened cakes and donuts. He picked up a pack of chocolate-covered cupcakes. "I told her."

"What?" Jace asked.

"Krystal. About you two. The whole friends crap." He grabbed a pink cupcake pack, too. "And now this *pretend* relationship. There's nothing pretend about it and you know it." He sighed. "Why are women so damn stubborn?"

"You're asking me?" Jace laughed. "See you in Austin."

Travis nodded. "Beef jerky." He headed to the massive

rack of dried jerky as Jace slipped out and crossed the parking lot.

"Hey, George." He nodded at the driver. "Anyone awake in there?"

"Check for yourself." He smiled.

It was dark inside the bus, the red glow of the emergency lights doing only so much. Once his eyes adjusted to the gloom, he walked to the end of the hall—Krystal's room. Light spilled out from under the door. He knocked and Clementine barked.

"Just me," he whispered.

She shushed Clem, her words and footsteps muffled until she opened the door. "I'm pretty sure you're on the wrong bus." But she didn't look or sound irritated—just curious.

"Maybe." He held out the bag. "I brought you something. Both of you. Thought you might want a snack."

She stepped back, waving him in, then closed the door. "You bought dog biscuits?" That had her smiling. "Look at that, Clementine. He knows the way to a gal's heart. Dog treats and chocolate caramels. Oh, wait, Red Vines and sour gummy bears?" Her smile grew. "You must want something."

"Nope." He held his hands up. "I come in peace. No ulterior motives."

"Hmm. We'll see." She gave him a full toes-to-head assessment.

Her long hair was down, no makeup, rainbow-striped fuzzy socks, and a massive T-shirt with a unicorn on it.

She looked adorable. Until he read her shirt. "I'm a unicorn. I will cut you." He frowned. "That's…cute."

"Travis. He thought it was hysterical." She shrugged and flopped down on her bed. "You can stay, but I'm sort of in the middle of something." Papers covered her bed—scraps of paper, note cards, a napkin, some sheet music highlighted and scribbled notations in a variety of vibrant colors.

"World domination?" The sheet music caught his attention.

"That's next on my to-do list." She stared up at him, green eyes flashing. "If you stay, I might tell you."

"I'll take that as an invitation." Which was good because this was exactly where he wanted to be.

"Sit." She patted the bed. "I could use a fresh set of ears." She sat cross-legged, tugged her shirt over her bare knees, and scooped her guitar off the ground. "Working on the melody mostly. I have a few ideas." She pointed at one sheet. "But I'll know what I want when I hear it." She tapped out a soft beat against the side of her guitar.

He nodded, his eyes scanning the music. It was the music she'd been humming that night in her kitchen. "This is the pie night song."

"Pie night?" She laughed, her fingers stopping. "You remember that?"

"Damn good pie." He winked her way before reading over the lyrics. "You want to play it for me?"

She hesitated, chewing her lip again. With a nod of

her head, she said, "If you open those Red Vines, I might consider it."

He opened the bag and held one out to her. She leaned down, mouth open, to bite the end of the Red Vine. But she changed direction and leaned farther forward, planting a quick kiss on his cheek. Red Vine in her mouth, she sat back, grinning.

A kiss on the cheek and he was happy. Damn happy. "What was that for?"

"Nothing." She shrugged, the Red Vine hanging from the corner of her mouth. Her fingers strummed over the guitar strings, her gaze moving over the pages in front of her. "I'm thinking this." She plucked out the notes, pausing now and then to try a different chord or tempo.

"Faster but lower." He nodded when she got it. "That."

She leaned forward, her Red Vine almost gone, to scribble more notes on the page. "I like that."

"I've held her forever, right here in my arms. Protect her and love her and keep her from harm. From my baby girl to the love of his life. More than my daughter, now she's his wife." He paused. "The sunshine, the flowers, the smile on her face. A walk down the aisle, to her favorite place. Standing beside the one who she loves. Exchanging promises before the man up above."

He paused, reading ahead. "Wait…"

"That's the chorus." She tapped the paper with her Red Vine.

He nodded, hummed, then sang. "She's smiling, she's happy, in her pretty white dress. And I gave her up, 'cause

I knew he was best…" He glanced up at her, then back at the page. "We both love her, need her, will put her first. But it's his turn now. I'm watching her dancing, dancing, in someone else's arms." He stared at her. "Father-daughter song?"

Krystal nodded, another Red Vine in her mouth. "For my daddy. If he likes it."

"He will." Jace stared at the words. "Might be a good wedding song? That whole daddy-daughter dance thing." He sat forward, grabbing a pencil from the pile of writing tools and jotting a note. "Fiddle. Right here?" He looked at her. "And guitar."

She picked up the page, her green eyes widening. "Yes. You are a genius." She stared at him.

"You won't hear me argue." He leaned back against the wall, lifting his arm so Clementine could make herself at home in his lap. "You heard her, right, Clem? That right there was a compliment. From your momma."

"Don't get used to it." She waved her Red Vine at him, yawning.

"Wouldn't dream of it." But he caught her Red Vine in his mouth and yanked it out of her hand.

"I thought those were for me?" Another yawn.

"I thought you'd share?" He lifted up Clementine. "What's that? You're disappointed in her?"

Krystal's smile faded a little. "Join the club."

It was like a punch to the gut. Not just her words, but her attempt at dismissing the slip that said so much. She didn't want his sympathy or his questions but she did want him. He'd work with what he had. He set Clem down on the bed beside him, stacked up the papers and note cards, and put them on the floor by the bed.

"What are you doing?" she asked, watching as he kicked off his boots.

"Getting some sleep." He stood, tugging off his shirt and opening her closet for a hanger. "Borrowing this." No answer. He hung up his shirt and turned to find her staring at his tattoos. She had a thing for his tattoos. "If that's okay?"

"Sleep?" she repeated, definitely staring at his tattoos.

At least he had her full attention. "Unless there was something else you had in mind?" He paused, the zipper on his jeans halfway down.

She shook her head.

"You sure?" He waited, hands on hips.

She shook her head again.

He grinned, pushing his jeans off and laying them over her dresser.

She giggled then. "What the hell are you wearing?"

He stared down. "Boxers." The green repeating pattern wasn't so bad. But over the front closure was the print of one large hundred-dollar bill.

"What is on them?" she asked, leaning forward.

"Money." He bobbed his eyebrows at her. "Gives a whole new meaning to 'show me the money.'"

Their eyes met. "I've seen it." Her voice was husky.

He nodded. In two long steps, he'd flopped onto the bed beside her. "Good damn thing, too. I'm worn out. All this pretend relationship stuff is hard work."

She was staring at him, conflicted.

He held his arms out to her. "Come here."

She hesitated. "To sleep?"

"That's the plan." He yawned.

"You came here to sleep?" She was crawling up the mattress, hair falling over her shoulder, fighting back a yawn.

He hadn't had a single expectation when he'd knocked on her door. "I came here to see you."

She sat, staring down at him. "Jace."

"Krystal." He reached up, running his fingers through her hair.

"This is pretend," she whispered, even as she leaned into his touch. "We agreed."

"I know." *You keep telling yourself that.*

"You're making things all...mixed up." Her gaze was mapping his tattoos. Then her finger, slowly, along the outside of his arm to the inside of his elbow. She shuddered.

"How?" He murmured, the dilation of her pupils and hitch in her breath challenging the whole sleep and comfort thing. He'd have to be dead not to respond to her. But, tonight, he wanted to hold on to this different, fragile intimacy building between the two of them.

"Now. Doing...this." She shook her head, blinking. "Being...you."

He caught her hand in his. "I knew you weren't a fan of the name..."

She laughed, her hand squeezing his. "Stop."

"I'm not doing a thing." He tried to pull his hand away, but she held on. "I'm trying to sleep."

With an eye roll, she lay down, her head resting on his chest. "Fine."

"Fine." He stared up at the ceiling, smiling.

Her hand rested lightly over his heart.

"Good?" He couldn't resist pulling her closer, resting his hand on her side, turning into her, burying his nose at her temple.

She nodded, her fingers pressing against his bare skin. "It's growing on me."

"Oh?" Her scent flooded his nostrils.

"Your name," she whispered, draping her arm across his waist.

He chuckled, pressing a kiss to the top of her head.

Chapter 13

KRYSTAL WOKE TO THE STOP AND START OF THE BUS. She peered at the clock. Almost seven. If they were on track, they'd be turning onto the long drive of her family home within an hour.

She stared down at Jace, who was snoring softly.

An hour before the rest of the world interrupted.

She rested her chin on his chest, studying him in the dim light slipping through the blinds of her window. Where had he come from? How had he wound up here? And how was she ever going to get over him? The last question hurt. Whether she liked it or not, she cared about Jace. She'd practically attacked him onstage because she'd missed him so much. Not his body, him.

His voice. His honesty. The way he looked at her—the way he saw her.

What am I doing?

He was gorgeous. Every inch of him. He'd thrown his arm up over his head, showcasing muscles and ink. His face, turned toward her, had dark stubble along his jaw. A thick, chiseled, manly jaw. His mouth? That was one of her favorite features. Not only could his smile turn her to mush, but the man could kiss.

What am I doing?

She should get up, take a shower, get dressed, and do

her best to put some distance between them. She wasn't ready to admit the damage was done between them; she couldn't. Jace Black wasn't meant to wind up with someone like her. She tore her gaze from his face, doing her best to get a handle on the very real, very overwhelming sense of joy and dread, hope and loss, want and self-loathing.

"What am I doing?" She lay back on the bed, her heart aching.

The bed shifted and Jace was leaning over her. "Kissing me good morning."

She nodded, cradling his face—his beautiful face—in her hands.

A crease formed between his brows. Cautious. Maybe even a little bit concerned.

She pulled him down, her lips catching his in a lingering caress. One hand pressed to her cheek, his thumb stroking her cheekbone. He was gentle with her, like she was something to treasure. His smile, against her lips, was impossible to resist. His mouth, the sweep of his tongue, his soft moan against her throat.

Terrifying or not, she was falling for him.

His kiss deepened, slow and leisurely.

She shuddered, her hands sliding down his back.

"You okay?" he whispered against her cheek.

She nodded. "I…" She swallowed, needing him. If she didn't get out of her head, her heart would lead her down a path she'd never survive. He would leave her. She couldn't love him. She couldn't love. Even if he made her wish she could.

He pressed a kiss to her forehead, the tip of her nose, her chin.

"Please," she whispered, aching for him. All of him. So much.

He smoothed her hair from her face and stared down at her, the fire in his eyes tempered with something infinitely more powerful. And binding.

It was different this time. His invasion was slow and sweet, filling her completely. Her fingers dug into his hips, reveling in the weight of his body against hers. Every thrust was deliberate, stroking something deep inside, demanding her response. Her body clenched and he paused, his breath powering out of him. He kissed her, his gaze boring into hers as he started to move again.

Would he still look at her like this if he knew what she'd done?

She pressed her eyes closed.

"Krystal." His lips moved over hers. "Hey. Look at me."

Her eyes fluttered open, her hands resting on his shoulders as their eyes locked.

He smiled down at her, one hand sliding beneath her shirt to lift her hips. Between the torturous rhythm he'd set, the kneading of his hands on her hips, and the look on his face, she had no choice. It was too intense. Too perfect. Too real. And it rolled over her with a ferocity she wasn't prepared for. "Jace." She gasped. "I'm coming." In that instant, she split into a million blissful pieces— and every single one of them loved him.

He groaned, bending forward to kiss her and holding her against him. Watching his release was mesmerizing. His jaw locked, nostrils flared, the cords in his neck... He held nothing back from her and it left her shaken.

It took a few minutes to realize the bus was no longer moving.

"Shit." She stared up at him. "Shit. Shit."

"I'm taking it there's a problem?" He was grinning, so damn gorgeous she was almost willing to ignore the fact that they could be discovered at any moment.

"The bus." She squeaked. "Jace. We're not moving."

He rolled off her. "Got it."

He was dressed in no time, smoothing the bed and feeding Clementine before she'd found something to wear. "I'm going to take this little lady out to do her business."

Clementine danced on dainty feet, whimpering.

"I think she'd appreciate that." Krystal nodded.

With a wink and a nod, he and Clementine left her alone. She sat on the edge of the bed, more than a little unsettled.

"Hey." Emmy Lou poked her head in. "We got behind last night so we're fueling up. Still an hour or so out."

Krystal moaned and flopped back on her bed. "Good."

Emmy laughed. "Don't be too relieved. Travis and Daddy brought breakfast."

Krystal covered her face. "Great."

The bed sank beside her and Emmy Lou took her hand. "I'm pretty sure you're the only one in denial at this point."

She didn't answer. There wasn't a single thing she could say.

"What were you two working on?" Emmy asked. "Looks like you got a lot done."

Krystal peeked through her fingers. Her sister wasn't the type to make sex jokes. That was when she saw the music sheets in her sister's hand. She giggled.

Emmy shot her a look. "Daddy seen this yet?"

"We just finished it." She sat up. "Think he'll like it?"

"He's going to love it." She handed her the pages. "You should show him."

"As a distraction? Or because you think the song is ready?" There were so many notes, scratch throughs, and rewrites, she was amazed Emmy could make out any of it.

Emmy blushed. "It can't hurt to show him the song."

With a sigh, Krystal followed her sister down the hall to the main cabin. Her father, Travis, and Jace were all eating sausage rolls and laughing. Apparently, she'd been worrying for nothing. She and Emmy exchanged a "whatever" look.

"Hungry?" her father asked.

"Probably starving," Travis said, smiling up at her.

"I am." Krystal took a sausage roll. "Here, Daddy. Jace and I wrote this."

"Don't believe her," Jace interrupted. "She had it all figured out—"

"You fixed the tempo," she interrupted.

"That's nothing." He was grinning and staring at her.

Her cheeks felt hot. "It's something." She spun away

from them and made herself a cup of coffee, humming softly while the little coffee maker filled her favorite "The best breed is a rescue" coffee mug. But when she turned back, they were all watching her.

Except her father—he was poring over the sheet music.

Travis appeared to be in shock.

Emmy was a little happy and a little worried.

And Jace... She wasn't ready to interpret what that expression meant. All she knew was that it made her feel good. Special. Worthy.

What am I doing? She took a sip of her coffee and prayed the last leg of the trip went fast.

But when the bus pulled down the long Spanish-oak-lined drive, Krystal's panic returned—like a sledgehammer to the chest.

"Luke says it's close to the studio," Jace was saying. "I can't keep taking advantage of your generosity."

It was no big deal. Jace should have his own place, some privacy. She just wished she'd had a little heads-up to get used to the idea of not having him around all the time.

"I wish Luke had said something." Her father was shaking his head. "We've got plenty of room. Hate to see you throwing money away."

"Wheelhouse is paying for it." Jace shrugged, the fabric of his T-shirt pulling tight across his shoulders.

She'd miss those shoulders.

Her father nodded. "Of course they are." He glanced

her way. "Probably best. You two keep spending too much time together, you might start to believe you're a couple. And that would be terrible." He chuckled.

Her daddy was teasing her about Jace? "I can give that song to someone else." She held her hand out.

Hank shook his head, reaching out to tuck a curl behind her ear. "I'm not giving it up. Sometimes I marvel at the things you put to music. You did good, baby girl."

Her daddy's praise had always mattered. She held on to it as the bus doors opened and they climbed down the steps to a world far removed from their life on the road. Probably for the best. Real life always caught up in the end. Better to let things cool down between them before they headed out on the next leg of the tour.

Luke was waiting, leaning against the same four-door diesel pickup truck Jace had driven before.

"Looks like you've got a ride," Hank said, holding out his hand. "I'll see you at the studio in the morning, son."

Jace shook his hand. "Yes, sir."

By the time the bus was unpacked and they were the only two hedging their goodbyes, Krystal's panic was barely under control. She had no reason to go to the studio in the morning. No reason to spend time with him between now and their first ACMF rehearsal. And it felt…wrong. For the last few weeks, she'd come to rely on him. His presence, his voice, and his touch had become a necessary part of her day. Now she was supposed to be okay without him?

He stared down at her, his light brown gaze wandering

over her face. "You're not going to make this easy, are you?"

She didn't know what that meant. Or what she was supposed to say. If she could manage to say a damn thing.

The corner of his mouth quirked up. "I don't want to go."

She could breathe a little easier. "You don't?"

He shook his head.

"Why?"

He swallowed, stepping forward to run his fingers through her hair. Their gazes locked and held. The way he looked at her—unflinching and intense—had her pulse racing. "You know why."

No. No, she didn't. Nothing her far-too-imaginative brain could come up with made any sense. The other options, the ones that made her heart swell with hope and want, were too unrealistic to believe. No matter how much she might want to believe…Jace, caring about her—really caring about her—was terrifying. Deflecting was what she did best. "There aren't any reporters around, Jace." She rolled her eyes and tried not to hyperventilate.

"If you're not prepared for the answer, you shouldn't ask the question." His hand settled on the back of her neck as he stepped forward to kiss her. She should move away, turn her head… Instead, she put her arms around his neck.

A kiss goodbye was not a big deal. Or a few gentle, soft, lingering kisses.

"Dammit." He was pulling her close then, kissing her

until holding on to him was the only thing keeping her on her feet. "I'm gonna miss you." And he let go.

She stood, frozen in place, as his boots carried him farther away. When he climbed into the truck and started the ignition, she kept waiting for him to stop, to look her way and wave goodbye. He didn't. He and Luke and that massive truck drove down her driveway and disappeared around the bend.

Clementine barked and ran around in a circle, tail waving like a poof-topped flag. Krystal scooped her up and held her close. "He didn't say goodbye to you," she whispered, preferring anger to this…this ridiculous sadness she was feeling.

"I've got a few pictures that might help you two deal with your separation." Travis was looking all kinds of pleased with himself. While everyone else had the common decency to give them a moment alone, her brother remained—to tease her without mercy. Why hadn't she noticed?

Right, because she'd been too caught up in Jace to know or care if they had an audience of a thousand. What was wrong with her? She knew better than to put herself in this position. To put Jace in that position. Right here, in front of her house, with her mother and who knows who else looking for some tidbit of information to be used against her. If she wasn't more careful, Jace would definitely fall into the to-be-used-against-her category. "Travis." She snapped, so wound up she didn't know what to say or think. "I'm warning you, I'm not in the mood."

"I hate to break it to you, Little Sister, but that's pretty much your mood every day." He draped an arm around her shoulders.

"Why are you still here?" she grumbled.

"I dropped this." He held out his lucky pocketknife. "Wasn't after more pictures or anything. Not saying I didn't get a few."

Her eyes were burning and her throat felt tight, so she glared up at him.

"I'm teasing." But he wasn't smiling now. "Come on, Krystal. He didn't know. Daddy thought he was staying with us—pretty sure Jace did, too," he said, leading her to the house. "Luke called when you were still getting dressed. If it makes you feel any better, he didn't look too happy about it, either."

It shouldn't matter. It shouldn't. But, somehow, it did. She stared up at her brother. "Really?"

Travis stopped, his expression shifting. Sheer incredulousness widened his eyes. "Holy shit."

She frowned, pulling away from him and hurrying toward the front door.

"You have got to be kidding me." He was fast, running to catch up with her. "Krystal." He grabbed her arm and spun her around. "You realize Momma will eat him alive if she thinks this is real."

"It's not." She nodded, trying again—with all-too-forced conviction. "You know it's not." *It was. It is.*

Travis started laughing. "I don't know who I feel sorrier for: you or Jace."

She yanked free, tucked Clem close, and braced herself for the reunion with her mother.

"I don't need all this." Jace looked around the fully furnished apartment a few miles from the studio and about twenty minutes from Austin.

Luke chuckled. "You need to stop thinking like that. It's not all about need anymore."

He glanced at his manager. Luke Samuels was a decent enough guy but there were times Jace knew they'd never connect. Luke had never wanted for a thing. Jace had learned to make do without wanting. "I'm not wired that way." Jace opened the refrigerator. "Who did the shopping?"

"Wheelhouse hired a personal shopper." Luke didn't bother looking up from his phone. "Tomorrow is booked solid so try to get some sleep tonight."

Luke rattled off his itinerary. Studio, lunch meeting with a cologne company, studio, and Austin Country Music Festival mixer. "Did you get all that?" Luke asked.

"Yeah." He nodded. Luke had been downright crabby since they'd left the Kings' place. It wasn't like Jace had made his feelings about Krystal a secret. Then again, Luke hadn't kept his feelings a secret, either. "Might want to look these over." He pulled some magazines and newspapers from his ever-present messenger bag and spread them on the marble kitchen counter.

Jace nodded, eyeing the collection of print with him and Krystal covering the pages. "Huh." He picked up one especially good picture of Krystal, hard-pressed not to smile.

"I've got a meeting." He sighed, looking at Jace. "The place is yours, man. Do what you will with it. You're somebody now. That can be a good thing." He clapped him on the shoulder. "It also means you have options." He nodded at the magazines then. "I'll see you in the morning."

"Or you can tell me where to meet you for the lunch?" Jace offered, hoping Luke would take the hint. He needed a break from…everything.

Luke nodded. "Even better. Cool. I'll text you the address, man."

Once the front door closed, he did a slow spin, taking in the town house the record label had rented for him. Three bedrooms—why did he need three bedrooms? Two bathrooms. It'd be nice not to have to share when Heather arrived. The hot tub in the small, high-walled garden out back was a nice surprise. A massive grill, too. Even better since the chrome-and-marble kitchen was full of gadgets he had no idea how to use.

He headed to the refrigerator, his stomach grumbling. For real food. A steak sounded just about right. Hopefully this personal shopper had thought to get some. He rummaged through the refrigerator and came up with a package of two petit sirloins.

"Those are some sad-looking steaks." He sighed.

One magazine caught his eye and he picked it up, skimming the article about their blossoming relationship. Seeing himself side by side with Krystal was a dose of reality.

She was Krystal King. He was some overnight reality show singer. For the last couple of weeks, he'd forgotten that they came from different worlds. To him, Krystal was a damaged, creative soul, and he was the damn fool falling head over heels in love with her.

His phone vibrated. He set the steaks aside and pulled out his phone from his pocket.

Hey big brother. Can't wait to see you.

He nodded. **Me neither.**

She peppered him with questions. What should she pack? Where were they going? Who would they see? He answered as best he could.

Wow. You are like no help. And a laughing emoji.

I'll ask Krystal. Love you.
Love you too.

There was that picture again, the bowling alley one. Seeing her that way, relaxed, in his arms, filled him with a sense of rightness. Right or wrong, he had it bad for this woman. Damn near spilling his heart out in the driveway of the King homestead wasn't part of the plan. He'd be seeing plenty of her over the next few days. Then they'd be back on the road together for the East Coast leg of the tour. But that hadn't made leaving her this morning any easier.

He sat on one of the kitchen stools, spreading out the magazine and papers Luke had left. A dozen different pictures of them, but one thing never changed. He wasn't the only one looking at her like she was the air he needed to breathe. She looked at him like, maybe, he was important. Maybe he was a fool for falling for her, but there wasn't a damn thing he could do to stop it.

His phone vibrated.

Krystal.

Somehow, seeing her name made the new surroundings and quiet not seem so alien to him. He wasn't sure what he'd been expecting, but a close-up picture of Clem, a tiny pink studded bow clipped in the poof on top of her head, was not it. **She's upset you didn't say goodbye.**

Getting out of there had been a top priority. Saying goodbye to Clementine? Not so much. The dog was cute and all, but it was her owner he was interested in. A whole hell of a lot.

Nothing a dog biscuit can't fix.

He waited for her response.

Another picture. Clem, dog biscuit in her mouth, and Krystal, a Red Vine in hers. He smiled, running a finger over her face. There was nothing prettier. Nothing.

Never cared much for Red Vines before.

That's plain sad and wrong, Jace Black. I'm not sure I can associate with someone who can't appreciate the delectable yumminess of a Red Vine. Then another text. Before what?

Caught that one?

He chuckled.

Before you. You free for dinner?

It took a minute for her text to come in.

Not a good idea. Momma's on the warpath. I'd like to keep you out of the line of fire.

He frowned, then dialed her number. FaceTime.

"Hello?" Her hair was in a tangled bun on her head. "What are you doing?" She was walking quickly across the marble hallway.

"Calling you." He smiled.

She rolled her eyes. "Why? You left, like, an hour ago."

"Figure I should set the record straight." He slid off the kitchen stool.

"That sounds ominous." She was practically running down the hall.

"Where are we going?" he asked.

"My room." She glanced back over her shoulder. "Hold on."

He did, his view alternating between her bare feet and

the tile floor. Once they were in her room, it was white carpet and then her face. "Okay, go ahead."

He smiled. She smiled back.

"Hi."

She flopped onto her bed, holding the phone up and over her.

Just like he'd been this morning. Braced over her. Staring into her eyes. Making love to her. In that moment, he'd have given just about anything to have her within reach. He cleared his throat.

"What record are you setting straight?" Against the muted green of her quilt, her eyes were bright, more mesmerizing than ever.

"It's not your job to protect me from the media or your mother."

She blinked. "That's why you called me?" Her forehead wrinkled.

"Maybe I miss...having company." He shrugged.

Her eyes narrowed. "Company?"

"You."

She smiled. "Oh."

"I know you miss me, too. You don't have to say it." He shook his head.

She was still smiling. "I didn't say a thing. How's your place?"

He shrugged. "Big. Too big for just me. Empty."

"You need a dog." Krystal turned away as Clementine ran into view, doing her best to bathe Krystal's face in doggy kisses.

"I'm good. Wouldn't want Clem to get jealous." He paused. "If I were going to find a good steak place, around six, where should I go?"

She nibbled on her bottom lip. "Are you looking for a recommendation? Or trying to get me to meet you?"

"A man's got to eat."

She rolled over, her phone resting on the bed and looking down at him. Most of her hair had slipped loose. He liked this view just as much. Better if she were naked and here with him. "Damn," he bit out.

"What?" Her green eyes sparkled.

"Nothing." He shook his head.

"Daddy's favorite steak place is Frank's Steakhouse."

"Frank's it is." He stood up. "Guess I'll get cleaned up and head that way."

She sat up. "Jace." She cleared her throat.

He nodded.

"Guess I should practice at this pretend thing a little?" She cleared her throat again. "I miss you."

"Maybe I should come over." He'd come up with a reason—other than needing to see her.

"No." She shook her head. "You are not."

He nodded. "Yep."

"Jace, please."

She'd said that to him this morning, too. Breathless, clinging. And just like that, his blood was pumping; memories of this morning—deep inside her—kicked in. "Hearing you say please does things to me."

Her eyes fluttered shut. She rolled onto her side,

propped her phone on the pillow beside her, and stared at him. "Good." It was a whisper.

He shook his head, content to stay as they were.

"Heather texted." She smiled. "I'm going to take that girl shopping."

He groaned, thinking about the schedule Luke had for them. "Pretty sure I don't have time for that. Besides, she has clothes."

"I didn't say you were invited." She rolled her eyes. "You'd just slow us down."

He laughed. "I see how it is."

She grinned. "I gotta go."

"I'll see you tomorrow? At the mixer thing?"

"Maybe." But that look set in, far-off and remote, like she was fighting something only she could see. "We'll see."

"I only called to talk to Clem, anyway. Since she was upset with me." He smiled.

"Oh, really?" She held the phone out to Clem, who cocked her head at an angle. "Say goodbye, Clem."

Clementine stood up, her tail wagging.

"Bye, Clementine. You take care of your mommy for me." He waited, hoping she'd turn the phone around again.

"You tell Jace your mommy doesn't need anyone to take care of her, Clementine." And the phone went dark.

He hoped she'd show up at Frank's. She didn't.

He hoped she'd come over to his apartment. He didn't sleep for shit.

He and Hank put in a solid three hours at the studio the next morning, but no Krystal.

Luke's luncheon was a hit. He didn't mind the sample of cologne and aftershave they gave him, and the dollars were impressive enough, but Luke asked for a few days to mull over their offer.

A few more hours in the studio and he headed home to change for the mixer.

Luke was there. With Calvin Laramie.

"No," he said. "No offense, Cal, but you and I have a different notion of how I should look."

Calvin was definitely offended.

"Studio sent him." Luke crossed his arms over his chest. "The team is upstairs, waiting to get to work on you. Don't fight it, man."

Jace glared at Luke and headed upstairs, Calvin trailing behind.

The good news was the stylist had learned from his last visit. This time, he embraced Jace's clean-cut, low-maintenance vibe. He didn't say a word over the jeans Jace picked out. They were grey, not black, but they'd do. Jace was partial to his well-worn boots but Calvin handed him a pair of hand-tooled black Luccheses that made his mouth water. He wasn't sold on the black rodeo-cut shirt with stitching, but he let it go. When his hair was sprayed to hell and back and his stubble was deemed groomed enough, he climbed into his truck and headed to the Grand Old Texas Opera House off the famous Sixth Street in downtown Austin.

Crowds of cameras and folk armed with microphones lined the dark blue carpet leading into the Grand Ole Opry recreation. Luke had drilled him with questions to and from their luncheon, hoping to prepare him for the questions he'd likely be asked a couple dozen times or more.

He didn't miss a beat. Smile in place, lots of handshakes, a few awkward hugs. He could do this. And, yes, questions. Most were things like "How does it feel to be here tonight?" or "Who are you most excited to meet?" or "Where is Krystal?" That last one came up a lot. He was beginning to wonder the same thing. He found himself scanning the arriving vehicles, looking for a flash of sparkle and long blond hair.

Inside, the pace slowed.

It wasn't the first time he was struck by how out of place he was. He had the clothes and the hair and boots that cost more than his bills for six months. That didn't mean he fit. A sea of faces he knew through the albums and singles he'd played for hours straight. Clint Black. Tammy Wynett. Dierks Bentley. George Strait. Willie Nelson. Some good, some legends, and others he'd never quite figured out how and why their records were made.

Luke handed him a cold beer and helped guide him around the room. About an hour into the evening, same bottle in his hand, he was ready to call it a night. But he waited, knowing the Kings would show. She was worth the wait.

"Jace? You're Jace Black?" Tig Whitman approached

him. "Good to meet you, son. Nothing makes an old dog like me happier than seeing someone young and talented rise above the crowd." He was shaking his hand with a mighty grip. "Pure talent, son, pure talent."

"Thank you, sir. Good to meet you, Mr. Whitman." He nodded, torn between flattery and suspicion. If Hank King wasn't a fan of the man, there was a reason.

"Aw, now, my friends call me Tig, son. And I'm hoping we'll be friends. This here is my latest discovery. Becca, come say hello." He waved the teenager forward, draping his arm around her shoulders.

"It's nice to meet you." Becca smiled, her voice pitched low. "I'm a real fan of the show. And you."

"I hear you'll be singing?" he asked, leaning forward to hear her better.

She nodded. "Uncle Tig has this way of getting people to give him what he wants." But her tone was flat. Like maybe, that wasn't a good thing. "I'm so happy and excited to be here."

"You deserve it, sugar." Tig patted her head, beaming at her with pride.

There was something about her expression that made Jace ask, "You had a chance to check out the stage yet?" He paused. "They're setting up the stage out back."

She shook her head.

"I can take you." He glanced back and forth between Becca Sinclair and Tig Whitman.

"I'll be back?" It was a question, like she was asking permission.

"Sure, sure." Tig patted her. "You two go on and have some fun."

Jace wasn't sure what made him more uncomfortable, the relief on Becca's face or the slight narrowing of Tig Whitman's gaze.

"Water," he said, sliding his still-full beer back across the counter.

"Scotch on the rocks." Becca shrugged.

"Aren't you a little young for that?" he asked.

She shrugged. "I'm not that young." She knocked back her drink and slid her glass back across the counter. "It helps, you know? With nerves."

He didn't know. He'd never been much of a drinker. After Nikki and Ben, he'd never thought to take up the habit.

Once her drink was refilled, they slowly navigated the room and out through the oversized barn doors to the outdoor amphitheater.

"Fresh air." Becca sucked in a deep breath. Then downed a good half of her drink. Her giggle was nervous, brittle. "That's it?" She pointed at the stage.

"This time tomorrow, wall-to-wall fans." He nodded. "That's what I hear, anyway."

She was staring into her drink. "Never been a fan of crowds. Don't mind the studio, recording stuff…but this part." She shrugged. "Uncle Tig says I'm made for it, though. He knows what he's talking about?"

He wasn't sure what she was asking him. "You should switch to water."

"Okay." She nodded. "Can I get you something?"

He held up his still-full glass of water. "I'm good. Thanks."

He watched her go, beyond puzzled by the whole exchange. For someone so happy and excited to be here, she was awfully eager to get drunk. Nikki had been the same.

Not going there.

He took a sip of water. Over the rim of his glass, he saw the person he'd spent the last twenty-four hours aching to see. In a bold red dress that dipped low in the front, Krystal was drawing plenty of attention. Not that she noticed. From the way she was scanning the crowd, he knew she was looking for someone.

Or someone to avoid.

Mickey Graham was here—Luke had seen him.

And then there was Tig Whitman.

Whether or not she liked it, he wanted to be at her side when she ran into either of them.

She saw him before he got to her. If someone had told him she'd light up like a Christmas tree and make a beeline for him, he wouldn't have believed it. But she did.

"Hi." She stared up at him, inches away.

"Hi yourself." He slid an arm around her waist and kissed her. It wasn't nearly as long and deep and lingering as he'd have liked, but it was perfectly acceptable for where they were. "You look good enough to eat," he murmured in her ear.

"Promise?" Her eyes flashed.

His breath caught and he shook his head.

"Jace." Hank was shaking his hand. "How's your evening going?"

He was still recovering from Krystal's invitation to say more than "Fine. Good."

"Looking a little rough around the edges." Travis nodded at him.

He shrugged. "I've been here an hour."

Travis took his glass and sniffed. "You're not drinking. That's the problem. I'll get you something."

Krystal hooked her arm in his. "Anyone of interest here?"

"Everyone?" he asked. "I'm pretty sure everyone who's anyone is here." His fingers threaded with hers. "Mickey was playing pool a while back. But you and him and a pool cue might not go over too well for him."

She smiled up at him. "I like how you say that without an ounce of judgment."

"Not one." He couldn't stop looking at her. Or touching her. He let go of her hand long enough to slide an arm around her waist. He rattled off a few more names, including commentary on a few wardrobe choices that had her smiling.

"Anyone else?"

She swallowed. He knew—from the look on her face, he knew.

"Tig is here." He frowned. "I know he and your daddy have some sort of gripe. Might want to give him a heads-up."

She stepped closer to him. "Probably should." But she was staring around the room with wide eyes. Nervous. Beyond nervous. "Or I can text him and we can sneak out for that steak you were craving?" She faced him, smiling too bright. Something was wrong.

"Give me a sec." He squeezed her hand. "I'll go tell Luke."

"I'll go with you." Her hands held on to his, ice-cold. "Okay? Let's hurry."

That was when he noticed Tig Whitman, staring their way.

Chapter 14

IT HAD BEEN TEN YEARS SINCE SHE'D SEEN HIM. TEN years of nightmares and cold sweats, panic attacks and migraines, eating disorders and self-loathing. And he hadn't changed one bit. He was all smiles, charm, and booming laughter.

When he wasn't watching her.

When he was, she wanted to scrub every inch of herself clean with pure bleach.

Made worse by Becca Sinclair. How old was she? Young, that was clear. And more than a little lost.

Jace was doing his damnedest to get them out of there. Just when he'd managed to talk them out of one conversation, someone else was waiting. But they weren't the sort of people he could brush off, either. A partner at Wheelhouse Records. Two radio music execs. Luke and a rep for some cologne company Jace was thinking of being a spokesman for.

She did her best to smile and nod and act like she was engaged in what was going on. But sweat was trickling down her back and a powerful throb had started up at the base of her neck, winding a band of tension around her head.

It didn't matter if it was real or not; she couldn't shake the feeling of being watched.

"Good to see you, too." He was shaking hands again,

this time with a tattoo artist who admired his ink. She agreed wholeheartedly. And, right now, she needed some one-on-one time, held tight in his beautiful ink-covered arms.

"He has good taste." She tugged on his arm. "In tattoos."

He laughed, leading her toward the back. "Luke said they moved the truck around back. Thought we'd want a faster exit." The hall was long, dimly lit, and lined with concert posters from the last several decades.

"I appreciate that." She did. It was no secret that Luke wasn't her biggest fan.

"The faster the better." Unfortunately, he wasn't in a hurry to get her out of there for sex. He was getting her out of there because of her initial moment of terror. As bad as it was, and it was no picnic, she was proud of how well she was holding herself together. Now.

"Are we really getting a steak?" She had to run to keep up with him. "Or are you showing me your place?"

They passed the bathroom, dodging the door as it swung open and two tipsy women stumbled out into the hall, laughing.

He glanced back at her. "I'm not sure what we're doing."

She frowned. "That doesn't sound like much fun."

"Shit." He stopped. "He has the keys."

"Who?"

"Luke." He stared back at the chaos inside. He pulled out his phone from his pocket.

"He won't hear you." She argued. "Just go."

He shook his head, dialing his phone. It rang and rang. "Shit," Jace bit out. "I'm sorry."

Being a mixed-up mess of emotions had her scrambling for control. With Jace, that was always a struggle. "You have nothing to apologize for." She pressed a hand against his chest. "Nothing." It was important he know that. Because, of everyone in her life, it was true.

"Krystal, are you o—"

Kissing him was the best way to change the subject. No, she wasn't okay. But she would be. He could help with that. The way he saw her, the way he made her feel—like she wasn't something damaged and broken. It was a bittersweet fantasy that couldn't last. But, for now, she was going to enjoy every minute of it.

His hands were tangling in her hair as he spun her, pressing her against the wall. "Good try," he murmured against her lips. He cradled her face between his hands. "You can talk to me."

She wanted to. Oh so much. But she wasn't ready for this to end. "Go, get the keys. I'll fix my hair...or something." She headed for the bathroom, the fluorescent lights shockingly white after the near-gloomy hallway.

To the left was a powder room, likely one of the original dressing rooms for larger performance groups. To the right, the bathroom. She turned left and sat in one of the old, velvet-covered armchairs, her reflection staring back at her from one of the floor-to-ceiling mirrors.

"I saw you come in here." Becca Sinclair stood in the

door. "I just had to meet you. I mean, you have no idea what your music has meant to me. Your songs."

"Thank you." Krystal smiled. "Have a seat. It's a lot quieter in here. And cooler."

Becca hesitated, one arm wrapped around her waist. She was super skinny. All long limbs and big eyes. "Sure." She sat, her knobby knees peeking out from her frayed and studded white denim skirt.

"I like your skirt." Krystal studied the girl, fully aware that Becca was studying her right back. "And your boots."

"Jace seems really nice." She shook her head. "And you two? That's so cool."

"You met him?" she asked.

"He and Tig were talking." She shrugged. "You know how Tig is. Never met a stranger." Her gaze wandered, bouncing off the sconces mounted near the mirrors, the pictures and prints hanging on the wall, and the rings and bangles hanging off her own arms.

"He's always loved the sound of his own voice."

Becca stared at her, then burst into laughter. "Good one."

It would be too much to hope Becca would just come right out and say Tig was a good guy and had never done anything inappropriate to her. To anyone. Sixteen, twenty-one, to sixty and beyond. It didn't matter. But knowing he wasn't like that now, that her fear hadn't given him permission to move on to some other love-starved girl, mattered a whole hell of a lot.

"How long has Tig been handling you?" she asked.

Becca was wide-eyed. "Handling?"

"Representing?" She clarified.

"Oh." Her laugh was forced this time. "A couple of years. I was, gosh, seventeen? About?" She nodded. "He knows how to get things done." She was doing that avoidance thing, looking anywhere but Krystal.

And it made Krystal want to cry. "You know there are managers you could consider? If you're interested?"

Becca was playing with her bangle bracelets. "Why? He takes care of me." Her dark eyes met hers then. "After everything he's done for me, that wouldn't be right." She stood. "Anyway, I just wanted to say I'm a real big fan of yours. Real big."

Krystal smiled, her fingers gripping the arms of the chair. "I know this job can be hard sometimes, so if you ever want to talk, I'd be happy to listen."

"You mean that?" She took a deep breath. "Really?"

"Really." She nodded. "Us girls need to stick together. Here." She handed Becca her phone. "Plug in your number."

Becca did.

Krystal called her. "Now you have my number." She smiled. "Call me, for whatever. Whenever."

"Okay." Becca had a really sweet smile. "Okay, I will. Thanks." With an awkward little wave, she left.

Krystal sat forward, elbows on her knees, and covered her face with her hands. She didn't want to read into every little thing Becca had said or done. It was pointless and likely to drive her crazy. There wasn't much more she could do or say.

Wrong. She stared at herself again.

"You should have said it." She hugged herself. "Told her."

And if she was wrong? And Tig Whitman only had been her own monster? What then? Becca could go to the press—to Tig—and share Krystal's torment with the world. There was no damage control for that. She'd be labeled a liar. Her family? Their careers? Jace? All gone.

She curled up in the chair, resting her cheek on her knees, willing this all to go away.

"Krystal?" Emmy Lou touched her shoulder. "You okay? Headache?"

She nodded.

"You want to go?" She crouched down at her side. "Jace has the keys."

Krystal nodded again, looking her sister in the eyes. "You know I love you, right? That I'd never do anything, say anything, that would hurt you?" She swallowed down the lump in her throat. "I'd never make something up for attention?" It was still a whisper.

Emmy took her hand and stared at her. The sheen in her twin's eyes was bright, raw. "I know."

Krystal squeezed her hand.

"Are you okay? I know, with Mickey here, it had to be awkward." She wrinkled her nose.

"Mickey's here?" Krystal laughed.

"And Tig." Emmy Lou was watching her closely.

"I noticed." She gave her sister's hand another squeeze. "Daddy okay?"

"I don't know." She shrugged. "That vein in his forehead?" She waited for Krystal to nod. "It's all popped out. His cheeks are all red."

"Not good." Krystal stood. "Jace and I are going to Frank's. Try to get him out of here. We'll get a big table."

Side by side, there was no denying they were twins. Krystal spent more time in the gym, she was stronger, curvier than Emmy Lou. But working out was one way to burn off some tension—something she had more than her fair share of. Emmy Lou had a willowy quality, fragile in all the ways Krystal wasn't.

"Krystal." Emmy stopped her. "I know you think I can't handle whatever is going on but you're wrong. You're my sister and Daddy's my daddy, too. I hate that you're both eaten up with something. I might not be able to do anything, but I'd rather know—"

"No, you wouldn't, Em. Trust me." She hugged her sister. "I promise." She kissed her sister's cheek. "Text me about y'all joining us at Frank's?"

Emmy Lou nodded and followed her out of the powder room and out into the hall. "See you later." She waved and headed back down the hall to the party underway.

Jace was leaning against the hallway, jaw clenched tight.

"What happened to you?" she asked.

"Mickey Graham." He pushed off the wall.

She waited, staring up at him. "Care to elaborate?"

"I'm sure you'll read all about it in the paper tomorrow." He ran a hand over his face. "You ready?" He took her hand and led her to the door marked "Exit."

She nodded, doing her best not to smile. "Did my Gentleman Jace defend my honor?"

He shot her a look but didn't slow.

"And I missed it?"

Another look—but this time there was a ghost of a smile on his lips. He held the door open for her.

"Did anyone see?" That could be bad news. "Jace, I hope you didn't do anything stupid." She yanked him to a stop in the gravel parking lot.

He spun to face her. "Stupid? I'm pretty sure that ship has sailed." He opened his mouth, so close to saying something. Instead he shook his head and said, "But knocking Mickey Graham flat on his back wasn't it." His hand pressed against her cheek. "That he had coming."

Even though she was a strong, independent woman, his urge to protect her was a huge turn-on. "You know something, Jace?" Her hand covered his. "You are so hot."

His shock gave way to laughter. Deep, rich laughter that warmed her from the inside out. "You are a constant surprise."

He hadn't meant it as a reminder—he had no idea. But she did. And it left a bitter taste in her mouth. "You have no idea." She stood on tiptoe and tugged his head down, needing him to blot out everything else.

His arms were tight around her, crushing her against him as his lips met hers.

The click and flash of cameras had her pulling away. "Let's take this someplace more private."

He rested his forehead against hers. "I don't give a shit. Let them take pictures."

"I'm pretty sure we don't want pictures of what I want to do to you floating around." Her hands gripped the front of his shirt.

He groaned. "Nope." A final kiss and he was leading her toward his truck, parked on the edge of the lot, by the exit.

"Luke totally scores brownie points." She smiled, letting him help her up into his truck. "This brings back some memories, Mr. Black."

"I think you called me Jack or John or Justin then?" He shook his head, slammed the truck door, and came around to climb up and in beside her.

Halfway to Frank's, Emmy texted.

"Emmy says they're not coming." And Krystal was more than okay with that. Nothing sounded better than time, just her and Jace. "What's the plan?"

"Food." He looked at her.

With their milkshakes, burgers, and fries bagged up to go, they drove the rest of the way to his place, singing along to the radio.

"Nice," she said, sliding out of the truck and climbing the steps to his town house. "New construction?" The row of townhomes was finished and, except for his, there were no signs of occupancy.

"Don't ask me." He smiled, unlocking the door. "I just live here."

While he set up their drive-through dinner on the stone-topped dining table, she did a quick walk-through. "It's nice."

"It's…okay." He shrugged. "Sorta weird to live someplace I had no say-so in."

She nodded, sitting at the table and devouring her burger. "This is so good." Her vanilla milkshake was even better.

He was watching her, the bone-melting smile she'd come to expect from him doing just that. Until he said, "We need to talk."

She set her milkshake cup down. "No, that is absolutely the last thing we need to do." She shook her head for emphasis. "I need something from you, but it's not talking."

His laugh was reluctant. "Why won't you talk to me?"

"I don't talk to anyone." She leaned across the table, grabbed his shirt, and pulled him forward. "It's part of my charm. Besides, I thought most men weren't into all the touchy-feely talking stuff."

"I'm not most men." His kiss was light.

"Oh, I know." She was up, coming around the table to pull him to his feet. "I'd like to take the time to fully appreciate how not like most men you are." She unfastened his jeans, tugging the fabric open, and she dropped to her knees. She smiled up at him. "Starting now."

Jace was exhausted. Every time he attempted to have a conversation with Krystal, she'd used sex to make him forget everything except her hands, fingers, tongue, and mouth on his body. As far as a distraction technique went, it was highly effective.

But her determination to distract him only confirmed his suspicions. Whatever was bothering her, whatever the secret, it was at the root of her fears. From intimacy to confidence, it was all tied up in one another. And, dammit all, he was no closer to figuring it out.

She was sound asleep on her stomach, her hand on his chest.

That was something else he'd noticed. Her sleep was restless. Unless he was touching her or she was touching him. Almost as if knowing she wasn't alone kept the bad dreams away. Considering how little sleep either of them had the night before, he stayed in bed as long as he could. When the room was filled with sunlight and his stomach was growling, he slipped from the bed, pulled on his boxers, and headed downstairs to make breakfast.

The personal shopper nailed the breakfast thing. Bacon. Eggs. Crusty bread, sliced thick, for toast. Butter. Strawberry jam. Orange juice.

His phone was dead, so he plugged it into the charger and connected it to the sound system wired into the house before getting to work. His phone started blowing up with alerts about the time the front door opened and Heather walked inside.

"Heather?" He ran a hand over his face. "Dammit. I'm sorry." Messages from Heather.

"For what?" she asked, running over to hug him. "Smells good."

He chuckled, hugging his little sister tight. Damn, he was a bastard. More pinging. Messages from Emmy Lou. And Travis.

"Better be enough for all of us." Emmy Lou came in. "Travis brought donuts, but this smells way better."

"You cook, too?" Travis held two bags and was pulling one on wheels. "Come on, man. You can't cook in your underwear. It's not hygienic."

Jace was at a loss. He couldn't express how grateful he was to them for taking care of Heather. Since he was wearing nothing but his boxers, now probably wasn't the time to try.

"Travis." Emmy shook her head.

"I have every right to give him crap." Travis kicked the front door shut. "He forgot his sister."

He sighed. "I didn't forget. My phone died." He smiled down at Heather. "Pretty sure that wins me the worst brother of the year award."

"Yep." Travis grinned. "Totally."

"I figured." Heather sighed. "When I couldn't get ahold of you or Krystal, I called Emmy."

"Thank you, Emmy Lou." He smiled at her.

Emmy smiled, taking care not to look at anything below the neck. "I'll take over the bacon; you go find some clothes."

He nodded, taking the stairs two at a time—and running into Krystal hard enough to knock heads.

"I was about to say good morning." She sat down on the step, rubbing her head. "I knew you were hardheaded, but damn."

"Krystal." He shook his head. "We have company."

"Hope you're dressed, Little Sister. There is a minor present," Travis called up the stairs.

She froze. What? she mouthed.

"Travis, knock it off." Emmy Lou sighed. "I'd like to say he's not always this obnoxious, Heather, but I'd be lying."

"At least I've never forgotten you or Krystal," Travis snapped back.

"Heather?" Krystal looked just as horrified as he felt. But when she stood up and headed down the stairs, he grabbed her arm.

"I'm not complaining about the outfit here—for me."

She glanced down, as if she hadn't noticed how short and tight his shirt was on her. "Right." She nodded and ran up the stairs, her every step revealing the curve of her bare ass.

He closed the bedroom door and started tugging on jeans.

"What happened?" she asked.

"Heather." He pulled a shirt on. "My phone died. They picked her up from the airport."

"This is my fault." She picked up her red dress from the floor. "You didn't get much sleep—"

"It's not your fault I didn't charge my damn phone."

He opened his drawer, throwing some workout pants her way. "Might be better than the dress."

She dropped the dress and tugged on the pants, pulling the drawstring tight. "Thanks. Is she upset?"

"Heather?" He shook his head. "If she is, she's not acting like it. Pretty sure having your brother and sister pick her up from the airport makes my being a dick brother okay."

"You are not." She hugged him. "You need to charge your phone. Or maybe get an alarm clock. But you're a good brother."

He sighed, accepting her kiss on the cheek before they ran down the stairs.

"Nice pants," Travis said.

"Thanks." Jace laughed, knowing damn well he was teasing Krystal.

"Krystal." Heather was hugging her. "It's so good to see you."

"You too." She hugged his sister. "I can't believe you got Travis out of bed before noon."

Heather shrugged. "Well, I appreciate it."

"So do I," Jace added.

"Thank you. Seems to me you should be too, Little Sister?" Travis's brows rose. "Instead of poking the bear. You're going to poke this bear? The bear who knows and sees all?"

Jace saw the exchange—Krystal's panicked look and Travis's triumphant smile.

"I think Travis is the bear," Heather whispered.

Emmy Lou laughed. "Siblings," Emmy Lou murmured. "Bacon's almost done."

"Toast." Heather was spreading butter on slices she'd already toasted.

"I'm hero of the day, so I'm eating," Travis said, sitting in one of the leather recliners.

Heather giggled. "Want some coffee?"

"That'd be nice, Heather." Travis was all smiles. "And I will share my donuts with you."

"You and your donuts." Krystal opened the pastry box. "I think there's enough for everyone in here. To have two. Or three."

"What?" he asked. "I like my donuts."

"I like my eggs." Jace chuckled. "Scrambled okay?"

"Sounds good." Heather nudged him. "Feels like old times."

He winked. "Especially if you leave your dishes piled in the sink."

Heather shook her head. "Well, now you have a dishwasher so that won't be a problem."

He chuckled.

"You didn't have a dishwasher?" Travis looked dumbfounded. "What the hell kind of place did you live in?"

"Travis," Emmy chided.

Jace shrugged. "My grandmother was a diner waitress; she didn't have much." He'd never be ashamed of where he came from. "It was a clunker of a trailer, but it had its charm."

"Charm? With its leaking roof, rusty window panes,

and air conditioning unit that squealed?" Heather shrugged. "I have to say, this place is a little nicer. And don't forget how it leans to one side. And rocks like a seesaw when the wind picks up."

"When you put it like that." Jace nudged her. "Still, it is—it was home."

"And you never see anything but the good stuff." Heather hugged him again. "Which I miss, like, a lot. Because college kids are all 'let's talk about the meaning of life and be depressed.' Not fun." She paused. "Wait? Was?"

He shrugged. "I'm not sure where I—we—go next." Which was true.

"Hotels and buses." Emmy Lou nodded. "And then there's this."

"Which isn't you," Krystal said, setting the table.

"It's not?" he asked, more than curious to hear what she considered 'him.'

"No. Of course not." She seemed almost offended that he was doubting her. "You're a country boy at heart. You might not need much on the inside, but you don't want to feel fenced in on the outside."

"You nailed him." Heather smiled.

The pained expression on Travis's face was almost comical. Almost. But he wasn't ready to start making sex jokes with Jace's little sister around. And, shockingly enough, Travis managed to stop himself from running with Heather's unintentional slip.

With the breakfast spread, they sat at his stone-topped

table and ate, listening as Heather filled them in on dining hall food—she was too skinny still—and how her roommate Brenna's favorite time to study was two in the morning, with the lights on.

"See, Emmy Lou? You thought we missed out by doing everything online." Travis added another scoop of scrambled eggs to his plate.

"I wouldn't mind that." Heather glanced his way.

"Eat." Jace handed her another piece of toast. "You're going back, kid. I'm not dragging you all over the place when you're where you need to be. If we need to figure something out with food and housing, we will. But you know I'm right." He might be "living the dream," but this life came with no guarantees. He wanted security for Heather—nothing would change his mind on that.

"He's all crabby, like a grown-up," Travis stage-whispered.

"He's always been like this." Heather nodded, spreading jam on her second piece of toast. "But it means he loves me."

Jace nodded. "You know it."

Krystal was studying him, elbow on the table, chin resting in her hand. She smiled slowly, like whatever she was thinking about was a good thing. He could only hope like hell it was him.

"What about you all? Krystal?" Heather asked. "Miss being home? Since y'all are on the road so much?"

Krystal shrugged, her gaze falling from his. "Not particularly."

"Home gets pretty damn crowded, oh, say thirty minutes after we get there." Travis crunched on a piece of bacon.

Emmy Lou and Krystal nodded. Jace had been there, he knew firsthand how strung-out the energy was. Long-term? It would take a toll. A serious toll.

"Why don't you move out?" Heather asked. "Get your own places?"

"I'm not sure." Emmy Lou laughed. "We spend so much time together, work and all, it seemed convenient to stay put."

"For me? Lazy." Travis grinned, taking the last piece of bacon. "Besides, I'm not the one getting picked apart. Krystal here?" He had that look—one that said he was up to no good. Jace braced himself as Travis said, "You should get your own place, Krystal. Hell, I bet you could move in here. You and Jace, shacking up?"

Jace sighed. He was beginning to accept that he and Krystal, when it came to their relationship, were in different places. If he pushed, she'd take a step back—not forward. Travis wasn't pushing. He was shoving.

He saw the tic in Krystal's jaw, the way she avoided his gaze. Any second, she was going to do that defensive head tilt thing and change the subject. Damn Travis anyway.

"I am impressed with the food." Krystal winked at Heather. "Is this the norm?"

Which was the last thing he'd expected her to say. Now she was smiling and talking to Heather about their

shopping trip later in the weekend, like Travis's suggestion wasn't some way to get her worked up. She wasn't.
Not in the least. Maybe it was for Heather's benefit? Or
maybe, hopefully, it wasn't.

Chapter 15

"NOTHING CHANGED BUT THE LOVE I HAD FOR YOU..." Krystal sang, strumming through the last notes while Emmy Lou belted out the chorus again. When the music faded, there was a smattering of applause from the festival workers and a select few members of the press given early access.

She took a long swig off her water bottle and waited. As far as she was concerned, their set sounded good. They'd tweaked the amps, adjusted their sound reverb, and made accommodations for the outdoor acoustics. Since they were singing tried-and-true fan favorites, it wasn't like they needed more practice.

"Y'all good?" Travis asked.

Emmy Lou nodded. "You?" she asked Krystal.

She gave a thumbs-up, her gaze sweeping the mostly empty audience. Her father was there, with Heather and Luke, waiting for her and Jace to do a quick run-through. As soon as that was over, they had a couple of hours before the show tonight. They were slated to perform and emcee Sunday's awards and benefit, but it had been *implied*, meaning expected by the label, that they put in a rehearsal appearance.

While Emmy Lou and Travis packed up, Jace walked across the stage carrying his banged-up Martin

Dreadnought acoustic guitar. His tractor brand T-shirt did all the right things for his broad chest and shoulders and showcased the network of inked designs on his arms. His faded jeans, well-polished boots, and a Roughnecks football cap made him one sexy country boy. Sweet, talented, and smiling at her. Damn, but he made her so, so happy. She should stop staring at him, she should, but it wasn't going to happen.

"Anyone ever tell you that Jace guy is a lucky son of a bitch?" he asked when she was within earshot.

"Why is that?" She took a few steps closer, his smile reeling her in.

He tipped his cap back. "He gets to do this," he murmured, snagging an arm around her waist and pulling her in for a kiss. "Right here." His mouth brushed hers.

"If you think this makes him lucky, I'd love to know what last night made him." She kissed him.

"Worn out. Sore." He chuckled. "With no complaints."

"You two going to sing?" Luke called from one of the wooden seats in the amphitheater. "Or is this a new act?"

The audience laughed.

"Is that why we're here?" he asked, still nuzzling her.

She teased. "I guess we should sing then."

"If you say so." With a sigh and a kiss on the nose, they ran a quick sound check and Jace tuned his guitar.

Krystal turned, bending for her water bottle, when she saw Becca. The girl was standing in the shadows, watching. Krystal waved and she waved back.

"Who are you waving to?" Jace asked.

"Becca." She took a sip. "She said you two met last night?"

He nodded, a crease forming between his brows.

But questions would have to wait until they were done here. They weren't the only ones lined up for some rehearsal time. After tonight, the stage would be in constant use for the next seventy-two hours. Two smaller stages had been set up in the fields behind the Opry building. These weren't the headliners, but they were the perfect place for new bands to get heard and seen. And ACMF was all about that. Nonstop, round-the-clock music with nonstop, round-the-clock food and beverages and a whole hell of a lot of merchandise tents set up.

"Ready?" he asked, his fingers strumming their song from his guitar.

She loved watching him play. Loved watching him sing. And loved Heather for entering him in the reality show that landed him right here, with her, singing their song. Each performance was different somehow, channeling their dynamics—fueling their hunger and sharing it with their audience. Singing with him was personal, intimate, and freeing.

Jace didn't hold back. Whether he was singing or making sweet love, he did it with one hundred percent of his focus and energy. Which was why singing—or making love—made him unforgettable. The song ended and she and Jace wound up tangled up, breathless, so close it would be easy to wind her arms around him and—

"Get a room," Travis yelled from the audience. "No one wants to see that."

Jace laughed. "Everyone is a critic."

"They're jealous because of all the sex you're getting," she teased.

"How do they know?" His brow cocked. "It's not like I posted a scorecard on that Insta-thing."

She was laughing then. "That would be awesome."

He took her hand as they walked offstage, to find Becca there, pacing, a mic in her hand. She wore what looked like an extra-long men's western shirt. Her braided leather and silver belt was clasped with a massive belt buckle. Her boots had a fringe of silver running down the back. And the only makeup she wore was too-bright pink lipstick.

"You up?" Krystal asked.

Becca nodded, looking more anxious than excited. "I've never sung in a place this big."

Krystal couldn't remember a time when she wasn't performing for a crowd. Even before they'd officially become the Three Kings, she and her siblings were singing. County fairs and craft shows. A few local rodeos, then a few worth noticing. She'd only been fourteen when Three Kings was born.

"Helps if you can focus on something," Jace offered. "Or someone. When I was on *Next Top American Voice*, I'd find my sister and if I got jittery, seeing her would calm me down. Same with singing with Krystal. One look at her, and I know we're good."

Becca blinked. "I don't have anyone."

Krystal hurt. As much as she hated to, she asked, "Where's Tig?"

"A meeting? I think." She shrugged. "It's just a rehearsal." But it wasn't *just* a rehearsal—not to Becca. Beads of sweat lined her upper lip and forehead. Her face was so white, her lipstick was almost clown-like.

"I'll stay." Krystal smiled, squeezing Jace's hand. "I've been wanting to hear you sing."

Becca shook her head. "No. No, you really don't have to."

"I know." She shrugged. Pressuring the poor girl wasn't going to help. "But I'd like to?"

Becca shifted from one booted foot to the other, undecided. "I'm fine."

"You sure?" Krystal asked. "Try closing your eyes. People think you're lost in the music, but it gives your mind a break from the noise. Or stare over everyone, not at them."

Becca nodded, sniffing. "Okay. I can try that." Her smile was wobbly. "See you two later."

They weren't down the steps of the stage before Jace asked, "I'm guessing we're staying?"

"Oh really?" She was a fan of the cap thing. He could pull it off. "You think you've got me all figured out?"

He reached the wood-chip-covered ground and turned to face her. "Hell no. Not in the least." The corner of his mouth curved up. "Doesn't mean I'm going to stop trying."

"But we are staying." She paused. "Or y'all can go on and I'll catch up. It shouldn't take long."

He rubbed his cap back and forth on his head, his eyes warm on her face. "I'm where I want to be."

They headed into the amphitheater seating. Jace headed toward his sister and her family, but Krystal sat up front, where Becca could see her.

Becca was a wreck, staring wildly around, her hands shaking so hard around the mic that it picked up the noise. Krystal sat, willing the girl to look at her, so she'd know someone was rooting for her. When Becca's dark gaze bounced right over her, Krystal worried the girl was too worked up to notice. But she had. And when Becca looked at her, all surprise and relief, Krystal knew she'd made the right choice.

The band counted to five and Becca started singing, eyes closed.

"Momma said don't waste your wishes on flowers and coins…" Her voice was deeper than expected. Deep but smooth. "Four-leaf clovers wilt and shooting stars burn out…" It was a sing-along kind of song. A song that would get stuck in folks' head, to hum along to. Becca kept on singing, her eyes opened and she blinked, searching, then smiling at Krystal.

Krystal winked.

"But I'd plant clover and dandelions, collect every coin, and buy a telescope so I could wish every wish on you-oo-hoo-oo. All for you-oo-hoo-oo." Her posture was easing, one foot tapping along.

The girl could sing. And this song was radio gold.

"She's something, isn't she?" Tig Whitman said.

She hadn't heard him sit behind her; she'd been too focused on Becca. Becca—who needed her to stay put.

"She reminds me a lot of you. A lot of heart. Eager to please." He chuckled. "Damn talented."

She leaned forward, not wanting his voice in her ear or his breath on her skin.

The song ended and Krystal was up, running toward the stage. "You did great, Becca."

Becca cradled the mic to her chest, beaming. "I know I said you didn't have to stay but thank you, so much. It meant a lot. So much."

Krystal nodded. "Like I said, I wanted to hear you sing. I'd heard good things—they were all right."

"Course they were." Tig was back, not in the least deterred. "I know talent when I hear it."

"I'll see you later?" Pretending he didn't exist was Krystal's only option. Otherwise, she'd have to talk to him or look at him and neither of those seemed like productive options at this point. She was holding it together, no point pushing it. "See ya." With a wave Becca's way, she walked—not speed-walked or ran—away from Tig and toward the seats where her family and Jace had been sitting.

"Emmy and Heather went to look at T-shirts." Jace smiled. "If she buys a shirt for all the bands she likes, you might not have to take her shopping after all."

She forced a smile, taking Jace's hand in both of hers.

It helped. It always did. But a quick survey left her chilled to the bone. "Where's Daddy?"

Travis nodded toward the stage. She'd run up the far aisle, away from Tig. Her father had headed down the other aisle, to get to her.

"Shit," she whispered.

"I'm guessing this is bad?" Travis asked, pushing up out of his chair. "I'll go." He trotted along, smiling, making sure the whole world knew there was nothing worth noticing up front. Not one tiny little thing.

She watched—in slow motion—as Tiger Whitman turned to lock eyes with her father. Her easygoing father was strung tighter than a guitar string about to snap. Even from this distance, she could see the muscle clenched tight in his jaw.

"Don't do it." She didn't know if she said the words out loud or not. "Don't."

Jace's hand tightened around hers.

Tig Whitman was fearless. Or clueless. Or both. He was heading for her father, smiling his best smile like they were still the friends they'd once been.

"He's got him." Jace's hands held her shoulders, rubbing up and down her arms. "Travis is there."

She nodded, breathing easier when her brother nudged her father. Even aisles away, she could hear Travis carrying on about them being late to a meeting and how the car was waiting out front. For a split second, she saw her daddy's face and it scared her. Not of her father, but of what the twisted, raw fury on his face could lead to.

Because of her.

Head down, Hank walked back up the aisle and out of the amphitheater, Travis wise enough to trail a few feet behind.

Jace didn't say a word until they were out of the amphitheater. Even then, he seemed to be considering all the possible explanations for what the hell he'd just witnessed.

"Heather and I think we need food before we do more shopping." Emmy Lou held out a large plastic bag.

"What did you buy?" Travis asked. "What's even open yet?"

The festival wouldn't officially kick off until that night.

"I guess vendors see Emmy and are like, 'Oh my gosh, I'm going to sell a shirt to Emmy Lou King,' so they open. And wind up selling a shirt to Jace Black's sister." Heather giggled. "It was pretty awesome."

"Food?" Her daddy sounded gruff. "I could eat."

"Me too." Travis nodded. "Someplace with cake."

"Donuts for breakfast and cake for lunch? Well, okay." Heather nodded.

"Eat like a King." Travis winked.

Heather thought it was hilarious, but the rest of them groaned. Except their father—he surprised everyone by chuckling.

"I could go for some cake, too," he agreed, casting a glance her way. "What do you think, Krystal?"

She nodded, leaving Jace to slip her arm around her father's waist. "That sounds perfect."

"I know a place." Sawyer nodded.

"Of course you do." Travis grinned.

"You two are spending too much time together—you're doing the same thing." She pointed between them. The posture. The eyebrow. The slightly condescending half grin. "All of it." They were even starting to look alike.

They loaded up into the big black SUV with Sawyer behind the wheel. It was a tight fit, but no one complained.

"I left my purse." Emmy Lou squealed from the back seat.

"We'll go around," Sawyer offered, driving around to the back of the amphitheater to the lot behind the row of trailers set up as temporary dressing rooms. Since their bus, the Kings' Coach II, hadn't been fully detailed this afternoon, Krystal and Emmy had used the dressing rooms. She didn't mind the whole communal dressing room thing, but it did get crowded. And, for whatever reason, women tended to overshare a lot when they were getting their hair and makeup done. She'd been all too relieved to see their bus parked and ready, their own personal oasis from the enthusiastic chaos that was the Austin Country Music Festival.

"I'll get it," Krystal offered, closest to the door. "Five minutes. Then cake." She was still smiling when she ran into the dressing room.

The empty boxes, used tissues, makeup wipes, powders, and every sort of hair implement and torture device had been tidied and stored away. Which meant Krystal had to dig through cabinets and shelves before finding

Emmy's large multicolor fringed purse. It was tucked under a box of hot curlers on the far corner of the counter. A bright pink sticky note with Emmy Lou's name on it hung from the designer label. She was headed back to the front door when something made her stop. A noise. Something bumping into a wall? A slap. Something muffled and shuffling and—another slap?

Noises. A man. Definitely sex noises.

"Gross." She spun, hoping to sneak out undiscovered, only to trip on the metal foot of a makeup chair. She fell, landing on her knees and dumping Emmy's bag all over the linoleum floor. She was on her knees, shoving everything back into the purse when the restroom door opened.

Becca.

Crying hard.

Makeup smudged down her face. Her too-bright pink lipstick smeared.

Behind her stood Tig. Eyes closed. Leaning against the wall. Panting hard.

His pants around his ankles.

Krystal was frozen, processing, fighting what she saw. Fighting the truth. She wound up sitting, staring at Becca, so many words clogging her throat. "Becca?" she whispered. "Are you okay?"

"Oh." Becca floundered, wiping at the tears streaming down her face. "I…um…"

Of course she wasn't okay. Krystal knew that— knew exactly what this girl was feeling. Fear. Confusion.

Shame. And no one to tell, no one to turn to—no one to believe her.

She has me. Krystal stood slowly, sliding Emmy's bag to her shoulder. "We're going to get something to eat. You should come." There wasn't a thing she could do about the tremor in her voice.

Becca shook her head.

"Please, Becca."

"I can't," she whispered, glancing toward the open bathroom door. She was terrified.

"Yes. You can." Krystal held her hand out. "Believe me, you can."

Tig chose that moment to push the bathroom door wide. He was buckling his belt, breathing hard and sweaty and completely oblivious to Krystal's presence. "That was good. Real good."

For the first time, she wasn't afraid. Inside, she was raging. Ears roaring, eyes stinging, lungs aching to scream—long and loud and in his face.

But Becca was crying softly, her gaze falling to her feet. She wouldn't thank Krystal for becoming her avenging angel, not yet. Right now, she was too caught in it. Trapped in her fear.

"No more of that now, Becca, honey." He sighed. "You know you're my—"

"Special girl?" Krystal finished, the words all too familiar. "Come on, Becca. Let's go."

His shock was more than a little empowering. Mouth gaping, eyes searching, looking beyond her... To see if she was alone? His gaze locked with hers, his surprise and panic fading as his brows scrunched together. "She's not going anywhere with you. She's right where she wants to be."

Bastard. "Yes, she is." Krystal stepped forward, still holding out her hand. "Becca?"

"Becca? We talked about this, remember?" Tig whispered. She knew that sweet, cajoling voice all too well. Damn him, climbing into her head—Becca's head—and making her doubt that what he'd done was wrong. After all, how could someone so sweet, so caring do something so bad? Those words had run through her head long before her mother dared to say them out loud.

Because he is a monster. "You don't have to listen to him."

"I'm fine, Krystal." Becca sniffed, wiping her nose with the back of her hand. "I'm just…emotional. So…so excited about tonight. And the rehearsal." She was shaking all over.

"Don't lie." She pleaded. "It won't—"

"I'm good." Becca cut her off, pressing her eyes shut. "You don't understand."

"I do." She'd meant to yell. To scream. But her voice, her words, were flat and hollow.

Becca was staring at her.

"I *do*," she repeated, harder this time.

"Your momma said you were spiraling. Might spend more time on getting your head straight than things that don't concern you." Tig sighed. "Becca knows all about you, Krystal. How unbalanced you are. The accusations you made. All your mistakes. You go on now." His smile was almost sympathetic.

"The only mistake I made was staying quiet." She faced Becca. "I won't make that mistake again." Her words hung in the quiet. Tig Whitman could bluster and stare and insult her; he didn't matter. Becca did. She stared at Becca, willing her to listen—to hear her.

"I appreciate the concern." Becca's gaze darted from her to Tig and back. "But I'm fine."

"Because she knows I'll always take care of her." He nodded, looking every bit the doting uncle and nothing like the predator he was.

"You know this is wrong. You have to know that." Becca wasn't a kid but that didn't make this okay. Regardless of age, this was never okay. Never. "Becca—"

Becca pressed her hands over her ears. "Go, Krystal." She headed back to the restroom and slammed the door behind her.

The look on Tig's face was straight out of her nightmare. That smug fucking smile. Gloating. He'd won and he knew it. Score one for the monster. The monster she was now alone with.

She was out the door, stumbling down the metal steps of the trailer and hurrying across the lawn—away from him. Away from the memories and fear and helplessness. Not for herself—not this time. But for Becca. There had to be something she could do. Some way to get through to Becca.

But first, she had to calm down. Alone. No cake or questions or well-intended hugs or smiles of encouragement. It would make it that much worse.

She pulled her phone out and texted. **Have purse. Met up with Becca. Send Sawyer back to get me in a few minutes.**

Will do. Have fun. Thanks. Emmy responded with a string of kissy-face emojis.

By the time Krystal reached her bus, she was dripping sweat and having full-body shakes. She downed a bottle of water and crumpled to the floor, curling in on herself. Hands pressed to the ground, she took slow, deep breaths. It didn't help. Visualizing her happy place was impossible. Her brain had Becca and Tig and memories she'd locked away for years cycling over and over. "Asshole." She lay flat, staring up at the ceiling. "Damn you."

If Becca didn't want her help, she couldn't force it on her. But she couldn't leave her to fend for herself. When Krystal had stayed to hear her sing, it had meant something to the girl. Becca was love starved and lonely—perfect victim material. It might take time to show Becca she had a way out—options that didn't include debasement and emotional abuse—but it was worth it.

It took effort to peel herself off the floor. Once Krystal was up, she leaned against the wall and headed to the bathroom. She washed her face and hands, ran a hand over her braid, and stared herself in the eye. "You're strong. Be strong." Fear had controlled her for so long.

"No more." Her hands were trembling, so she shook them out, splashing more cold water on her face and neck. "This is going to take some work."

Sawyer would be here soon. She was suitably recovered to make it through the evening—she hoped. There was no way to erase tonight, but letting it shut her down was letting Tig win somehow. Head high, she walked back down the hall, shaking her hands and breathing deep. Heather and shopping and cake and fun, all reminders that the world wasn't all bad.

"See George is still your driver. Good poker player." Tig was there. In her bus.

Time seemed to stop, the thump of her heart drowning, deafening.

"I'm here to clear the air." He sounded calm and rational. Not a care in the world. "Before you go off the handle and make a mess of everything."

He'd already done that. Why couldn't she breathe? She was strong, dammit.

"Nothing to say now?" He smiled. *Smiled.* And it scared the shit out of her. Not that he could know that. "I'll talk, you listen."

The command in his voice was just what she needed to snap out of it. "Leave." Her voice didn't break. Didn't waver. Strong. "Now."

Tig didn't budge. "Becca and I have something special."

"She was crying with joy?" Being angry made this a hell of a lot easier. "And the slapping I heard? That was a conjugal high five?" Why was she talking? Listening? Letting him stay? "Leave, Tig."

"She's twenty-one." His brows rose.

"Not fifteen. Or sixteen." She shook her head. "Get off my bus."

"Your bus?" He ran his hand along the oak paneling, stepping toward her. "You think you got this bus from your talent alone? It was me, sugar. Uncle Tig. Talking you up and selling the Three Kings like you were the best thing since sliced bread. I helped make you who you are today."

He had no idea.

He shrugged. "Think of our time together as payment. Pretty sure I got the short end of the deal."

"You think you had a right to do...what you did to me?" She shook her head, the roaring in her ears returning. "Get out."

"You remember it how you want. I know you liked it." He paused. "You begged me, remember? On your knees and begging. Is that what bothers you? That you wanted it so bad?"

"Because you said Emmy Lou was next." She remembered every detail of that night. How he'd threatened Emmy Lou when she'd tried to resist. He was calm and rational about it. Like getting to Emmy Lou would be easy. And she believed him. He'd made her apologize, made her beg for his forgiveness. And she had. After, she'd gone to her parents to tell the whole awful truth. And her already broken world imploded. "You hurt me.

Me. It wasn't enough that you made my body feel dirty. You made me feel dirty, too. I wasn't going to let you do a thing to my sister, you son of a bitch." Stop talking. "Get off of my bus."

"I think you couldn't stand sharing me with someone else." He smirked. "The truth can hurt. Thank me and move on. I taught you what it takes to get ahead. How to survive." He was standing over her, stealing the air and crowding her. "Tell your story if you want. Tell them how I used your sweet, young body, taught you how to please a man, and *you* let me get away with it. You did that." He sighed. "Go on and tell. And you'll spend the rest of your life wondering who's staying out of pity. You think Jace won't always wonder? That he'll stay because he cares? How can he leave you after this? He's stuck—with damaged goods. You'd do that." His eyes narrowed. "You destroy your family and their careers, go on. Emmy, you know how fragile she is. And Travis? Kid's always been hotheaded. You gonna trigger that?" He was closer, breathing on her. "All that and truth? No one will believe you now. No one. Even if we both know it's true."

"Get out." She was on the verge. "Get out, damn you." Screaming now. "Get out!"

Tig put his hand over her mouth and she lost it.

Who hit who first, she didn't know or care. His hands were on her and she had to get them off. Had to get away. He kept grabbing her, telling her to be quiet...but panic blinded her and she fought like a trapped animal, mindless in her panic. She was falling, her head slamming against the bus floor hard enough for her to see stars.

She blinked, confused as Tig Whitman went sailing through the air.

Sawyer was leaning over her, a little hazy around the edges—but there. "Krystal?" He leaned closer, too blurry to see now. "You okay? Did he hurt you?"

But she passed out before she could answer him.

It had only been a few nights since he'd moved into his own place, but he'd missed the chaos and energy the King family had. And the loyalty—strong and unwavering. He'd been disappointed that Krystal wasn't with them, but he suspected she was where she needed to be.

Something about Becca troubled him. She seemed on edge—all the time. Like it wouldn't take much to break her spirit. Maybe Krystal could help her with that. He'd never met anyone as strong and fearless as Krystal—unless it came to committing to a relationship. But he was working on that.

Hank's phone started ringing the minute the cake arrived. "Talk about timing." With a smile, he left to take the call. "Leave me something."

"No promises." Travis rubbed his hands together.

"Best meal ever." Heather stared at the assortment of cake slices on the tray their waiter carried.

Jace was hoping there was a nice big steak in his future.

"Dessert first is never a bad idea," Emmy said. "Don't you dare touch the strawberry shortcake." She wielded her fork with menace.

Jace chuckled. "Partial to strawberry shortcake?"

"Krystal's favorite." Travis shrugged. "You snooze, you lose."

He needed to remember that. He was pretty sure his grandmother had a recipe she'd bragged about winning awards with. He'd have to check.

"Don't be a jerk." Emmy Lou frowned. "My favorite is carrot cake. Which I don't have to defend because—"

"Carrot cake isn't cake," Travis finished. "Cake isn't even part vegetable. Am I right? Cake is the antithesis of a vegetable."

"Antithesis, huh?" Emmy giggled. "You're working hard for your cake, aren't you?"

"Y'all are awesome," Heather piped up. "Thank you, like so much, for all of this. I know Jace can be a pain sometimes, so knowing he has people looking out for him is a big deal to me. Especially since I can't be around very much."

"Ouch." Jace pressed a hand to his chest. Heather's lack of a filter wasn't always a good thing.

"Which part?" Travis used his fork to scoop off something chocolate. "The part where she's thanking us for being your friend or the part where she's apologizing about you being a pain?" He was laughing.

Emmy was too. Hell, even Heather was now.

"I'm not sure." Jace shook his head, his gaze darting to his phone.

"She'll be here." Travis sighed. "It's been less than an hour, man. Show some dignity."

It was his turn to laugh.

"I think it's super cool she's taking Becca Sinclair under her wing. Thank you." Heather took the plate with sample bites from Emmy Lou. "She's like this orphan with a grandpa who's super old and Tig Whitman heard her singing at some berry festival thing or something and saw potential and now she's singing with you guys."

"All that?" Jace nudged her.

"How old is she?" Travis asked. "She looks, like, twelve?"

"She better be legal." Jace shook his head. "She downed two drinks at the mixer like they were water." And today, her nerves. A little performance anxiety was one thing, but what the hell was Tig Whitman thinking, putting her on the big stage? Maybe when she wasn't dripping sweat and white as a sheet, but now? It seemed unfair to her and the fans looking for a good show.

"Something going on there." Travis nodded.

"I think it's sweet." Heather sighed. "Not that she has baggage, but that Tiger Whitman is going to help her dreams come true."

"Any second now, a singing cricket in a top hat is going to come in and sing about wishes and hopes and dreams." Travis took a massive bite of cheesecake.

"Pinocchio was his favorite," Emmy Lou explained. "He went as Jiminy Cricket for Halloween one year."

Travis glared her way. "I suddenly have a craving for carrot cake."

"Aww." Heather was a little too starry-eyed over Travis King. "I bet you looked adorable."

"I was all about the blue fairy." Travis shrugged. "She was hot."

"And just like that, the awws fade away." Emmy Lou sighed. "You're supposed to be sharing."

"I only want what I want."

Travis had managed to pull most of the plates directly in front of him. He was taking random bites and swatting her fork away with his.

Jace's phone vibrated.

Not coming. Sorry. I'll see you tomorrow.

"She on her way?" Travis picked up his phone. "Oh, hey. Dad texted." He stopped eating and set his fork down. "We need to get home."

"What's wrong?" Heather asked.

"He just said home 911. Which means get our asses home." Travis flagged down the waiter. "Can we get to-go boxes?" He glanced at his phone. "Says Sawyer is en route. Will drop y'all at home on the way."

Is everything okay? Need anything?

Krystal didn't respond to Jace's text. By the time he and Heather were delivered to their front door, the mood between Travis and Emmy had declined into long silent stares out the window and the occasional obligatory response to Heather.

"I'm bummed out." Heather waved the dark SUV off. "Think everything is okay?"

"I'm sure it's fine," Jace lied. Something was up; he could feel it.

"I need your help." Heather tugged him up the stairs and opened her suitcase. "What do I wear?"

He and Heather spent the next few hours picking out different outfits, talking about her classes, the "hot" TA in her Western Civilization class, and how badly she wanted a cat.

"No to the cat and *hell* no to the hot TA. What's wrong with this?" He held up a feed store shirt. "It's a concert, not an awards show. That's Sunday, so we've got time to get you whatever it is you need for that. Hopefully Krystal or Emmy can help with that. If not, I'll call Calvin." He'd told her all about the quirky stylist.

She grinned. "You're not performing tonight, right?"

"Nope, just walking in, shaking some hands." He tossed the T-shirt at her. "Maybe after we can go see that movie with the chick from outer space who—"

"Meaning you're not dying to stay and watch the whole show?" She dropped her T-shirt on the bed. "Isn't, like, *everyone* going to be there?"

He shook his head. "It's more an opening-act kind of night."

"But *you* are playing with the headliners on Sunday." She smiled. "That doesn't freak you out? Like whoa, that is my brother up there." She flopped onto the bed beside him. "I mean, I still think of you as shy, super-private—"

"That went out the window when *Next Top American Voice* made my life into a viral video." He tugged a strand of her hair.

"Sorry." She did look sorry. "But, you know, it all worked out." She picked up the feed store shirt. "Are you sure about this?"

"Nope." He smiled. "Why do you think I wear black all the time? And it's in my contract."

She laughed. "Guess I'll get ready."

He nodded. "Sounds good." He closed her door behind him and headed for his room. Sending Krystal another text. **Is a feed shirt something Heather can wear tonight?**

She didn't want to answer a question about what was going on, maybe she'd answer a text about Heather. He put his phone on the charger and took a quick shower. As he toweled off, he checked—still no message from Krystal.

"Dignity?" He put the phone back on the charger. It'd help if he could shake the unease knotting his stomach.

"Fine." He pulled out the box of grooming supplies Calvin had left for him.

When he'd gently but firmly told Calvin he could get himself ready for ACMF, he'd expected a protest. Calvin didn't protest, but he did leave a detailed list on "the right way" to do his hair and his wardrobe for the entire festival.

"Ten steps?" He stared at the how-to list for his hair. "What the hell is pomade?" He dug through the pin-striped bin Calvin had taken great care in organizing. "Screw this."

His phone pinged. Krystal. **Feed store shirt is perfect. Does she have boots? She needs boots.**

He grinned. "Needs, huh?" Heather had boots. Whether she brought them with her was another story.

I'll see what I can find. Did Travis eat your cake?
No cake for me. My butt is getting too big—Travis says.

He frowned, his thumbs flying. **Travis is full of shit. You can tell him I said so. Your butt isn't too big. It's just right.**

I hope you and Heather have fun tonight.

He leaned against the counter. *Be better having you on my arm.* He hesitated. **You okay?**

Call me when you get home. We need to talk.

There was nothing comforting about those words. He went from uneasy to worrying. If he hadn't promised Luke he'd put in an appearance, he'd be asking Hank if he could stop by. But he'd promised, so he dressed in his Calvin-approved attire and frowned. "Seriously, man?"

"You ready?" Heather called. "I sent Krystal a pic and she approved."

He pulled the door open. "Looking good." He glanced down at his skin-tight black shirt. The damn sleeves were short and rolled tight. "Well, I'm pretty sure this is my stylist's idea of revenge for telling him I can dress myself."

"What's wrong with it? Your arms look superhero huge and impressive." She grinned. "Just don't breathe out or all your buttons will pop."

"Ha-ha." He gave her a once-over. Her feed store shirt was on the snug side, so were her jeans. Then again, she was his little sister and he wasn't ready to accept that she wasn't all that little anymore. She wore sparkling hoops, a long, fringed leather necklace, and her boots. "You look nice, kiddo."

"Great." Her sigh was telling.

"What?" He tugged on the sleeves of his shirt.

"I'm almost nineteen. The kiddo thing is getting old." She shrugged.

"I hate to break it to you, Heather, but you're always going to be my kid sister." He kissed her forehead. "Always."

Heather's phone went off; she pulled it out. "Brenna. I sent her a picture of what I was wearing, too. And tonight's program—" She stopped talking, her smile fading. "Wait." She picked up the remote on the counter and stared at the buttons. "How do you work your television?"

"Might not even be hooked up—"

The screen came to life. "Guess you don't know what channel *TNM* is?"

He shook his head and headed back into the bathroom for his phone. "What sort of moron rolls up their sleeves this high?" he asked.

"Jace?" Heather called.

He headed back into his bedroom. "We need to leave pretty quick."

"Look." She pointed at the television, grabbing his arm. "Jace, I'm serious. Look."

He did.

"An eyewitness says the altercation took place in the bus behind me. Miss King was taken by an ambulance to a nearby hospital, but details are still coming in." The reporter turned to her coanchor.

Footage of the Kings Coach II appeared, several police cars parked at angles, forming a perimeter around it. He waited, the unease he'd been grappling with all night grabbing hold.

The footage cut to a reporter, standing beside one of the police cars. "Yes, that's right," he said. "The Austin Country Music Festival was slated to kick off tonight but things have come to a screeching halt until law enforcement can confirm the threat is contained." He paused, glancing over his shoulder. "The only thing we can confirm is that Krystal King was attacked in her bus by an unidentified assailant earlier this evening. We're waiting for more information—"

Jace was running out the front door, boots in one hand, keys in the other. "Heather," he called. He needed to see Krystal, to know she was okay. *Be okay. Please, please, be okay.* She had to be.

Chapter 16

HER HEAD HURT. A PULSE IN HER EYES. THE WHOLE side of her face, really. She lay there, trying to make sense of the strange beeps and low voices, and why the hell was it was so cold? The hard, mean reality of what had happened came slamming to the forefront of her brain.

Where the hell was she? More importantly, where was he?

The spindly fingers of dread were working their nasty fingers around her lungs, the beginning flutter and press of anxiety setting in. That tremor along her spine. Clammy palms. That odd sense that time was speeding up. Out of control. Her hands fisted.

No more freaking fear. *No more.* If she let this go on, she was giving him control—letting him win. It wasn't just her in this beyond fucked up situation. It was up to her to try to end it. If she didn't try, there could be others like her. And that was sad, wrong, devastating.

Reaching up, her fingers encounter a well-padded gauze wrap around her head. "My head hurts," she managed.

"Krystal?" Emmy. "Hey, Sissy. Are you okay?"

She forced her eyes open. "I'm not sure." Hospital. Hospital room. Hospital bed. The cold made sense. "People." Not just people. Police. All her empowerment self-talk was getting an immediate challenge. Holding off the whole panic attack was going to be harder than she'd expected.

"People on your side." Her father's voice was gruff. Damn, he looked old. Worn out and shell-shocked.

"Okay." Her attempt at a smile ended in a wobbly wince. Her fingers lightly traced over her temple, eyes, and cheek. "Bad?" Her gaze shifted from her daddy to Travis.

"Sure as hell isn't good." Travis was red-faced and stony. Something about her jovial, teasing, ass of a brother strung tighter than a guitar string hurt. It wouldn't take much to trigger a full-on explosion. He couldn't be here for what was about to happen.

"Okay." She didn't try to smile this time.

"I want to ask if you're okay." Emmy. "But you have a black eye and stitches in your head so..." Poor Emmy— the tears she wiped away kept coming.

Tig's warning. About Emmy. And Travis. If she did this, there would be no turning back. How could she? *Because of Becca—and who knows how many others.* Because someone needed to stand up for them. She only hoped her family would support her.

Sawyer stood, silent as always, watching her. What would have happened if he hadn't been there? That was a dangerous question. He had been there. And he'd stopped...everything. His nod was stiff, nostrils flared and jaw clenching tight.

"Krystal." Her father spoke up. "The police have some questions for you."

Questions that had big, life-altering answers for every single person in this room. Questions that should have been asked, and answered, ten years ago. "Okay." Her fingers pleated the thin white sheets covering her legs.

"Give her a minute." The female officer held her hand up. "There's no rush here."

Two men and one woman. Police officers in full police officer uniforms. Because calling the police was the right thing to do when someone is attacked. A flash of his hand on her mouth streaked across her mind. Her stomach clenched tight, bile rising up in her throat.

"Where are we?" The answer was obvious but the question came out anyway.

"You're in the hospital." Emmy sat on the side of her bed, taking her hand.

Because she was hurt. Black eye and stitches? That's what Emmy had said. Which matched with the slamming pulse in her face and eye. She didn't feel much in her head—probably shot up with something to numb her for the stitches. She was drained, like after one of her marathon workouts. Wrung out.

Because of Tig… Another flash. Him over her, being pinned on the floor. Her heart rate picked up. Thanks to the monitor she was hooked up to, everyone knew it, too. The rapid beeping had one of the policemen staring at the monitor with concern. For some reason, she wanted to giggle. Since that probably wouldn't be okay, she pressed a hand to her mouth.

Which reminded her of her face. The pulse throbbing in her cheek and eye.

"It's okay." Emmy smoothed her sheets, not in the least okay. Her sister's lower lip was quivering and she was sniffing, doing her best not to fall apart completely.

Would it be? Would it ever really be okay again?

Yes. It would.

Sawyer was fidgeting. The man she'd begun to think of as more robot than human was shifting from one foot to the next, looking...out of sorts. He was never out of sorts. His master poker face was failing. Big-time. It was unnerving as hell.

"He called the ambulance." Emmy's words made it ten times worse.

"Ambulance?" She closed her eyes and hissed, reaching up to touch her face, but that hurt, too. "Dammit."

"You think you can answer some questions?" Her father stood at the foot of her bed.

She stared at the three strangers, then her family. "Probably best if I do this alone."

Travis shook his head, his face turning a dark red.

"I'd like to stay," Emmy whispered, her hand tightening on hers.

"Emmy." She blew out a deep breath. How could she protect her sister now? The truth was going to come out. It had to. "I can't sugarcoat this. Can't make this easy." She swallowed. "I can do this on my own."

"I know." Her sister's gaze locked with hers. "But you shouldn't have to. We all want to be here for you."

Words were the easy part. It was after they were said that things changed—when the actual words faded but their impact remained. "Are you sure?"

Emmy nodded.

"We're all sure." Her father's blue gaze searched hers.

Fine. There's no way to hide it this time. "Okay. Let's get this over with."

"I'm Officer Washington. That's Officer Cruz and Officer Ramos." Officer Washington stepped closer to the bed, her dark brown eyes sweeping over Krystal's face. Her attention lingered, briefly, on Krystal's eye. "First, we'd like to do a rape kit. Check for DNA samples under your nails, swab inside your mouth—"

"Fuck," Travis growled.

"I wasn't raped." Krystal shot her brother a look. "But I'm okay with you checking for samples. You'll need that, won't you? For a restraining order?"

Officer Washington nodded.

"Okay." Krystal lay her head against the pillow, then popped forward, away from a shooting pain at the back of her head. Too fast. Dizzy. "This is like the worst amusement park ride ever." She was gripping Emmy's hand, clinging to stability.

"You hit your head," Officer Cruz explained. "Hard. Concussion. A few stitches."

"That explains it." Her gaze caught on Sawyer, jaw tight and nostrils flared. Seeing him this way was unsettling. "Thanks, Sawyer. For taking care of me. And him."

"Him?" Travis jumped in. "Tig? Tig did this to you?"

Yes, Tig. She was going to have to stop freaking out every time someone said his name. "Where is he?" The question had her heart monitor climbing.

"Mr. Whitman is at the station." The female police officer said. "Can you recount the events leading up to your altercation with Mr. Whitman?"

"Altercation? How about assault?" Travis bit out. "Have you seen her face?"

"Travis." Krystal sighed. "You're stressing me out with the human volcano routine. Keep it up and I will make Sawyer drag your ass out of the room."

The two male police officers glanced back and forth between her, Sawyer, and Travis.

"Let's try to keep things as calm as possible. Your sister is going to need both of her brothers' support." Officer Ramos's low bass voice was just menacing enough to get Travis's attention. "All things considered."

"Sawyer isn't our brother." Emmy's glanced Sawyer's way, her lower lip quivering.

"No?" Officer Ramos didn't look convinced. "There's a…resemblance."

Krystal studied Travis. Then Sawyer. Officer Ramos had a point.

"Just security." Sawyer's tone was hard.

"Good damn thing he was there, too." Travis scowled, his lips parting. "What if—"

"Stop. I mean it." Krystal glared at him, which made her face hurt. Which made her react and cover her tender face. "Dammit." She shook her hands out. "Tonight?"

Officer Washington's forehead creased. "Let's start there."

I can do this. I have to do this.

The door to her hospital room opened and Jace was there.

Jace.

Her heart. Oh, her heart. He was here.

No.

His face. He hesitated, just inside, doing his best not to react. But that was reaction enough. His smile was for her, strained and broken but real. His light brown eyes searched her face before falling briefly away. When he looked at her again, he'd pulled himself together. Because he was Jace. Strong and beautiful. Here. For her. He was here for her.

On this point, Tig had been right. Jace was exactly the kind of guy who would stick now—out of misguided nobility. He'd want to ride in on a white horse, make it better, with his smile and his warm gaze and gentle hands.

She sucked in a wavering breath, her heart breaking in a million pieces. There was only one option here—one she could trust was right.

"You can't be here." She forced the words out, brittle and raw.

You are a liar. Tig's voice echoed in her head. She wanted Jace here, wanted his strength and support. Needed it.

"Not visiting hours?" he asked, frowning. "I needed to see you were okay."

Panic reared up. One touch, one look, and she'd cave. Because she loved him. It was stupid and useless but true. She loved him. So much. Too much to put him through this. And once he heard, everything would change. Tig's accusations had added bruising weight to her constant guilt. She'd let things go on—let Tig do those things to her. How could Jace look at her the same way? How could he leave her? He was a gentleman. And this time, it would be his downfall.

In his eyes, she was a better version of herself. Losing that? It would hurt. But there was no help for it; she needed to get used to pain.

She gripped Emmy, the bed, anything not to reach for him. He couldn't be here.

But he was headed toward her with a single-minded focus that demanded her response. He was all buttoned up and starched for a night out, looking seriously sexy and gorgeous and manly…staring her way, smiling her way, not acknowledging anyone else in the room. Not her family or the police officers or the out-of-control beeping of her heart monitor. Just her. By the time he was beside her, sitting on her bed, she welcomed his arms around her. Craved his scent, turning into him—even if it hurt. *Jace.* She couldn't get close enough. This. This was what she needed.

His lips pressed against her ear. "I don't want to hurt you." He could never hurt her. Ever. It was a truth she'd finally come to accept. He was, without fail, the man she believed couldn't exist. And, dammit, she loved him.

If you love someone, you put their needs first. Always.
Another bit of her gramma's kitchen counseling.

Jace had Heather. A fledgling career. The support of a
record company, endorsements in the works. Obligations
to fulfill. He didn't need to be front and center for the
media circus she was going to unleash. He owed it to
himself, to his sister, to see this through.

She had to stop hiding. Tig Whitman had to pay. And
Jace shouldn't be a part of that. She wouldn't let him.
Now she had to pretend she wasn't exactly where she
wanted to be, burrowed against the chest she adored, and
go full-on bitch mode. She shook her head. "Jace." She
forced herself away from him. Be strong. For both of their
sakes. Strong. And mean.

"Don't do it." His brow furrowed, those light brown
eyes searching.

Dammit. Tough. Not soft and achy. Mean.

"Please." He blew out a deep breath. "Let me stay."

Yes, stay. Hold on to me. No. *Stop it.* She cleared her
throat. "I need…" She broke off. She didn't want him
here—it wasn't what was best for him. But she *needed*
him. "Stay."

He nodded, staring at her so long and hard Krystal's
eyes were burning something fierce. "I'm not going
anywhere."

That look. Her heart hammered away. When he
looked at her like that, she could almost believe he cared
about her—that, by some miracle, he might care for her
no matter what. She knew better. They'd never make it,

never made any sense. He was too good for her. Once he knew the truth about Tig, he'd never look at her this way again.

Officer Washington watched the exchange—the whole room did. Clearly, she had some concerns about Jace's arrival. "If you're staying, Mr. Black, I'd like to get back to questioning?" She nodded toward the door.

He stayed at her side, his warm gaze sweeping over her face. "Stay strong. I'm proud of you," he whispered.

She closed her eyes and took a deep breath. His words echoed. And they made her strong.

"Miss King, I understand that this might be difficult. But you need to be as thorough as possible. Details, in this situation, can be key."

She nodded. Details. The bits and pieces that made facts into so much more. "You heard her, guys. Last chance to bail." It was a pathetic attempt to defuse the tension in the room, but she had to try. Hoping they'd go. Hoping they'd stay.

Nobody moved.

She stared at the whiteboard on the far wall, listing the nurses on duty and an emoji pain scale for patients to use when describing their discomfort. She stared at the "High Level of Pain" face—red cheeks, tears, forehead scrunched. On the inside, that was her. She focused on that, focused on only that. Not her family or the police officers or even Jace. Just that red-pained face, and started talking.

"Tig Whitman is an asshole. Make sure you write that

part down." She took a deep breath and started talking. If she distanced herself, made it more like a narration, on the outside, the words came easier. She spoke slowly, carefully, choosing her words. Narrating—not involved. Going in to get Emmy's purse. What she heard. What she saw. Becca. What she suspected. Becca shutting her down. Tig—smug and smiling. A tremor ran along her skin. She stopped there.

Officer Washington waited. "And then?"

Jace's hand rubbed up and down her back, encouraging her. Because he didn't know what was coming. None of them did. Her stomach clenched.

She flexed her fingers, shook her hands out. They were all watching. All waiting. She blew out a long, wavering breath. The "High Level of Pain" emoji was blurring now. Her words weren't as steady when she described running for her bus, texting them to pick her up later, panicking—no point denying she had. "I wanted space…I was upset. Needed to get my head right." More hand shaking. "He was on the bus." She focused on the light overhead. The fluorescent bulb had a slight pulse. "He…he kept saying things…" Her gaze fell, darting toward her father, then the sheet covering her legs. "Things…that happened a long time ago." A long time ago. The past. No more. Head up. No more secrets. She cleared her throat, the edge to her voice defiant—wavering. "I'm a liar, he said. No one believed me then. Why would anyone believe me now? The truth won't change the past." Her hands were so cold, tingling. No matter how hard she shook them, she couldn't stop the frigid stinging shooting from her fingertips up her arms.

"You have a past with this man?" Officer Washington asked.

Her heart rate had accelerated to jackhammer intensity so she tugged off the finger monitor and threw it on the bed. It was only going to get worse. "I do. He was my mentor. My father's best friend. Near family. And he…molested me for almost a year before I told anyone." The words choked her. But they were out. She'd said it—the truth. Eyes burning, stomach churning, shaking like a leaf—but she'd done it.

And now everyone knew.

Jace jolted, the whole bed jerking.

Jace knew. She pressed her eyes shut, bracing herself.

"Are you fucking kidding me?" Travis's voice rose. "Who did you tell?" His eyes widened. He knew, his gaze slamming into their father. "Tig Whitman put his fat, white hands on my sister? And you knew? You… Why didn't you do something?" He was hurt.

It had hurt like hell when she'd realized her father was human—flaws and imperfect and capable of making terrible mistakes.

"Travis." Krystal tried to sit up, gripping the railing on the bed to steady herself.

"Krystal." Jace's hands held her shoulders. "Slow. Easy. Careful with yourself."

"Mr. King." Officer Washington's voice dripped authority, her careful, methodical stare down of her brother and father impressive. "When did this happen?"

"Fifteen. Until I was almost sixteen." She glanced at her father, her devastated father. "I was a handful back then, a kid who made stuff up and caused all sorts of hell. Now I know I was the sort of kid someone like him would look for."

"Camp?" Emmy's voice broke. "Momma sent you to that camp? Because of... *this*?"

Jace's breathing was unsteady now, his hand against her back still.

"This is such bullshit." Travis was pacing. "It's not like you were setting things on fire, causing fights, or stealing shit. If you had? It shouldn't have mattered." He was glaring at their father again. "A parent should always believe their kid. A parent should always protect their kid."

"Mr. King." Her dark brows rose. "Last warning." Officer Washington paused. "Back to the facts—to tonight. Who initiated the assault? Mr. Whitman is making his own claims about tonight." Officer Washington paused again. "He says he was the victim."

Which was hysterical and horrifying all at once. But really, what choice did he have? He wasn't going to fall to his knees, confess, and ask for forgiveness. But her? Attack him? "Me and my superhuman strength? Since he's there and I'm here, I'm guessing I didn't hurt him all that badly?"

Officer Washington didn't answer.

She paused. "He was close, too close, and I panicked. I started yelling for him to get out. And then, he put his hand over my mouth and I tried to get away."

"I was there." Sawyer shook his head. "I don't know how it started, but I saw how it ended. He was on top of her. His hand was over her mouth and she was screaming to get away. Kicking, clawing, she fought—"

"I can't do this." Travis. Anger, sadness, and fury marred his normally carefree face. "I can't." He pushed through the hospital room, the echo of his boots rapid on the linoleum floor.

"Daddy." Emmy stood. "He shouldn't be alone. I've never seen him like that."

Her daddy was torn. He didn't want to leave her. But Travis was known to make poor decisions when he was upset. And he'd never been this upset before.

"Emmy's right." Krystal nodded.

"I'll go." Jace was up, jaw locked. "I'll stay with him." He looked at Emmy.

"I'll stay with her." Emmy nodded.

He nodded and stooped, pressing a kiss to Krystal's forehead. "You're amazing, you know that?"

It was hard to look him in the eye.

His thumb ran along her jaw. "You are. Believe me. I know." Another kiss to her temple and then his footsteps were carrying him across the room.

She looked up once the hospital door swung shut, the weight of his absence making her hold on to her sister that much tighter.

"Miss King, let's go over a few more things." Officer Washington was talking again.

Jace was pretty sure that not being able to remember how he got here was one of the reasons he didn't drink. Here, being here, facedown in a thick, fluffy white carpet. He turned his head, groaning, and hoped like hell the white fluffy carpet he was snoring on was located someplace familiar.

His first thought was Heather. His phone, near dead, was in his pocket. One text last night, saying she and Misumi were spending the night in the town house, another later, saying Emmy and Krystal were flying Brenna in this afternoon. A third saying she and Misumi were coming to the King house around nine this morning.

He had no idea what time it was. Or where he was. Or how the hell he'd get to where he needed to be, namely, wherever Krystal was.

It took far too much energy, and a hell of a lot of nausea-inducing movement, to roll from his stomach to his back. But he did it. He pressed the palms of his hands to his temples, providing enough counterpressure to offset the throb behind his eyes. A few blinks and he could see.

"You were snoring." Krystal loomed over him, sitting in a large black-and-white chair, her legs curled beneath her, a laptop balanced on her knees.

He was at the Kings'.

And she wasn't in the hospital. Maybe, here, she wouldn't be so quick to shut him out. Her face was an angry train wreck of color, but she looked so damn beautiful to him. "I'm sorry." He sat up and instantly regretted it, sliding back to his elbows until his head eased.

"Whoa there, cowboy." She was fighting a smile. "You're in for one hell of a hangover. You're the color of my Aunt Linda's pea soup. Meaning green. Bright, putrid green."

"And this makes you happy?" If poking fun at his expense made her happy, bring it. Seeing her smiling was balm to his shaken soul. He managed, slowly, to push himself into a sitting position.

"As long as you don't throw up all over Emmy's rug, sure. She took a lot of time decorating our office." She glanced at him. "I thought you didn't drink?"

He leaned forward, laying his head on the edge of a nearby chair, staring around the large room. There was a large glass desk with computers on either side. A wall covered in family photos—photos of Clementine too. Books, lots of books, a large TV and stereo, massive speakers, and a floor-to-ceiling rack of CDs and records. "I don't. Now I remember why."

She laughed.

What headache? She was laughing. Beautiful. Close. Safe. That was all he needed.

He'd spent most of the night, what he remembered of it, trying not to think about what had happened to her. Not to erase it or pretend it hadn't happened, but to give him time to process it without going after the man who embodied true evil. While Travis talked, fuming and raging and sharing details that cut deep, they'd polished off an entire bottle of Whiskey Honey-Jack.

Tig Whitman had done the unspeakable. And Krystal, according to Travis, had owned it, been shamed by it, for years.

And her parents? Her mother? Sending Krystal away… He hadn't exactly been a fan of CiCi King. Now? Well, he hoped there was a special place in hell reserved for her—and Tig Whitman.

Staring at Krystal, even banged up, offered some comfort. The bruise darkening her upper cheek and eye wasn't easy to look at, but it was still Krystal. Same bright green eyes, same sarcastic smile, same crazy, mussed blond hair he loved to run his fingers through.

"How's your head?" he asked.

She wrinkled her nose. "Better than yours, I'd imagine."

Clementine chose that moment to run across the room and hop into his lap, her paws on his chest as she panted in his face. "Morning," he managed, rubbing the white poof on the top of the little dog's head.

Krystal was watching them, looking strained. "Leave Jace alone, Clem."

Now the dog was off-limits? She was playing hardball. "Travis said you had a concussion. Why'd they release you?"

"I'm fine." She rolled her eyes, then winced—making him wince, too. "I couldn't stand being there. And, yes, I worried Clementine would be missing me." Her voice trailed off. "At five, the morning shift started and they discharged me. I came home to my dog, my work, and you snoring face-first into my sheepskin carpet."

"Is that what it is?" he asked, pulling lint from his mouth.

She nodded, her smile wavering.

It was amazing what that did to him. That flash of vulnerability had him up, aching to hold her close. She didn't have to be strong for him. Whatever she needed, he'd do it.

"Jace." She held her hand up. "Stop."

He stopped, running a hand over his face. "What changed? Why are you shutting me out?"

She stared at him. "I'm not sure we're on the same page, Jace. After last night…" She tore her gaze from his. "I need space. My family and I have a lot going on. You and I both have a job to do, the final leg of the tour. And the single. Let's focus on that." No inflection, nothing. "The whole pretend relationship makes things complicated—"

"Complicated?" Was she serious? Last night had been hell. Traumatic. She was skittish for good reason. He'd accept that she needed space, but he wasn't going to act like what he felt wasn't real. The throb behind his eyes rivaling the throb in his chest. "It wasn't complicated. It was…" Real. For him, anyway. But now definitely wasn't the time for that.

She stood, crossing the room to a large couch. Travis was there, mouth open, passed out. Not that Jace cared. "We're not going to talk about this?"

"I just did." She glanced his way. "Drop it, Jace. We're friends. I don't have room for...more than that. Can you be my friend?" She crossed her arms over her chest.

He nodded, reeling.

"I'm hoping you two didn't drive here?" she asked. "You smell like a liquor cabinet."

That was it? Five minutes of some lame-ass explanation and he was supposed to accept that what they had, what he knew was real, wasn't? No way. He wasn't buying it.

"Can you two keep it down?" Travis groaned.

Jace frowned.

"Did I forget to mention my brother passed out, drooling, on my custom, hand-tooled leather love seat shaped after my favorite guitar?" She sighed.

"We had Jerome with us. Driving." Travis's words were muffled. "I'm not a complete moron."

"Why do you have a love seat shaped like your favorite guitar?" Jace inspected the love seat, looking for something—anything—to lessen the ache in his chest.

"More inspired by it?" She shrugged.

He forced a smile. "Sure. Of course. Why not? I have a recliner designed around my grandmother's favorite banjo."

She laughed. "It was some sort of endorsement for a leather company. Momma used them to help outfit the Kings' Coach II and Daddy's man cave, and because the owner's daughter liked me and Emmy, he made us each something one-of-a-kind." For a minute, she was smiling at him. "Do you play the banjo?"

He nodded. Bruised or not, she was beautiful. Damn, but he loved her. Even when she was doing her best to drive a wedge between them.

"I didn't get shit," Travis added. "In case you were wondering. The girls both got stuff. Not me. Did you hear me? About Jerome? All of it? Don't mind me—no one ever does."

Jace laughed, then grabbed his head. "I am never drinking again."

"Good plan." Hank King walked in, looking bone weary and...old. "Alcohol is the root of many a mistake. Glad everyone is up."

Jace had a hard time looking at the man who had turned his back on his daughter. There was no excuse for it, none. And, as much as he'd like to deny it, it changed the way he saw the man.

"Krystal, you've got about two hours before Molly Harper gets here."

"Wait, hold up." Travis sat up, groaned, and flopped back onto the couch. "Why is she coming?"

"Morning," Emmy singsonged, carrying in a large tray. "I made breakfast."

Travis waved his hand. "Shh, you're too frigging happy. And loud."

She sat the tray she'd been carrying on the coffee table in front of Krystal's love seat. Loudly. The thump and rattle of china made Travis scowl and moan. "You're not getting any sympathy. Keep snapping and you're not getting any muffins, either."

"Emmy said she was doing your makeup?" Hank asked. "You sure?"

Krystal nodded. "I'm not really ready to face people, in my face and business. Not yet. But this way it's only on TV. Even with hair and makeup, I look terrible."

"You are beautiful." Jace said it before he thought better of it. No, dammit, she needed to hear it, audience or not. She was beautiful.

Her gaze met his and held.

"I'm still lost." Travis tried again to sit up. "Someone turn off the spin cycle in here. Hottie Harper is coming here, why?"

"Did you just call her Hottie?" Emmy Lou was horrified.

"Am I wrong?" Travis looked at him. "Back me up here."

Jace held his hands up in mock surrender.

"Damage control. Misumi's idea—and she set it up." Krystal turned away, eyeing the muffins Emmy had brought with disinterest. "She's kind of amazing. Like, needs-a-raise sort of amazing."

"Fine. I'll let you sort that out." Hank nodded. "Gonna need all the damage control we can find since that son of a bitch already issued a statement saying Krystal invited him back to her bus, then attacked him in a fit of jealousy."

"Are you kidding me? She's got that." Travis pointed at Jace. "Young and, according to the thousands of women screaming his name, a stud. And everyone is supposed to believe she'd rather have balding Santa? Who's gonna buy that?"

Jace was too raw to find the humor in the situation. He was figuring Travis out, and like Krystal, Travis used humor to defuse awkward situations. Better than blowing up again... The hangover would probably keep him in check. Hard to get all fired up and hostile when any and all movement was a challenge.

"He brought up the past." Krystal sat again, the oversized black-and-white love seat making her look tiny and, banged up like she was, fragile.

"Hold on." Travis held up his pointer finger. "I need to down a cup of coffee before anyone says another word. Maybe two."

Jace wanted to know. Sort of. If he was going to get his act together before Molly Harper arrived, he needed to know everything there was to know—no surprises.

"There's a pot." Emmy pointed. "You're welcome."

"I'm guessing Travis filled you in?" Krystal asked, that flat voice again. He didn't like it. Didn't like not being able to take her hand. "You can sit, if you want." She was staring at him again, nibbling the inside of her lip.

Fine, if she wanted him to sit, he'd sit. Beside her. He sat close enough that their thighs were pressed together, touching. She stared down at their legs but didn't move. Even though there was plenty of room to move. It helped him. Maybe, hopefully, it helped her, too.

Clementine, tail wagging, ran back and forth across

their laps before flopping down and rolling over, belly exposed. *That's right, Clem, make your mommy smile.*

She did. "Shameless." Krystal gave her canine baby a good tummy rub.

"Okay." Travis reached for a muffin. "Go."

Between the throb behind his eyes and the tension rolling off Hank King, Jace braced himself. Until last night, he'd thought of Tig Whitman as a pioneer. An advocate for artists and musicians. Now his name stirred a visceral reaction he wasn't quite comfortable with. He wasn't normally quick to anger. Then again, there was nothing normal about this situation.

"He says Krystal was infatuated with him when she was young—that's why her mother and I sent her away. To get help for her unhealthy attachment to him." Hank crossed the room and stared out one of the windows overlooking their sprawling ranch. "He's the biggest chickenshit I've ever met in my life, but he's not stupid."

Just when Jace thought his headache was easing, it did a full one eighty, leaving him worse off than before.

"That shit." Travis paused, shocked. "Mother fu—"

"Enough with that word." Emmy shoved a muffin in his mouth. "You have a vocabulary. Use it. After you've swallowed."

Jace laughed, thrown by Emmy's outburst. For Emmy, shoving a muffin in her brother's mouth counted as an outburst. Her efforts to be her normal chipper self were valiant, but no one was fooled. None of them were okay.

How could they be? Last night changed the world for them. Today would change everyone else's. And it was just beginning.

Jace shook his head. "What you're doing? It's the right thing. That's all you need to remember. Not everyone is going to be able to accept it—but you know the truth."

"He's right." Her father turned. "No matter what, Krystal, we're seeing this to the end. No more hiding."

"Glad to see you've finally figured that out." Travis stood, stretching, shoving another muffin in his mouth.

Hank's posture dropped. "What I did—"

"What you didn't do," Travis corrected.

Hank nodded. "It was wrong."

"Wrong?" Travis shook his head. "Daddy, you and Momma and Tig? Might as well have done the same thing. Betraying her." He was getting angry now, his cheeks going red. "How she could stand to look at you, every day, smile and hug you and act like you loved her when you knew what happened. Knew and did nothing."

Jace was heartbroken for Hank King, but Travis was right.

"Travis." Krystal was up, standing between her father and her brother. "If we fall apart, our family, that's on me. Whether or not that makes sense to you, it's true. This is on me. My fault." She pressed a hand to her chest. "I'm the reason this is happening. Don't make me regret coming forward with this, please. Don't make me the bad guy here."

Her words were enough to break Hank King. He

moved quickly, grabbing his daughter and pulling her into his arms, cradling her against him. "No, baby girl. None of this is your fault, you hear me? This is on me and your mother. We didn't listen—sent you away. And then you stopped talking. We did that to you. Left you alone when you needed us most." His voice broke then, and he was crying.

Krystal was sobbing. "Daddy."

Emmy grabbed Travis's arm and started tugging him to the door.

"Can you forgive me?" Hank said. "I know I can't."

Jace followed Emmy and Travis, closing the office door behind them.

The three of them looked at each other, wearing a range of expressions. None good. The only thing Jace could do now was be there for Krystal. So he would. No matter what. Even if she'd made it clear that that wasn't what she wanted.

"We all agree this is fu—" Travis stopped. "Messed up? And Momma's not even here yet."

Emmy sighed. "No, this time your words are right. This is all totally fucked up."

It didn't matter how bad Jace's head was hurting, they were all three laughing then.

Chapter 17

THE INTERVIEW WOULDN'T END. KRYSTAL DID HER best to stay calm without being distant, something Misumi said she had problems with. This was all about connecting with the audience and appealing to their emotions. Empathy. Sympathy. All that crap that made her want to run and hide.

What good was being emotional? It made it easier to attack, to tear people down, when they showed their weakness.

Krystal wasn't prepared for Molly Harper to cry. On camera. Not a single dramatic tear, either. It was more a "someone get her a box of tissues" sort of thing. Why that made Krystal cry was an even greater mystery. Maybe having her daddy sobbing in her arms had flipped some sort of crying switch, and now it was stuck in the on position? And Misumi's whole "be human and emote" thing wasn't helping. Whatever, it sucked—all of it. Big-time.

"You have your diary with you?" Molly asked.

"After Tig's statement, I found it. I wrote down everything, processing, trying to make sense of what was happening. I was almost relieved to see what I'd written—because I needed confirmation of what really happened. Even now, he has the ability to make me doubt myself and what I know is true." She tapped the book. "It was horrible. He is a liar. A liar who is playing on the persona the media has cultivated and enforced about me."

"Except for our show."

"You have been nothing but kind to me, Molly." She nodded. "It means a lot. Especially you coming here this morning."

"After what you've been through, you shouldn't be traveling." Her attention wandered to Emmy Lou's modest cover-up job. "When you say confirmation of what happened." Molly eyed the diary. "You are referring to *encounters* with Tig Whitman?"

Krystal nodded. "I got this from my sister on my fifteenth birthday. Our birthday. It was the first time Tig ever touched me in a way that I knew was wrong."

Molly was dabbing her eyes again. "Why didn't you tell anyone, Krystal?" She paused. "I think I understand, but for viewers out there who might be in your situation or have a similar past, maybe hearing from you can help them. Or give them comfort?"

Which was a mantle she wasn't ready to wear. She was broken and messed up—not in a position to help anyone. Still, she tried. "He said I was his special girl. It was natural to show the people you cared about, he said. And since there are different types of love, there are different ways to show it. To *prove* it." She shrugged. "I did love him. He was more or less my uncle. There was this disconnect between what he was saying, which made me feel loved, and what he did, which made me ashamed and dirty." She paused. "If I told, he'd stop—but my family would know and be sad and ashamed, too, maybe even embarrassed. I'd lose and hurt my family and I'd lose the praise and support he gave me—inappropriate behavior aside. Abuse like that isn't simple. Especially for the victim."

"What would you like to tell your fans?" Molly paused. "I know this is hard for you."

Krystal nodded, tears stinging her eyes. "My fans kept me going." She shook her head. Screw it. The tears weren't stopping. "Their love made me feel less... broken. And alone. I've had some dark days, a lot of them recorded, but it's hard to live with. This 'what I did' thing that has gnawed and gnawed at me until there's this hole inside."

"But it's a 'what was done to you' thing, Krystal." Molly was close to more tears. "Do you think your experience has impacted your ability to foster healthy relationships?"

Krystal stared at her lap. Her hands were shaking. "Definitely. I admit to being guarded. For me, love is another word for making okay things that aren't right. The great manipulator. Men—people—in my life have used that word right before they did something that had nothing to do with the emotion." She swallowed. "Or used me in the hopes of advancing their career."

"Has that been a worry with you and Jace?" Molly asked.

"No." She shook her head. "He is the real deal." He was everything.

Molly nodded. "Last question, then. What are you hoping to accomplish with this statement?"

"It's been ten years. I have reason to believe I wasn't the only one victimized. My hope is, by sharing what happened, others will find the courage to come forward to stop him. He's in a place of power, working with other powerful people. It's likely they know or suspect what he's done but, like me, they have somehow come to terms with his behavior for whatever reason makes it bearable for them. No one wants to hear about this stuff. No wants to believe someone liked and respected is capable of this. They need to look a certain way, act a certain way—not be the guy you have at family picnics or teaching your kid to drive. Victims know this. That's where the shame comes in. 'How could a normal person do something like this? Maybe it's me? I must have done something to make them act this way.'" She was staring at her hands but forced herself to look at Molly. "But that's the lie. It's not you. Me. The victim's fault. Don't fall into that trap. Don't believe. Trust your instincts. Parents, listen to your kids. If they're telling you something is happening to them, something is. Listen and do something about it."

"Krystal, I can't thank you enough for inviting me into your home. I am saddened by what's happened to you. And, like so many fans, I hope this long and likely complicated journey will lead to the closure and justice you deserve. You have support. We're with you. And we all wish you a quick recovery." She smiled. "And cut."

Krystal and Molly sat, staring at each. The sun was

pouring into the music room, casting shadows on all the framed gold and platinum records lining the walls. Molly said it offered the sort of ironic contrast that would add a punch to the setting. Even the most successful can be affected by sexual abuse—anyone could be. "You did really well."

Krystal stood, still hooked up to her mic. "Thank you, Molly. Really."

But Molly was hugging her. "My cousin. He was older than me."

And then Krystal was hugging her back, tight, a wave of compassion and understanding almost drowning her. This woman, sunny and together, was broken inside, too. It hit her then…had she said enough? Not just for herself, but for Molly—others? "I'm so sorry."

"Me too. For you. You are awesome." She stepped back, all smiles. "I'd really like to continue to cover this, if you're okay with it? Do some investigative work? You know, reporting?"

"Yes." Krystal nodded. She'd only find truth. How could that be a bad thing?

The tech was unhooking them when the door opened and her mother walked in.

"Shit," she whispered.

Molly turned. "I'm guessing this is the parent who didn't listen?"

Krystal wasn't going to throw her parents under the bus. This wasn't about them. This was about Tig. Her father was truly haunted by his actions; she didn't have it in her to hold his mistakes against him. But her mother? Tempting as it was, she wouldn't out her mother for the queen manipulator she was.

"Molly," her mother gushed. "I'm sorry I wasn't here to greet you."

"Mrs. King." Molly shook her hand. "It was so incredibly kind of you to open your amazing home to me and my crew."

"I only wish it were under less horrific circumstances." Her mother's sympathy was almost as good as her surprise. Krystal often wondered how much time her mother spent in front of her mirror practicing her emotional repertoire. Knowing her mother, a lot. She was a perfectionist when it came to delivery. If she was going for sympathy, Krystal wasn't buying it. Then again, she knew her mother all too well.

"Yes." Molly nodded. "Still, you have to be proud of your daughter for taking a stand. It's sad that there's still such a stigma attached to sexual abuse."

"Hank and I were just discussing that." Her mother nodded. "Please say you'll stay for some iced tea and a walk around the house and grounds?"

"Tea sounds lovely." Molly nodded. "Unfortunately, we have to head to ACMF soon."

"Of course." Her mother smiled. "Duty calls. Us career girls have to keep our eye on the prize always."

Over the years, Krystal had come to terms with her mother's career choice. Keeping the Three Kings on top, her family together, and her father relevant on the

music charts was, apparently, a full-time job—with lots
of overtime. How did CiCi King manage it all? Through
whatever means were necessary. She was ruthless in her
efficiency.

"They're all waiting for us in the kitchen," her mother
said. "Feel free to bring a camera, of course."

Of course.

"Are you sure?" Molly asked, excited.

"Certainly."

The three of them, cameraman in tow, strolled from
the music room and down the hall to the large family
kitchen. Her family was gathered around the massive
farm table in the kitchen, Jace and Heather included.
From the looks on their faces, her mother's invitation
had not been a family decision.

"Let's show our guest some Texas hospitality." Her
mother smiled.

Travis hopped up. "Miss Harper." He pulled the chair
back, smiling what he thought of as his smolder face.

Krystal sighed, her gaze instinctively bouncing to
Jace.

He winked. And her heart thumped. *Dammit.* This,
being a couple in front of Molly and her camera, was
going to be a challenge.

Emmy and Krystal made sure everyone, cameraman
included, had a tall glass of sweet iced tea. Homemade
ginger, oatmeal raisin, and pecan sandy cookies were put
on the table and, slowly, the strain of the whole surprise
eased. Molly shared some of her favorite assignments

while Travis hung on every word. Her father, still not quite himself, tried to engage. While Heather was too nervous to do more than give one-word responses about college and her brother's career.

Krystal was fully aware of Jace's arm draped along the back of her chair. Since they had an audience, it made sense to lean against him. She could breathe now. The interview was over, her nightmare ready to be shared with the world. It was horrible and real and done. She could breathe. For now.

But the minute the cameraman was done with his cookies and he'd begun filming, her mother was *on*.

"I wanted to thank you for coming out, Molly." Her mother assumed her concerned expression. Not too much of a furrow—her Botox wouldn't allow that. "We are just heartsick over this whole ordeal."

Jace's arm tightened, his other hand taking Krystal's. She held on. That's what you did. Held hands, sat close…

"You have to understand, that was a trying time in our lives." Her mother paused for dramatic effect. "I'd had a terrible accident and was taking those horrible pills— the ones they've taken off the market now—for pain?" She looked at Hank. "What were they called?"

No one answered.

She vaguely remembered her parents having an accident on the way back from an awards show. Her parents had only suffered mild injuries—but they were Hank and CiCi King so it had made front-page news. Was that what she was talking about?

What was she saying? What accident? What pills?

"Anyway." Her mother shook her head, appearing confused. "It was all a haze. All of it. Poor Hank had his hands full with my health, his mother's passing, his career, the kids and their career, and then Krystal." She shook her head. "We thought it was all over and done with. How were we supposed to know? She had come home from camp and said it was all made up for attention."

Krystal stared at her mother, stunned. Her mother was going to undermine her? Poke holes in her story instead of offering her support? Even now. What was her goal? Or was this true? Her daddy seemed to think so. It was easier to accept... But was this the truth? That was the question. Her mother always—always—had a master plan at work.

"No, she didn't." Hank patted his wife's hand. "You were still taking those pills then, sugar. Krystal never said that. I didn't know about the pills, you see. CiCi here, she likes to take care of all of us—she didn't want to worry me. If I had, things would have played out differently. Not a day goes by that I don't wish I couldn't go back and fix this all."

He smiled at Molly. "When Krystal came home, she wouldn't talk about it anymore. At all." He sighed. "CiCi is right about my mama passing."

"I'm so sorry," Molly murmured. "It sounds like a tough time all around."

"She and Krystal were real close. Bet you didn't know, but Krystal loves to bake. She's wanted to do a cookbook for years." He smiled at her. "But losing her gramma was hard on her, I think. That, on top of everything... It's no wonder she stopped talking, with no one to listen. I can't imagine what you went through, baby girl. Tears my heart out."

Krystal stared at her father in absolute shock. He'd defended her. Publicly. He'd taken away any doubt her mother's story might have caused.

Jace was rubbing her upper arm. "She's strong."

"She's awesome." Heather grinned at her. "A real-life hero."

"I agree." Molly nodded.

Backstage at the Austin Country Music Festival Awards was chaos. From the sheer number of acts rotating in and out of the Austin Opry to the mass of fans crowded in front and behind the venue, hoping to catch a glimpse of their favorite performers.

"I'm not sure I'm cut out for this." Jace sat on a stool, tuning his guitar. He and Krystal were supposed to perform their duet soon. Krystal, who'd been avoiding him since Molly Harper left the Kings' place. Krystal, who would barely look at him. They were supposed to sing their duet?

"Get out of your head." Travis clapped him on the shoulder. "She's fine."

Jace shot him a look. "What sort of reception is she

going to get here tonight? She could get booed off the stage, Travis. You think she'll be fine if that happens?" He waited. The interview with Molly was going to air that night, but the sound bites and commercials removed any doubt what they were going to talk about.

"You two have your first single dropping next week. This scandal sucks, but timing wise, it's not a bad thing."

Jace's fingers paused on the tuning peg. "I can't believe you said that."

"C'mon, man. It's called trying to find a silver lining in this pile of shit thundercloud, okay?" Travis threw his water bottle on the stage. "You think I want to be here?" He turned, his narrowed gaze searching. "I can't shake the feeling he's here. Restraining order or not."

"Not if he wants to live," Jace said. He wasn't one for violence, but he'd had some pretty vivid daydreams about pummeling the shit out of Tig Whitman. And they brought him great joy.

Travis chuckled. "Right?" He sighed. "She's putting you through hell, isn't she?"

He didn't answer.

"You really love her, don't you?" Travis's disbelief was irritating.

"Yes, I love her." He slid the guitar strap over his neck and stood, looking down the hall toward the side entrance. Krystal and her father had decided to stay in the bus until their performance. After that, they'd slip out. Jace would have gone, too, if Heather weren't in the audience with Brenna, her college roommate. No matter how many times Heather insisted she didn't need a babysitter, he didn't want the press getting to her like they were trying to get to him.

"This is hitting her hard," Travis said.

"I know." He nodded. "It kills me that she has to go through this. I just, you know, want to be there for her."

"You ready?" Travis asked, nodding behind him.

Jace turned to find Krystal headed his way. Seeing her tilted chin and defiant posture made him ache. He knew why she did that tonight—why she always did that. Better to keep everyone at arm's length than risk letting someone close again. After the hurt she'd suffered, it made sense.

But treating him like the rest of the world hurt like a son of a bitch.

With her body-hugging suede dress, fringes swinging around her thighs, her long blond hair hanging free, and boots reflecting the backstage floor lights, she was Krystal King—music icon. But when she was close enough for him to see her, the brutal reminder of her attack dark on her face, she was simply the woman he loved. Fierce and defiant. Strong and smart. Fragile and damaged. Outspoken and timid. All scrambled up inside.

"You're staring." She smiled up at him, uneasy.

"Have you seen how incredible you look?" He leaned forward, brushing her cheek with his lips. Maybe the crowds and the chaos would work in his favor. When they were "pretending" she seemed happier than when they were alone—like she needed the audience to let herself have this connection with him. "Beautiful."

"You look pretty good yourself. This is better." She reached up and unsnapped another button. "Give them a tease."

Sawyer, Krystal's constant shadow, sighed loudly. But they both ignored him.

He glanced down at the amount of skin and tattoo showing and shot her a look. "I'm not sure I want to be eyed like a piece of meat."

"Oh, you do, trust me." Travis nodded.

Krystal's smile faded, her gaze on the dip in his shirt.

He reached up to snap it closed, but she stopped him.

"Enjoy it." She pointed up and down his body. "Travis would be more than happy to introduce you around." Her gaze locked with his. "Until then, remember, this is a big night, Jace. You want to make the biggest impression you can. Wheelhouse isn't the only record label out there, you know. Options are good."

"She's got you there." Travis shook his head. "Play it safe, and lose the shirt. But wear the hat."

Krystal was laughing.

Emmy poked her head around one of the curtains. "Are you coming?" she called to Travis. "Come on." She smiled. "Break a leg, you two."

Travis trotted toward Emmy, dodging a sound tech and a tangle of cords as he went.

They walked onto the stage, but their rehearsed banter was loud enough to hear backstage.

"Hey, Trav, any idea who's up next?" Emmy started their introduction. "I think the name sounds familiar."

The audience laughed.

"I'm not going out with Travis." Jace leaned in. "Wouldn't that go against the whole committed relationship thing?"

Krystal rolled her eyes. "Fine. Work on your discretion."

Travis was up now. "Yeah. You're right. Very familiar." Pause.

Jace shook his head. Now wasn't the time or place for this conversation but, dammit, there were things that needed to be said.

"Right. I remember now." Travis snapped his fingers. "He won that television show. Jace Black."

A couple of whistles and a few screams.

Krystal looked up at him, then the dip in his shirt.

Emmy continued. "Um, Travis." She waited until the laughing died down. "I was talking about our sister? My twin? Krystal King?"

He felt Krystal stiffen, waiting for some backlash from her impending televised interview. Her accusations would have a ripple effect over the entire industry. There was no guarantee how tonight would go.

But the audience was clapping. A few fans screamed. Maybe not thunderous applause but a whole hell of a lot better than nothing.

She smiled.

"You ready?" He took her hand, squeezed it.

Travis and Emmy came back.

"It's all you two." Emmy smiled.

Jace nodded and led Krystal onto the stage, to the two stools set up mid-spotlight.

He gave her a hand up and onto the stool, earning a few whistles and cheers, then sat beside her. He waited for her slight smile and started to play, his gaze never leaving her face.

He sang, the words pouring out of him without thought. Her words. Her heart. Her story. Love, for Krystal, had never been free from suffering. "I remember you, standing in the sun, smiling at me, and suddenly my world caught fire. Blinding, beautiful fire."

Her green eyes were deep emerald, shining in the light, the light showing the whole world the damage Tig Whitman had done to her face. Her voice wavered as she sang the first words. With a slight shake of her head, she kept on, stronger. "Blinding, beautiful fire." The rasp of her voice rolled over him, mesmerizing him. She did that every time.

The fans sang along to the chorus so he held the microphone out and sang, Krystal smiling and clapping along to the beat. He glanced back and her eyes locked with his as she sang, "And your words, your lies, your promises were the sweetest pain of all."

He kept playing, kept singing, but stepped closer, needing to touch her. She reached up, resting one hand on his shoulder. Like she knew. Like she needed it, too.

"Love isn't love when the flames burn it down. There's

no hiding or forgiveness from the damage that it's done."
They sang the chorus together. "When the smoke clears
away, you'll still find me searching here. Searching for the
ashes of my heart."

By the time the song finished, the spark he loved—
the energy performing gave her—was shining back at
him. When the last note faded, the audience erupted.
He pointed at her, more clapping. She shook her head
and pointed his way. Another bow and he took her hand,
leading her off the stage.

"Y'all were amazing," Emmy said as she and Travis
hurried back onstage.

But Krystal was tugging him away from the stage, down
the hall, and out the side door. Sawyer, practically glued
to Krystal, didn't flinch, just followed a few steps behind.

"Where are we going?" he asked.

She glanced back at him, eyes blazing with hunger.

He stopped walking, staring down at her. He wanted
her. He'd always want her—but his heart was invested in
more.

Her gaze fell to his lips. "I need you." She blinked.
"Need to feel good."

"Me?" he asked.

She swallowed, her gaze falling from his.

Later, it would hurt. Right now? He scooped her up,
picking up the pace as they headed for the bus.

They were breathless when they stumbled inside.
Impatient, she pushed him against the wall of the stair-
well, her kiss desperate for more. With a tug, the snaps

popped wide. With a sigh, she stared at his chest. "I can't tell you how satisfying that is."

She had his shirt off before they made it up the steps—her boots, one of his, and his belt forming a path to her bedroom door.

He kicked the door shut, his hands spinning her around. "Not tearing it this time." He pulled the zipper down, his hands slipping inside. Her skin. Soft and smooth. He moaned, pressing his nose against her soft hair and nuzzling the base of her neck. His hands slid up, across the plane of her stomach, to cradle the full weight of her breasts.

She arched into his hands, the peaks hardening against his fingertips.

She wiggled free, shimmying out of her dress and turning to face him.

He leaned against the door, aching for her. But, dammit, aching for more.

She saw, the panic on her face tearing at him. Just before her green eyes fluttered closed, he saw what he needed. Hunger for him. More than that, tenderness. So deep and real it reached inside his chest and gave him hope. As long as there was hope, he'd never give up. She stood on tiptoe, breathless and nervous and hungry for his kiss. He welcomed it.

Light. Featherlight. A mix of breath. And instant heat.

"Don't let go," she whispered.

"I won't." One hand cradled the back of her neck, while the other arm pulled her in close. *Ever.*

His lips found hers, sealing them together. She arched into him, her fingers tightening in his thick hair as the tip of her tongue tasted the seam of his mouth. Her soft moan sent a frisson of heat along each and every nerve. He teased her, the tip of his tongue, the cling of his lips, bearing her back on her bed to explore every curve. The spot behind her knee. The bend of her elbow. The skin of her side. Her hip. He lingered over her breasts, until each tip was pebble-hard for his mouth. Her bra and panties joined everything else on the floor, and still he took his time. His unhurried exploration had her breathing hard and hanging on to his waist.

He shivered as her fingers traced—the lightest of touches—the pattern of ink across his chest and arms. His lips parted hers, and she gasped at the thrust of his tongue and the fervor of his kiss. He was barely holding on, the press of her knees against his hips a clear invitation. When she was gasping for air, his lips traveled to the spot behind her ear, down the length of her neck, to press hot, wet kisses at the juncture of her neck and shoulder.

He stared down at her as they came together, hissing as the tight heat of her body opened for him.

"Jace," she whispered, her nails scraping his upper arms.

If this was what she needed, being in his arms, he'd give it to her. She might not be ready to admit that there was a hell of a lot more than animal attraction going on here. But she would. When she was ready. Until then, he'd be here. Giving her what she needed. Loving her as best he could.

Chapter 18

"This one says I'm a soulless millennial exploiting real issues for a profit." Krystal skimmed the rest of the article. "All about how spoiled and entitled I am. Blah blah blah. Should be thankful for the people who've put me where I am—Tig Whitman included." She set the magazine aside and poked at her grapefruit half. "I am thankful. Not for Tig, but for how lucky I am."

"Um, luck might have something to do with it. But you know, there's that whole hard work and real talent thing that helps, Krys. Stop reading them." Travis pushed the magazine off the table and onto the floor.

She shrugged.

It had been a week since her interview. In that time, Tig had located two kids from the Wellness Ranch—people she had no recollection of—talking about how mean and dismissive she was of everyone else there.

One backup singer—whom her mother had fired—shared an episode confirming Krystal's "temper tantrum mentality" when she ripped off a costume backstage and screamed at her manager. That one was true. But Steve had insisted she wear a dress that didn't let her move. She'd almost fallen twice during her performance, so when she'd finished her set without actual bodily harm, she had taken it off and thrown it at him.

Even Misumi's mother had been sucked into it all, her comments edited to sound as if Misumi was overworked and underpaid. But that was only partly true. Krystal and Emmy had just given her a substantial raise and her hours were self-imposed. The girl didn't have an off switch.

Not all of these newly unearthed "close connections" were bad. The woman she'd volunteered with at the animal shelter had only nice things to say about Krystal. "I trust an animal's instinct over a human's any day. All the animals loved Krystal. I think what's happening to her is shameful."

Her choreographer praised how methodical and dedicated she was to her overall health and performance—not in the least bit relevant for this situation, but still nice to hear. Her daddy had always enforced how important being in shape was to a performer. Eating right, with the occasional splurge, and working out were a part of daily routine. A habit, not a chore or hardship.

Mrs. Charles, her favorite school tutor, had blasted the bad press. "That girl is tough because she's had to be. It's easy to twist things around when you have no idea what they've been through. She tells everyone what she's been through and people are still twisting things around." She had sent Mrs. Charles a thank-you note and some daisies, her favorite. Few people outside her family would dare to defend her so vehemently at this point.

She and her siblings' entire education had been conducted through tutors and online programs. Until now, she'd hated missing out on going to school, having friends, a lunch period, recess… Now, she was relieved. Who knew what sort of backlash Jimmy from second grade could use against her? As it was, there was no Jimmy from second grade.

"You need to focus on other things right now. Good things. The single drops tomorrow," Travis reminded her, pushing the grapefruit closer. "Eat something. You're getting all pokey looking."

She frowned.

Emmy appeared, sliding into the red vinyl booth beside her. "You should have ordered the waffles. With the strawberries and cream."

She nodded.

"Why is my magazine on the floor?" Emmy stooped.

"She was reading the article." Travis shot their sister a look. "It wasn't kind. Imagine that, considering the title and all."

"A Tragedy or a Tragic Liar?" It was Emmy Lou's turn to frown. "I didn't buy it for the articles." She flipped the pages and held it up. "There's a whole section on Halloween treats." She turned the page. "Look at these marshmallow ghosts. Aren't they adorable? And these cookie and pretzel spiders. We need to have a Halloween party so I can make all this."

Emmy's favorite holiday was Halloween. It was true, they had only the best memories of the holiday. Costumes made it okay for the family to go out together, without all the hubbub that would normally accompany a King family outing. As a child, having your daddy to yourself like other kids—even for one night—had made the night special.

"Halloween is a ways off." Travis stared down at the recipe. "Why would you combine a chocolate crème cookie with pretzel sticks and licorice?"

"Don't knock Red Vines." Krystal pointed at him with her spoon. "They are never a bad choice."

The bell over the diner door rang and she turned, like she had the last four times it rang, to see who had come in. Not that she was looking for someone in particular.

"He's not coming. Said he didn't sleep well. Or feel well. One of them." Travis sighed, leaning back. "You need to make up your mind, Krystal. You keep stringing him along, you're going to lose him. Guys don't like that shit."

"I'm not stringing him along. My mind is made up and he knows that." Not that she or her siblings believed a word she said. Her heart definitely didn't. With a sigh, she set down her spoon. "What's wrong? Is he sick? Or just tired?"

Travis shrugged. "He didn't want breakfast. I asked what's up. He said he 'feels like hell.'"

Checking on this would be bad. Denial or not, some of her behavior could possibly, probably, fall in to the stringing-him-along category. But it wasn't intentional. She tried to keep her distance, she did. But one look from him, one crooked smile, or the brush of his hand, and she was kissing him—then running away.

She stared out the front windows, the buses lined up

along the outside of the parking lot. "I should check on him."

"No. You shouldn't." Emmy Lou shook her head. "You told me to keep you away from him, remember? You can't get mad at me."

"You told her to remind you of what?" Travis asked. "What the hell is wrong with you?"

When it came to Jace, she had the best of intentions but zero willpower. Krystal slipped out of the booth. "Page seventy-eight will give you a laundry list to pick from." She went to the counter, ordered three bear claws and two black coffees, smiled at the starstruck waitress, and hurried to the boys' bus.

Hardy, the driver, opened the door and thanked her for the bear claw and coffee she'd brought.

"Breakfast?" she called out softly.

She walked to the back of the bus. Unlike her and Emmy's top-of-the-line model, this one was more basic. She and Emmy had their own rooms, snug but private. There was one sleeping compartment at the back of this one, but it was reserved for her father. Jace and Travis had the not-so-private sleeping bunks built into either side of the bus. When they weren't in use, the bunk folded up and out of the way. Efficient, her father called it. Uncomfortable, Travis countered, pointing out the inequality in the buses whenever he had the chance.

Jace was sleeping, hard. His face was turned away, sheet rumpled across his chest. She swallowed, marveling at that chest. Jace was…well, his body was impressive.

Not just the muscles, all of him. She sighed, hating how much she ached for this man.

One arm was draped out, his hand hanging off the edge of his bunk. A pencil lay on the ground, dropped, on top of sheet music. Sheet music she had no right to read. A glimpse down the hall told her there was no one around to know if she'd read it. And she and Jace had worked on several songs together, so there was a chance he'd share this one, too.

And she really, really wanted to read it.

She kicked off her shoes and sat on the other bunk, picking up the sheet music with care.

"Let Me Love You." She stared over the edge of the page at him, sound asleep. Her heart thumped so hard and heavy against her chest. What would she do if he ever said something like that to her? *Stop with the daydreaming.* Her eyes skimmed over the words, paused, then read them again—slowly—the music playing out in her head. "You say your heart is hard and there's no hope. Your world split wide and you can't cope. Words are empty and nothing more. Finding strength, a daily chore. I say, stop fighting to stand alone. Words can heal, hear my song. Don't let the world defeat you. Don't lock your heart away. See me standing here and let me love you." The words were blurring. "Through the dark of night and the light of day, I will love your troubles away. When you're cold and you've lost your way, I will love you home to stay. See me standing here and let me love you. Because I do. I love you."

She wiped the tears from her face and finished reading

the song. His writing was loopier at the end, almost too small to read. It was brilliant. He was brilliant.

She stared at him, sound asleep, his cheeks red. *I love you.*

She put the page back and knelt, resting a hand on his forehead. He was flushed. Maybe he was sick?

He jolted awake, sleep-filled eyes blinking as he turned to look at her. "Krystal?" He sat up, running a hand over his face. "What's wrong?"

"Nothing." She held up the bag and coffee. "Travis said you weren't feeling well. Wanted to make sure you were okay."

"Didn't sleep much last night," he explained, yawning. "New song…" He looked around his bed, then over the edge. "Here." He picked it up and placed it on the bed beside him, facedown.

Interesting. Not sharing then. Guilt kicked in. "I read it. It was there and I couldn't not read it."

He grinned. "And?"

"And it's amazing." She nibbled on her lip. "A perfect duet."

"Sort of what I was thinking." He stared at the pages. "This bit right here. It needs something."

"Maybe we can look at it later? If you want?"

His gaze met hers. "I do."

The longer he looked at her, the tighter her lungs felt. It was downright unnerving. "I just wanted to make sure you were feeling okay." She stood. "We've got all those press things tomorrow."

"*That's* why you're checking in?" He shook his head. "Thanks. I'll be ready for tomorrow."

Which wasn't what she meant at all. "No." She set the bag on his bed.

"No?" He stared up at her, stubble-covered jaw and wild dark hair. Shirtless. Gorgeous.

He truly took her breath away. "No." She repeated. His gaze locked with hers and an instant surge of heat caught deep in her belly, burning outward.

He grinned, one brow shooting high. "You're here for sex?"

"What?" Laughter erupted, startled and breathless. "No." She shook her head. "No."

"That's the fourth time you've said that." He pushed the blankets back and stood, his boxers hanging low on his hips. "At the risk of losing my man card, I'm not in the mood." His gaze swept over her face.

He shouldn't look at her like that then. Shouldn't look at her like she was something to eat. Shouldn't make her shake with longing. There was no bite in her words as she attempted to argue with him. "I'm not—wasn't here for se—"

He kissed her then, hands sliding through her hair and pulling her close. His warmth wrapped around her, melting whatever trace of resistance she had and setting her on fire. His teeth nipped her lower lip until her moan gave him access to her mouth. His tongue slid deep.

She wanted this, wanted him. Her hands wandered over the carved expanse of his chest. A delicious and hard chest she shouldn't be stroking. "Jace." She pushed away. "That's not… I didn't come here for this."

"You said that." He was breathing hard. "And you're not here because you were worried I couldn't do all the promotional stuff tomorrow?"

When he said it that way, she sounded like a horrible person. It wasn't about him being up for their promo spots tomorrow. Not at all. "Travis said you weren't feeling well." She was flustered now.

"And?" he waited, half-naked, flushed, and staring at her mouth. If he expected a coherent answer, he needed to stop acting like he was ready and willing to finish what he—she—they'd started.

Why had she come? "You want me to say I was worried? Fine." She shook her head, snapping. "I was worried about you. Not the stupid interviews." She glared at him. "I wanted to check on you. To make sure you were okay."

He was smiling. "Really?"

"Yes, really, dammit." She was beyond flustered now. What did it matter anyway? She pointed at the bag. "Food and coffee." She frowned, tearing her gaze away. "Don't choke on it." She spun, stomping down the hall toward the door.

Travis was halfway up the steps when she came down, brushing past him. "Problem?"

"Shut up," she snapped, heading for her bus, ignoring her brother's laugh.

What the hell was that? She had been worried about him. That was a human response, wasn't it? Then she'd been caught up in the beauty of his words. Next, she'd been tangled in the beauty of his arms, and then he... he... What did he want? Some sort of revelation? Did he think he was being cute by dragging some half-hearted admission that, yes, she cared about *him*, not just their working relationship? Why did he have to look so damn pleased about it?

"What's wrong?" Emmy Lou looked up from her computer. "You saw the news?"

"News?" Krystal repeated, still trying to make sense of that smile. Of course she cared about him. They were... friends. It's not like she was pouring her heart out to him, telling him how she really felt about him.

"Tig?" Emmy Lou turned her laptop around. "This just posted."

That name was more effective than having a bucket of ice water dumped on her head. "What?" Her eyes adjusted to the screen and read "Tig Whitman Plans to Sue King Family in Civil Court."

She sat in the dining booth before her legs could buckle. With a thunk, her forehead rested against the table and she stretched her arms out so her hands could dangle off the other side. What had she been thinking? Oh right, that she was doing the right thing. She shook out her hands.

Beyond the press, there had been an incredible outpouring of emails, letters, and cards from hundreds of survivors. They believed her. They thanked her. They wanted advice on how to keep going, how to live, how to let go. Answering them helped her feel stronger, reminding her of why she'd stepped forward. She never pretended to have the answers, she didn't. Every day was a struggle. Some days were harder than others. But surviving until it got easier was what they had to do—or their attacker still had control. She said that to them. And yet, here she was, letting Tig and his stupid threats get to her.

It didn't take long for Travis and Jace to climb on board their bus.

"I'm guessing you heard?" Travis asked.

She didn't move. Tig couldn't win. No one believed her; no one had come forward with stories of similar abuse. But, dammit, he couldn't win.

"Taking it well, then?" Travis asked.

She flipped him off. "Why did I... I'm stupid. I knew...I knew it was a risk—"

"A risk worth taking." Jace knelt by her, his hand resting on her thigh. "Don't second-guess yourself. Don't doubt what you did. It's never a bad idea to do the right thing, Krystal."

She'd known the media would pick apart her family's every action—but that hadn't made it any easier to see.

They'd started with her parents. Following the near catastrophe of her interview, her parents had one hell of a fight. Screaming, her mother; and doors slamming, her mother; and the shockingly calm suggestion that one of them leave for a while, her father, had ended with just that. Her mother decided now was the time to visit one of her sorority friends. In Italy. While the details of the fight hadn't made it to the press, there was all sorts of speculation about CiCi's sudden international trip— something she never did without her entire family. Was it over her drug addiction reveal? Was she still a drug addict off to some high-priced rehab center away from the public eye? Had she and Hank finally decided to divorce? Krystal didn't worry too much over her mother, but she worried about her father. Normally, he'd laugh off whatever the papers printed about him. But now? He hadn't been doing a lot of laughing lately.

And Travis? Well, a lot of that was just splashing pictures of his constant stream of rotating women. Not exactly news.

Emmy's was the hardest. Why the *Star Gazette* thought it was necessary to run an article on Brock and how lucky he was not to have wound up a member of the King family was a mystery. The only thing that mattered was how devastated Emmy Lou had been. Again. Brock didn't deserve that sort of love—he sure as heck didn't deserve her sister. Emmy Lou was the one who'd lucked out, not Brock. If a man wound up winning her sister, what else could he ever need or want for?

And then there was Jace. Nothing was off-limits. They'd tracked down his wife's relative who'd gone on and on about how deeply in love they'd been and how, after Nikki's death, they'd all worried Jace would harm himself. Another article had printed pictures of Jace with his son, Ben. He'd looked so happy—so much like a proud father. Knowing what he'd been through, what he'd lost, gutted her. How did he go on? How had his heart survived?

It was so hard. She'd never been in love before. There was something powerful about having him just walk in the room. Just that, and everything felt…easier. Like now, with his hand on her thigh and his words of support, he made this easier.

And the tug in her heart stronger than ever.

"It's never a bad idea to do the right thing?" Travis mumbled. "That was frigging deep."

Krystal flipped him off again.

"Krystal." Emmy sat across from her, taking her hand. "Look at me."

She shook her head.

"Please."

Her sigh was bone deep, but she looked at her sister.

"We'll figure it out." Emmy Lou squeezed her hand. "I'm not saying I have a single idea but…we'll come up with something. Okay?"

"Okay." Emmy needed her to say it, so she did. But she didn't necessarily believe it.

"Man, maybe you should think about Luke's deal?" Travis said. "It's not too late to save yourself from this sinking ship."

Krystal sat up, glaring at her brother. "Sinking ship?" She flipped him off again, right in his face.

Emmy and Jace laughed. Jace, who was kneeling beside her, the warmth of his palm seeping through her jeans and into her skin. She stole a glance from the corner of her eye. Lucky for her, he was now wearing a shirt. And pants. Not that it made him any less appealing. She sighed, tearing her gaze away.

"Wait." Her brother's words registered. "What deal?" Her gaze darted from Travis to Jace, a whisper of unease racing down her spine.

Jace stood, shaking his head. "Nothing."

His hand, his warmth, was gone. More than a whisper now—especially since Jace wouldn't look at her.

"I'm not sure a tour with Samson McCall, Aaron Jackman, and Martina Lambert is nothing." Travis shook his head. "Soda?" he asked, heading to the refrigerator.

"Water?" she called out. Because a painful knot was now lodged in her throat. "Why wouldn't you take that?" she asked. It was a no-brainer. They were three of the biggest names, regulars, chart-toppers. They'd banded together for a limited tour that sold out in less than twenty-two hours.

"I'd be opening for them." He shrugged.

"You're opening for us," Emmy Lou pointed out. "Don't get me wrong, you're like family now, Jace. But family looks out for one another. This seems like one of those don't-regret-this sort of things."

"Told you," Travis said, rolling a water bottle across the table to her. "Sinking ship." He pointed between the three of them.

Krystal took a long swig of her water bottle. It didn't help. If anything, her throat felt a little more shredded than it had before. Forget unease. Dread was more accurate for the hollow, stark hole devouring the place around her heart. "When does the tour start?"

His light brown eyes met hers. "I'd finish up here and have, like, two days."

Nod. Respond. Pretend to be happy for him. But she couldn't.

"But you get to finish with us first?" Emmy Lou nodded. "Then you have to do it, Jace. No conflict of interest. And Wheelhouse supports it? Since they're all about their artists?"

"Yeah." He sighed. "Luke said they'd mentioned a contract extension." He was still staring, still searching.

Krystal tore her gaze from his. He couldn't know how she felt. He'd stay. Out of obligation if nothing else. He was wired that way.

"What does Heather say?" Emmy Lou reached across and took a sip of Krystal's water.

"She's not too happy about losing visitation rights to Clementine." He nodded. "But I guess I should think about it some more. If you think it's a good idea—"

"It's a smart career move." Krystal nodded, her fingers slowly tearing the label from her water bottle. "As long as you have studio time worked into your contract, nothing should stop you."

"Maybe." Jace shrugged. "Up for working on that song now?"

She nodded. How could she say no? It was a great song. She hadn't seen much room for improvement. But now, she wasn't going to say no to time with Jace. She couldn't.

The tour had eight more performances. Eight. Then Jace would be gone.

————————

"But you see his point?" DJ Freddy Young was saying. "Men get accused of this stuff all the time. Some real, some not."

Jace was having a hard time keeping his mouth shut. "No. I don't. It's never okay for a man, for anyone, to be a predator—period. I'm pretty sure everything that comes out of Tig Whitman's mouth is a pile of sh—"

"Jace," Krystal cut in, her crushing grip on his hand reining him in. Which was good because he'd been about to tell DJ Freddy Young he was a fucking idiot. Who invited someone on their show, then proceeded to ridicule them for making sexual abuse *allegations* without proof? Apparently this asshole.

"There was enough proof to warrant a restraining order. That's a pretty good place to start," Krystal said. "Since the case is still pending, it's probably best if we talk about the single."

DJ Freddy nodded and turned to Krystal. "I hear it was originally for your sister to sing? With Jace? What happened there?"

"Emmy knew it was a special song." Krystal smiled. "She said she had a sore throat so I'd have to rehearse with Jace. My father was there."

Jace nodded. "He heard us singing and said that was

it." He looked at her. "I knew, after singing with Krystal, it wouldn't be the same. We have this thing—"

"Oh, I feel your *chemistry*." DJ Freddy laughed. "I've got the AC cranked up in here and it's still smoking hot."

Krystal's hand tightened again.

"You're not worried about what all this Tig Whitman stuff is going to do to your career?" DJ Freddy circled back around.

"No." Jace shook his head. "The truth has a way of coming out. Is it painful? Hell yes. But it's true. As long as people stay quiet, this sort of thing will keep happening. Three out of four assaults go unreported. Can you imagine? Living in fear? Hurting? That's wrong. I don't care who you are, who has done this to you, it's not okay." He held her hand against his chest. "That's what people should be saying. That's what matters. And I'm proud of Krystal for coming forward. I can't imagine how terrifying it is to go through it, then get ripped apart for trying to make sure it doesn't happen to someone else."

"We've heard about the emails and letters you've been getting," DJ Freddy said. "People of all ages? Sharing their story with you? Victims? Is that right?"

"It is. It's very humbling to have someone share something so personal with you. But I think it's easier to talk about it with someone who's been through it. They know. They understand. And there's no judgment." She paused. "I've been trying to answer most of them, but there's been a lot. And I'm not an expert. But there are some amazing resources out there, for victims and their families. I've posted them on the Three Kings website. And you can call this helpline, anytime, to get help." She read the phone number.

"We'll leave it with that. I wanna thank you two for coming in today," DJ Freddy said. "Now, here it is, their brand-new single, out today, 'Ashes of my Heart.'" He pressed a few buttons. "We're good. Thanks."

Jace and Krystal shook hands and were escorted, quickly, to the black SUV waiting outside. Sawyer climbed into the driver's seat and they were off.

"You controlled yourself." She sounded amused.

"Barely." He sighed. "Next?"

"We have a break." She stared out the window. "There's the afternoon talk show and the late show tonight."

He studied her profile, itching to take her hand. They'd made three stops already. And every time they got in the car, she'd turn away, shut down. The amount of pressure she was under was overwhelming. Between her family and the single and Tig… If there was ever a time to fall apart, it was now. In true Krystal fashion, she was holding it inside. She always had a shoulder for Emmy or Travis, but she would never think to burden them. She needed someone to talk to.

Dammit, he wanted to be there for her. "You can talk to me."

She shook her head, her phone ringing. She glanced at the screen, then answered. "Misumi?" She shifted, her skirt sliding up just enough to show off some skin.

He didn't deny himself the look. She had terrific legs.

Most of the time she wore boots, so her painted pink toes in high-heeled strappy sandals had him checking out her legs more than once over the course of the day.

"Are you kidding?" There was excitement in her voice. "Of course, I'd love to." She paused. "Yes." She sighed, shaking her head. "CiCi King is not my manager. From now on, I don't care what she says; I'm making my own decisions. I know that puts you in an awkward position—" There was a break in conversation—and she was laughing. "Good. I'm glad. Now?" Another pause. "Okay. Thanks, Misumi." She hung up the phone, all smiles. "The Sexual Violence Advocacy Group is interested in my charity cookbook idea." Her hand rested on his arm. "But they want to meet with me…now, basically."

"Let's go. Sawyer and I will find something to do." Seeing her light up and excited made him so damn happy.

"You're sure?" she asked.

He nodded.

She gave Sawyer the address.

Damn, her smile. "You better put that pie recipe in there." He paused. "Best damn pie I've ever had."

"You haven't had my strawberry cream." Her brows rose. "Or my berry cobbler. Oh, my key lime cake is to die for on a hot day."

"Sounds like I've got a lot to look forward to." His hand covered hers, loving the spark in her eyes.

Her gaze crashed into his, the instant spark.

"I like seeing you this way. With things to look forward to. Caught up in the moment." His fingers ran along the curve of her jaw. "You deserve more of that, you know? Doing what you want? What makes you happy. You have a right to that." She loved music. Watching her onstage, she was pure magic. She'd come through this stronger, with songs to sing and stories to tell, he knew it. As long as her mother didn't get in her way. "You ever think about breaking off on your own?"

Her eyes closed. "All the time." It was a whisper. "But now..." She looked at him, hesitant. "They're all standing by me, Jace. I worry about letting them down, you know? Momma's obsession with keeping us together is relentless, but it's kept us together. Is that a bad thing? I don't know." She shrugged. "We've been a team for so long..." She was leaning into his touch.

"It would be hard." Her skin was so soft. Now that the bruise was fading, it was easier to touch her. And, damn, he loved to touch her. "To live for yourself after worrying about everyone else for so long."

She studied him, a crease forming between her brows. "I guess we're the same in that way. Heather is—"

"My only family." He nodded. "But she has her own life. I want her to have that. I want her to be happy."

"Are you?" Her voice was husky and low. "Happy?"

He'd be happier if she'd stop fighting him and give them a real chance. Even now, as she was leaning into his touch, arching toward him, hungry for him, she was holding a part of herself away from him. The part he wanted—her heart. "Right now?" he asked.

She nodded, eyes flashing. She was on fire for him.

He gave in, clasping the back of her neck and meeting her halfway. His lips fastened on the column of her neck. His nose ran up, around her ear, so he could suck her earlobe into his mouth. The choked groan in the back of her throat had him holding a second longer.

"Feeling pretty good now," he said against her temple before letting her go.

Her gaze stayed fixed on his, breathing heavy, flushed, wanting more. If she asked, he'd give her whatever she wanted. Hell, he hoped she would. She didn't. For the remainder of the drive, she stared out the window—but she held on to his hand.

When Sawyer pulled over, Jace opened the door for her, escorting her inside the glass front building before he leaned in the passenger window of the SUV. "I don't know about you, but I'm hungry."

Sawyer nodded. "I could eat."

They located a burger joint a few blocks away, left the SUV parked, and walked. Jace and Krystal had taken a chartered plane to New York for the day. After the late show, they'd fly back down to New Orleans for a show tomorrow. It was a whirlwind trip, but the television spots were a big deal and Wheelhouse was a machine—it expected the artists to go above and beyond when it came to promoting their music. Considering he and Krystal were getting some one-on-one time, he had no complaints. They'd be dog-tired tomorrow, but he'd worry about that then.

Luke kept sending him sales numbers. He was

excited. Over-the-moon excited. Jace's relief had nothing to do with the song's success and everything to do with Krystal. Since the day Luke had handed him the sheet music, he'd known the song was special. But, with all that had happened with Krystal and Tig, there had been some murmurs about it taking a hit on the charts. If the song had tanked, she'd have taken it personally.

No need to worry there.

They were sitting down to their double patty, bacon, and cheese monster burgers when his phone went off. Email.

"Luke's going to give himself a heart attack if he stares at sales numbers all day." He opened his email and froze.

One sentence: *There's video footage of her attack with his audio confession.*

He stared at it.

Read it again.

Not Luke's email address. Whose was it? It was series of numbers and letters, nothing recognizable. Was it spam? He hoped like hell it wasn't. "You were in computer stuff in the military, weren't you?"

"Cybersecurity." Sawyer nodded. "Some counter-intelligence."

"Can you tell me what this is?" He handed Sawyer his phone.

Sawyer's brows rose and his green-blue eyes went wide. "Dummy address. Some hub out there—probably no way to trace it." He shook his head.

"I thought the security cameras and audio were turned off?" Jace eyed his burger, no longer hungry.

Sawyer stared at him. "Hank said something about turning them on. Reports of break-ins around the festival grounds. Guess he called the security company? Had them turn it on?"

Jace remembered then. That day, talking about ways to get Krystal out of performing at ACMF. Hank had said he'd turn it on. "Guess he did. That's the only way there can be footage, right?" He waited.

Sawyer nodded.

"Hank's been so stressed out, he probably forgot. Or didn't want to watch. Not his daughter." He ran a hand over the back of his neck. "It was CiCi's idea to install the cameras, wasn't it? Never thought I'd be happy about something CiCi King did."

"She's…interesting. And my employer, so that's all I'm going to say." Sawyer took a bite of his burger.

Jace chuckled. "Fair. Can you figure out who sent this? Hack in, something?"

Sawyer set his burger down. "Does it matter who sent it?"

Jace stared at him for a minute, noting the slight tilt of the other man's head. The tilt of his mouth. Almost defensive. Oddly familiar. "No. As long as we can get to the video."

"I can get into the system. I was the one who installed it. It's password protected, but that's not a problem. That's why she hired me. I had the field experience and the tech."

Jace took a moment to process that. "I don't want to think this, but what if it's been deleted by someone?"

"I can recover it." Sawyer shook his head. "I admit I've allowed myself to get invested in this family and this thing with Krystal—" He broke off, the hardening of his face intimidating as hell. "I can't really afford to lose my job."

"Understood. I'm calling Hank, forwarding him the email. You won't get fired when you help him clear Krystal's name." Of all the questions spiraling through Jace's brain, only one needed answering: Did this tape exist? Because, if it did, Krystal would finally have the peace she deserved.

Chapter 19

THE FLIGHT FROM NEW YORK TO NEW ORLEANS was a little over three hours. Krystal had planned to spend that time working on a song she'd had bouncing around in her head for the last few days. Instead, she'd fallen asleep. One minute, she'd been sitting across from Jace, watching him pick out a few notes on his guitar, the next she was opening her eyes to him standing over her, smoothing the hair from her forehead.

"We're here." His voice was soft, his gaze warm.

She nodded, stretching and sitting up. His jacket, rolled up, slid down the seat back. She looked at it, then him.

He took the jacket, shook it out, and slid it on. He paused, turning into his shoulder. "Smells like you."

She wasn't awake enough for this. Him. Resisting. "Sorry," she murmured.

"No complaints." He shook his head, holding out his hand and pulling her to her feet. "Good nap?"

She nodded, then shrugged. "I'm not sure I'm fully awake yet."

He smiled. "Sleepwalking?"

"And talking, apparently." Don't smile back. Don't stare. Don't... She was smiling. "You?"

"No nap. Or sleepwalking. Or talking." He shook his

head. "Sawyer and I played some cards. I finished a song."
He shrugged, stifling a yawn. "Skyped in to a few international peace summits. That sorta thing."

She laughed; she couldn't help it. "Now I feel like a
total slacker."

"You should." He nodded. "Got everything? Sawyer's
getting the car."

Once she'd shoved everything back into her back-
pack, she turned on her phone and followed Jace out
the door and down the long set of stairs from the plane
to the waiting SUV. Normally, there were no photogra-
phers. Even with the uptick in interest from the whole
TW Gate—Travis thought he was being funny but the
nickname meant she didn't have to say his name, so she'd
taken to using it—most journalists didn't camp out at
airports in the middle of the night.

"Why the turnout?" she asked. "It is like three in the
morning, isn't it?"

Jace nodded.

"People need to get a life." She yawned, taking his
hand to climb into the SUV. "Always the gentleman."

He climbed up beside her. "No breaks, time off for
overtime, either."

"You're way too chipper for this time of
night—morning."

"Feeling good." He shrugged.

"Nothing like finishing a song." She nodded, resting
her head on the headrest, another yawn. She had no
idea when she dozed off again, but she woke up to the

sound of humming. She blinked, adjusting to the dark. Her head was in his lap, which explained why she was so comfortable. His arm lay across her chest, warm and strong, anchoring her in place. It hurt to feel so much for someone after she'd convinced herself something this sweet couldn't really exist. There was no way to talk herself out of it; it was too real, too embedded in her heart to ignore.

Eight more performances and he was gone.

She rolled onto her side, burying her face in his stomach.

His fingers slid through her hair in long, slow strokes. His humming, deep and smooth, almost lulled her back to sleep. But the lights got brighter and the car slowed.

"Krystal?" he whispered.

"I'm awake." She stared up at him.

He stared back.

And, if it wasn't for the flashes of light and sound of voices outside, she would have stayed like that. But Sawyer's curse, followed by his calm but effective threat to "Step back" had her sitting up and staring out the window.

"What's happening?"

His hand was on her back. "Something big."

She nodded, sitting back. "I can't anymore, Jace." She shook her head. "I know I'm supposed to be strong, but you know, I'm not."

"Hey." He cradled her face in his hands. "This could be good?"

She shot him a look.

He laughed. "Damn, you're beautiful. Let's get inside, away from this. Okay?" He took her hand and, slowly, opened the door.

Sawyer and Jerome did their best to push their way through the crush of reporters and cameras, but it didn't stop her from hearing their questions.

"Now that the video has been leaked, what are your plans?"

"What do you say to those suggesting this video was held until your single was released?"

"Will you press criminal charges against Mr. Whitman?"

"What is your response to Mr. Whitman's statement?"

She clung to Jace, sliding her arm around his waist and holding on. What were they saying? What video? What statement? By the time they were safely inside the hotel, she was shaking.

"Jace?" she whispered.

"Keep going." Sawyer was at their backs, steering through the kitchens and to the elevator.

"What's happening?" she asked as soon as the doors closed. "We were on the plane for three hours." She pulled out her phone. "Dammit." It was dead.

"Your family is in the penthouse suite." Sawyer glanced her way. "I think Hank wants to explain everything."

She blinked. "But everyone is okay? Right? There's nothing wrong?"

Sawyer was almost smiling. Almost. "Nothing is wrong, Miss King."

The doors opened and she headed straight for the penthouse. But Jace hung back.

"I'll see you tomorrow." He smiled.

"You're not coming?" She frowned.

He hesitated. "After last time—"

"Jace." She swallowed. She didn't want to think about last time. Last time, she knew what she had to say. Now? She had no idea what was happening. Having him at her side helped. "Don't leave me, please."

He nodded, following, Sawyer trailing behind.

"You good?" he asked, waiting for her nod before opening the door.

Inside, it was quiet. Her father was sound asleep in a recliner. Travis's legs hung off the end of the couch, his arm thrown across his face. Emmy was curled up in the corner of the couch, wrapped up in a fleece blanket covered in unicorns.

She pressed a finger to her lips and shook her head. They'd been waiting up for her but...

The television was on. Muted. But that didn't matter.

"That's..." She stared, horrified by what was playing out on the television. "How did this happen?"

"Baby girl?" Her daddy sat forward. "We tried to call."

She couldn't answer, couldn't look away.

"Her phone is dead," Jace said.

Tig's face, his mouth moving. She knew what he was saying. And then, she couldn't watch anymore. At least she knew, the whole world knew, he started the physical altercation. Even though it had been a week, the force of his blow remained.

"When did this happen?" She sank onto the couch, trying not to see the television.

"A couple of hours ago." Her father was standing beside her. "It got leaked to the press and, well, hell, it's all over the place."

"Daddy, turn it off," Emmy whispered.

"You okay?" Travis sat up and slid closer, nudging her. "I mean, I know it's been a week, but seeing it?" He put his arm around her. "No one can doubt you now, Krys. No one."

It was a shock, yes. Seeing herself flopping around like a rag doll was one hell of a shock. But he was right.

"He said…" She was up, staring at Jace. "He said it was true. He admitted—"

"He did." Jace's jaw was locked tight.

"You knew?" She frowned.

"It didn't feel right to say something without your family." He shrugged. "I'm sorry."

She didn't remember moving—making the choice to move—but she was. And she didn't stop until she was pressed tight against him. She held on, soaking up the strength and warmth only Jace could give her.

"I didn't need to see the tape to believe you. I've always believed you. I always will." His arms were tight around her. "Whatever you need." It was a whisper.

The first wracking sobs were a surprise. She didn't cry. Fine, that was a lie. Considering the tears she'd cried over the last week, it was clear she *could* cry. But she didn't like it. This was different.

"It's okay, Krys." Travis was worried. "It's okay now."

She nodded, smothering her face against Jace. Get control. "I'm tired. This is a lot."

Jace was rubbing her back. "That's an understatement."

"I know it is, baby girl." Her father's voice was soft. "I'm not saying the road will be straight and smooth from here on out, but there's no denying his guilt. I admit, I can't watch it, but according to Sawyer, all the proof we need is on this tape. Whoever sent this tape, they're your guardian angel. One day, I hope I can thank them in person."

Of course, Sawyer knew, too. Sawyer knew everything. Took care of them.

Squished as she was against Jace, she could see Sawyer. He stood by the door, quietly watching her father. It was a hard look, full of judgment and condemnation and anger. But there was something else, too. Raw and broken and desperate. She'd seen that look on Travis's face more than once. A son, hungry for approval—even though they hated themselves for needing it.

Sawyer. A couple of years older than Travis. Same height. Same build. Sandy colored hair, not blond. Blue eyes, like her father.

Officer Ramos had planted the seed that horrible night in the hospital. A stranger had seen what was right there, staring them all in the face.

Gently, she pulled herself from Jace's arms and headed

straight for him. The moment he realized it, his expression cleared—blank and impartial. When they were toe to toe, she stared at him, studying every feature. He noticed, enough for his jaw to clench tight.

She shook her head. "Thank you," her voice cracked.

And so did his blank and impartial shield.

She hugged him and he hugged back. One arm only, but strong and hard enough to lift her off the floor before he let her go. She knew, in her heart, who he was. How could she not? A King, yes. Her brother, too. And, she suspected, her guardian angel. She hoped, eventually, he'd let their father know that. But, for now, she'd leave things as they were. She, of all people, respected that everyone's timeline differed when it came to working through personal baggage.

"If you're all good here?" he asked, having a hard time looking any of them in the eye.

"You go on, Sawyer," her father said. "Can't thank you enough for what you've done for me and my family."

Krystal saw the slightest tightening at the corner of Sawyer's eyes. He nodded, glanced her way, and left the hotel room.

"He's pretty cool," Travis said. "You know he can play the guitar?"

Krystal smiled, walking back to her family and collapsing onto the couch. "Imagine that." Music was in their blood. She had a brother. A big, burly, sort of scary brother. Which meant, somewhere out there, was a woman her father must have cared about.

"We're lucky to have him," her father said.

"We are." She nodded, wondering if her father knew he had a son. It didn't match with the man who had raised her—dedicated to his children. But then, she'd never imagined her daddy's personal life before he met her mother. Now she had questions. Who was Sawyer's mother? Had she been someone special? And why hadn't Sawyer told their father?

"You okay?" Jace asked, his voice low.

She nodded, blowing out a deep breath. "More than okay. Is it wrong to say I'm hungry?"

"About time." Travis reached for the phone.

"What does that mean?" She frowned.

"You're getting skinny." Emmy sat beside her, cuddling close.

"Strawberry shortcake," Jace said, sitting on her other side. "It's her favorite."

Chapter 20

IT WAS ALL LIKE A CAREFULLY PLANNED DOMINO chain. The first one gets tipped, and they all go down, one on top of the other, faster and faster until the very last one. Over the next few days, five other women came forward.

Five.

Becca was the sixth.

Krystal cried for them.

She wasn't the first. Two came before her—women he'd damaged so badly they'd walked away from their chance at stardom.

Wheelhouse Records disavowed any connection with Tig Whitman. They asked for a meeting, so she and her father had driven into Austin to listen to their plan to support her charity cookbook. Not only would they donate a portion of sales from any musician who chose to participate, they were also planning a charity concert. The whole ride home, the ghost of a new song was flitting through her brain. A new song. A survivor's song.

"What's the verdict?" Emmy Lou asked when she walked into the kitchen. "Are we hired, fired, or temporarily unemployed?"

Krystal laughed. "We've been extended. Internationally. Twelve stops."

Emmy clapped, pouring hot water from her teapot into her mug. "Want some peppermint tea?"

"I'm good, thanks." Krystal started pulling out ingredients.

"What are we making?" Emmy sat on the stool.

She shrugged. "Not sure."

"You can talk to me, you know. I'd really like it if we had the twin thing that people talk about."

"That's harsh." She stared at her sister. It took a lot to get Emmy Lou riled up. "But you're right. I'm sorry."

"I know I'm right." She nodded. "Now talk to me. We don't want to go to Australia? We don't know what to make for dinner? We don't want to lose Jace but we're still borderline emotionally constipated and think we can't have him even though he clearly wants to be had… by you?" She shook her head. "You get what I'm saying."

She blinked. "Who are you and what have you done with my sister?"

"I'm right here." She smiled. "I've always been right here." She stared into her tea. "And I might have read something this morning that made me really, really wish you would see what a great guy you have waiting for you."

"What did you read?" Yes, she would ignore the rest of the statement for now.

"Brock is divorced."

Krystal stopped cracking eggs. "Oh." She didn't know what else to say. "Are we happy?"

"Of course I'm not happy." She shook her head. "I

want him to be happy. It didn't work out, but at least he tried. You and Jace—"

"Em, you can't honestly believe I could make him happy? I'm me. A mess." Krystal sucked in a long, ragged breath. "I'm trying to come to terms with the fact that tomorrow might be the last time I ever really sing with him. That, after tomorrow, I won't see him or his tattoos or his smile or get comfort from him just being…there. And you know what? I hate it. I hate that I feel all these things because I know…I know…"

"What?" Emmy pushed back.

"That it can't be real." She slapped the wooden spatula against the bowl, her frustration mounting.

"Why?" Jace's voice. Because Jace was behind her. In the kitchen. Listening.

She froze, staring at her sister in horror. "Emmy Lou King," she hissed.

Emmy's little shrug was not in the least bit remorseful. "You love me." She picked up her mug and practically ran from the kitchen.

Krystal risked a glance Jace's way. "What are you doing here?"

"Your dad invited me." His gaze never left her face, the muscle in his jaw flexed tight. "You keep holding out on me." He ran his fingers through his hair. "Holding out on us."

"There is no us." Her heart. Her damn, traitorous heart that loved him. Only him. All of him. There was no doubt. No hesitation. Only the inescapable acceptance of the truth. She loved him. *No no no.* This couldn't happen. She couldn't let this happen. "You're you, Jace. I'm me. With everything my…stuff put us through, it felt real." She swallowed. "Maybe too real?"

He shook his head and faced her. He was pissed. Arms crossed. Leaning against the counter. His head cocked at an angle. And his jaw clenching, the muscle pulled taut. "Because it is real, Krystal."

Something in his tone tipped her off. "Jace…don't do this." She wouldn't stop shaking her head. "We're going to Australia. You've got your new tour. There's no point. Don't say something you can't take back. Don't say something you can't mean."

As much as she wanted to forget everything about the night of her attack, she couldn't. Tig's words were indelibly etched into her heart.

"That's what scares you?" He closed the distance between them, staring down at her. "That I love you? You think it doesn't scare the shit out of me?" He swallowed. "It does. But I do. Love you."

He'd said it. The words were out and she was staring at him like an idiot. "No. No. You can't."

His brow rose. "I can." He brushed a curl from her shoulder. "You can't do a thing to stop me."

She pressed a hand to his chest, frustrated. "Jace." She broke off, pressing again. Why had he said it?

"I get you've been hurt. But I won't hurt you."

"I'll hurt you." Her voice shook. "My whole life, I've wound up hurting those I care about. You've already had your heart ripped out. Now you want me to believe that three words can make everything better?"

"If you let them. If you believe in what they mean." He shook his head. "I see *you*. And I love what I see." His fingers stroked along her cheek. "Don't let fear stop this. You're this brave, strong woman. Be brave for me."

She opened her mouth, then closed it, pushing against his chest again. "I don't know if I can." The hurt on his face pushed her from the kitchen, down the hall, to the safety of her bedroom, mumbling something about answering some letters.

She waved away the call to dinner and Emmy's invitation to come watch a movie. She couldn't face him, couldn't stand the hope and longing his words stirred.

About midnight, doubt kicked in. And regret. What if she was wrong? What if he really did love her? And his devotion wasn't due to some overdeveloped sense of honor but honest-to-goodness love? How could someone like Jace love someone like her?

At two, she stopped pacing her room and went back to answering letters. If she couldn't sleep, she'd do something useful. Some were fan letters. Others were long letters that had her sobbing.

"Krystal?" Her daddy knocked on the door. "Can I come in?"

"Yes."

He surveyed the mass of letters all over her bed. "I figured you were avoiding things." He sighed, holding out a plate. "Strawberry shortcake."

Her stomach growled.

He chuckled and sat on the edge of the bed.

While she devoured her cake, he read over the cards.

"What do you say to them?" he asked, setting a card aside. "How do you even know what to say?"

She scraped the frosting from her plate. "I don't have the answers, I start with that. But…" She set the plate down. "Some still feel like their attacker controls them, even months or years afterward. For those, I tell them living a full life, without fear, taking chances, is the only way to move on." She shuffled through the letters. "Others have a hard time taking compliments, that it's easier to believe the negative things—it makes what happened more logical. But listening to the people who really love you makes more sense that believing the person who hurt you." She shrugged. "Like I said, I'm no expert."

He smiled. "Sounds like you have a pretty good understanding of what you're talking about."

"Dinner go okay?"

"You were missed." He nodded. "Jace and Emmy made the cake for you. His idea."

She shook her head. "He's…stubborn."

"You wouldn't know a thing about that." He chuckled. "He loves you, I know that much."

She kept right on shaking her head. "He can't."

"Krystal. You're giving this wonderful advice to strangers. Telling them to live without fear, to take chances, to listen to the people who really love them—not the ones who hurt you." He shook his head. "Why aren't you doing those things? You write the most beautiful songs and I love hearing them. As your daddy, I'd rather you were living the most beautiful life—so I could see you truly happy." He took her plate.

"I love you, Daddy." She smiled. "You totally just pulled a *Sixteen Candles* move on me."

"*Sixteen Candles*?" He paused by the door, thinking.

"You know, the scene in the movie where the father gives her the pep talk and makes it better?"

"Oh, right." He smiled. "Well, damn, I did good. Get some rest, baby girl."

"Thanks for the cake." As soon as the door closed, she flopped back on the bed.

Clementine stirred from her bed.

"I can't believe I'm taking relationship advice from my father." She stared up at the ceiling. "The thing is, Clem, he's right." She covered her face with her hands. "I don't want to lose him. I love him. And…" She swallowed, resisting the urge to squash all the happy. Instead, she let the joy bubble up and flow freely. "He loves me." And it felt incredible.

Jace and Luke stood on the side of the stage, watching the Three Kings do their thing. He and Krystal's duet was up next. After last night, he didn't know what sort of reception he was going to get. He'd scared the crap out of her last night—but he didn't regret it. He'd regret not telling her more. Life was too short to live with regrets.

"I still think you're making a mistake." Luke scrolled through the messages on his phone.

"I know." Jace smiled. "I'm in a good place here. I'm happy."

Luke looked at him then. "Well, man, that's what life is about, right?" He smiled. "It's not like you're going back to the oilfields."

Jace chuckled. "I am thankful for that."

Emmy and Travis came offstage.

"You're up." Travis nodded. "She's on high-energy mode."

Emmy was all smiles.

"I don't know what that means." Jace gave them an odd look and carried his guitar out and onto the stage.

The lights came up and Krystal started playing, leaving him confused. He sat on his stool, the melody familiar but not "Ashes of My Heart."

"Before we sing our song, there's something I need to ask Jace." She stared out over the audience. "If y'all are all right with that?"

He smiled at the roar of approval.

"That okay with you?" she asked.

He crossed his arms over his chest. "Yes, ma'am."

The crowd went crazy.

"I was hoping you'd say that. I know you said it wasn't ready but...well, it really is. And I am. So, here it goes." She faced him, took a deep breath, and sang, "I say my heart is hard and there's no hope. My world split wide and I can't cope. Words are empty and nothing more. Trying to find strength is a daily chore."

He stared, blindsided. His words, her words. She knew—knew this was them. Knew what she was doing. Scared or not, she was putting herself out there. Being brave for him. He swallowed hard against the lump lodged in his throat.

"You say—"

He kissed her, surprising everyone—including himself. But he recovered and picked up where she left off. "I say stop fighting to stand alone," he sang, smoothing the hair from her cheek. "Words can heal, hear my song. Don't let the world defeat you. Don't lock your heart away. See me standing here and let me love you."

Tears were streaming down her face as the chorus spilled out of them both.

"Through the dark of night. Through the light of day, I will love your troubles away. When you're cold and you've lost your way, I will love you back home to stay. See me standing here and let me love you."

She pressed her fingers to his lips and sang the rest alone. "Because I do. I love you."

He closed his eyes, smiling. "It's about time."

The audience laughed.

He didn't care—he was kissing her again. He knew they had a show to do; no one seemed to mind their detour. Cameras were flashing; there were plenty of whistles.

"We've got to finish the set." She was breathless.

He nodded.

After that, "Ashes of My Heart" was a blur. All he could think about was getting her backstage, alone. They finished the song, Krystal hopped into his lap, and the lights went down with her twined around him.

"This needs to be the fastest concert in history," she said against his lips. "Wait for me?"

"I'm not going anywhere, Krystal." He kissed her nose. "Except Australia. With you." He dropped another kiss on her lips and left the stage before the lights went back up.

"Well, that got people talking." Luke was laughing. "What the hell was that?"

Jace smiled. The best damn night of his life.

By the time Krystal burst into her dressing room, he'd been pacing for an hour.

"Hi." She closed the door, leaning against it. "What's this about Australia?"

"No, I think we're starting with you loving me." He grinned.

"I love you." Her green eyes never wavered. "Chances are it's never going to be easy."

"You think I don't know that? Nothing about you is." He reached for her. "My choice to make." His arms tightened around her, pulling her close.

Her head rested on his chest. "I didn't have a choice when it came to loving you, Jace Black."

His hand ran up and down her back. "I thank my lucky stars for that."

"Your heart is on overdrive," she murmured, looking up at him.

"It does that when you're around." Another long, slow stroke down her back. His hand was shaking—ever so slightly. She had no idea the effect she had on him.

She smiled. "It does?"

He nodded, kissing her temple. Like it was the most natural thing in the world. Natural and right.

"And you're not leaving?" Those green eyes were blazing. "You're going to Australia with us?"

"I'm going to Australia with you." He shook his head. "I love you and want to be with you. Pretty straightforward stuff."

"Good." He'd never seen anything as beautiful as her smile. She whispered, "Because even though I'm still not sure I'm in love with your name, I am very much in love with you."

"You keep on telling yourself that." His lips brushed her nose.

KINGS OF COUNTRY

BROCK

Chapter 1

"OPEN, DAMMIT!" EMMY LOU PUSHED THE BUTTON again, smacking the pink and white polka-dot umbrella against her thigh. It still wouldn't open. The sky rumbled overhead.

"Ooh, language, Emmy." Her twin sister, Krystal, laughed. "Next you'll be saying shit or ass or fu—"

"No, I won't." Emmy spoke into the mic on the earbuds she had plugged into her left ear, while her sister continued to laugh. "But this might be a little easier if I wasn't face-timing you right now." Umbrella in one hand, phone in the other, she started walking.

Krystal held her phone closer, flipping her lower lip for a full-on pout. "But I miss you."

"I miss you too." Emmy said, blinking raindrops from her lashes. "Enough to walk through a parking lot, in the rain, with an umbrella that won't open, *and* keep talking to you." She kept pressing the button on the handle, but it didn't help. Of course, the rain was falling faster now; big pelting drops.

"Where is Sawyer? Why isn't our bulky, scowling bodyguard carrying a massive bulletproof umbrella over your head? Or have you wrapped in bulletproof bubble-wrap? Or, at least, driven you *inside* the coliseum versus dropping you off in the rain, in the back forty?" There was a hint of accusation in her sister's voice. "I assumed he'd be Velcro-ed by your side since you're his number one person to protect. And that's his job."

"Be nice to Sawyer." Being a bodyguard for the Kings couldn't be easy. This last year especially—with all the drama. But he'd stuck it out and stayed with them. Either he was super loyal or her daddy paid him really well. Maybe both. "He wanted to be here." Emmy wiped the rain from her eyes. "He had to go pick up Travis down the road—because our brother ran out of gas." She sighed, clicking the button on her umbrella again. "And I'm getting soaked because this thing is broken."

"You're probably just not doing it right." Krystal was all innocence. "Are you pressing the button?"

"Are you serious?" Emmy Lou stared at her sister, coming to a stop.

"No." She burst into laughter. "But you sort of set yourself up for that one."

"I should hang up." Emmy laughed, peering at the stadium through the rain. Rain that was getting heavier and faster.

"But you won't." Krystal leaned forward. "Then again...you are starting to look like a wet rat. Walk faster."

Emmy stuck out her tongue at her sister, her steps quickening. "Where is Jace? Normally you two are glued at the hip."

"You have *no* idea." She bobbed her eyebrows and giggled.

"And I don't want one, thank you very much." She was jogging now, weaving around the parked cars.

"He's doing an interview for an Australian magazine. They really love him here." Krystal grinned. "What's not to love?"

Emmy smiled. "He *is* pretty lovable." She adored her sister's boyfriend. Jace Black was a good guy *and* he loved her sister with the perfect mix of tender and fierce. And Krystal? Emmy had never seen her sister like this. Happy. Smiling. At peace, for the first time in so long.

"Isn't he, though?" Krystal was gushing. She never gushed. Not before Jace, anyway.

"I'm glad you two are having such a good—"

The squeal of brakes had her jumping a good ten feet in the air. A truck, going way too fast in a parking lot—in a torrential downpour—skidded to a stop mere inches from where she stood. It happened too fast for her to move. Too fast to do anything but curl in on herself, dropping her umbrella and holding her other hand, and phone, out to protect herself. Which, considering the vehicle was massive and she was not, didn't make any sense but… it was instinctual. She braced herself on the truck hood, her knees knocking so hard there was a high likelihood she'd collapse onto the slick concrete at any moment.

"Holy shit," Krystal was saying, the phone now face down on the hood. "Emmy! Emmy? Can you hear me? Are you okay? Answer me."

She could have been hit… Almost was. *But wasn't.* Emmy flipped the phone over. "Here." But she was gasping for breath. Her heart pumped madly, reaching what had to be the maximum beats per minute. "Fine."

She was vaguely aware of the truck driver's side door opening wide, followed by rapid footsteps plashing in newly formed puddles. But she was still grappling with the whole near-death experience to process the arrival of her almost assailant.

"Where is the driver? Are they getting out? Hold your phone up," Krystal growled. "I want to see what this asshole has to say about nearly running you over."

"Are you okay?" said the mountain of a man heading her way.

"I'm fine." She answered, rubbing water from her eyes. Her hand shook. Her voice shook. But she *was* **okay.**

"You didn't see me coming?" he asked, stepping closer. "My truck?"

"Seriously, Emmy Lou, hold up the phone," Krystal snapped. "You couldn't see her? In her bright-yellow and pink, daisy-covered raincoat? Because, honestly, she might as well be wrapped, head-to-toe, in reflective tape. Asshole."

"Krystal," Emmy whispered into the mic hanging from her earpiece.

"Hold up the phone. You might need a witness." Krystal sighed. "Emmy Lou, I'm serious."

Emmy held up the phone, unable to avoid the constant trembling.

The man came around the hood of the truck and stopped. His eyes widened and his mouth opened, but he didn't say anything. Shock probably. Complete and total shock. Not just because he'd almost turned her into a smudge in the stadium parking lot, but because he was who he was and she was who she was and they were standing face-to-face...staring, at each other, in the rain...

"Brock?" Krystal sounded just as stunned. "Is that Brock? Is that you?"

No, there was no way that was possible. Emmy was not equipped for this. Not right now. Not in the least. She should be; it had been years. *Years.* This shouldn't be a big deal. Seeing him, that is. Being almost run over by him—by anyone—*was* sort of a big deal.

"Hey." Brock nodded, barely glancing at Emmy's phone and Krystal. His gaze was pinned on her.

"I'm..." Her voice broke. She was what? "I..." No better. *Just stop. Pull it together.* This was silly. "Hi." She forced a smile. "So..." She could do this. Talk. Breathe. *In and out.* Easier said than done.

His mouth opened, then closed and the muscle in his jaw clenched tight. The staring continued.

I can't do this. She couldn't breathe, let alone string words together into something coherent. Especially since he just stood there, rigid, wearing an odd expression on his face. A face that, all weirdness and near-death experiences aside, she knew well. *All too well.*

Adrenaline was kicking in now. Enough to get her moving, anyway. And that's exactly what she was going to do. Move. Away. The sooner, the better. "Okay." She hung up her phone, shoved it into her pocket, and started walking—*do not run*—toward the stadium door. No looking back. Just moving forward.

Did she almost slip? Yes. Did she go down? No. Had she managed to save a shred of dignity? Probably not. She pulled the door wide, stopping just inside to scan the signs and arrows that indicated what was where.

"Bathroom?" she whispered to herself, scanning the sign until she found what she was looking for—at the same time her phone started ringing. She didn't have to look at it to know it was Krystal. But she did wait until she'd closed the door on the restroom and locked the door before she answered. This time, she denied FaceTime and kept it strictly audio. Her twin knew her too well to hide the maelstrom of emotions kicking her insides around and playing out on her face.

"Emmy?" Krystal asked. "Are you okay?"

"I didn't get hit—"

"I know, I know but…it was Brock."

Yes. Brock. She shrugged out of her raincoat and sat in the chair placed next to the diaper-changing station. "I know." Her heart was still beating way too fast. Sitting wasn't good. She stood, smoothing her pale blue blouse and staring down at her jeans, saturated below the line of her raincoat. She wiggled her toes in her rain boots, water squishing.

"This sucks." Krystal cleared her throat. "I wish I was there."

"I do too." She stared at her reflection. "But I know what you'd do if you were here."

"I'm not so sure."

"You'd remind me I made a promise to myself not to let him get to me anymore. You'd remind me that I already spent too many years and too many tears on him." Which was true. Their breakup—rather, his sudden and complete disappearance from her life—had almost broken her. She'd cried until she was sick and Krystal knew it too. Krystal was the one who rocked her into the wee hours. Krystal was the one who pushed her to get up, to keep going, every day. Krystal was the one who told her it was okay to be angry with him for deserting her without a word. And when Emmy Lou was more herself, Krystal had turned all the tears and sadness and anger into their double-platinum single, "Your Loss."

"And you'd be right."

"True." Krystal paused. "But, after I was done telling you all that, I'd get up in his face and chew him out for almost running you over. And that's just to start."

Emmy smiled, using toilet paper to dab away the smeared make-up from her eyes. "I'm sure you would."

"Then I'd tell him to stay the hell away from you," she snapped. "Like away *away* from you. And I'd tell Sawyer to punch him in the face if he didn't. Or the gut. Maybe not the gut, if he's still solid muscle, the big oaf. Wherever it would hurt the most. I'd leave it up to Sawyer to decide—he'd probably know."

Brock had made a habit of staying away from her so that wouldn't be a problem. Starting six years ago—when she'd still been sending letters to him, begging him to tell her why he was suddenly cutting her so completely out of his life. She covered her face with her hands. *Humiliating pathetic letters.* They should have burned, not mailed.

"Emmy Lou. Is there anything I can do?" Krystal sighed. "I mean, besides booking a flight home—which I will do as soon as we get off the phone—"

"You will not." Emmy sighed. "You and Jace deserve some time off. Enjoy each other. Away from…everything." As in the latest media circus revolving around her sister. "I'll be more upset about you two cutting your vacation short than running into Brock." Which was mostly true. "I'm not going to fall apart. Okay, he's here. Now I know. The chances of us running into each other again—"

"Literally," Krystal interjected.

"Are slim. And, if we do, I won't be dripping wet and suffering from shock so I won't do what I…just did." She shook her head. Meaning mumble a bunch of incoherent gibberish before running away? *What was that about anyway*? "Promise me you won't come home. Finish your vacation."

Krystal sighed. "Where is Daddy anyway? Why isn't he with you?"

"He had a meeting and I didn't want to sit and wait on him. I had Sawyer. Well, until Travis called. I'm fine." She tugged the band from her hair and twisted, wringing out the water. "You're right. I do look like a drowned rat."

"Whatever. You're you, Emmy. All you have to do is walk into a room and the clouds part and angels sing."

Emmy laughed. "I can't believe you just said that."

"But you're smiling now," Krystal said. "And it's true," Krystal whispered, the words muffled. "Jace is here." There was a smile in her voice.

"I'll let you go, then." Emmy put her bag on the counter. "Tell Jace I said hi, okay?"

"He says hi. And he will so kick Brock's ass if he needs to." There was a pause. "No, you don't know him… Yes, the football player… *That* Brock." Another pause. "He said he would totally kick his ass."

Emmy shook her head, but she was smiling. "I'm pretty sure that won't be necessary. But I appreciate the offer. Love you."

"You too, sissy." Krystal made a kiss-sound. "Talk later."

"Okay." Emmy dug through her bag, pulling out her brush and make-up bag. Her momma would have a fit if she saw the state of her daughter. CiCi King was all about a woman looking her best—at all times. *Best might be pushing it.* But that didn't stop her from attempting damage control.

Besides, she needed to remember why she was here. Her sweet Daddy had found a way to combine her fledgling solo career with working on a cause she believed in. She was the new face and voice of every Sunday night football intro anthem—and she would serve as one of the American Football League's Drug Free, Like Me ambassadors. The AFL's charity program helped raise funds for drug addiction prevention, treatment, and recovery programs as well as outreach education in schools and sports camps. Between her millions of fans and followers and the several million more football devotees, this was her chance to do something that mattered.

Little things like squishy socks, limp hair, or running into the boy—man—who'd crushed her hopes and dreams and heart didn't really matter.

"Don't you dare get water on my wood floors, Brock Nathaniel Watson." Aunt Mo's voice carried all the way down the hall from the kitchen.

Brock stepped back outside the front door, kicked off his still-soaking Racer sneakers, and left them on his aunt's covered porch. His socks were just as saturated. With a sigh, he tugged them off and rolled up the cuffs of his jeans. The damn rain continued to pour down, thick sheets hammering the roof and ground with surprising force. A crack of thunder split the air and rolled across the grey-black sky.

A flash of Emmy Lou, wide-eyed and shaking, with rain dripping off her nose and chin, rushed in on him. Again. He couldn't shake it—shake her.

She'd been scared stiff. For damn good reason. If his brakes had locked up? His truck had skidded? The crushing pressure against his chest had him sucking in a deep breath, his eyes narrowing as he peered out into the storm. She was okay. Shaken, sure, but okay.

Hell, he was damn near in shock. She was the last person he'd expected to see. And this? Well, running her over wasn't exactly the sort of reunion he'd imagined.

Not that he'd spent much time thinking about her. Of course not. That—she—was ancient history. Once that door shut, he'd locked it up tight and never opened it again.

Her band, The Three Kings, were probably doing some concert or something. Football wasn't the only thing that happened at the stadium, he knew that. But, in the six years he'd been playing for the Houston Roughnecks, he'd never run into a single performer.

Of course, it would have to be Emmy.

"You coming in?" Aunt Mo's voice jolted him back to the present.

He stepped inside, pulling the door shut behind him.

"Your shoes out front?" Aunt Mo called out, the steady beat of her footsteps coming down the hall. The moment she saw him, she shook her head. "Look at you,

Brock. Did you swim here? Go on, find something dry to wear before you catch pneumonia."

"Not just worried about your floors after all?" He grinned.

She rolled her eyes and offered up her cheek. "Don't you give me any sass, young man. You give me a kiss and get yourself changed for lunch."

"Yes, ma'am." He leaned down and kissed her cheek, then headed down the hall to his old room, and closed the door behind him.

"I made you some brisket to take home. And some meatloaf." She was on the other side of his door. "I remember you said the boys liked my oatmeal cookies so I made five dozen for you to share."

He tugged off his wet clothes, shaking his head. "Training doesn't start for another two weeks, Aunt Mo." She knew that. As soon as training, pre-season, and games dates were posted, she knew. Half the time, she knew about things *before* he did. Her large-print calendar was marked up with a rainbow of permanent marker ink. Aunt Mo never missed one of his games. She was a die-hard football fan. No, she was *his* fan, and it meant the world to him.

"Is that right?" she paused. "Well, I guess you'll have to take them. You can share with Connie."

He didn't have the heart to tell Aunt Mo his agent was a vegan. And a health fanatic. He'd only ever seen Connie eat salad. Without dressing.

"Connie could use a cookie or two. She's all skin and

bones. You tell her to send Trish over here so I can teach her partner how to cook."

"I'll tell her." He chuckled, tugging on some jeans, socks and boots, and pulling on one of the starched button-up shirts hanging in his closet. He ran a hand through his hair and pulled the door open. "Better?"

"It is." She hooked her arm through his. "Come on and eat. I'm guessing you didn't have much of a breakfast?"

He'd told her most of his meals were prepared for him by his trainer—something she'd clucked her tongue over. But it took a hell of a lot of effort, and about nine thousand calories a day, to stay in peak shape. Being six five and almost three hundred pounds of muscle wasn't easy. "I ate." At six, he'd consumed five eggs, oatmeal, wheat toast with peanut butter and honey, an apple and a banana. At eight, he'd eaten nearly as much. Six meals a day, every day. All a necessary part of his fitness regimen.

"Not enough, I'm sure." Aunt Mo patted his forearm. "Sit yourself down and tell me what's what."

This was his Wednesday routine. Every Wednesday, he'd fly his Cessna 350 from Houston, or wherever else he happened to be, to Austin. At eleven thirty sharp, Aunt Mo had lunch waiting. Not just any lunch either. To her, making sure he was well fed was her way of contributing to the team. Some days, he brought some teammates along—and Aunt Mo loved that. She'd cluck over them all, remind them of their manners, make them clean their plates, and send them all off with an invitation to come back anytime they liked. That was Aunt Mo. When his mother had left them, it was Aunt Mo who had stepped in to take care of him and his father. She saw a need and she filled it, no questions asked.

"Anything new and exciting happening?" She started pulling serving dishes from the top oven rack and placing them on the hot pads placed all over her nice linen table-cloth. "I could use some excitement."

He took his time loading up his plate, waiting for her to make hers before picking up his fork. He scooped up some roasted sweet potatoes from a cast-iron skillet. "I almost ran over Emmy Lou King in the parking lot today."

Aunt Mo's eyes went round and she set her fork down. "What, now?"

He swallowed and took a sip of tea. "She was there, today. At the stadium. I was heading here."

"Brock." She placed her hand on his. "Land sakes, boy. What happened?" Her well-lined face creased with concern.

"Nothing." He shook his head. "It was raining hard, I wasn't going fast—but she came out of nowhere, I slammed on the brakes and stopped close enough for her to put her hands on the hood of the truck. I...I didn't see who it was."

Aunt Mo pressed both hands to her chest. "Oh my. Goodness."

"I got out and...it was Emmy." He cleared his throat, cut a large bite off the grilled chicken breast on his plate, and started chewing. It gave him time to get the lump out of his throat and the image of Emmy, wide eyed and star-tled, out of his head.

"What did you do? She must have been in shock. Of

course she was. What did you say?" Aunt Mo was watching him. "After you were done apologizing, I mean."

Had he apologized? Had he said a thing? Once he'd seen it was her, he'd sort of blanked out. A damn fool, standing in the rain, staring down at her as if he'd just suffered a blow to the head.

"Brock?" Aunt Mo patted the back of his hand, the crease between her brows deepening.

"I'm not sure," he confessed. "We both stood there, getting soaked, and then she ran off." He shrugged, wondering why he'd decided to share this with Mo. The whole damn thing had a dreamlike quality to it. But it was no dream. If it was, he wouldn't have her bright pink and white polka-dot umbrella on his passenger seat.

About the Author

Sasha Summers grew up surrounded by books. Her passions have always been storytelling, romance, and travel—passions she uses when writing romance novels and novellas. Now a bestselling and award-winning author, Sasha continues to fall a little in love with each hero she writes. From easy-on-the-eyes cowboys, sexy alpha-male werewolves, to heroes of truly mythic proportions, she believes that everyone should have their happy ending—in fiction and real life.

Sasha lives in the suburbs of the Texas Hill Country with her amazing and supportive family and her beloved grumpy cat, Gerard, the Feline Overlord. She looks forward to hearing from fans and hopes you'll visit her online. Facebook: Sasha Summers Author, Twitter: @sashawrites, or her website: sashasummers.com